STEALTHY STEPS

VIKKI KESTELL

NANOSTEALTH | BOOK 1

Faith-Filled Fiction™

STEALTHY STEPS

Nanostealth | Book 1
Vikki Kestell
Also Available in eBook and Audiobook Format

BOOKS BY VIKKI KESTELL

NANOSTEALTH

Book 1: *Stealthy Steps*
Book 2: *Stealth Power*
Book 3: *Stealth Retribution*
Book 4: *Deep State Stealth*

A PRAIRIE HERITAGE

Book 1: *A Rose Blooms Twice* (free eBook, most online retailers)
Book 2: *Wild Heart on the Prairie*
Book 3: *Joy on This Mountain*
Book 4: *The Captive Within*
Book 5: *Stolen*
Book 6: *Lost Are Found*
Book 7: *All God's Promises*
Book 8: *The Heart of Joy—A Short Story* (eBook only)

GIRLS FROM THE MOUNTAIN

Book 1: *Tabitha*
Book 2: *Tory*
Book 3: *Sarah Redeemed*

The Christian and the Vampire: A Short Story
(free eBook, most online retailers)

STEALTHY STEPS

Gemma Keyes was an ordinary, unexceptional young woman with a lackluster life until an overheard conversation ends her budding career—and her loyalty to an old friend puts her very existence in jeopardy.

My name is Gemma Keyes. Other than my name, I am utterly forgettable—so those who never paid much attention to me in the first place haven't exactly noticed that I've *disappeared*. Vanished. Oh, it's much more complicated than it sounds. And let me tell you, *invisibility comes with its own set of problems.*

I should tell you about Dr. Daniel Bickel, world-renowned nanophysicist. We used to work together, but I'll be candid with you: *He's supposed to be dead.* Well, he's *not*. (Imagine my surprise.) Instead of the proverbial "six feet under," he's subsisting in an abandoned devolution cavern beneath the old Manzano Weapons Storage Facility on Kirtland Air Force Base here in Albuquerque.

"I need to show you what I'm protecting here, Gemma," he insisted.

I stared into the clear glass case. I could hear . . . humming, clicking, buzzing. A faint haze inside the box shifted. Dissolved. Came back together. It reminded me of how mercury, when released on a plate, will flow and form new shapes. Only this, this *thing* was "flowing and forming" *in midair*.

"Do you see them?" Dr. Bickel asked.

"Them?" I was confused. My mouth opened to a stunned "o" as the silver haze dissolved into blue letters.

H E L L O

Dr. Bickel hadn't pressed any buttons. Hadn't said anything. Hadn't gestured.

He grinned. "Ah. They've noticed you. They know they haven't seen you before."

"Well, I wish they *wouldn't* notice me!"

And I need to warn you about General Cushing. The rank and name likely conjure images of a lean but muscled old soldier, posture rigid, face cemented in unyielding lines, iron-gray hair cut high and tight.

Let me disabuse you of that impression.

General Imogene Cushing is short and a tiny bit plump. *She* wears her beautiful silvered hair in an elegant braid knotted at the nape of her neck, and she knows how to smile sweetly.

With the deadliest of sharks.

You wouldn't suspect a two-star general, *an Air Force O-8*, of being a traitor, would you?

DEDICATION

For Conrad,
in celebration of our first collaboration.
Building the science and technology backbone
of this story was a great adventure!
Stealthy Steps owes a lot to you.

ACKNOWLEDGEMENTS

Many thanks to my wonderful team,
Cheryl Adkins, **Jan England**,
and **Greg McCann**.
I am honored to work with such
dedicated and talented individuals.
I love and value each of you.
Our *gestalt* is powerful!

Thanks also to
David Barr,
Ph.D., material science,
and to
Rose May,
M.S., nuclear physics,
for their technical review.

Cover by
DogEared Design

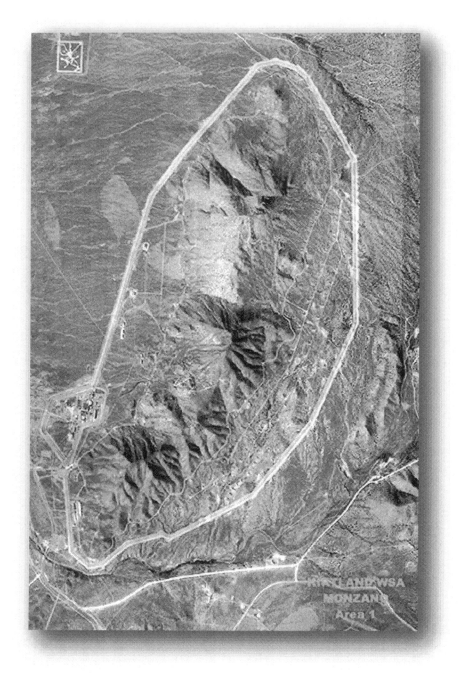

Figure 1. Manzano Weapons Storage Area, Google Earth 2008. Retrieved January 27, 2015, from The Living Moon.

FOREWORD

After World War II, the U.S. Armed Forces Special Weapons Command constructed a weapons storage facility in the foothills of the Manzano Mountains on the eastern edge of what is now Kirtland Air Force Base, just outside Albuquerque, New Mexico. The storage facility, originally named Site Able, was renamed Manzano Base in February of 1952.

At the onset of the Cold War, four research plants, multiple warehouses, and miles of tunnels—many large enough to drive trucks through—were hewn out of the mountain. For a time, a large part of America's nuclear stockpile was stored in the Manzano complex. (The weapons were stored in reinforced concrete and steel bunkers apart from their nuclear warheads.)

The facility had other intended uses: During President Eisenhower's administration, the military built an emergency relocation center deep inside the mountain. The Manzano facility was designed to serve as a devolution command post for the president and his staff in the event of nuclear attack.

The military built one hundred twenty-two magazine bunkers around and into the foot of the mountain to protect the complex. Forty-one of those magazines provided direct entrance to the facility via tunnels. Two electrified fences and an intrusion zone surrounded the mountain; armed forces guarded the perimeter.

That was then. Today the facility sits mostly empty and unused. The primary tunnels (comprising a fraction of the complex) are employed to train military and Department of Energy personnel. While America's nuclear arsenal is now stored elsewhere and the Manzano facility is essentially abandoned, the many secrets of the mountain remain largely unknown.

To most people.

⌘⌘⌘⌘

PROLOGUE
MID-SEPTEMBER

The first explosion shook us from our seats.

Dr. Bickel and I—Gemma, his "girl Friday"—jerked our eyes in the direction of the blast. The force of the overpressure roared into the cavern, tumbling us to our knees. Dirt and pebbles cascaded from the cavern's wide roof and filled the air with choking dust.

The shockwave rumbled from the tunnel Dr. Bickel had termed *his decoy door.*

"They're blasting through, Gemma!" Dr. Bickel shouted.

Dr. Bickel had warned me; he'd sensed General Cushing and her men closing in. He'd cautioned me—but I had closed my ears. I hadn't wanted to believe him.

And now they were coming.

"What do you need me to do?" My ears rang from the concussion, and I screamed my question. Dr. Bickel beckoned as he ran from his small living quarters toward the laboratory—*toward that all-important glass case.*

The lights circling the cavern flickered then died; when they came back on, they were dimmer under backup power. A pounding *thump-thump-thump* reverberated from far down the decoy tunnel. Dr. Bickel trotted ahead of me on his thin, underused legs. He was more nimble than I was; I stumbled over fist-sized bits of debris and almost fell as I followed behind. The dust-laden air choked me, and I fell into a coughing fit.

"My lab book, Gemma. Get it!" Dr. Bickel rasped, pointing.

Cushing would give her eyeteeth for that book—Dr. Bickel's scientific journal containing the irreplaceable observations and notes on his most recent work.

I clenched my jaw: We couldn't let it fall into her hands.

I felt my way along the lab's tables and swept up his current lab book and some loose papers. Dr. Bickel was in the habit of typing up his notes every evening and uploading them to an encrypted remote server somewhere in the cloud, but his lab book was in his own writing. It was proof positive of his accomplishments.

A more valuable proof of his genius was found in the glass case ahead of us—the tall, transparent case in the far corner of the lab. Cushing wanted the contents of that case. She would stop at nothing to get what she desired.

Dr. Bickel had emphasized how crucial it was to save *them* from Cushing and others who would misuse them—use them, perhaps, against America and her citizens.

Another explosion shook the cavern. More dirt silted from the ceiling. I spat grit from my mouth as the pounding resumed.

"It will take time for Cushing's people to overcome my delaying devices," Dr. Bickel called over his shoulder. He reached the glass case and fumbled in a cabinet beneath it, pulling out two hefty carryalls.

I knew what the bags were for. He had described them to me: luggage he had specially constructed to transport *them*. In fact, Dr. Bickel had brought the first of them here in these two carryalls.

Did he intend to put *all of them* into the two bags? I couldn't imagine how he would manage it.

I waited not far from him, shivering, hugging his lab book to my chest, watching him connect white, flexible tubing—the sort I've seen on dryer vents only not as wide—to a rigid port in the first bag's side.

"Don't worry, dear girl. They will flow into the carryalls," Dr. Bickel shouted. Amidst the chaos, he had still sensed my question before I had asked it.

He had just clamped the tube onto the second carryall's port when yet another blast rumbled into the cavern. It knocked me backwards and I clutched at my ears. For all practical purposes I was temporarily deaf.

Chunks of rock fell and demolished precious equipment. A stone bounced off my head; another one grazed me. I looked stupidly at the blood oozing from a scrape on my arm.

Dr. Bickel grabbed the edge of the nearest lab table and pulled himself to his feet. He pivoted as though listening, dropped the tubing, and ran toward the front of the lab. There he would have an unobstructed view of the tunnel where it emptied into the cavern.

I shook myself and climbed back to my feet, but I was dazed—stunned by the glancing blow to my head. Dr. Bickel staggered back toward me, toward the case. He gestured. I couldn't hear what he shouted. His mouth moved, but I heard nothing. Anxiety etched his face.

My ears popped and cleared right then and I heard him shout, "—coming through, Gemma! Soldiers! Lots of them! My tactics didn't slow them down long enough! *I don't have enough time!*"

I nodded but stood rooted, unsure of what to do.

"Go, Gemma! Go! Get out now!" As he reached me, he gave me a little shove in the right direction.

I nodded again. Still my body would not move—it felt as though my brain's commands were disconnected from my limbs. Instead, I watched Dr. Bickel do something quite curious. He yanked another object from the cabinet below the glass case. When he stood up he wielded an aluminum baseball bat.

I blinked. *What?*

The case was strong; Dr. Bickel had designed it himself. Did he really think to shatter the glass? Obviously, Dr. Bickel had stored the bat under the case on purpose—had he foreseen this day? This necessity? And why? Did he intend to just *release them*?

With more strength than I had credited to my sedentary friend, Dr. Bickel swung the bat toward the glass. He connected with his target—not the surface of the glass, but rather a corner of the case. The bat rebounded.

I stared into the case. I could see *them*—the faint haze of their trillions bunched and crowded into the corner farthest from the blow Dr. Bickel had delivered. The cloud shimmered, alternating from silver to crimson. Their deepening colors conveyed a frantic quality—except they were not capable of feelings, of emotion.

Shouts echoed from far down the decoy tunnel. The intruders were through! They would be in the cavern itself in moments. Fear jarred me from my daze.

"Dr. Bickel! Hurry!"

He swung the bat once more, and the case's corner seam split apart. Instantly the air filled with an unnatural hum.

"Hide!" Dr. Bickel shouted. Red-faced, he waved his arms in the air. "*Nano! Hide!*"

Hide? He had trained them to that one-word command—but where could they possibly hide here? They needed continuous power and they could propel themselves only short distances.

Yet I saw the swarm as it—*as they*—left the case. They poured like vapor from the wide-open seam. Once clear of the glass, they gathered themselves into a dense ball, packed themselves together closer and tighter than I thought possible—and shot into the air. The silver-blue haze of the nanocloud shimmered ever so slightly—and vanished.

The tramp of boots and shouted orders drew closer.

"Thank God," Dr. Bickel said aloud. He whirled around—and stopped short when he saw me.

"No! What are you still doing here, Gemma? I told you to go!" His mouth twisted in fear, but not for himself. He shoved me toward the cavern's back wall, toward my exit.

"Go! Before they see you, Gemma!"

I realized then that the intruders probably knew nothing of *my* involvement with Dr. Bickel—likely did not know of my presence in the lab today! Could I get to the back wall before the soldiers spotted me? Their shouts grew nearer.

"Hide!" Dr. Bickel shrieked. "Hide, Gemma!" His eyes compelled me to go.

I tore my gaze from his dear face and ran, expecting him to follow.

If we can reach the back wall of the cavern without being intercepted, we will be safe! I told myself. I knew where to slip between the close-set rock walls. I knew the way out, and so did Dr. Bickel. *The intruders didn't.*

Soldiers would round the lab tables any moment. Rubble covered the floor of the cavern along our path toward the exit. If either Dr. Bickel or I stumbled or put a foot wrong and went down? I kept my eyes on the cavern's rock floor so as not to trip or stumble, but I glanced up once to pick out the little landmarks I used to find the narrow, overlapping cleft by which I exited the cavern. I swerved left to correct my course and sprinted straight toward the cleft and the tunnel that led away from the lab.

So close!

I heard Dr. Bickel shout again, from a distance. "Hide! Hide, Gemma!"

Why isn't he right behind me? I slowed and started to turn.

Gunfire erupted in the cavern. *So much gunfire!* Rock and stone amplified the harsh, rapid pops.

Why are they shooting? Why would they? No one is shooting at them! Why—

Something hard slammed into me, struck me between the shoulder blades, pierced my back. The blow drove the air from my lungs and flung me onto my belly. My hands and face skidded in the debris covering the floor. I tasted blood.

I've been shot!

I started to rise, but a hot, numbing weight pulled me down. I crumpled to the rock-strewn ground. It hurt! *Oh, it hurt!* Every part of my body burned! My skin stung as though stabbed by countless fiery needles.

I could not inhale, could not seem to catch my breath. I was drowning in the fluid that clogged my nostrils and mouth and surged down my throat. I gagged and could not dislodge the flood that gushed into every pore, every opening. Every part of me.

Consciousness was slipping away. From a far distance I heard more gunfire—rapid and fierce—followed by a man's scream of pain.

Dr. Bickel! No! Oh, no!

I protested the horror of my friend's death with my body's last bit of oxygen. Sight and sound faded.

Dr. Bickel . . .

***

Why is my head pounding so?

My entire body ached like someone had worked it over. *With a hammer.* Every inch of my skin radioed distress to my brain. My muscles and joints throbbed; I pulsed with fever.

Why?

I lay on my side. Sort of. My legs, cramps shooting through them, contracted toward my chest. My arms clutched my middle.

I struggled to recall where I was, yet my thinking was soupy, disjointed, as though the synapses refused to fire in the right order. I couldn't quite pry my eyelids open.

My eyes hurt. I was relieved to frame a complete, coherent thought. *I'm cold, too.* I shivered and shook.

Was I in a car accident? Am I in a hospital? Or am I home sick in bed? Why am I so cold?

A sharp, bothersome buzzing somewhere behind me did nothing to relieve my confusion and mounting anxiety. My right index finger—the only part of my body that seemed willing to respond to my commands—tapped my mattress.

Wait—what?

Again, tentatively, I tapped and then scratched at my mattress.

It was *not* my mattress.

I was *not* at home in my bed or lying in a hospital. *I was lying in dirt.* And I didn't know why or where. My thoughts skittered from one plausible scenario to another but nothing seemed to fit or fill the gaping void in my memory. Panic bubbled up, got stuck under my rib cage. And squeezed.

Stay calm, Gemma. Just. Stay. Calm.

The intense, allover pain threatened to splinter my self-control. I scrabbled to hold in the shrieks building in my chest.

Take slow breaths. Slow. In slow. Out slow. In. Out. Slow.

The buzzing-chittering somewhere behind me seemed to be coming *closer.* And the closer the worrisome buzzing, the more excruciating grew the "whanging" in my head.

I gasped and bit my lip; nothing I'd ever experienced compared to this agony. *Or this anxiety.*

Adrenaline pumped through my body and, in a rush, took effect: I managed to sit up, groaning as I did. My eyes popped open. They darted about, hoping to spy something familiar. Anything.

It was night and I was outside. *Where?*

I turned my gaze upward and squinted. The sky was the deepest, inkiest blue-black imaginable. Stars speckled the heavens, but no moon lit the sky.

Off in the distance the lights of houses winked through the dark. The houses were not close, but their presence was comforting nonetheless.

I rolled over onto my knees and winced. Sand, dried weeds, stickers, and bits of gravel crunched under me. Getting up so abruptly might have been a mistake, because as soon as I rose onto my knees, my stomach clutched and heaved. I threw up until my ribs ached, until only acrid bile came up.

Still I retched. I couldn't remember when or what I had last eaten, but I was convinced that I'd thrown up everything back to the "iffy" potato salad of July Fourth a few years back. I spat to rid my mouth of acid and longed to rinse the bitter taste away.

I didn't want to think about the tendrils of hair that had been hanging down when I spewed.

Ugh.

As bad as the nausea and vomiting were, the pounding pressure in my head—*and that infernal humming*—were worse. I gripped my head with both hands.

"Oh, please," I moaned with eyes squeezed shut. "Please! The pain is killing me. Please stop."

I pressed harder. Under my digging fingers the torturous hum slowly dulled and retreated, as a lazy wave withdraws from the sands. I held perfectly still. I didn't move, fearful the breakers would rush back to crash upon my fragile shore.

I must have dozed off or passed out again because I woke with a start. I cracked open my eyes and struggled to my feet. The noises that had plagued me were gone, and I was grateful—but the night was still very deep and I was still very lost. As my eyes adjusted to the starlight, I picked out the darker shadows of rocks and boulders and a hillside sloping away from me.

I have to be somewhere in the open space around Albuquerque, somewhere in the foothills. But where?

I clawed at a chest-high boulder to steady myself. While my headache had diminished significantly, my skin still burned and throbbed. I could not resist resting my forehead on the rock's cool, granite surface.

I may have spent five minutes leaning against the boulder before I pulled myself up and tried again to take stock of my surroundings. The night told me nothing: It was dark—so very dark!—and the shadows of giants loomed near. I had the sense that I was close to a massive rock outcropping. If not for the twinkle of lights in the distance, I might have gone full-on bonkers.

I swayed and reached for the boulder to steady myself. I shivered, looked off into the murky night, and shook my head to clear it.

Gemma, I don't know how you got yourself into this mess, but you've outdone yourself this time, I informed my inward self—as if *she* were completely uninformed on my current situation!

I wasn't ready to confront the obvious, more pressing problem: As dark as the night was, how in the world would I find my way down whatever foothills I might be in?

"Where am I? How did I get here? Shouldn't there be a path somewhere around here?"

My whispers floated unanswered into the night, but they had spawned a spasm of coughing. My throat was rough. Rusty. Scraped raw. My lips were dry and cracked. A keen yearning for a sip of cool water tormented me. When was the last time I'd had anything to drink?

My left arm, in particular, throbbed. My fingers found a tender, sticky spot, but I couldn't see the wound or recall how I'd gotten it. The palms of my hands felt scraped and tender, too.

Think! Think, Gemma! I tried to concentrate but it was like wading through wet cement, and my thoughts wandered.

I need to get down from here. Get home and tend to myself.

I closed my eyes. Made myself focus. Hikers and off-road bicyclists loved the high-desert mountains bordering Albuquerque on the east and south. The foothills were laced with well-worn trails. The agencies in charge of the "open areas" had smoothed and marked many of the trails. I only needed to stumble upon *one* of the trails and follow it. Eventually I would find a trailhead and a parking lot at the base of it—and my car?

I looked down to take my first step and gasped. A moment ago the ground had been shrouded in darkness—now the softest glow illuminated the ground a foot out in front of me.

Someone's found me!

I whirled to see who was casting the light—and stared into black night.

"What in the world?" My breath got stuck in my chest; the scratchy words barely reached my own ears.

I swiveled forward—and there it was again: *that soft light.* Darkness cloaked my feet, yet a tiny bit of hillside opened ahead of me, illuminated by the pale glow. I dragged one foot forward and then the other.

The glow seemed to focus ahead, a little beyond me. Did it move *with* my feet or *ahead* of them? I was all in a muddle and couldn't decide. I inched forward anyway.

After a few steps, I staggered to a stop. The effort had resurrected the fierce pounding in my head. I reached up to massage my neck while I stared out into the darkness. The light by which I had taken those few steps didn't reach higher than my knees. In fact, I thought the light dimmed when I lifted my eyes to look out into the night. But when I pointed my gaze toward my feet, the glow out ahead of me brightened.

Are my eyes playing tricks on me?

I stood still, befuddled. Getting nowhere. The only constant was the agony: Muscle and bone beat a throbbing rhythm in concert with pounding head.

You have to move, Gemma. No matter how you feel, you have to pick up your feet and get moving if you ever hope to get home.

The comfort and relief of my own bed, of my own pillow and covers, called to me. I shuffled ahead. One cautious step at a time, I traversed a steep, rock-strewn hillside. The ground leveled out some, and I turned left, thinking or sensing that I should follow the slope in that direction.

My rubbery legs had taken but one step when the faint light illuminating my path dimmed—and went out. I was enveloped in darkness.

"No!" My raw throat croaked the one-word protest.

What dangers lay on the shadowed, sloping hillside? I couldn't see hand in front of face—so how would I avoid unseen pitfalls in the dark? Shaking, I backed up a step and rotated—slowly—to the right.

The glow near my feet flickered and reignited.

"Thank goodness!" I breathed. I inched ahead.

For another fifteen minutes, by the light of—what, *my shins?*—I threaded my way around cactus, rocks, and other hazards until I reached a flat, sandy ledge. Ahead, straight across the shelf, loomed a dark void.

Perhaps because I was testing a theory—however implausible it *had* to be—I edged closer to what I hypothesized was the ledge's rim.

The light went out.

I sank onto the loose dirt. On my hands and knees, I crawled forward and, with cautious hand extended, felt along the ground out in front of me.

I hadn't crept more than eighteen inches or so before my fingers traced the crumbling end of the ledge. I couldn't see into the abyss beyond my fingertips, but I had no desire to find out how far I would have fallen had I kept going in that direction.

I crawled backwards, stood, and faced the drop-off. On quivering legs I pivoted until I faced left of the ledge.

The ground ahead of me brightened.

I trod slowly on, but I was thinking. Pondering. Was I being guided away from danger by whomever controlled the light?

And what of the noises? The humming, buzzing, or ticking (whatever it was!) had petered out, but every once in a while I heard a faint click or thrum nearby—weak and indistinct, but still there.

What are those sounds? What's making them? My delirious notions—I was convinced that I was feverish—wound round and round in my head as I tried, in vain, to recall where I'd been and why I'd been there.

Why, why, why in the world would I be out in the foothills at night? Nothing I came up with made any sense.

Caught up in my thoughts, I came close to stepping into a wide crack, but—scant inches from the gap—my guiding light winked out. Shaken from my trance, I stumbled to a halt. I got on my knees, felt forward, found the obstacle, and skirted it.

When I was safely on the other side of the crack, I stood and the glow brightened. I picked stickers and grit out of my hands, slapped the same from my jeans, and continued on a steady left-handed angle downhill, meandering to navigate the many natural obstacles.

And then I was standing upon a narrow road. I looked one way and the other, confused and, again, a little anxious.

Why am I anxious about this road?

I had no answer, but I crossed over the road and kept moving downhill, the soft glow lighting my footsteps. I came to a waist-high, barbed wire boundary, slid between the strands, and kept to a descending course until I crossed yet another road and arrived at a wide swath of dirt.

I hobbled, unsure, onto the broad swath. It seemed to stretch forever in either direction, but the most curious part was another fence.

Its chain-link height stretched far above my head and was topped with nasty-looking razor wire. Through the links I spied the shadow of an identical fence some yards beyond. The fences ran parallel to each other down the smooth swath where they disappeared into the night.

If these fences are electrified, I'm in deep trouble—not that I'm not already in it clear up to my neck. And even if these fences aren't electrified? I'm still on the wrong side of them! How on earth do I get through?

I stretched tentative fingers toward the fence, ready to jerk them back at first contact. My gesture was accompanied by a frenzy of the annoying chittering-buzzing phenomenon. A mere hair's breadth from the fence, the clamor ceased.

I swiped my fingers across the fence.

Not electrified.

I didn't know that I'd been holding my breath until I let it out.

One obstacle down. Now to find the gate in this thing.

Except there didn't seem to be a gate—or any way at all through the fences.

But I just want to go home!

I was starting to whine, and I detest whining. I made myself take some calming breaths. Then I started walking the fence line. I walked perhaps half a mile, growing more anxious with the passing time.

No gate.

I turned back and retraced my steps until I thought I was at my starting point. Then I followed the fence line in the other direction.

Almost immediately I noticed something across the dirt road, something that seemed sort of *familiar*: the shadows of a three-boulder formation—a very large rock that was taller than me and, butted up against it, two rocks about half the first one's size, but one piled atop the other.

I stared at the rocks, clueless as to why I was drawn to them. I walked over to them and then turned toward the fence.

You've heard of muscle memory? I walked in a straight line from the rocks to the fence. By the glow ahead of my feet I saw that dirt had been recently swirled around the base of a fence post. It took me a minute, but right above the brushed dirt I found a line of severed links in the fence.

I dug my fingers into the links and pushed the section of cut fence away from me. I shoved it outward until I could crouch and scoot through. On the other side, I pushed the section back into position and, without thought, smoothed the dirt with my hands where the bottom links had scraped it. My hands paused.

I've been here before. I've done this before.

I was elated to recall something—anything!—if only a scrap. But the more I tried to add a "when and why" to the morsel, the harder it became to grasp the tattered threads and pull them together. I sighed and walked toward the second fence. I looked for and found cut links in this fence, too.

Moments later I was safely outside the fence line and across another road. I started moving downhill. I encountered a road that ran in roughly the same direction I was headed. I didn't walk on it, but I followed it, keeping it on my left.

I kept moving and lost all sense of time as the night grew darker. I was slowing down, though. My body ached and I was weak. Growing weaker.

Was that movement not far ahead? I sucked in my breath and stood stock still. A dark form slunk toward me. I couldn't make it out but, by its size, it was either coyote or cougar. The predator waited, stock-still, head down, and I caught the gleam of eyes.

I'm too weak to fight it off. Too weak to run. I shook from illness and fear.

A wisp drifted by my cheek. I cringed and waved it away—only to jerk at the loud *clack* that resounded out in front of me. I can't describe it better. It was a *clack*. The sound, utterly foreign to the foothills around me, startled the creeping creature, too. It turned tail and loped from view.

I swallowed with difficulty. I was parched and fear clogged my throat. After gulping air until I calmed, I licked my peeling lips and walked on.

My pace was slow but determined, fueled by my raging thirst and my longing to be home   home where I could collapse into bed and sleep off the sickness thrumming in my bones. I staggered on unsteady legs, and the glow out in front of my feet kept me—many times—from sprawling over obstacles.

I stumbled upon another road. This one ran crosswise to my heading. Across the road, yet another fence loomed: one more barrier I so obviously had no business being on *this* side of.

What have I been doing?

I was scared to answer my own question.

I searched along the fence to my left. I turned back and searched to my right. I was starting to panic again when the ground dropped down into a dry arroyo. I followed the fence line down into the dry gully and found that water had washed the earth out from under the fence. I pushed under it, crawled through the low branches of a scrub piñon tree, and scrambled back onto level ground. I kept moving, more afraid of stopping than of what lay ahead.

My guiding light flickered and went out. I knew what that meant.

I stopped and turned in a slow circle. When the glow brightened I was surprised and then relieved to see that I was, at last, standing very close to a manmade trail—a trail relatively free of trip hazards. I stepped onto the trail, turned left toward the lights I'd seen earlier and, with growing confidence, picked up my pace.

Perhaps fifteen minutes later I spied lights ahead. I hurried toward them and into a parking lot above a residential area. The parking lot, too, looked familiar, and I struggled to "place" it but could not.

The lot was empty. A sign proclaimed that the open space was closed after 10 p.m. and that hikers were subject to video surveillance. The second statement was worrying.

What time is it? And where is my car? I couldn't have set out hiking without first driving here.

I stumbled down the middle of the street, searching for the familiar outline of my Toyota, but I was near the end of myself. My strength was flagging, my thirst almost unbearable. I trod forward at a sluggish pace, hunting for my car.

That's when I realized that the night was not quite as dark as it had been. Weary and hurting, I squinted at a dark shape around the next corner. It was my car, parked along a curb in the shade of an overgrown tree.

I blinked, stupidly, at my aging Corolla. *Why did I park down here, three blocks from the trailhead? Why would I do that? Why can't I remember?*

I glanced around, feeling paranoid. *Is anyone watching me?*

I frowned. *But why would they be?*

Maybe because you weren't supposed to be inside those fences, dimwit?

Well, yeah. There was *that*.

I tried the driver's door and flinched when it opened with a soft *scree* and the interior light came on. Compared to the dead quiet of the foothills, the creak of the door could have been a gunshot.

Gunshot.

In my spotty memory, something sparked, fizzled, then died. I tried to revive it, but couldn't.

I slid into the driver's seat and slammed the door shut, grateful for my car's familiar feel and smell. I groped under the seat where I often hooked my keys on the seat's frame when I went hiking. It was an automatic gesture that was rewarded by the cool, solid feel of metal as my fingers grasped the dangling keys.

The engine turned over and I pulled away from the curb. A tree limb brushed the roof of my car and I had the strangest *déjà vu* moment, an almost surreal recollection: *That same tree limb brushed the top of my car when I parked under these trees,* I realized. *Like it did just now.*

It was another tickling thread in my spotty memory, but that was all it was. A loose thread.

Not knowing which direction to take, I switched on my headlights and swung the car into a U-turn and drove. Three turns later I recognized where I was. It would take me a few minutes to get to the freeway, but I felt better already. I knew how to get home from here.

I took the I-40 exit west at Central and Tramway. From there, what should have been a simple, twenty-minute drive *took an hour and a half.* I mean, all I longed for in the entire world was to go home, crawl into my own bed, pull the covers over my head, and forget this nightmare.

Except there was nothing simple about that drive.

I came close to rolling my car around the Carlisle exit. That close call scared me—but not nearly as much as *why* I almost wrecked my car.

I pulled over and onto the shoulder of the interstate then. *I had to.* I slammed the gearshift into park and sat, sobbing and shaking, for close to an hour.

You see, it wasn't fully dark anymore.

My hand on the rearview mirror shook as I adjusted the glass this way and that way, each adjustment more frantic than the last.

The mirror reflected my car's back seat and back window. *Nothing out of place.*

Through the rear window I studied my car's trunk and the shoulder of the highway behind my car. *All as it should be.*

And I could see the driver's seat headrest behind my head. *I could see it just fine.*

I touched the reflection in the rearview mirror and stared, bewildered, at what I *couldn't* see.

I couldn't see myself. Not any part of me.

I was standing on the crazy ledge, toes hanging far over it, no saving handhold in sight, the dark bottom a long, distant ways down. It took me a while to talk myself off that ledge.

It took longer before I could drive on.

⌘⌘⌘⌘

PART 1:
INTO THE TUNNELS

CHAPTER 1
THE BACK STORY

Dear Reader,

I apologize for interrupting. I dropped you smack in the middle of my story's most traumatic episode, precisely because it *was* the most traumatic episode. What took place on that mountain—the violent death of my friend and *what happened to me*—well, what took place there is the key event in my story, but it isn't the beginning, and beginnings are important.

And so, I'm sorry for yanking you around like this, for taking you back to the beginning.

I've begun to write it out now, and I want what I put down to be complete and believable. So I'm going to fill in the missing parts before moving on—the parts like properly identifying myself and providing a proper background.

I don't know how much time I have to write. It depends on how long it takes General Cushing to figure things out. She is looking for me, although she does not know she's after *me*.

Yet.

I don't doubt that she will put the pieces together eventually. And when she does? She will set her soldiers to hunt me, the same way she hunted down Dr. Bickel.

I can't ensure that this record will survive should I be captured, but I still choose, for my own sanity's sake, to record everything that has happened. All of it.

So while I can, I will write. When my account is complete—or when Cushing closes in, whichever comes first—I will hide the file somewhere, perhaps "out there" in the ether. The way Dr. Bickel hid his research notes in the cloud.

It's not the best plan, I know, but it's the best I can do for now.

This account is my insurance, just in case things go badly wrong.

Not that they haven't already.

My full name is Gemma Ellen Keyes. It's been a month since that awful day in Dr. Bickel's lab under the mountain. It's been a month of hiding and a month of coming to terms with my new "normal," with what I cannot fix or change.

You should know that I'm not a special person. I'm not brave. I'm not smart. Nothing unusual ever happens to me—quite the opposite, in fact!

When I was growing up, I always believed the most remarkable thing about me was my name: *Gemma (*pronounced "Jem-muh") comes from the word *gem* or *jewel*, right? And gemstones are beautiful—sparkling and prized—all the things I was not and never would be.

What I mean to say is that I have always been *ordinary*. Common. Nondescript.

I am twenty-six and single, and when this all started I was a woman of average height and weight, average hair and eye color (brown*ish*), average facial characteristics, and underwhelming prospects in life.

There. That's a better way to start my story.

I might be recording these events for personal reasons, too. I don't know. So much has happened in such a short span of time that I need a way to keep all this craziness straight in my own mind.

When I wrote "for my own sanity's sake" up above, you thought I was exaggerating, right? Let's see if you still think that after you've read my account.

I never intended to get involved in the mess I'm about to describe to you. I mean, I had no idea what Dr. Prochanski and Dr. Bickel were *really* working on—so how could I have known better?

Yes, I made some mistakes and I will confess to some major misjudgments. But how could I have known *this* would happen?

All right. Enough with the excuses. I need to get on with it.

You should know that I have always been unnaturally shy. My average appearance combined with the way I tend to hide quietly in the background were why people frequently overlooked me. And because people overlooked me, they often underestimated me.

That might be why I'm still alive at this point.

But it's also what got me into this fix.

Because other than my name, I am utterly forgettable—so those who never paid much attention to me in the first place haven't exactly noticed that I've disappeared. Vanished.

Actually, it's much more complicated than it sounds.

Yes, I'm still here.

But I have changed.

Sorry. I keep getting ahead of myself. I want this record to be thorough and complete, and already it reads like the ramblings of a paranoid schizophrenic. I apologize for the "stream of consciousness" approach. I'll try to keep my account simple and straightforward from now on.

Hang in there with me. I think you'll find it . . . interesting.

Before all this started, I lived in the house my aunt left me after she died. It's as though the little house knew me before I came to live here, because it, too, is unremarkable: A small*ish* two-bedroom stucco in a rundown neighborhood not far from old downtown Albuquerque.

I still live in my little house—for now. It sits at the back of a cul-de-sac, straight ahead as you follow our street until it curves and ends at my house. Everyone in the neighborhood calls it a cul-de-sac but, to be fair, it's really an unremarkable dead-end street.

Aunt Lucy said "cul-de-sac" sounded nicer than "dead end." I can't disagree with her there.

Aunt Lucy was our dad's older sister. Her married name was Lucia Reyes—which is close to the spelling of her maiden name Keyes but is pronounced "Ray-yez." No matter. We simply called her Aunt Lucy or sometimes Aunt Lu.

Aunt Lu's husband, Eduardo, died when he was only thirty-two. Aunt Lu and her husband didn't have any kids, and Aunt Lucy didn't get married again.

That's where we came in, my twin sister Genie and I. Aunt Lucy was maybe in her forties when she got us. We were sent to live with Aunt Lucy in this house, in this neighborhood, after our parents died in a fire. Genie and I were nine years old.

One of my strongest memories is of Aunt Lucy folding me into her soft bosom, stroking my hair, and crying with me over the loss of my mom and dad. The pain—*the agony*—of losing them was a deep, bleeding hole in my heart. I was just a kid and I didn't understand grief or how to survive it. If it hadn't been for Aunt Lucy and her love at that crucial time in my life, I don't know what would have become of me.

Once in a great while I still feel the fingers of that despair reaching out to grab hold of me. When I sense those sinking feelings trying to latch on, I run to my memories of Aunt Lucy. In that place I can smell her fragrance, feel the soft cushion of her breasts, and hear her heart beating under my cheek. Eventually the hopelessness backs away.

The three of us, Aunt Lucy, Genie, and I, lived together in this house until Genie left for college back east when she and I were eighteen. Then it was just Aunt Lu and me.

I could have gone away to college, too; Dad and Mom didn't leave us much family, but they did leave us a little insurance money for our educations. That little bit grew over time. I didn't go away to college, though; I stayed with Aunt Lucy and attended nearby UNM instead. I didn't want to leave Aunt Lu by herself because she wasn't well, and I was afraid something serious was wrong with her.

Genie may have realized something was wrong with Aunt Lucy, too, but she didn't feel the way I did about Lu. When Mom and Dad died, Genie hadn't grieved like I had, either. Genie is different. She doesn't love anyone, I'm afraid, except maybe herself.

Aunt Lucy took us to church every Sunday while we were growing up. I think she hoped and prayed that church would fix Genie—*as if!*—so we attended faithfully for years. I'm afraid that Aunt Lucy didn't understand. She didn't *see*. Didn't see what Genie was.

I hoped for a while that Genie would change, but she didn't. I lost faith that God could fix *that*.

I'll write more about my sister later. I don't want to, but I will have to.

It was because of Genie (I will get to her; I promise), that fading into the background became a habit for me. Even before our folks died, I'd learned, like a wild creature, to go still when danger was near. By middle school I'd adopted a fixed, vacant expression.

It was smart of me to look stupid.

I didn't realize until much later that this "trick" I'd picked up in my childhood was a gift of sorts: I could disguise or hide my feelings as I wished. Unless I chose to show my emotions, they stayed tucked away on the inside. It was how this twig was bent; it was how I grew.

Anyway, back to Aunt Lucy. After Genie left for college, I begged Lu to see a doctor and she reluctantly took herself. It wasn't good news. They told her that she had breast cancer, and it was advanced.

We did all the treatments anyway, and they gave her two more years. The treatments were hard on her, but I am so grateful for those two years.

Aunt Lucy took out a mortgage on her house to pay the medical bills and, with help from hospice, I took care of her myself as the end neared. I did my best and loved her dearly—but love alone cannot hold back the ruin of such a disease.

I dropped out of school the semester before she died so that I could be with her, so I could let her know how much I loved her.

It was during Aunt Lucy's decline that Jake came to live with us. Lu insisted that God had sent him. I disagreed. Why would God pick such an ugly cat to comfort someone as special as Aunt Lu?

Ugly. Not just unsightly, not merely run-of-the-mill unattractive, but full-on "you even-scare-your-mamma" ugly.

Jake was maybe three years old when he crawled up on our side porch in the middle of the night. He set up a wallering fit to raise the dead. He sure raised us from a good night's sleep! Jake's left ear and eye were mangled and he was mostly skin and bones—held together by the combined efforts of a large population of vermin.

That tabby had the biggest, meanest, tomcat mug I'd ever seen—and the charming personality to match! Still, Lu begged me to help him. So, for her sake, I prepared to do battle with a brigade of fleas.

I bathed that cat—and he clawed the mess out of me. (I should have donned raingear and chainmail first.)

I doctored him—and myself afterward.

I fed him—and the ungrateful monster sank his teeth into me!

Over my protests, Jake spent his convalescence on the bed next to Lucy, and she drew a great deal of comfort from his affection. And me? If I so much as walked by Lu's bed, that wretched excuse for a cat would snarl and swipe at me.

Lord forbid I should try to pet him! Heaven help me if I should show a little kindness! *To this day,* my hand bears the scars of those misguided advances.

Miserable brute!

I doubted that God would pick the ugliest, nastiest cat alive to comfort someone as special as Aunt Lu, but I was wrong. Jake had been what she needed after all.

After Aunt Lu died, Jake stalked around the house for days yowling and crying for her. He still lives with me. Or maybe he allows *me* to live with *him.*

The vote is still out on that one.

I said earlier that my sister Genie didn't love Lu like I did. I meant that. Genie didn't visit when Aunt Lucy got sick. She didn't come home when Lu passed.

Later, when I told Genie that I needed to dip into our education fund to pay the bills that Lu's new mortgage hadn't covered, she responded by pulling her share of the money from the joint account. I wasn't the least bit surprised—I was only relieved that she hadn't taken my share, too.

So I took care of the remaining bills and paid for Aunt Lucy to have a nice shady spot in the cemetery. Then I dragged my sorry, grieving heart back to school and eked my way through another semester.

I'm sitting at Aunt Lucy's old kitchen table under the dining room window right now, typing up this account on my laptop. Once in a while I look up and glance through the window. I tell myself that I'm admiring the early mums, but I'm really watching our street as it curves and empties into our "cul-de-sac."

From this window I can see all vehicles coming or going.

From this window I will know when they come for me.

While I keep watch, I observe Mr. and Mrs. Flores, my neighbors on the right, and nosey Mrs. Calderón, next door on the left. I watch the Tuckers two doors to my left, on the other side of Mrs. Calderón.

I watch my old friend, Abe Pickering, who is three doors to my right. He lives on the curve where the street empties into the cul-de-sac, so his house is almost opposite mine.

I keep watch as I type up this account, and I'll stay here as long as I can. Until the day someone stands on my doorstep and demands to see Gemma Keyes.

"Seeing" Gemma is the problem, of course. When that day comes—the day I can't produce Gemma for those demanding to *see* her—I'll have to leave.

I don't exactly have a plan for that day yet.

Without actually giving directions to my house, I can say that sometimes on a hot summer day when the wind is right, I catch the wild, warm, moist scent of animals from the Rio Grande Zoo. If you know old Albuquerque, you might be able to visualize how our neighborhood looks: corner bodegas, vivid murals painted on stucco and cinder block walls, narrow streets and tiny houses with patchwork yards owned by the same families for generations, lots of driveways and curbs cluttered with cars (always one or two vehicles in some state of disassembly), sidewalks haunted by transients and, of course, a growing gang presence.

Hmmm. As I type I keep saying "you" as though I'm writing to one particular person, someone I know—which is crazy, because who would that one person be? I trust few people in this world, and I would be crazy to get any of them involved. If things go sideways, they would likely suffer the same fate as I—and I won't have that.

But as I type away, I find that it is easier to explain what happened if I fix on one person reading my tale. One person who will care about all this. *Who will care what becomes of me.*

So, Dear Reader, if I keep typing "you" in my story, would you do something for me? Would you pretend that you—*whoever you are*—that you and I are sitting at my tiny kitchen table under my tiny dining room window, sipping on some hot, sweet tea? Would you pretend that we are looking out my front window, looking past my Texas sage and lavender bushes and over the "dead end" my shabby little neighborhood calls a cul-de-sac?

Would you imagine then that I'm looking you straight in the eye as I tell you this story? And would you try to believe that nothing I say is the product of a crazy person?

Could you do that?

Would you do that?

If you are at least willing to try, I thank you from my heart.

Where was I? Oh, yeah.

Like I said, I took time off from school to take care of Aunt Lu. I was about a year behind, but eventually I earned dual bachelor's degrees in history and accounting from UNM. History was my love, but accounting was more likely to pay the bills.

Genie had finished her degree the year before and already had the first year of law school under her belt when I graduated. I could easily picture her as an attorney. I felt sorry for those who would someday pit themselves against her in court—I knew I would be scared to go up against her.

I was twenty-three when I graduated. I'd earned pretty good grades in college, but what kind of decent, interesting job can you get with history and accounting degrees?

In probably the best career move I could have made, I had applied for an internship at Sandia at the end of my junior year. "Sandia" as in Sandia National Laboratories, a big federal R&D complex on the Air Force base here in Albuquerque. Sure enough, my accounting studies are what got me in the door.

I worked as a part-time intern for Sandia the last month of my junior year, full-time the summer after my junior year, and then part-time again during my senior year. Mostly I did administrative work. Unremarkable, non-career-boosting administrative "stuff."

The weird thing is that *thousands* of people work at Sandia, including some of the brightest minds in the world. So how is it that *I*, out of all those thousands, landed in this mess?

And for the record, *I am not a traitor*. I will name a few people later who *are* traitors, but I am not one of them.

You have to understand that since those who are searching for me have all the power, this account may be my only opportunity to proclaim my innocence: If they catch me, I'll likely disappear, never to be heard of again.

I have to tell my side of the story while I can.

You should probably have some background on the area I worked in at Sandia so that I don't lose you as I explain how things unfolded. In a nutshell, we taxpayers pay the federal government to conduct different kinds of research and development at Sandia. The Department of Energy oversees the work.

You may not know this, but DOE isn't only about "energy." Its mission has three parts. Yes, the first part is all that stuff about energy and energy conservation, but the second part is *science and innovation,* and the third part is *nuclear safety and security.*

The second and third parts are important to this story.

After World War II ended, the world got caught up in the Cold War and the nuclear arms race. Some smart people in the government (I don't think we have those anymore) decided that no single government entity (meaning the military) should have complete control of America's nuclear weapons.

Yes, the Department of Defense "owned" and maintained the weapons, but to ensure the nation's "nuclear safety and security," the nuclear pieces of the stockpile were given to an agency that would, eventually, evolve into the Department of Energy. Basically, DOE controls the "special nuclear material"—the part that makes a bomb or missile nuclear—while Defense manages the conventional weapon and its delivery.

Why keep them separate? Because without the special nuclear material, a nuclear weapon can't make a big boom with a mushroom cloud.

Just a regular boom.

It's a much safer world that way.

DOE makes sure that special nuclear material isn't put into a weapon without a direct Presidential order. DOE also safeguards nuclear materials so they don't fall into the hands of terrorists or rogue nations. It's a big job with a lot at stake.

DOE "rents" space on Kirtland Air Force Base here in Albuquerque for Sandia and for a few of its other programs, like its National Training Center and a hub for the Office of Secure Transportation. The Air Force base provides a secure place for DOE's activities.

Win-win.

By the way, I don't know if the whole "nuclear weapons" thing makes you feel more secure or gets you up on a soap box, but I'm not endorsing either view. I'm merely providing context so that you'll understand where and how my problem happened.

Anyway, the Air Force owns about 52,000 acres of high desert on the south end of Albuquerque. The base includes some of the foothills of the Manzano Mountains on the east. (*Manzano* means "apple tree" in Spanish. I read somewhere that early Spanish explorers found an apple orchard somewhere in these mountains when they first arrived—which is curious, since apples aren't native to America.)

As a nod to the nearby mountains, one of Kirtland's early names was "Manzano Base." You'll want to pay attention to this next part, *the part about the mountains*.

In the late 1940s, the military decided that the foothills inside Kirtland's perimeter were good for tunneling. They carved out huge tunnels in the mountain—tunnels big enough to drive trucks in and out—and stored a lot of America's nuclear stockpile there inside blast-proof, underground steel vaults. The tunnels and storage caverns were dry and stayed basically the same temperature all of the time—a perfect environment for weapons storage and stability.

They called the mountain facility "Site Able" at first and later renamed it the Manzano Base Weapons Storage Facility. They also dug a big presidential command post inside the mountain in case of nuclear attack. The underground post was supposed to keep the president safe and allow him to direct the government from there in time of war.

The military circled the whole mountain complex with *one hundred twenty-two* concrete munitions bunkers and what was called a "Perimeter Intrusion Detection and Assessment (or Alarm) System," or "PIDAS," monitored by armed guards. The PIDAS was more than the tall, razor-wire-topped fences (one of which was electrified) that ran parallel to each other around the mountain. Between the fences they graded a great swath of dirt. They laid wire mesh on the ground and covered the mesh with a layer of dirt. If intruders stepped on the wire mesh, sensors in the mesh would detect and report the intrusion.

For a while, as you might imagine, that facility was a Very Big Deal.

Later, with the advent of *thermo*nuclear weapons, the government realized that the mountain couldn't withstand such an attack, so they abandoned the presidential command post. Eventually they also moved the weapons out of the mountain and into a hardened underground storage facility called the Kirtland Underground Munitions Storage Complex—pronounced "Koom-Sec."

Where is KUMSC exactly? Apparently "everyone" knows a big slice of America's nuclear weapons arsenal is stored south of the Albuquerque Sunport's runways. (Think of that the next time you fly into our fair city.)

Many of the weapons stored in KUMSC are in a queue awaiting disarmament. That said, out of fifteen states "hosting" nuclear weapons, KUMSC still has the largest stockpile.

Well, it's nice to be recognized for something.

Back to the Manzano storage facility. After the military removed the nukes, they no longer had a use for the facility.

Today the facility sits empty for the most part—but the tunnels are still there. The vaults and research plants are still there. Lots of rooms and tunnels and munitions bunkers and stuff are still there. It's all still there. And these days the base provides only minimal security to the mountain.

Those are the parts you should remember.

Now more about Sandia. Many of Sandia's programs apply to our nation's nuclear weapons, but other big programs are listed on the science and innovation side. I interned in an area called microelectromechanical systems or MEMS.

Microelectromechanical systems is a mouthful, but please don't glaze over! Cut "micro/electro/mechanical systems" into four pieces and think about each slice separately.

"Micro" means really tiny—*micron* tiny. Micron-sized things can't be seen with the naked eye. In fact, you need a scanning electron microscope to see micron-sized particles.

I think we all know what "electro" refers to: Whatever the gizmo is, it runs on electricity.

Now add "mechanical" to micro and electro and you get "a really tiny mechanical device that runs on electricity."

A mechanical device may be, technically, a robot—not a cartoon robot that acts as a household servant and not a scary AI that runs a space ship and intones, *I'm sorry, Dave. I'm afraid I can't do that*, in a creepy, emotionless voice. No, I'm talking about a teensy-tiny *gadget*.

(Side note: I'm not saying that teensy-tiny gadgets can't be disturbing and scary. I should know.)

Don't disregard the last part, "systems." A single device is one thing; a system is much more. I looked up the definition of "system," and the one I think best applies to MEMS is, "A group of interacting mechanical or electrical components." A system in this situation means a group of microelectromechanical devices interacting and acting in concert.

Now, think of that entire system as *smaller* than a micron—*submicron* in size. At a thousand times smaller than a micron, it's called nanotechnology.

Of course, *smart* nanotechnology, *adaptive* nanotechnology is supposed to be futuristic. Fantastic. Sci-Fi.

Riiight.

Yes, I'm mocking.

Do I understand the science behind MEMS and nanotechnology? I bombed chemistry in high school *and* college, so no. I don't understand it all. You don't need to understand it, either.

Just remember *really small stuff*. I'll fill in the details as we go along.

Now you know what I mean when I say that I worked as an intern in the MEMS program—but not in a lab or doing science stuff. I just performed "administrivia"—making appointments, ordering supplies, scheduling meetings, typing agendas and minutes, filing, etc. And likely, the most I could expect Sandia to offer me after graduation was a full-time admin position. Doing more of the same.

Although it would have been a good paying job, did I really want to be a glorified secretary my whole life? Even I—average, ordinary Gemma—rebelled against the idea. What kind of future was that to look forward to for forty years?

The thing was, Dr. Prochanski, the lead scientist of one of the teams, suggested that I had an aptitude for project management—and project management seemed a much brighter career path. I did some research and found that project managers or project controls specialists can earn a pretty good living and can work on lots of different, interesting projects. So, during my senior year, I took a PM certification night course through UNM Continuing Education.

It was rough, managing twenty hours of work a week, all of my graduation requirements, and a night course, but I stuck it out. I might be average, but I'm tenacious. In the end, my tenacity paid off.

After I earned my degrees *and* my PM certificate, Dr. Prochanski sent me a link to a contractor position in his lab! Sandia often hires a subcontractor company to fill certain staffing positions, usually when staffing needs are temporary or are financed through grants or limited-life funding.

I was okay with being a subcontractor. Lots of Sandians start as subcontractors and then are hired as regular Sandia employees.

I applied for the job, and the subcontractor company, Global Staffing Alliance, offered me an entry-level project coordinator position on Dr. Prochanski's team. I was stoked!

The job was part administrative assistant, part inventory and project controls, but my position title meant I was logging real hours in project management. All I had to do was keep learning and in three years I'd be able to sit for my Project Management Professional certification exam.

I want to say a few words about Dr. Prochanski since he plays a large role early in my tale. The man was a demanding boss and a stickler for detail, but detail was something I did well. Because I seemed to always have a handle on "the details," he grew quite affable toward me. That was when he suggested that I study project management during my senior year.

As a young intern I found it hard to believe that anyone actually noticed and *valued* me enough to advise me. I felt honored that Dr. P had taken a personal interest in me. And maybe because my dad had died when I was a kid, Dr. P's attention spoke to a need I had.

I could count on one hand the number of people who had extended a helping hand to me as I grew up, so is it surprising that I felt a strong sense of gratitude and loyalty toward Dr. Prochanski? Can you blame me for trusting him?

I don't think you can fault me, but it was still a huge mistake.

⌘⌘⌘⌘

CHAPTER 2

I had been working in the MEMS program about a year when I first laid eyes on General Cushing. I arrived at work that morning, put my things away, and started brewing coffee for Dr. Prochanski and myself. I wasn't late to work; in fact, I was ten minutes early, but Dr. P already had a guest.

"Gemma, this is General Cushing. Please bring us coffee as soon as the pot is ready, will you?"

Cushing's rank and name likely conjure images of a lean but muscled old soldier, posture rigid, face cemented in unyielding lines, iron-gray hair cut high and tight.

Let me disabuse you of that impression.

General Imogene Cushing is short and a tiny bit plump. *She* wears her beautiful silvered hair in an elegant braid knotted at the nape of her neck, and she knows how to smile sweetly.

With the deadliest of sharks.

You wouldn't suspect a two-star general, *an Air Force O-8*, of being a traitor, would you? And yet she has proven herself to be merciless, unscrupulous, and unrelenting—and no great supporter of our nation's Constitution. If or when things here go wrong, *she* will be the one coming for me.

I made the coffee and took two mugs into Dr. P's office. General Cushing smiled at me, her pointy teeth gleaming brightly. Her dark eyes bored holes in my back as I set Dr. P's mug on his desk.

"So you're Gemma. Dr. Prochanski has been telling me how *helpful* you are to him."

It was my first encounter with Cushing, and I didn't like her. The way she dragged out the word "helpful"? It was demeaning, in a sort of sly, backhanded way.

Many of my female professors had raged against "the glass ceiling" and against the men in high places who keep women down. What those professors *didn't* address were the women who'd made it, the women who'd broken through that glass ceiling, the minority who were breathing that rarified air—and who preferred to keep it that way.

My feminist profs encouraged us to *Lean In*—as the book of the same name urged—but the instructors forgot to warn us of the *women* who would sabotage us when we tried to. They didn't mention those who wanted to remain one of the *few* women with power, the ones who were determined to keep their lofty heights uncluttered by other female competition and who viewed other women as potential threats.

Men keeping women down might be a real problem, but my profs should have encountered General Cushing. What a workshop that would have produced!

I blinked, and my ever-ready shuttered expression snapped into place. "Yes, ma'am. Will there be anything else?" When I met her gaze I was confident she'd see nothing more than an inane government drone. No threat at all.

Her eyes narrowed briefly but she smiled again and murmured. "No, that will be all. *Gemma.*"

Ugh!

And that will be all about General Cushing for the present.

Except this: She and Dr. P didn't talk long that morning. He escorted her to the front door and, on his way back, said in passing, "Do not mention the general's presence here today, Gemma."

Odd, I thought, but I readily answered, "Of course, Dr. Prochanski."

In my role at Sandia I held a security clearance and worked in a restricted area. As part of my job, I often handled classified matter (classified documents or information) or was privy to classified meetings.

I was trained in classified matter protection and control—the proper marking, handling, and protection of classified information. For that reason, I will cloak the details of my account with enough ambiguity to avoid ever being charged with the intentional release of classified matter (a.k.a. *treason*).

Remember, Sandia does MEMS research *and* development. Our MEMS lab was part of the Microsystems and Engineering Sciences Applications (MESA) complex at Sandia, which also included MESA's semiconductor fabrication facilities (fabs), located in nearby buildings.

One of MESA's fabs is strictly for the production of military semiconductor applications; the other fab is for civilian applications. On the civilian side, DOE is big on "tech transfer," a licensing process that allows the public sector to transfer the technology DOE labs develop into real-life uses.

New, first-to-market technology spells BIG MONEY, so technology espionage is a real thing. Other industrial countries (China in particular) are always conniving to steal new discoveries and advances. Technology espionage makes tech transfer *über*-complicated, given the level of security that is needed.

Enter Dr. iel Bickel.

In my last weeks as an intern, before I was hired as a full-time contractor employee in the MEMS program, a new scientist joined Dr. P's team. From the get-go, I could tell he was going to be trouble because he and Dr. P did *not* hit it off.

Dr. Bickel was perhaps fifty-five with a tiny pot belly, spindly legs, and thinning, rust-colored hair and a scraggly beard of the same. In contrast, Dr. P was in his late forties, a large, bullish, robust man with a big, gregarious voice and personality. He loved to be in command—frankly, he wouldn't have it otherwise.

Sandia greeted Dr. Bickel's arrival as a real coup and made the announcement with a lot of hoopla. We were told how very world-renowned he was in his field and how lucky Sandia was to get him.

Rumors circulated about Dr. Bickel's personal wealth. According to the grapevine, he could have worked in industry and made a pile of money, but he chose not to—because he already had a pile. A large one. He was, by all accounts, not "merely" rich, but "filthy" rich.

Weirdly enough, as enthusiastic as the bigwigs were to have Dr. Bickel, I thought the unremarkable-looking scientist was, himself, less than thrilled to "have" Sandia. He seemed annoyed by the fanfare and his notoriety. And he was unquestionably displeased that he would be reporting to Dr. P.

More on that soon.

From his first day, Dr. Bickel held himself aloof. Perhaps wary is a better word. I never saw him chat or joke. It wasn't that he was in a *bad* mood. He just kept to himself and hardly spoke to anyone except his two techs, Rick and Tony. They came with him when he joined Sandia.

As Dr. P's admin and project coordinator, I interacted with everyone on Dr. P's team, for one reason or another. My desk was the hub of department business "stuff." I developed what I hoped was a relaxed and occasionally fun relationship with all of Dr. P's staff.

Not so with Dr. Bickel. From the beginning, he kept his distance from me. If he had a task for me, he left voicemail or scribbled messages on my desk after work. If he needed supplies, he preferred to shoot me an email rather than speak to me in person. Dr. Bickel's standoffish attitude hurt my feelings more than a little. I wondered why such a prestigious scientist hadn't taken a job where he'd be happy—'cause he sure didn't seem happy at Sandia.

Dr. Bickel had his own lab space that only he and his two techs used. It was a small lab and I was surprised that the trappings of his "world-renowned" work were so Spartan, given the reception he'd received when he joined Sandia.

About six months after Dr. Bickel arrived, Dr. P announced in a staff meeting that Dr. Bickel and his team would be transferring their work to a new program. The program would be housed in a recently completed laboratory attached to our building. Dr. P said that the new program and lab had been given the acronym AMEMS for Advanced Micro-electromechanical Systems. Then Dr. P said that he would be the program's supervisor.

Apparently, Dr. Bickel was developing some innovative, cutting-edge MEMS manufacturing approach that didn't require semiconductor fabrication. I picked up a bunch of glowing but vague references to three-dimensional printing opening the door for this new approach. I also heard that this new method would render conventional semiconductor manufacturing obsolete.

How *printing* and MEMS *manufacturing* were related didn't make sense to me, but Dr. Bickel was supposed to be 'the bomb' when it came to 3D R&D. Everyone was hoping his theories would result in some major breakthroughs.

A personal comment about the AMEMS lab: I might not have known the science, but I thought the name redundant. I mean, Sandia already touted its MEMS R&D program as "advanced." Did this announcement mean that the newly established AMEMS R&D lab was more advanced than "merely" advanced?

Pffttt.

Anyway, Dr. Prochanski and Dr. Bickel and his staff moved into the AMEMS lab—to continue their work that was more advanced than the already advanced and cutting-edge R&D of Sandia's "regular" MEMS lab.

Yes, I'm being snarky.

As for me? I was delighted and a little surprised when Dr. P brought me over as admin/project management support for the AMEMS program. It was a lateral move but it came with a small in-grade increase. The new level meant a little more money, which was welcome. I was grateful and more indebted to Dr. P.

The new program inspired a high level of activity and anticipation. The AMEMS lab was larger than the space Dr. Bickel had in the MEMS lab, so he added two post-docs and a small team of techs to assist him and the ever-present Rick and Tony. All I knew was that the pace of Dr. Bickel's work picked up and generated lots of excitement.

Do you recall my saying how much Dr. Bickel despised Dr. P? Part of Dr. Bickel's disdain was for Dr. P's pompous personality; part of it was over "the science"—or the perceived lack thereof—on Dr. P's part.

It was no secret how low an opinion Dr. Bickel held of Dr. P's academic credentials, yet Dr. Bickel had to report his progress to Dr. P during staff meetings. The result? Every staff meeting was as contentious as (or more than) the last.

I know. I know because I took notes at those staff meetings.

In those meetings, Dr. P asked a great many technical questions, and those questions only stirred up Dr. Bickel's impatience and contempt. Sometimes when Dr. P questioned Dr. Bickel, Dr. Bickel took the opportunity to subtly (or not so subtly) criticize and buck Dr. P's authority and/or decisions.

Dr. P, for his part, couldn't abide having his authority questioned, and Dr. Bickel's outbursts were sometimes nothing short of open rebellion. And still Dr. Bickel continued to work under Dr. P—which, again, seemed odd since Dr. Bickel could have worked anywhere in the world he chose.

As an aside, the work of the AMEMS lab was highly classified. Demonstrations and detailed discussions of the research included only those people actively involved in the work. These were people with the appropriate clearances *and* a need to know.

I did not have a need to know. I just handled administrivia and inventory and project controls: I recorded progress in the AMEMS lab against the project goals, deliverables, and timeline. I often handled classified documents that concerned the research in the lab, but I didn't read them. Their scientific mumbo-jumbo was nothing I could fathom—or cared to.

The move to the AMEMS facility happened a little more than two years ago. Everything about my job in the new program was great except for Dr. Bickel's standoffishness—and one new expectation: Dr. P tasked me to provide him with regular reports . . . reports of a discreet nature.

The fact was, Dr. P expected me to spy on Dr. Bickel. Oh, not on his work, but on his whereabouts and other activities—which was bizarre, right? I mean, didn't they work together? Why would Dr. P need me to report on Dr. Bickel's movements? *And why me?* Dr. Bickel wasn't comfortable with me like the rest of the staff was; he didn't talk to me anymore than he did the others on the team—with the exceptions of Rick and Tony.

Over my feeble protests, Dr. P set up a standing weekly meeting between the two of us. He required that I track Dr. Bickel's whereabouts every hour of every day and bring a printout that showed his movements to each meeting.

I tried to follow Dr. P's instructions. I tried to insert myself into Dr. Bickel's good graces. I tried to keep track of the seedy little scientist, but Dr. Bickel worked long hours, sometimes late into the night and sometimes on weekends. Then again, he frequently left the lab for hours during the day. To say that he kept an odd schedule would be an understatement. And when Dr. Bickel left the lab, how was I supposed to know where he went? How was it any of my business?

With grudging compliance, I did my best to monitor and track every minute of Dr. Bickel's day. If he left the lab, I asked him to tell me where he was going and when he expected to return—so I could let people know in case they asked. Yes, he was out of the lab a lot, but he always had plausible reasons and seemed not to mind when I asked. Once in a while he'd turn a very penetrating look on me and I, not knowing what else to do, dummied up.

I did my duty and, to the extent I could, provided Dr. P with the requested weekly account of Dr. Bickel's schedule and activities, making it as detailed and complete as possible. At each meeting Dr. P studied the schedule and questioned me, asking me if Dr. Bickel had said anything about this or that, or if he had met with anyone.

Dr. P's inquiries during our weekly meetings were exhaustive—and exhausting. If I answered, "I don't know," to any question, his reply was, "Then find out, Gemma. I expect you to know everything there is to know about Dr. Bickel."

His demands didn't sit right with me at all, but I couldn't dredge up the internal fortitude to refuse Dr. Prochanski. I felt that I owed him a lot, and I didn't want to disappoint him. So I kept dogging Dr. Bickel.

Had I been in Dr. Bickel's shoes, I think I would have resisted the questions asked of me. I also questioned Rick and Tony about Dr. Bickel's whereabouts. They might have been stone bookends, one on either side of Dr. Bickel, for all the progress I made. Of course they were closemouthed about the work, but about Dr. Bickel himself? I wondered why they were tightlipped about him, too.

Under growing pressure from Dr. P, I took to looking through Dr. Bickel's office in his absence. As I spied for Dr. P, I learned some of Dr. Bickel's habits—such as how he never went home without first typing up his lab notes for the day and how, after he finished, he locked his lab book in the small vault in his office. It was classified matter, so that was perfectly understandable.

Then there was the one time he returned while I was in his office. Talk about awkward! I was smooth, though: smooth, blank-faced, and unflappable—all while shaking inside.

Dr. Bickel studied me with that thoughtful, knowing look and smiled. It was a tiny smile, and he added, "I hope you're being careful, Gemma."

What does he mean by that? Is he trying to warn me? I nodded and returned to my desk.

And later I started detecting *patterns*, patterns in when he'd be gone and when Rick and Tony would also be gone. Patterns in late work nights, early morning arrivals, and a few "all-nighters." I started paying closer attention to what Dr. Bickel wore to work—particularly when it was the same thing under his lab coat two days in a row.

Over time, the relationship between Dr. P and Dr. Bickel deteriorated. At the same time, my role as spy grew more onerous and my feelings about what I was doing worsened.

As I studied Dr. Bickel I noticed how exhausted he appeared most mornings. I started to see worry lines growing on his forehead and around his eyes. I maybe started fretting about him, Just a little.

And I stewed about how Dr. Prochanski intended to use my reports. Soon I was wondering if he planned to use them as ammunition to discredit Dr. Bickel.

I grew to resent the position Dr. P had placed me in. The more he demanded, the more reluctant I became. That's when I grew selective about what I gave Dr. P.

I started leaving out bits and pieces of things I *could* have reported to Dr. P but intentionally chose not to. After a while, "bits and pieces" became big chunks.

It wasn't much of a rebellion and it didn't do a lot to assuage my conscience, but it was what I could manage.

I just re-read those last several paragraphs. Seeing what I did for Dr. P, seeing it spelled out in cold, plain text, looks horrid. Because it was. It was *wrong*.

I'm ashamed of myself.

I guess my only excuse, Dear Reader, is that I was young and gullible. Naïve. I could have refused. I could have gone to HR and complained. In the end, though, I have to confess the truth: *When it began, I was motivated by my need for Dr. P's approval.*

Dr. P had a way, a way of making me feel valuable and trusted, a way of making what I did for him seem *right*. And once I started, I couldn't find a way to stop.

I know better now. I know Dr. Prochanski used me for his own ends.

I fell for his lies. I swallowed them, along with the proverbial hook, line, and sinker.

⌘⌘⌘⌘

CHAPTER 3

Dear Reader,

Remember the opening scene of my account, the attack on Dr. Bickel's lab? The next chapters of my narrative occurred about six months prior to that. I was closing out my third year as an employee at Sandia, still working on Dr. Prochanski's team, and studying hard for my PMP exam.

It was March, early spring. Spring in New Mexico is wonderful, but spring winds are *not*. I'm not grousing about gentle breezes. Oh, no. I'm talking *fifty-mile-an-hour gales*. It was a blustery spring day like the one I described above. I blew into our building on a blast of freezing wind and set to work making coffee.

And just like that, the last day I worked at Sandia began like any other.

One of my responsibilities was to take notes during our department's formal, unclassified meetings. I used my Sandia-issued laptop and typed the notes as the meeting took place. Before the meeting, I would pass out the agenda, which consisted of business left over from previous meetings, action items due at the present meeting, and items Dr. P told me to schedule for discussion.

That morning I passed out the agenda and waited for Dr. P to start the meeting. Nothing out of the normal there. What *was* out of the ordinary was that only Dr. P and Dr. Bickel were scheduled to attend the meeting. Dr. P had directed me to uninvite the other scientists and techs on the team.

That's when my antennae went up. Since only Dr. P and Dr. Bickel were scheduled to attend this meeting, I figured a confrontation was looming.

Scary.

I smelled trouble in the air, but I knew enough to keep out of it. I positioned myself in the corner of the room, away from the conference table. Out of line-of-sight.

Dr. Bickel entered the conference room first, seated himself, and looked around. "Where is everyone, Gemma?" He appeared tense and tired, and I was surprised when he spoke to me so familiarly. I didn't think he had noticed me, sitting in the corner, ready to take notes.

I cleared my throat. "I'm certain the, um, other attendees will be along shortly, Dr. Bickel."

I flicked a second glance at him. He was not one to care overmuch about his personal appearance, but I was again surprised and a bit concerned at how disheveled and tired he appeared. Exhausted.

And yet he'd been out of the lab a great deal in the past several weeks. I presumed that when people weren't at work, they were resting up at least *part* of that time. Dr. Bickel's appearance was puzzling, because he looked worn to a frazzle. I wondered if he were experiencing personal or family problems.

Does he even have a family?

I couldn't remember him ever mentioning anyone, but then he wasn't one for chitchat, personal or otherwise.

Dr. Bickel stared at the conference room clock. It read 10 a.m. straight up and he and I were still the only meeting participants in the room. Then he turned penetrating eyes on me.

I bent my head toward my keyboard and kept it there, but from under my lashes I observed Dr. Bickel nod to himself. To no one in particular he murmured, "And so it begins."

Dr. P charged into the conference room at exactly 10:05, his big, bullish presence filling the doorway. "Sorry to keep you waiting, Doctor," he boomed.

Did I detect a note of scorn in Dr. P's greeting?

Dr. Bickel said nothing. His expression was as impassive as mine was.

I shrank farther into the corner.

Someone followed Dr. P into the room. I stopped breathing when I saw who it was. *General Cushing*, smiling her shark-toothed smile, stepped inside the conference room and waited until Dr. P closed the door behind her.

It was only the second time I had encountered General Cushing. She hadn't changed much in the two years since our first meeting—and neither had my visceral reaction to her. My sense of self-preservation kicked in. I licked my suddenly dry lips.

Of course I hadn't known she would be attending the meeting—she wasn't on the invitee list, after all. Apparently, Dr. Bickel hadn't known she would be attending either. His expression turned to stone.

General Cushing, for her part, locked eyes with him as Dr. P ushered her to a seat opposite Dr. Bickel. Dr. P took the seat next to her. The general's and Dr. P's backs were angled toward me.

"Imogene. I wasn't expecting to see you today." One corner of Dr. Bickel's mouth turned up a fraction. I halfway expected his stony face to split from the effort.

"It's lovely to see you again, Danny."

I couldn't see Cushing's and Dr. P's faces now that they were seated—I was in the corner behind them and off to their left, after all—but I shriveled, visualizing General Cushing's smile growing wider, her pointed, sharky teeth gleaming.

And what was all this "Imogene" and "Danny" business?

Dr. P coughed into his hand. "Now that we've exchanged pleasantries, let's call this meeting to order, shall we?"

Dr. Bickel said nothing; Dr. P's fingers fluttered with the papers in front of him. After a moment, he opened a manila folder and extracted a document that he passed across the table.

Dr. Bickel did not reach for it. He did not so much as glance at it. He simply stared—with contempt, I might add—in General Cushing's direction. I could not see Cushing's expression, but she kept her back ramrod straight.

Dr. Prochanski's big voice echoed in the nearly empty room. "Dr. Bickel, your *involvement* in the research and development work of the AMEMS lab has been outstanding. I appreciate your *contribution* to our breakthrough, the successful development of the world's first-ever *smart*, multi-functional nanobots."

Whoa! I knew the work in the AMEMS lab had been racing toward a notable success, but it was all very hush-hush. I had heard rumors, but I was not cleared to know exactly what that success might be.

I was troubled, however, by how Dr. P addressed Dr. Bickel. The way Dr. P phrased it, Dr. Bickel was only a gear in the AMEMS machinery, a useful but replaceable cog. I might not be the sharpest stick in the stack, but I knew from Sandia's welcome of him that Dr. Bickel's theories and work were what drove the lab.

Right then my admiration for Dr. P slipped a notch.

Dr. P continued, "Under my leadership, the work of the AMEMS lab has flourished. Our results have attracted the admiration and attention of many in the federal government. Of course, I am humbled but gratified that our government has taken notice of my lab."

Wait. What?

It almost sounded like Dr. P was taking credit for Dr. Bickel's work?

He continued, "It is now time to take the next step and apply our work to an arena where it is much needed."

"Oh, yes," General Cushing murmured. Staring at the back of her head, I could still picture pointy teeth sliding over plump lips and oily words slipping out from between them. "The Pentagon has agreed to fully fund the next leg of AMEMS development. They are *quite* enthusiastic.

"We will enhance Dr. Prochanski's staff with our best and brightest minds and accelerate the rate of nanobot production."

"Not with me, you won't."

Dr. Bickel, growing as red as his fading hair must once have been, pushed away from the table and stood up. The chair in which he'd been sitting rolled away from the table and banged into the wall.

"I refuse to participate. My contract with Sandia stipulates that *none* of my research is to be transferred to the military. You already know, *dear Imogene*, that I will not allow you to appropriate any part of my work for military or 'national security' purposes. The matter is closed."

As though to punctuate his last word, Dr. Bickel stormed from the conference room and slammed the door behind him.

Yikes!

My hands froze on my laptop's keyboard.

"That went quite as you predicted, Doctor," General Cushing purred.

Cushing drew her chair closer to Dr. P's. The intimate manner in which she bent her head toward Dr. P and he leaned toward her made me want to upchuck. I forced myself to keep typing, "10:24 a.m. Dr. Bickel left the meeting," while listening.

"Yes. Dr. Bickel is nothing if not predictable."

"And how will you manage without Dr. Bickel's cooperation?" I could visualize her words oozing through the gate of her spiky, white teeth.

Dr. P chuckled. "During Dr. Bickel's entire tenure at Sandia he has kept two sets of data—one set he 'allowed' me to access and one he *thinks* he has hidden from me. He believes he has kept his progress secret, but he has not."

He leaned closer to Cushing.

Gag.

"The bots he has developed are adaptive, cutting edge, as you wished, and I have taken pains to copy all of his data—*his hidden data*. He doesn't know it, but his every movement in the lab has been recorded. Since he refuses to cooperate with us, I will simply assign him to other tasks and we will carry on his work without him."

My esteem for Dr. P crashed to the ground.

Cushing thought for a moment, tapping a fingernail on the conference room table. "Doctor, oh, my dear Petrel, I have quite an unsettled feeling about all this. The nanobots are too precious, too important to trust to Dr. Bickel in his present state of mind. I sense that we need to protect them, perhaps remove them from Dr. Bickel's oversight sooner than we planned. What do you think?"

Dr. Prochanski nodded vigorously. "If you think so, then yes. Of course, Dr. Bickel might present a problem when we do—he has many powerful friends in the scientific community, you know, and he would likely raise an outcry. I take it you've managed the contractual issues he spoke of so that the legal end is covered?"

Instead of answering, Cushing sighed and murmured, "Still, perhaps we should consider whether if, at this time, Dr. Bickel has served his purpose altogether."

Huh. What?

It was spoken so carelessly, so cavalierly, that its import took a moment to sink in. My hands slowed.

Dr. P didn't need a moment, though. "I confess that I have similar concerns. I'm confident that, with the proper resources, I can oversee the development of the nanobots to the next level and, as we've discussed previously, we should really consider how to, ah, *remove* Dr. Bickel, er, permanently."

I wasn't typing anymore. My hands shook on the keyboard.

Is he saying what I think he's saying?

And then a second chill washed down my back as I realized how stupid I'd been.

Neither of them realizes that I am still in the room—directly behind them, overhearing every word of their whispered conversation!

I should have stood and excused myself as soon as Dr. Bickel had stormed out. But it was too late! It was too late to excuse myself now.

I swallowed and forced my quivering fingers to move over my laptop's keyboard, but I wasn't typing. Instead I was berating myself for getting into this mess—and I was scrambling to figure out how in the bloody blue blazes I was going to get out.

Snap.

My game face clicked into place and my mind scrambled. I pulled up several bookmarked pages and kept my eyes on the laptop's screen.

With my eyes on the screen and my "who, me?" look locked in place, I coughed. I coughed the teeniest, *tiniest* little cough I could manage.

Cushing swiveled her chair to confront me. "Oh, dear, Dr. Prochanski. What have we here?" She asked her question with sickening sweetness, but I pretended not to notice and I didn't look up, seemingly engrossed in the pages before me.

"Gemma."

I looked around, affecting confusion. "I'm sorry, Doctor. Did you need something?" My tone was apologetic and every bit as sickeningly sweet as Shark Face's.

Cushing raised an eyebrow. "What are you doing here, *Gemma*?"

I had the grace (and the foresight) to blush. "Oh, I simply take the meeting minutes, ma'am, but I stopped taking them when Dr. Bickel left. Was that a mistake?"

She smiled and flashed her pointy teeth. "Then what have you been doing the last few minutes, *Gemma*?"

She wasn't buying what I was selling.

I blushed again, looked down, and stammered, "Just, um, things, ma'am. Nothing important."

Cushing held out her hand and snapped her fingers. "Let me see."

"Dr. P?" I appealed to him, but found only a troubled skepticism in his eyes.

"Hand her your laptop, Gemma. Now."

With feigned reluctance, I handed it into Cushing's grasp. She skewered me with a triumphant look and turned her eyes to my screen. Only to frown.

"What is this?" she demanded.

Dr. P glanced over her shoulder and glowered. "Answer the general, Gemma."

I stared at my folded hands. "It's Pinterest, ma'am."

"What is . . . *Pinterest*?" she hissed.

"I, um, I—"

She doesn't know what Pinterest is? Does she live under a rock?

"It's, uh, like a picture-posting and sharing website. People create boards of what they're interested in, you know, stuff they like. I-I like history and like to collect black and white photographs." I gestured toward my laptop. "Those are, um, early images of New Mexico's Pueblo Indians. It's-it's a hobby."

I bowed my head, but I could still feel Cushing's dead, dark shark eyes gauging me, weighing what I'd said. Assessing the threat.

I kept my expression neutral and sent my heart into survival mode. I went "there," into that safe, distant place, instinctively. After all, I'd survived much worse than Cushing.

What is this, Gemma?

That's my diary, Genie! It's private! You have no right—

*Your **diary**? Why, what do you have to write about? You're the most boring person I know.*

Give it to me! I shrieked. Aunt Lucy wasn't home. No one could hear me. Or help me.

I grabbed at my diary—the one place my twelve-year-old heart felt safe to confide its secrets and feelings—but my sister yanked it out of my reach.

Don't tell me what I do and don't have a right to do, Gemma, you inferior thing, she sneered. Then her visage turned uglier. *Wait. Have you been writing about me?*

She began to scan through my precious book. I made another, desperate, grab for it. This time, Genie slapped my cheek. The crack of her open palm rang in my ears and I recoiled, my hand covering my stinging skin.

Was it bad luck that she turned to the worst possible page she could have found? When she finished reading what I'd written about her she smiled.

Yes, Dear Reader, I'd seen evil smiles before.

Her smile growing wider, my sister studied me. *Why, I'm surprised at you, Gemma. You have more insight than I gave you credit for.*

Still watching me, her eyes gleaming, she began tearing the pages from my diary. Her breath quickened and I knew why: It gave Genie pleasure to make others suffer.

I screamed and threw myself at her, but she dodged away and kicked me. I stumbled and fell face down on the floor of our room.

That's when Genie began beating me. With the book. With her fists. Blow after blow rained down on the back of my head. I squirmed and tried to get out from under her, but she knelt on me.

As you might imagine, a little diary won't leave discernable marks on the back of one's head. Neither will a twelve-year-old's fists. She used both on me until she was exhausted.

Aunt Lu, Gemma's got a terrible headache, Genie, full of solicitous concern, reported to our aunt that afternoon. *I think you should give her some ibuprofen.*

Aunt Lucy looked into my tear-stained eyes and down my throat. *Does your throat hurt, Honey?*

No, Aunt Lucy. Just my head.

Genie peeked from behind Aunt Lucy and smiled.

Oh, yes. I'd seen evil smiles before, and I knew how to survive them.

So that day in the conference room I had zero problem "conning" the general. I played the beaten, clueless role just fine, *thank you very much.*

Shark Face narrowed her eyes and changed tactics. She huffed. "Really, Dr. Prochanski. I'm surprised that you allow your employees to waste precious government resources on frivolous, non-work-related pursuits like this."

He glared at me. "I didn't think Sandia's IT settings allowed access to social media."

(Actually, Sandia doesn't allow access to *unsecured* sites. Typing in a single "s" after "http" overcame that small hurdle.)

"I'm very disappointed in you, Gemma."

Well, I was more disappointed in him than he would ever be of me.

I managed a, "I-I'm sorry, Dr. Prochanski. It won't happen again," without breaking a sweat.

He looked at Cushing and then back at me. "You may go, Gemma." He handed me my laptop.

"Thank you, sir."

At the end of the day I was about to shut down my computer when Dr. P appeared at his office door and called to me. "Gemma, I need to speak with you."

I picked up a notebook and pen. When I entered his office, he, motioned to a chair in front of his desk.

He folded his hands on his desk and said, "Gemma, I'm very sorry to tell you this, but we are letting you go."

I was stunned. Shocked. His tone was sincere, but I didn't recognize the look in his eye. And I couldn't process his words.

"I'm sorry? What do you mean?" Not an original response but, dismayed as I was, it was all I could come up with.

"The contract under which you were working has lost its funding, so your position here is terminated, I'm afraid. Effective immediately."

They say the stages of grief and loss are denial, anger, bargaining, depression, and acceptance. I was validating the first stage of that model.

"I-I-you can't be serious? I'm sure the contract has enough money on it for two more years!" I *knew* it did; my company's management kept me apprised of the state of the contract that funded my position with Sandia.

Aaaaand then there's bargaining. I seemed to have skipped over anger for the moment.

"Is it something I've done? It can't be that I was looking at Pinterest! Please let me fix this?"

"My dear Gemma, this is not a termination for cause. Your contract position has been eliminated. Budget cuts."

His "my dear Gemma" grated over my nerves and I didn't believe him. Not for a moment.

I was crushed, but I crammed my "cards-close-to-the-vest" onto my face and studied Dr. Prochanski. I was certain *he* saw nothing more than my normal, vacant expression.

But what did I see?

His eyes had narrowed when he said, "not a termination for cause." His lips had stiffened and he'd glanced away, very briefly, when he said, "Your contract position has been eliminated."

He was lying.

They were getting rid of me because of what I'd overheard him and General Cushing discussing in the conference room. *What I heard was important,* I reasoned, still masking the hurt of my smashed ego.

It didn't matter, though, did it? They were getting rid of me and I couldn't do a thing about it.

He hesitated and then added, "I'm sure this topic will be covered in your exit interview, Gemma, but the policy is serious enough to bear reiteration: Everything you have read, seen, and heard in your work here is classified and cannot be spoken of outside these walls. To anyone."

Dr. P's voice had the tiniest edge to it, and I was certain he'd placed emphasis on the word "heard."

"I'll pack my things," I said, with no emotion.

"Very good." He picked up his phone. "Please send security to do the exit interview and escort Ms. Keyes off base."

I stumbled back to my desk and started emptying my drawers of personal items. I found an empty box by the photocopy machine and loaded it up.

"Gemma?"

I glanced up, still keeping my expression blank. Dr. Bickel approached the cubicle wall fronting my desk, his thinning red hair more disheveled than normal. Something in his demeanor spoke of stress, and I could feel tension oozing from him. His body language was like a guitar string wound far too tight.

"Yes?" That single word was as detached as I could make it.

"I heard what happened, Gemma. I'm very sorry."

How? How could you have heard? Dr. P told me I was being let go only moments ago.

I allowed none of those questions—or my astonishment—to flit across my countenance.

"Thank you." I added a photo of Aunt Lucy to the box. I was still cool. Still in control.

"If you need a recommendation, I would be pleased to write one for you."

I lifted guarded eyes to his, surprised to see compassion there. Was it possible that he had no idea of my "other" role in this department? That I'd spied on him? Again, I merely whispered, "Thank you."

"Here's my card. I've written my personal phone number and email address on it."

As Dr. Bickel leaned over the cubicle wall and placed the card on my desk, the officer from Sandia's security department came through the door. I glanced in the officer's direction and then back to Dr. Bickel.

At the last possible moment I leaned toward Dr. Bickel and mouthed, "Watch your back."

I don't know what prompted me to issue such a cryptic warning, but I didn't regret it. I turned away from him and waited for the security officer's approach.

As simply and as quickly as that, my career—my whole life!—went down in flames. I drove home and sat in my dark living room.

Thinking. Thinking. Thinking.

⌘⌘⌘⌘

CHAPTER 4

Dear Reader,

Are you still with me? I hinted that you would find the journey worthwhile.

The first person I told about losing my job was Abe, of course. I got up the following morning, still dazed, and shoved the box of stuff I'd hauled home from work into the coat closet. I couldn't bear to sort through it.

I looked down the street and saw Abe sitting on his front porch. I grabbed a sweater, two cups of coffee, and headed out the door.

I'm not sure how old Abe is, but he's getting up there. He's a vet—fought in Viet Nam, I think—and he still has what he calls "a fire in my bones." True to his military training, Abe keeps his yard trimmed, his house tidy, and (one of his quirks) his blinds closed at all times. I've been in his house and I can testify that it is meticulously clean and organized. *Spit-spot*. Not a speck of dust; not an object out of place.

What else should I say about Abe? Abe and Aunt Lu were the best of friends for as long as I could remember—not in a romantic way, though. They went to the same church and were kind to each other in simple, practical ways. Like, Lu took Abe a hot meal about once a week and Abe took care of things around our house when they broke.

I will never forget Abe, tears flowing down his black cheeks, when we buried Aunt Lu.

Abe was wonderful to Genie and me, too, especially when we first came to live with Aunt Lucy. He still looks out for me, I think, and still tries about once a month to get me to go back to church—but *that's* not gonna happen.

Sure, I have "friends," people my age I went to school with and hung out with growing up, but I'm not close to any of them. I don't trust or confide in them.

Abe is the person in my life who stands in the gaping hole left by Aunt Lucy's passing. He holds a precious place in my heart and is the closest thing to family I have left.

Well, there's Genie, of course—but that's a ball of mess I *never* touch on purpose.

So when I saw him sitting on his front porch, I beat a path across the cul-de-sac.

"Hey, squirt."

Abe patted the seat on the swing next to him. He'd built that big old wooden swing himself, and I'd spent many hours swaying back and forth on it when Genie and I came to live with Aunt Lu.

Abe had sat through lots of heartaches and tears with me that first summer as I came to terms with my folks' passing and, years later, with Lu's passing. That kind of bond is what I'm talking about when I say he's the closest thing to family I have left.

Abe's glossy face has a wealth of wrinkles around the eyes and mouth that enhance what I love about him. He has the deepest, blackest eyes I've ever seen and a smile that lights them up. He smiled at me right then and some of the weight I was carrying slipped off.

I plopped down on the swing, handed him one of the cups, and pulled my feet up under me. Abe set the swing going and we sat together for a long time.

Back and forth. Back and forth.

"I lost my job yesterday, Abe," I finally whispered.

"Huh. Did ya, now?"

Back and forth. Back and forth.

"Yeah." I was not going to tell him why. And I was not going to tell him about spying on Dr. Bickel—the part I was ashamed of.

He nodded.

Back and forth. Back and forth.

"You're young. Lots of livin' ahead. God'll see ya through."

Back and forth. Back and forth.

"Not the worst thing could happen to ya, neither."

Back and forth. Back and forth.

I took a deep, cleansing breath. *Not the worst thing could happen to ya, neither.*

"You're right. Thanks, Abe."

He patted my hand. I squeezed his hand back.

***

I'd been unemployed for all of three days.

"Gemma, dear, I'm so sorry. I heard you lost your job?"

Crud. I was cornered.

Like I said, I'd been off work for all of three days—and Belicia Calderón, the nosy neighbor on my left, jumped on me like a chicken on a grasshopper! I figured Mrs. Calderón had gleaned the news from Mrs. Flores, the neighbor on my right.

Abe was much too discreet to provide the *Cul-de-Sac Calumny Queen* with fodder for her flapping jaws. Mrs. Flores, whom I'd visited with yesterday, had likely let the news of my unemployment slip without realizing she had armed *The Queen's* guns—that's how good Mrs. Calderón was at prying out bits of information.

It wasn't that I was hiding the fact that I was unemployed. Not at all. But Mrs. Calderón was a relentless scandalmonger who dug for dirt where no dirt existed—and who kept digging and digging and digging. If she couldn't find dirt, she'd fabricate juicy details and add them to established facts, creating chaos, ruining reputations, and causing division between friends wherever she went.

I'd been to Walgreen's, and all I was doing was putting my car in the garage. Had the door up. About to drive in. Mrs. Calderón took that as license to waddle around the little wall between our properties.

Did I say waddle? Let me tell you something about Mrs. Calderón: *Everything* about her waddles. When she talks, that flabby skin-thingy hanging under her chin waddles. When she's excited, her sizable breasts roll side to side and jounce up and down.

I know; I'm *so* sorry for the image. I can't help it.

When she bends over (*Nooooo!*) her auburn wig shifts precariously. I'm shooting in the dark here, but I doubt that Mrs. Calderón *ever* had hair the dazzling shade of red her wig is. I'm pretty sure *no* one has. I tremble to imagine what might be revealed should the hairpiece ever slide off!

Besides all that waddles, there's her *tongue*. It wags! Trust me on this: She is one very *determined* gossip. When Mrs. Calderón has you in her sights, she cannot be put off, put down, or deterred. This morning, like a British ship-of-the-line flying under full sail, she bore down upon *me*, a hapless dinghy bobbing in the sea without mast or motor. She rounded the wall, waddled up the drive, and stood *right in front* of my car as I pushed up the door.

Which meant I couldn't drive into the garage until she waddled out of the way.

Grrr.

"But I thought you were doing so well at Sandia! Weren't you close to that nice doctor—your scientist friend?"

Dear Reader, I have never spoken of my work at Sandia to anyone in the neighborhood except Abe, so perhaps you'll understand why, mentally, my jaw dropped. Outwardly, though, I laughed as if I had not a care in the world.

"The contract ended, Mrs. Calderón, so my position was no longer funded." I glanced at my watch.

Wait. I don't wear a watch. All right, then. I glanced at my bare wrist.

"Oh, goodness! I'm so sorry. I need to run. It was very nice talking to you."

I jumped in my Toyota and started the engine before she could say another word—No! She *was* talking! I was in the car with the door shut and still she talked! Unbelievable!

She didn't budge, either. She kept talking and talking and blockading the driveway between the open garage door and me.

I looked down, pretended to fiddle with something on my dash, pretended I didn't see her still standing in the way. I eased my foot off the brake and my car moved forward.

With my peripheral vision, I saw her huff and waddle to the side of my drive. While she was still turned away, I hit the gas and my car jumped into its little stall. I threw the gearshift into park, turned off the engine, and raced to pull down the garage door—*and she was standing right there. Under the door!*

Arghh!

"But jobs are so hard to come by these days, Gemma."

News flash! Wow. I totally did not know that.

"I can't see how you can possibly make it in this economy. Oh, dear. Do you have any savings?"

"Pardon me. Could you move back a tad?"

I started pulling down the door. She glanced up and backed up. A tad.

"But aren't you discouraged, dear?" The door was coming down between us. "I'll look in the papers for you. Perhaps a waitressing job while you are looking for something more, ah, suitable. But you mustn't be too picky or presumptuous, Gemma. I know Lu didn't leave you anything, what with all the medical bills. Why, you're probably still digging out from under them! I don't know how you'll survive."

I slammed the door down in her face and shoved a big screwdriver into the door's track with more force than needed. I could have been more polite—Aunt Lucy had *taught* me to be polite no matter what. I *would* have been more polite, but when she dragged Aunt Lucy into her gossip?

I about lost it.

I strode out the garage's side door, up the steps, and into the house without a backwards glance.

***

I'd been officially unemployed for two weeks when a news ticker jigged across the TV screen. I shook myself out of a stupor: An explosion of some kind at the national laboratories on Kirtland Air Force Base. As the local anchor reported more information, my mouth fell open.

"Bob, we've just been told by a Sandia spokesperson that an explosion has taken place on the campus of Sandia National Laboratories in one of its laboratories within the MESA complex.

"The spokesperson stressed that the resulting fire has already been contained and presents no danger to other buildings nearby, but he also warned that the explosion did result in loss of life. No names have been released at this early point in the investigation."

I was holding my breath.

"Ted, when do we expect to hear more on this breaking story?"

"Bob, this information was released with approval of the lab director. The spokesperson expects the director to deliver a prepared statement sometime in the next hour. Live from outside the Eubank gate, this is Ted Martinez for Action 7 News."

A laboratory within the MESA complex! My heart plummeted into my shoes.

I stayed glued to the television all that afternoon and into the evening. News units outside the base caught additional fire trucks and ambulances racing to support the Kirtland department.

Of course, the base was shut down. Until a security assessment determined that the explosion and fire had not been a deliberate act and that the event posed no further danger, the base would remain under lockdown.

News helicopters could not fly over the base so they hovered as close to the boundary as allowed, which was not close enough for me. From far outside the base perimeter the news chopper's camera picked up only a thin plume of white smoke—all that remained of the fire.

I stayed riveted to the coverage all day and into the evening. That night, under bright lights, the lab director and the base commander held a press conference outside the base's Eubank gate. The lab's director, a tall, well-spoken man, addressed the cameras, his arms folded across his chest. He was not a happy camper.

However, rather than the director addressing the crowd, the base commander stepped to the microphone and spoke to the cameras. He didn't look much happier than the lab director.

Through pinched lips he announced, "Working laboratories deal with volatile materials and, for that reason, we have strict safety protocols in place. However, mistakes do happen."

He looked down and then back into the cameras. "Our initial assessment indicates that the incident was caused by human error and affected only one laboratory. The investigation is, of course, ongoing. We can, however, with heavy hearts, tell you the names of the two Sandia personnel who perished in this tragic accident."

I swallowed, not wanting to hear, but not able to tear myself away.

"Long-time Sandia employee and respected scientist, Dr. Petrel Prochanski, and his esteemed colleague, Dr. iel Bickel, perished today. We are told that their deaths were immediate. We can provide no further information at this time. Our hearts go out to their families, friends, and coworkers."

The commander stalked away from the microphone, ignoring the barrage of questions. The lab director, grim and silent, followed behind, and they were surrounded by their people as they filed through the gate and onto the base where reporters could not follow. My view on the television changed to a camera following their passage through the crowd.

As he had pronounced the names of the dead, I had leapt to my feet, crying, "No! Oh, no! No, no, no!"

Then, through my hot tears, *I saw her.*

General Cushing, her mouth curved in a tight smile, her eyes hard and glittering, stopped the laboratory director and spoke to him. The man tried his best to get free from her while maintaining his temper—that was apparent. Then Cushing placed one hand on his arm and the director looked her in the eye.

I don't know what she said, but its effects were immediate. The director flinched. Cushing, her hand still on his arm, smiled again and spoke further.

The director nodded. His lips were stretched thin, but he nodded.

I knew a beaten man when I saw one.

⌘⌘⌘⌘

CHAPTER 5

The first sting of horror lasted a week. Then the pain that had been cutting so deeply began to numb. After that I had to turn off the news, had to stop watching. It wasn't as though the news had any *new* news to report anyway. I could almost mouth the reports as the anchors spoke.

A strong conviction grew in my gut that General Cushing—and whomever she reported to—were the actual figures in control of the investigation, in which case anything the news reported was exactly what Cushing wanted the public to know.

It wasn't hard to imagine *Shark Face*—plump lips lifting to reveal white, gleaming teeth— pulling strings, asserting her will and that of her superiors, and manipulating the lab's federal oversight and contractor employees. I'd seen her exert her power over the lab director and, no doubt, she'd done the same with the base's commander.

She has to be well connected to wield such power, I mused. I sneered as I pictured her.

I made a meatloaf for Abe and carried it over to him for his dinner. Of course he'd seen news coverage of the explosion in the lab and we'd talked at length about my relationships with the two scientists who'd perished in the accident.

That afternoon, though, I finally confided what had really happened my last day of work, and I started by confessing how I'd spied on Dr. Bickel for Dr. Prochanski. Abe listened without saying anything, nodding once in a while to show that he was following.

Once I'd aired my guilty conscience and expressed my regret, a dam broke loose inside of me. I had to tell Abe everything—it was eating me up inside.

I described General Cushing, including my sense of her as a person (I use the term "person" loosely), and I described that fateful meeting between Dr. Prochanski, Cushing, and Dr. Bickel in the conference room. I whispered what I'd overheard Dr. P and General Cushing decide—the real reason I'd been let go.

When I had finished unburdening my heart, Abe's countenance was grave. I'd never seen him so serious.

"Girl, you have no experience with the military like I do. This General Cushing? You are well served to be away from her—you can be thankin' God for that. She's no one to ever mess with, I can tell from the way you described her." He shook his head.

"Thank the Lord, you don't have to worry 'bout this woman anymore. Now, let's talk 'bout you." He studied me, and I didn't like what I saw reflected in his black eyes.

"You got you a good conscience, Gemma. Lu made sure of that. But just *sayin'* you wish you hadn't done somethin' don't fix it. Don't make it right an' don't make your heart light again."

I swallowed. He'd hit my sore spot. Exactly. "But I don't think I *can* fix it, Abe. They-they're dead." I was thinking of Dr. Bickel in particular. I couldn't apologize to him, couldn't ask his forgiveness. Somewhere in a corner of my heart, I felt a twinge of responsibility for his death because of how I'd so dishonored him.

"No, you can't fix what you done, but you can still be forgiven for it."

I didn't want to hear what was coming next.

"You can ask Jesus t' forgive you, Gemma. That's the only way to get shut of the guilt."

I nodded but didn't say anything. It was far easier to feign agreement with him than to answer back.

***

I attended the memorial services for Dr. P and Dr. Bickel—closed casket, of course—before their bodies were shipped to their home towns for burial. The powers-that-be held the services off base so that access to the service wouldn't be a problem for attendees. It pained me to see my old coworkers again and to know I wasn't part of their everyday life anymore.

I felt adrift, lost at sea.

I wasn't part of anyone's everyday life anymore.

***

It was mid-May when I grew a wild, ambitious hair. Before Aunt Lucy got sick, she and I had xeriscaped the front yard, replacing the old, thirsty grass with colorful gravel and adding some big rocks for accent along with a few drought-tolerant shrubs and plants like lavender and sage. This year I wanted to do something different in the backyard: I decided to plant a little vegetable garden.

I wanted to grow simple stuff that would do well in the summer heat—squash, tomatoes, cucumbers, peppers, and a little patch of corn. The only problem? Aunt Lucy had never grown anything in her backyard except grass.

Well, I had a good shovel and a strong back. Just add elbow grease, right? That's when I discovered that the backyard's soil was composed primarily of unyielding "hardpan" clay—much like cement.

You know: *concrete.*

Did I mention I knew next to nothing about actual gardening?

I staked out the area I intended to plant and worked at digging up the sizable patch of grass for four days. Each day my vision for the size of my plot shrank. At the rate I was going I *might* have enough ground turned and tilled to plant a couple of tomato plants.

Jake came to investigate my efforts. He sniffed around the dirt but stayed out of range of my hands. God forbid that I should try to *pet* him let alone *touch* him! Anyway, I'd earned enough stripes trying to pet him. I knew better.

Jake sniffed a patch of dirt and turned around over it a couple of times—

"Get out of there!" I tossed one of my gloves at him. He hissed at me before stalking away.

"He's probably planning to come back and use my garden as his new litter box just to spite me," I growled. "Devil cat!"

I kept at my digging, though. Finally I had a plot about twelve-by-twelve turned, weeded, and ready. I bought some pepper, tomato, cucumber, and squash plants at Home Depot, put them in the ground, and called it good.

Whew.

It was hot already, too. Once the sun fully rose and it was too hot to work in the yard, I retreated indoors. I was grateful for the relief my old swamp cooler afforded. However, by late in the day the vintage evaporative cooler barely kept the house livable. It did the job, but just.

Most days after coming inside, I would sit in the dining room at my little table overlooking my front yard and the cul-de-sac. The swamp cooler blew air from a back window through the kitchen into the dining room, making my perch the most comfortable in the house. I'd spend a couple of hours searching for jobs on my laptop and applying to the scant few positions I found.

While I worked, I'd keep watch through the dining room window. I told myself that I was just admiring my blooming lavender bushes and the creeping sedum in my rock garden, but I watched the other houses in the cul-de-sac.

I watched Mr. and Mrs. Flores, I watched nosy Mrs. Calderón, I watched the Tuckers, and I watched Abe.

I talked about this earlier, but I should add a few more details. You see, in my neighborhood that's what we did: We *watched*. All around our cul-de-sac the neighbors watched each other—and everyone watched everyone else watch them back. It didn't used to be that way, but these days it was a necessary evil.

I've already told you a lot about Abe and Mrs. Calderón. The folks on my right, Mr. and Mrs. Flores, are very simple folk. They have three grown children and a busload of grands, but the kids and grandkids live in other states. Usually the Floreses go to see them instead of the other way around. I don't blame them, given the deteriorating condition of our neighborhood.

These neighbors I've mentioned? We mostly watch out *for* each other. The reason for our constant vigilance comes in the person of the one neighbor I haven't yet described, our local gangbanger, Mateo Martinez.

The rest of us? We all watch him and his girlfriend, Corazón, who live on the other side of the Floreses, in the house between the Floreses and Abe. We keep tabs on Mateo's gang buddies who roar in and out of our cul-de-sac on a daily basis. Some of the neighbors probably keep one finger on their phones, ready to dial 911.

Abe does *his* watching from his front porch, usually with an old revolver next to him on the swing. (Abe is retired military and of the anti-gang persuasion—and New Mexico is an open-carry state.)

APD publishes a list of the two hundred and fifty gangs operating in Albuquerque. Of course, some gangs are larger—and scarier—than others are. I don't know what Mateo's gang is called. I know them by their shaved heads and distinctive tattoos, and I know they are a blight on what had once been a cozy, happy neighborhood.

I remember when this was a quiet, safe place to be a kid. Now the only kid left on the block is Mateo's nephew, Emilio, who moved in with his uncle about a year back.

Emilio. That kid, Mateo's scrawny nephew and the burr under my saddle, spends more time outside than in. All weekend and before and after school (if he actually goes), he perches on the curb in front of his uncle's house.

Doing guess what? *Watching.* And chewing his lip, a shrewd regard darkening his eyes. He watches us and he watches his uncle's gang members come and go. Of course, we watch him, too.

Now that school is out for the summer, he's always there, hunkered down on the curb, shifting his spot on the sidewalk as the shade progresses. His shade comes from the hedge of untended, overgrown juniper bushes that grows between his uncle's yard and Abe's.

Emilio usually fiddles all day with a pocketknife and a scrap of wood. The kid has eyes in the back of his head, a surly temperament, and—for some reason that escapes me—an abiding grudge against *yours truly*.

Emilio is ten or eleven, I think. He's dark-haired and dark-complexioned, skinny, and perpetually sour. He's the reason I use a hefty screwdriver to secure my garage door, why I paid an arm and a leg for some guys to mount bars over my windows, and why I insisted those same guys install metal security doors on the garage's side door and the doors to my house.

The kid hasn't tried anything recently, but the first six months he lived in the neighborhood? Someone broke into my garage at least twice, and I'm sure it was Emilio. He stole some unopened jugs of motor oil the first time and all my tools the second. Abe had to *give* me the big old screwdriver I use to fortify my garage door because all *my* tools were *gone*.

So that's two thefts on the garage. The next time Emilio broke in, it was my house.

It was spring last year. I had been at work, fighting a cold that morning. Exhausted, I'd finally given up the fight and gone home at noon.

I'd come in the side door like always—and caught Emilio red-handed, in my kitchen, going through my cupboards, and eating the leftover pizza I'd planned to have for dinner. He had a plastic grocery sack stuffed with whatever he'd pilfered from me.

We'd both been surprised—stunned—but for two to three seconds we'd just stared at each other. Then anger and hate had sparked in his eyes. And maybe something else? I don't know, and I don't know what he saw in my eyes that made him hate *me* with such vehemence.

Anyway, he'd grabbed up the bag, hit my front door, and lit out across the cul-de-sac and around back of his uncle's house. I called Abe. He came over and we debated calling the police and discussed the likely ramifications of riling up Emilio's uncle.

"Aint' goin' to be worth messin' with that fool uncle o' his," Abe advised. The unspoken caution involved Mateo's gang. They hadn't bothered any of us in the cul-de-sac and, in return, we had not "rocked the boat" with regard to their bothersome presence in our neighborhood. It was an uneasy, unarticulated "truce," but a truce nonetheless.

The next week Abe got a friend to put up the bars on my windows and doors—and not for cheap, either. He managed to get me a discount at least.

While the guys worked, Emilio had sat on the curb across the street. He'd watched, whittling on a stick and sneering at me. Two days later, "someone" spray-painted some nasty words on my garage door. Abe was painting over them when I got home from work that evening. From his regular seat on the curb, Emilio had glared, defiant and bold, shooting obscene hand gestures in my direction . . . and I wondered, not for the first time, why Emilio had been going through my kitchen cupboards.

As I said, Emilio spent more time outside than in. I guess I didn't blame him; it couldn't have been any picnic living with Mateo and Corazón.

If Emilio was the prickly sticker lodged in the bottom of my foot, then Mateo was the thorn in the whole cul-de-sac's side. More than once, we'd witnessed his volatile temper as he'd shouted orders to his gang pals or personally issued a beatdown on one of them. I'd seen for myself the evidence of his violence in the bruises Corazón tried to cover up. I hadn't seen any marks on Emilio, but then, the kid was pretty fast on his feet.

In one way, we (the neighbors) should have been grateful, because the situation could have been much worse. Mateo used his house (and our cul-de-sac) for drunken parties and, for the most part, kept the parties down to a dull roar. Occasionally, when his crew got out of hand, one of us called the police. They cited Mateo a couple of times, but they never found anything to arrest him for—because Mateo kept illegal activities involving his gang far away from his own "crib."

And I guess we could be grateful for that part.

So we watched Mateo and his gang come and go—with their tricked-out, low-rider cars and pounding music—but what else could we do? Mateo had inherited his house from his father so he had a right to live here. Mateo's older brother, Vicente (Emilio's dad) should have inherited the house. Vicente died before his father did, though, so Mateo got the house.

I remember Mateo's dad, Mr. Martinez. He had always been kind to Aunt Lucy, Genie, and me. I also remember the worried creases between his eyes and his disappointment as Mateo grew from rebel teen to defiant criminal and gang member. Back then we had overheard more than a few shouted arguments between Mateo and his dad.

If our old neighbor could see what Mateo was doing now—how his son had spoiled our neighborhood? Well, Mr. Martinez would be spinning in his grave.

***

May passed into June without incident, but also without a new job. Money was getting tight. My unemployment checks kept the clichéd wolf from the door, but on the other side of that door I worried that my gas and electric would be shut off—right after the Internet. I just could not manage all the utility bills on top of the mortgage and a much-straitened grocery budget. Soon I would have to choose between lights to see by and gas to cook by. Or my cell phone.

Aunt Lucy would have terminated the Internet and phone by now, but you can't find a job without those any longer. Without Internet, finding a job was impossible, and if I didn't have a phone, potential employers had no way to contact me.

One morning in mid-June I decided to tackle the weeds in my vegetable garden. I had done a good job keeping them at bay, but in the heat they were getting away from me. That day I resolved to really clean them out.

I soaked the garden to loosen the weeds. I might have—and I'm just saying *might have*—soaked the garden a bit too much. I only mention this because while the water loosened the weeds, it also turned the natural clay soil to a slick, sticky bog.

I had been working since before six in the morning in what felt like wet cement. Fearful that I might lose them forever, I had taken off my shoes. I was wearing good gardening gloves, but they—and the rest of me from my elbows down—were covered in layers of dripping, drying, and dried mud.

I figured the time to be around nine, and I still had a third of the weeds to go. I was flagging but determined to finish. The hardest part was getting the shovel down into the ground so I could turn over the wet, heavy soil.

"There you are. I rang the doorbell but no one answered so I thought I'd check back here. Hello."

Mind you, I'm no vision on a good day, but that day I was on my knees, spattered and slimed with mud. I was hot, sweaty, and filthy.

Not so the man who stood a few steps away. Oh, no. *He* was clean and tidy, casually dressed in jeans, a polo shirt, and a lightweight suit jacket.

And, I should add, *very good looking*.

I swallowed and willed my expressionless mask to drop. "Yes?"

He raised his hand from his side as though he had planned to offer a handshake, but if he *had* planned to offer his hand, I'm pretty sure he thought better of it as soon as he eyed my mud-caked gloves.

"Sorry to disturb you. I'm Zander Cruz. Are you Miss Keyes?"

"Yes, I am." I stood up.

Mistake. Mud trailed from my shorts down my legs.

Oooh. Stunning, I'm sure.

"What can I do for you?"

He considered me for a moment. "I think that can wait until after we finish up here." Without another word, he stripped off his suit jacket, put it to the side, and picked up my shovel.

"This patch here?" he asked, indicating the last unturned portion of the garden.

"I . . . um, yes."

It took him five minutes to turn over what would have taken me another twenty or thirty, and then he dropped to his knees and started knocking clods apart and sorting out weeds.

I didn't say anything. He didn't say anything. We just weeded.

He obviously knew what he was doing, and I tried not to stare as he made short work of what was left.

"Um, I think that does it." I stood up and so did he.

"Great. Where do you want all this?" He pointed to the pile of weeds.

"In the trash. I'll get the wheelbarrow."

"Show me; I'll fetch it."

He brought the wheelbarrow over from the rickety garden shed and together we piled it full of weeds and the mud clinging to them. He wheeled the heavy mess to the trash and shoveled it in.

"Now. Where were we?" He held out a grimy hand. "I'm Zander Cruz." A grin lurked around his eyes—gray in color—but he didn't let the grin reach his mouth.

That is, until I laughed and shook his hand with my equally grimy glove. "Gemma Keyes. Thank you for your help."

"My pleasure." He grinned with me now.

"That was hot work. I suppose I should offer you something cold to drink. Iced tea all right? And what was it you wanted to see me about?" I liked the looks of this guy, liked his attitude.

"Yes to the tea. I just wanted to meet you, introduce myself. I'm the new associate at DCC. I'll wash my hands and rinse the shovel and wheelbarrow while you get the tea."

DCC. As in *Downtown Community Church*. DCC was Aunt Lucy's old church, the church she'd dragged us girls to for years.

If I weren't so good at concealing my feelings, I'm certain the guy would have seen irritation and disappointment alter my demeanor. *Abe!* This Zander Cruz guy was only here "to meet me" at *Abe's behest*—probably because I'd confided my spying guilt to him.

I dearly love the old guy, but this crossed a line, you know?

There's a lot to my "church story" and the many reasons I wanted nothing to do with it or its people. Most of my reasons began with Genie—of course.

From the first day Aunt Lucy had taken us to service at DCC, Genie played the "Hi! I'm the perfect child!" role and played it . . . well, *perfectly*. She had smiled and charmed, said the right things, done the right things, and was always delightful and helpful—when all the while she was laughing at the DCC folks behind their backs.

I know; we had shared a bedroom and I'd heard her ridicule them often enough.

Genie enjoyed hurting others. She'd select a kid from church and cotton up to the poor soul until he or she trusted and confided in her. Then at home in the privacy of our room, Genie would (out loud!) pick them apart until she found the ideal weakness and the means to exploit it.

Genie hadn't kept her plots to herself. No, I was always privy to her cunning—because Genie relished my horrified reactions as much as she relished the malicious, gleeful destruction she sowed.

After she'd picked the boy or girl apart and found what she was looking for, she would find a way to drop an embellished hint or a juicy morsel (*always* something hurtful or offensive) into one of the other kids' ears. Before long, the kids in Sunday school had been at each other's throats. Every week it was some new drama.

Yes; wherever Genie had gone, damaging strife followed—and she loved it.

For extra points she had particularly loved pointing the finger at *me*. When chaos inevitably ensued and the adults got involved, Genie would always be the convincing, innocent bystander—and somehow *I* would come under scrutiny. No one could seem to figure out where the problem originated, but I remember Aunt Lucy and Abe turning sad and disappointed eyes on me. The memory of their mistrust still stings.

Had the people at DCC really been that blind? Had *Aunt Lucy* been that blind? Maybe. But Genie had also been that "good." Not one person at DCC ever saw through her deceptions or how artfully she'd poisoned everyone against me.

Whatever. I would not be darkening the doors of DCC again. Not in this lifetime.

Do I sound bitter? Paranoid? Well, you haven't met Genie yet. But perhaps now you can understand why I had found it safer to hide in the background and let Genie be the pretty, vivacious twin while I played the plain, stupid, silent one. I stayed out of trouble that way.

Oh, and by the way. Belicia Calderón and Genie have been thick as thieves since Genie and I were girls. If you think Mrs. Calderón taught Genie bad habits, think again.

It was the other way around.

I stripped off my gloves and stood on an old towel I'd laid on my kitchen floor while I washed my hands and arms. I scrubbed them harder than I needed to: The old memories still had the power to work me up.

I took a cleansing breath and shoved those dark feelings away. I don't like to let them intrude anymore. Then I filled two tall glasses with ice and took a pitcher of tea from the fridge. With my hands full, I pushed the fridge door closed with my hip.

Mistake number two. A rump-sized schmear graced the refrigerator door.

Argh!

Then I wondered—and glanced at my reflection in the back door window.

Mistake number three. Mud droplets spattered my face and hair.

I looked like a plague victim.

What do I care? He's (shudder) *an associate pastor,* I told myself. *And besides, he's been looking at me like this for an hour already.*

When I took the tea outside, Jake was sitting next to Zander, pushing his yellow tomcat mug into Zander's hand, purring and relishing a good scratching under Zander's fingertips. I glared at the horrid creature, amazed and disgusted at the same time.

Of course when I sat on the porch—at least three feet from Jake—he hissed, raised his back, and stalked off, our animus intact.

Zander and I sat on the back porch drinking our tea and talking. I have to admit, it felt comfortable. Our conversation was light, he wasn't preachy, and I felt that I didn't have to hide myself—which was unusual for me.

He's seen me at my worst, I thought. *That leaves nothing to hide.*

Zander, "Short for Alexander," he told me, grew up outside Las Cruces in southern New Mexico. "My folks had three acres and we planted pretty much what you have here. A lot more corn, though, to dry and grind for masa. We had pecan trees, too. Nothing stacks up against a real, homemade pecan pie."

My stomach rumbled in agreement. "Ice cream. Pecan pie has to be served warm, topped with vanilla ice cream."

"Of course. Not legal without it."

After about thirty minutes we'd drained the pitcher and he stood up. "I have to go now. I enjoyed talking with you, Gemma." He tipped his head just a hair. "I like your name. *Gemma*. It's perfect for you."

I may have gawked, but he didn't notice; he was putting on his jacket.

"I'm sure you've figured out that your good friend Abe Pickering sicced me on you. I apologize for ambushing you the way I did, but he set his teeth in me three Sundays ago and would not let go of my ankle until I said I'd call on you. Chewed right through my socks, he did." Zander was grinning with his eyes.

I smirked and then had to laugh. It was too vivid of an image—and too true-to-life—not to chuckle, "Yup. That's Abe."

"Forgive me, then?"

I nodded. "Thanks for pitching in. You came along just as the bog was about to suck me under—never to have been seen again."

If only I'd known how prophetic those words were.

Zander threw back his head and laughed. His unfeigned good humor earned a smile from me in return.

"I'm glad I came at the right time," he said. "Glad I could help."

Then he looked me in the eye. "Here's where I'm *supposed* to throw out my obligatory pitch and ask you to come to church Sunday, but no, I'm not going to do that. Instead, I'll just say: Gemma, you are very loved by God. Not in a 'God loves everybody' sense, but in an individual, personal sense. He loves *you*, Gemma Keyes."

My mask clicked on. Effortlessly, seamlessly. "Thanks again for coming."

He smiled. The corners of his gray eyes crinkled. "I'm glad I did."

⌘⌘⌘⌘

CHAPTER 6

Like most summers before the monsoons arrived, late June was hot and dry and miserable. Three months of unemployment had passed, three months had gone by since Dr. P and Dr. Bickel died in the tragic incident in the AMEMS lab. And what of that tragedy? Three months of "dedicated investigation" had elapsed, and the explosion that took their lives remained inadequately explained to the public.

I had just completed my weekly unemployment certification. I applied to four jobs that week, all four with government contractors, and all four positions below my qualifications. Still, I doubted I would hear from any of them.

I nursed a growing suspicion that General *Snaggletooth* had flagged my security clearance. If so, the most cursory scan of my profile in eQIP, the government's security clearance database, would warn off all potential government contractor employers.

You see, you can't get a decent DOE job without a security clearance, and I'd held a "Q," which equates (roughly) to a Top Secret clearance on the Department of Defense side. If Cushing had flagged my file in any negative manner, I'd never work in government again.

I logged into my email anyway. Not much popped up: A message telling me my bank statement was ready to view.

Great. As if I weren't disheartened enough already.

The subject line on the other new message caught my attention: "Re: Your Job Application."

It was a better day already! I clicked it open and read the single line inside the email.

Sorry for the spam.

"Huh?" I didn't recognize the sender, and I was in no mood for games.

What spam? I thought this was about a job!

Apparently it wasn't.

I scowled, clicked open my spam folder, and perused each email diverted there by my Gmail spam filter. I scrolled by the usual pharmaceutical offers, ignored six or seven letters from the Federal Minister of Finance of an impoverished African nation (or variations on that theme), and disregarded lots of "deals" and "re-fi" offers and some "FedEx" or "USPS" delivery notifications that were, in reality, phishing scams.

One message with the subject line that read: *You'll Love My Photo.*

I stared at the message for a few seconds, debating whether or not to open it. Opening the email was not where the danger lay: If the email contained malware, it was inside the attachment—inside the photo they were so sure I would "love."

The photo might be porn, and I didn't want to deal with that. In addition to the porn, the sender would have embedded a nasty virus or some other kind of malware in the photo. If I opened the picture file, it might execute the virus.

I clicked on the message and opened it. I glanced at the attachment, a .jpg file, and then gulped. Right there, in the message, was the same statement: *Sorry for the spam.*

My eyes narrowed. I closed the message and clicked "delete."

When the screen cleared, the email with the subject line, "Re: Your Job Application," stared back at me.

Sorry for the spam.

I didn't want to admit it, but something in the cryptic message intrigued me.

I looked at my external hard drive. I didn't write data to my computer's hard drive. The only things on my computer were the operating system and installed software. I saved all my data to an external hard drive and then backed up regularly to my Acronis account in the cloud. I also backed up my system image on Acronis because I'm a little OCD.

If I opened the photo and a piece of malware propagated across my system, I would have to wipe the drive and start over. It would take me a couple of hours to restore the system image from Acronis.

Was it worth it? Just because I was "intrigued?"

Well, did I have anything more pressing on my busy social calendar?

My hands, practically of their own volition, reached for the USB cable that connected my computer to the external drive and pulled the cable out.

Guess I was going to open that photo file.

I dragged the email from my trash folder and put it back in my inbox. Then I inserted a USB flash drive into my computer. Without opening the email's image attachment, I saved the file to my flash drive, opened my virus scanner, and scanned the drive.

The scan results came back quickly: *No virus or malware detected.*

I studied the icon of the image for a few seconds and then clicked on it. It opened. I stared at the photo in front of me from under raised eyebrows. It was merely a picture of Sandia Crest, the big Sandia Mountains uplift that dominated Albuquerque's eastern foothills!

Nothing special, no spectacular sunset, *no porn* and, as far as I could see, not relevant to anything?

I sat back, thinking.

You'll Love My Photo.

Oh, yeah? And why is that?

I figured the file either contained malware so sophisticated or new that my virus software did not detect it (in which case I was in deep doo-doo) or the image was hiding something.

I'm no hacker—I don't know what the "darknet" means, let alone how to navigate it. I'm maybe head and shoulders above the average user, but I'm no hacker or technogeek.

On the other hand, while working for DOE I had heard of steganography, the practice of hiding data files within an image. That's how those who sent destructive emails hid strings of malware in an image. We were warned at Sandia not to open or download images from the Web, for fear we'd bring malware onto our network.

I spent twenty minutes browsing the Web, looking for a simple means to open the .jpg file without triggering an executable file. I ended up downloading a trial version of WinRAR. Once I'd installed the WinRAR program, I followed the instructions on one of those "how-to" sites and sat back and stared. Again. Only this time, I was staring at a file named, "Read_Me_Gemma.zip."

Whoa.

I put my hand over my mouth, puzzled, and a little freaked out.

Well, I was not about to unpack the zipped file without scanning it first, so I did so. That scan came back clean, too, so I unpacked the zip file.

It was a letter. To me!

I scanned to the bottom for the signature, and my mouth fell open.

But it couldn't be!

My Dear Miss Keyes,

If you are reading this message, then you truly are the intelligent, savvy young woman I took you for. For whatever reason, you always seemed to undervalue yourself and allowed others to do the same. But despite that remarkable, "flat" affect you habitually present to the world, I recognized that there was much more to you than you were willing to reveal.

As regards to this message? I had to find a way to communicate with you, Miss Keyes, and it could not be out in the open.

They are hunting for me, you see, and I could not take the chance that they might be monitoring you. Not that I think they are, mind you, but I could not risk it.

You see, you and the rest of the world think I'm dead.

"No kidding!" I muttered.

Unfortunately, Cushing knows better.

*Gemma (I hope it is all right that I call you by your first name as we did at Sandia?), you were aware that I was doing advanced and classified R&D on the civilian side of things at Sandia. Dr. Prochanski liked to report on the state of "our" work, but the truth is that it was all me. I was doing the work; all the theories and efforts were **mine**. Dr. Prochanski may have led the AMEMS lab, but Sandia brought me in because **my** research in MEMS was, quite accurately, years ahead of anything **his** puny mind could conceptualize.*

Dr. Prochanski, that underachieving braggart, couldn't grasp the progress I was making—let alone the science behind it! I should say, "the progress I made." Yes, I finally achieved the breakthrough I had theorized about and sought for more than thirty-five years. Thirty-five years of hard work, of dedicated research, design, and development! I, at last, achieved my breakthrough goal.

You also might not know that Dr. Prochanski kept our DOE oversight in the dark about the state of my projects. Now I'm going to tell you why you lost your job—and why I had to "die."

*Dr. Prochanski had a secret deal with General Cushing—a secret deal he **thought** I knew nothing about. You see, I objected to any military appropriation or national security application of my work. Prochanski knew that and General Cushing knew that. They plotted to get my breakthrough to a prototype stage and then seize it for national security purposes—take it from the civilian side at Sandia to the military side.*

And they believed I was only at the "prototype" stage! They were the ones in the dark, despite Prochanski's efforts to monitor, record, and steal my work.

Gemma, when we worked together at Sandia, I stayed aloof from everyone. As a person trying to hide my true agenda from Cushing and Prochanski, I couldn't help but notice you, to a degree, doing the same thing.

Yes, though you were an excellent member of the AMEMS team, you kept your little shield up all the time. I concluded that you had a need, just as I had a need, to protect yourself. I don't say I understand your motives, but I recognized a kindred spirit in you.

Dear girl, I am so sorry that you lost your job. Prochanski was one of the most egotistical individuals I've had the displeasure to know. I tried to warn you, Gemma, (in the most subtle manner) that he could not be trusted, but you were, quite understandably, loyal to him and could not see how evil a man he was.

Yes, he truly is dead. Again, I am sorry for your loss.

On the last day you worked at Sandia, when you overheard Prochanski and Cushing's unguarded conversation in the conference room, you were no longer of any use to Prochanski. In fact, you became a threat, a liability to their plans. So Prochanski decided to get rid of you, and Cushing arranged to besmirch your security clearance. You'll never work for government again.

"I knew it," I growled.

I hope that sad experience ripped the blinders from your eyes? But all is not lost! I told you that Dr. Prochanski kept our DOE oversight in the dark about the state of my R&D. Well, guess what? I kept him in the dark, too. I have much to tell you on this topic, but can divulge nothing more in this message.

You must be wondering why I'm reaching out to you, Gemma. Here I must admit that I'm in a bit of a spot. To be plain, I need help and have no one in the immediate locale I can trust. Because we share a kindred spirit, I am willing to trust you. Will you trust me?

I stopped reading. It was a bit hard to reconcile this open, quite human person to the aloof, taciturn Dr. Bickel *I* knew. Oh, I recognized the brilliant-but-arrogant braggart in the first part of the message, but this "kindred spirit" stuff? All new to me.

On the other hand, if Dr. P was—had been—as underhanded as Dr. Bickel wrote, then yes, I could understand why Dr. Bickel had maintained a rigid distance from his coworkers. I could understand completely. I skimmed the last few lines and then re-read them, studied them with care.

I can't risk another email landing in your inbox. If you are afraid of getting involved, I won't blame you. Imogene Cushing is that scary. But if you are willing to take a chance or at least take another step, look for another piece of spam tomorrow.

Sincerely,

Daniel Bickel

PS: Delete this message and purge your email's trash folder.

I stared at the document, processing all Dr. Bickel had written— processing the fact that he was alive!

So whatever disaster occurred in the AMEMS lab, Dr. P died but Dr. Bickel got away?

General Cushing had managed to cover up the absence of Dr. Bickel's body in the lab's rubble—making Dr. Bickel dead to the world. I pondered the implications of such an "accomplishment" and didn't like what I came up with.

The stakes in this game are high, I thought, *high enough for Cushing to declare a man dead who wasn't, and high enough for Cushing's superiors to give her the support she needed to pull off such a cover-up.*

I was saddened again over Dr. Prochanski's death, but then I replayed the scene in the conference room on my last day at Sandia. I recalled every nuanced word and every denigrating remark that had come out of General Cushing's smiling mouth. I remembered how she had arched her eyebrow and smiled—and how Dr. P had revealed his true colors.

Oh, I remembered it all.

Dr. Bickel is right. Cushing is scary, I thought. *Scary and evil.*

But you, Dear Reader? You recollect when I wrote about that day that I'd seen worse. You remember that, don't you? Yes, Cushing was scary and evil.

But I'd tackled worse.

The doorbell rang. It jolted me out of my deep reflection. I closed down my laptop and went to the door. I peeked through the peephole.

Dark hair and gray eyes stared back at me.

Holy crud. Zander Cruz.

I cracked open the door.

"Hi, Gemma. I hope this isn't a bad time?"

"Um, no. It's fine." I opened the door for him to come in. Instead, he gestured to the front steps.

"I prefer to not give the neighbors anything to gossip about."

I instantly pictured Mrs. Calderón's pudgy chin and nose flattened against her front window—just before she waddled over to my yard to poke her nose into my business. "Agreed, but the resident gossip has a bird's-eye view of my front porch. How about we sit on the back steps like before?"

"Sounds good." He took the steps two at a time and headed around the side of the house.

I ran to the kitchen, dropped ice in two glasses, and grabbed a jug of lemonade from the fridge. When I opened the back door, Zander was studying my garden.

Jake was winding his way in and out of Zander's legs. I hardly knew what to think of Jake's taking to Zander. I shot the cat a malevolent look. He put his nose in the air and strutted away.

"What do you think?" It was an inane opening to a conversation, but it's what came out of my mouth.

"I think it's doing as well as can be expected." He took a glass from me. "Thanks! I've been on the road all morning. How did you know my throat feels like roadkill broiling in the sun?"

I nearly spewed lemonade. "Um, quite the colorful description."

He laughed. "Sorry. That's just me. I'm never what folks expect."

I wondered what he meant but turned the conversation back to my garden. "What did you mean by 'as well as can be expected'?"

He walked over to the plot and pointed at my tomatoes. "Well, it's the hottest part of the summer, so your plants are struggling just like everyone else's are. On the other hand, your soil is just too much clay. Clay is dense. You have to water way too much before the water soaks down to your plants' roots, and the roots themselves are probably rotting. They are crowded and waterlogged."

"Well, what can I do about that?"

"Amend the soil with some mulch and garden soil. You really need to do that in the spring before you plant, but you have time to work some in this season."

"Okaaay."

He laughed again. "If you're not doing anything, let's hop in my car and I'll show you what to get."

An hour later we were back with bags of garden soil, an expense I couldn't afford. I bought them anyway. Zander and I talked the entire hour to and from the store and never ran out of things to say. Of course I didn't mention the astonishing email from a dead scientist I'd decoded and read before Zander had arrived, but it wasn't far from my mind.

As he was leaving Zander asked, "What's the deal with the boy across the way?" He tipped his head in the general direction of Mateo Martinez' house.

I glanced over. True to form, Emilio huddled on the curb in the tiny patch of shade the overgrown shrubs provided. He was fiddling with something in his lap and I glimpsed the flash of a blade. He was whittling again.

Emilio, as though sensing us talking about him, glared at us from under his dark brows. I frowned. He reciprocated.

"That's Emilio."

"He was sitting out there when I pulled up the last time I was here and was still there when I left. Is he always out on the curb?"

I shrugged. "Pretty much."

Zander gave me a quizzical look. "Does he live around here?"

"Sure. Right there. He lives with his uncle and his uncle's girlfriend."

"Do you think he's being taken care of properly?"

I was starting to feel a little defensive. I shrugged again. "I don't know—his uncle runs with a gang, so everyone in the neighborhood steers clear of them. And Emilio has broken into my garage twice and my house at least once. He's the reason I have all these bars on the windows and doors."

Zander stared at me unblinking, and I had the impression that I'd given a disappointing answer. It didn't help that I heard Aunt Lucy's voice echoing in my head, *It's our job to help those whom God places in front of us—especially those who are defenseless.*

I shoved her words into a dark corner and set my jaw: *No way this kid qualifies as "defenseless." He's a little thief. A little gangster-in-the-making.*

Zander studied Emilio across the cul-de-sac. Emilio shot Zander a fierce snarl in return. Zander murmured a preoccupied goodbye to me and strode toward his car. I shrugged again and turned to go inside.

When I didn't hear Zander's car start I looked out the window and, openmouthed, watched Zander striding across the cul-de-sac. He held what looked like a couple of Powerade bottles in his hands. He walked up to Emilio and squatted in front of him.

I couldn't hear what they were saying but I watched, trying to understand what Zander was doing. He and Emilio exchanged a few words. Zander held the drinks toward Emilio who, after a moment's hesitation, took them.

Zander said a few more words and Emilio looked away but ducked his head in assent. Then Zander clapped Emilio on the shoulder and stood up. He waved his hand once at Emilio and came back across the road and got in his car.

He saw me in the window and waved once to me, too. I lifted my hand in return, but I was watching Emilio. He was chugging one of the bottles.

Aunt Lucy's voice returned with more insistence. *It's our job to help those God places in front of us—especially those who are defenseless.*

Zander: *Do you think he's being taken care of properly?*
I don't know—his uncle runs with a gang so everyone in the neighborhood steers clear of them. And Emilio's broken into my garage twice and my house at least once. He's the reason I have all these bars on the windows and doors.

I realized that I was holding my breath and blew it out. Frustrated and disquieted, I stepped away from the window.

***

I waited until after three in the afternoon the next day to check my spam folder. There I found a message with the subject line, *Don't Wait! Refi Now—Federally In$ured!*

"Clever, Dr. Bickel," I whispered.

I opened the email and scanned its brief contents: a very questionable link and another image. I picked the image, saved it to my flash drive, and ran it through the same processes as I had with the picture yesterday. I discovered another zipped file hidden in the image, named "read_me.zip."

After I'd scanned the zipped file and extracted its contents, I found two items: a text file named "read_first" and a PDF file named "print_me." I scanned the files for viruses and then opened the text file. The only words in the file were, "Print other at once and delete all."

My venerable old HP 5P spit out the PDF file in seconds. I made sure the copy—several pages long—was complete before I deleted the files from my flash drive, deleted the email from my spam folder, and deleted the *deleted* email from my email's trash.

The last thing I did was to reformat my flash drive—not that I thought that taking those precautions would be enough if someone were inside Google's main servers where their email backups are stored, but at least a cursory glance would flag nothing out of the ordinary.

I picked up the three printed pages and skimmed them. The first page contained a map? The other two pages were printed instructions—no, *directions*—with references to the map. I read the directions and followed them with my finger on the map, my mouth widening in disbelief.

"You've got to be joking," I breathed. "Oh, Dr. Bickel! What have you done?"

⌘⌘⌘⌘

CHAPTER 7

If you were to use Google Earth as I did and follow Tramway through Albuquerque as far south as far it goes, you would pass over a shopping area and then various housing developments. Beyond those housing developments lay the mountain indicated by Dr. Bickel's map.

The mountain on Dr. Bickel's map is pretty innocuous as far as mountains go: rounded, unimposing, not terribly high. I'd hiked and climbed around in Albuquerque foothills that were more challenging. Still, I studied the mountain to become familiar with its peculiarities.

From above I scanned all around the mountain and counted the ring of bunkers built into the mountain's flanks. I spied the road that banded the mountain, connecting the bunkers. And there was no missing the PIDAS at the base of the mountain, not far below the road. The PIDAS and the patrol roads on either side cut a wide swath out of the mountain. The tall, razor-wire-topped fences running parallel around the mountain were the main attraction.

The satellite details were a little fuzzy, but one thing was quite clear: all of what I studied lay *inside* Kirtland Air Force Base's perimeter fence.

And he wants me to follow this map and his directions?

I'd done my research, too. I knew that the mountain had housed weapons back in the day. Supposedly the place was riddled with tunnels carved out by the military. Supposedly the mountain wasn't guarded all that well any more.

And supposedly Dr. Bickel *hadn't lost his mind.*

Still, sane or not, Dr. Bickel was asking me to come—to trespass on the base and enter the mountain. He was asking me to risk *a lot.*

Because I don't want to be responsible for anyone else attempting what I did, I won't record exactly where my approach to the mountain began. It's enough to say that I followed Dr. Bickel's map and directions, including his advice to wear good boots and gloves.

It was evening, past dusk. I drove slowly through one of the residential areas that butted up against the foothills along the base's border. The foothills here are designated Albuquerque open space. Hiking trails wind through the open space, open space that adjoins and follows the base's perimeter fence.

Signs at the trailheads proclaim that the open space closes at 10 p.m. and announce that hikers are under video surveillance. I didn't know how long I'd be gone, and I didn't want to leave my car at the trailhead where it would attract unwanted attention, so I decided to park a couple of blocks away from one of the trailheads.

I found a good spot on a side street, shouldered the small rucksack I carried, and headed uphill to the trailhead. All was quiet as I set out on well-used paths leading from the trailhead into the open space.

The days were long now, so it was already late. The scent of grasses and warm dirt wafted to me on the evening air. Off to the west, the last glow of the sun silhouetted the west mesa and faintly outlined *the mountain* west and south of me.

I angled a little east through the open space, passed through a hiker's gate in a barbed wire fence, and kept going. I walked under darkening skies, following various markers on the map, then slanted south, toward the base's fence.

The base's boundary line wasn't far, actually. It took me only another five minutes to reach it. I followed the fence line for about a quarter mile more.

Dr. Bickel's map and instructions told me to look for a scrub piñon up against the fence. He described the tree's shape and other markers nearby. I found the tree without any difficulty: It was down in an arroyo, what New Mexicans call a gully or a "wash."

His instructions told me to crawl under the branches of the bushy tree. I would find, he wrote, that flash floods had washed the earth from around the tree's roots and scoured the soil out from under the fence. I donned my well-worn pair of leather gloves, climbed down into the arroyo, wriggled my way under the low branches, and came smack up against the fence—just as Dr. Bickel had said I would.

The arroyo was strewn with rocks and gravel; the bottom of the fence was, at its most accessible point in the arroyo, perhaps a foot off the ground—room enough for me to squeeze under if I pushed my rucksack ahead of me first.

I peered through the chain link. On the other side the patrol road ran parallel to the fence. However, the arroyo's terrain was rough and its edges crumbling, so they had pulled the patrol road away from the arroyo's banks. The road was farther from the fence line here than it had been before I reached the piñon. From the bottom of the arroyo I could no longer see the road—and neither could someone on the road see the bottom of the wash. Or me.

Dr. Bickel's notes insisted that the base ran patrol infrequently and that the fence wasn't closely inspected. That said, from this point on, there would be no doubt of my being in an area where I had no business being.

I took a deep breath to calm myself—and stalled out.

Right there, under the inky sky, I almost bailed. It would have been easy to turn around and go back home.

Was I scared?

Well, was I planning to trespass on a U. S. military base?

Was I, furthermore, preparing to venture into a restricted government area without due authorization?

Um, *yeah*. So right-o, I was scared. The base might not post armed guards around the mountain 24/7 anymore, but I didn't care to compile a list of all the laws I was about to break.

This wasn't the first time I'd gone over this moral and legal ground. But each time I held argument with myself, a reaction in the pit of my stomach—a response more powerful than merely "scared"—egged me on. The gut-level truth was: *I was angry.* I was angry with Dr. P and General Cushing—angry that *their* schemes had cost me my livelihood and angry that, through no fault of my own, I had been embroiled in plots and plans *I had nothing to do with.*

Angry people do rash things, sometimes foolish and rebellious things. Aunt Lu's cautioning voice resounded in my head, warning me not to allow my emotions to dictate my decisions.

Yet on the other side, the rash side, along with my anger, surged a conviction: What Cushing and Prochanski had intended to do to Dr. Bickel was wrong. Criminally wrong. *It was murder, plain and simple.* Now Dr. Bickel said he needed my help. He was the innocent party here, and if I could help him, shouldn't I? And if I could do something to stop General Cushing, shouldn't I do it?

Really? The voice of reason sneered, heavy on the sarcasm. *Really? **You** do something? You might as well be a gnat nipping at a bear's behind, for all the effect you could hope to have on an Air Force major general and a federal government program run amok.*

I'd ridden this train of thought enough times that I was becoming efficient at shutting down my internal scruples.

I know, I know. Not smart at all.

Right there, huddled at the bottom of a washed-out gully, I used my anger and sense of "justice" as the tool to lever caution aside. Again, I acknowledge: *not smart at all.*

The good news was that I would live through this ill-advised course of action.

The bad news?

I would live to regret it.

The night was darkening; if I was going ahead, I needed to get moving.

I pushed my rucksack under the fence. It took me longer to wriggle through, scraping against the rock-strewn arroyo bed as I went. A few minutes later I was officially trespassing on the base.

An owl called somewhere out in the night as I knelt and leaned against the wrong side of the fence. Then I crawled up the side of the arroyo and ran across the patrol road. Crouched in the dark, I opened Dr. Bickel's map.

I needed enough light to see the map and the directions I was to follow. A dependable Maglite hung from my belt but, it was not for use out in the open. I had no idea who, civilian or military, might be watching the backside of this mountain. If I switched on a flashlight in the starry night, I would be painting a target on myself. I palmed a tiny penlight to illuminate the map; my hand would shield its light from observing eyes.

Not far away from where I knelt, another patrol road intersected the one following the fence line. For the first part of my trek I was to follow the intersecting road as it led south and west, in the general direction of the mountain. Once I had my bearings, I crept along, not on the road, but alongside it. The ground undulated with holes, cracks, and dry beds where runoff had scored deep cracks in the sandy soil. I walked in the low spots as much as possible. Then the terrain began to slope upward.

Above me I saw the outline of the old PIDAS. I headed directly for the fences. The route sloped upward the entire way, but I kept the PIDAS in front of me. When I drew close to it, I ducked down behind some brush to consider my next move.

A patrol road ran alongside the PIDAS on its outside perimeter; another road ran along its inside perimeter. Between the roads, the military had graded a great, wide swath of ground. Atop the ground, they had laid a mesh of interconnected sensors and spread dirt over it. They had erected the fences along the length of the swath. The roads, the sensors, and the parallel fences completely enclosed the mountain.

Back when the government stored weapons in the tunnels, one of the fences had been electrified and the sensor system under the graded dirt had been active. Dr. Bickel said the PIDAS wasn't active anymore, but that didn't make the fences topped with razor wire any less intimidating.

I estimated the distance straight across the patrol roads and the PIDAS to be fifty yards or more. Fifty very long yards where I would be completely out in the open with only the night to hide me. I shivered a little. At least the wire mesh and sensors laying under the swath were no longer active.

Says here in fine print.

(Skepticism alert!)

I consulted Dr. Bickel's map. It took a while to find the markers indicated on the map and align myself with them. I walked five minutes south in the brush below the PIDAS before I spotted the three rocks on the opposite side of the PIDAS and the other patrol road: One of the rocks was as tall as I was. The other two, one piled atop the other, were just shorter than the first.

Before I stepped onto the smoothed earth, I followed Dr. Bickel's instructions and tore off a branch of sagebrush. Then I faced the three rocks straight on and marched toward them. I crossed the outside patrol road and continued toward the fence, wagging the piece of brush in the dirt behind me to scuff my footprints. When I reached the fence I shone my penlight down. There, along the closest fence post, I saw nearly invisible vertical cuts in the links.

Clever.

My instructions said to push the section of fence forward, not pull it back. I did so, and tossed my rucksack ahead before squeezing through myself, dragging my piece of sagebrush with me.

I pushed the fencing back into place, taking care to line up the cut links, and brushed the dirt around the fence bottom, scuffing out the scribed marks the fence section had made in the dirt. I wasn't terribly worried about my footprints or the marks the fence made. The swath, perhaps once well-tended, was now dotted with desert grass and small brush that, from its looks, the military probably mowed once a year.

Then I scuttled through the no-man's land to the second fence, sweeping my footprints behind me. I found similar cuts in the second fence and pushed through just as I had with the first one. I shoved the fence back into alignment and smoothed out the dirt.

I got to the other side of the dirt swath, crossed the inside patrol road, and looked back to see if my brushed footprints showed. If they did, I couldn't tell. It was too dark.

I stowed my "broom" behind the three rocks and climbed the slope above me. Next I would reach the road that banded the mountain and connected the bunkers.

I crested the slope, slipped between barbed wire strands, and stepped onto the road. I didn't waste any time there. Heart pounding, I crossed quickly. From there my track angled to the left and was steeper.

I pushed on.

Fifteen minutes later I stumbled in the dark toward the next marker, a flat ledge. On the right, shadows played over sagebrush, boulders, and weeds. To the left of the ledge and straight ahead hung a black void. The map warned me of an abrupt drop-off, so I approached with caution.

When I at last stood on the flat ledge, the map pointed me right, at an oblique angle. My route was all steeply rugged now.

According to the instructions, my objective was above me: a rocky outcropping on the side of the mountain. When I reached the rocks I was breathing hard—it had been a challenging climb. I stepped behind a boulder and sat back on my heels to rest and study my next moves.

The penlight on the now-grimy sheet illuminated the words, "Head for the middle of the outcropping. When you see the tallest pillar, go behind it. There you'll find a door."

A door in the middle of what was basically a wall of rocks? I drank some water and waited for my heart rate to slow.

I found "the tallest pillar" in a field of boulders. The only way to get *behind* it was to crawl over and around a bunch of other very large rocks. It took me a while—in the dark with only my penlight to guide me—to arrive "behind" the tallest pillar.

Dear Reader: I particularly detest the idea of climbing around in a pile of rocks—in the dark—with the specter of scorpions and snakes lurking on, around, and under every rock. I had to force myself to crawl and climb. Dr. Bickel's instructions to wear good hiking boots and leather gloves were never more appreciated. Regardless, I kept my hands away from cracks and niches.

At last—no mean feat!—I was behind the tallest of the rock columns. I played my tiny light over the wall behind the pillar and saw nothing. I looked again. On my third scan I glimpsed the barest glint of metal. I pointed the light at what might be an edge of some kind. I clambered over another rock and around an unexpected curve—practically a left-hand turn. I followed the unexpected turn and was confronted by a thick metal door. It was cleverly angled away from the pillar so that only its edge had hinted at it.

Whoever had installed the door had made sure it would not be easily seen, even in daylight, and whoever had constructed the door had done so a long while ago. Its exterior was weathered and corroded—and quite without handle or any visible means of opening it. I referred again to my instructions.

"With your left toe, press the lower left corner of the door. At the same time, press the upper right corner with your hand," I recited.

I'm not that tall. I stretched myself out, as far as I could, left toe and right hand, corner to corner across the door. I pressed fingers and boot toe where indicated. Nothing happened—and then under my fingers I felt something give. Still, the door did not open. I pushed with my booted left toes with the same result—*nada*. Frustrated, I pressed my fingers over the upper right corner of the door and *kicked* the toe of my left hiking boot into the door's lower left corner.

Click.

The door eased outward an inch or so, just far enough for me to wrap my fingers around the frame. A cool breeze flowed from the other side of the door. I wrenched it open—and then I was inside.

I won't kid you: I was convinced that the heavy door would slam shut behind me leaving me with no way to reopen it from the inside—leaving me trapped inside the mountain. Because that's what happens in every scary movie, right? Well, I was *not* going to be the expendable, no-name character, the "red shirt" in this scenario.

I unclipped the Maglite from my belt and wedged it between the door and its rusted frame, propping the door open. With my penlight I searched the inside of the doorframe and the door.

I heaved a sigh of relief: The inside door had a wheel of sorts connected to a series of flat bars. I grabbed the wheel and turned it in a half circle. The bars, similar to gears, pivoted and rotated, and my penlight picked up the movement of bolts, top and bottom, sliding out of the door's thick core.

Closed position. I spun the wheel the other direction and the bolts retracted. *Open position.* I retrieved my flashlight and allowed the door to swing shut.

I don't know how the makers managed it, but I observed the wheel spin on its own and heard the bolts slam home, sealing the door, making it one with the mountain. For an awful second, terror overcame me—until I spun the wheel again and, with a hiss, the door opened.

I restarted my heart, nodded to myself, and pulled the door closed once more. The wheel turned. The bolts slid home.

I was emotionally sapped, but I was, *finally*, inside the mountain.

Time to move on.

I glanced at Dr. Bickel's cryptic instructions and followed the only passageway, a narrow thing, leading away from the door. After three turns, the passage narrowed further, but ahead I glimpsed a welcome glow of light. The light came through a crack at the end of the passage.

I pushed my way through the crack and out from behind a massive iron beam into a wide tunnel with a high ceiling. Dim electric lights mounted along the walls lit the tunnel.

I looked around. Other beams supported the walls and ceilings of the tunnel. As tunnels went, it was large enough for my Toyota—and a slew of other vehicles—all at the same time.

I was in one of the mountain's main tunnels.

I'd downloaded and studied old maps of the mountain's storage facility that I'd found on the Internet—and that's not saying much, because there aren't that many. The maps showed four large "plants" within the facility. They were connected by main tunnels. *This* side of the mountain, however, housed only one of the plants. If the maps were accurate, that plant was far south of my location. So why the tunnel? Where did it lead and why wasn't it on the map?

And yet it's here, I reasoned. *It has to lead somewhere.*

Not wanting to "lose" the beam that hid the crack from which I'd emerged (and thus lose my return route), I scraped a faint line on it near the stone floor.

My instructions told me to proceed down the tunnel, so I tiptoed on, nervous and shivering, not with cold, but with anxiety. It wasn't that I was scared *of* the tunnels in the mountain—the tunnels had been there for generations, after all. I wasn't concerned that they would collapse, and I wasn't walking along in total darkness.

I was maybe a *little* worried that I could get lost, but not too much so. From the diagrams I'd found on the Internet, the tunnels, while extensive, had not been constructed as a maze. Four primary tunnels ran straight, two north and south, parallel to each other, and two east and west, parallel to each other and perpendicular to the other two. A few branches on the north end angled away from the north/south and east/west tunnels.

My concern was that Dr. Bickel's instructions had already taken me into *uncharted* tunnels. I'm talking about the passage from the outside door leading here and "here" not showing up on the map. Would I run into more unmapped tunnels and passages? Who knew what kind of winding warren those might prove to be? But how could Dr. Bickel remain undetected inside the mountain unless he was hiding in an uncharted, unused area?

I had a little anxiety, too, about what I would find when I reached the map's terminus. What was Dr. Bickel concealing there? More importantly, why had he "invited" me to help him? What help could I, Gemma Keyes, possibly give him?

The inside of the tunnels reminded me of the last Terminator movie I'd seen. John Connor and his girlfriend were directed into an underground bunker where they *thought* they would find the means to end SkyNet before it took over the world.

In reality, they'd been sent to an abandoned bomb shelter—an old devolution site, a safe place for the heads of our nation to survive a nuclear war and still carry out the functions of government.

Was I headed to a similar location?

(And did you know most of that movie was filmed in and around Albuquerque? Not the most reassuring factoid.)

I stared at the map, startled to realize I'd overshot the next marker. "Crud!"

To my consternation, my whisper echoed down the tunnel. I shut up and backtracked, looking for . . . another steel beam with a mark on it?

There. On the opposite side of the tunnel. At least I hoped it was the beam noted on my map. A soft scrape at its base identified it. Behind the beam and mostly obscured by the beam's width, I located a narrow hole in the rock that opened about a foot off the floor of the tunnel.

"That's a lot smaller than the last crack I crawled through," I grumbled.

Did I say the hole was narrow? It was perhaps two and a half feet high, less than a foot wide. I shone my light inside, but the hole was so narrow that I couldn't get my head positioned to see what the light revealed.

I'm supposed to squeeze through that?

I certainly was *not* inclined to "squeeze though" into an unknown situation. Cramming myself through a small space to reach a large, well-lit tunnel had been easy. Leaving the large, well-lit tunnel to squeeze into the unknown—the *dark* unknown—was not a happy prospect.

I dithered one or two minutes before deciding I would reach my hand inside and feel around. Again, I was grateful to be wearing gloves. Whatever creepy crawlers might be inside the crack, the gloves would protect me from them.

Right?

Riiight.

(Liberal dose of acerbic irony sprinkled here.)

I plunged my hand inside the tiny crevasse and felt nothing but air. I leaned in, inserted my arm up to my shoulder, and moved my gloved hand about, searching for a sense of what lay beyond, for anything solid.

Nothing.

It's okay then, I said to convince myself. *It's another tunnel and it opens up once I'm past the icky squeezy part.*

I took my rucksack off and held it in my right hand. I shuddered and then ducked behind the beam. I had to put my left arm and shoulder through first, followed by my head—an idea I was *not* fond of—but I gritted my teeth and pushed into the hole, pulling my rucksack after me.

On the other side I was able to stand straight away—which was good since I was almost hyperventilating. I shone the tiny light around and found myself in what looked like a skinny fissure in the rock. Rather than a tunnel, the fissure appeared to be a naturally formed, really narrow crack in the mountain. At least it afforded more than enough headroom for comfort. My pulse and breathing slowed.

I glanced back, saw the faint glow of the tunnel lights from the other side of the beam, took a few more minutes to steady my galloping heart, and then started walking in the only direction I could.

I pointed the tiny penlight at my feet and advanced with caution, one step at a time, making certain that the floor did not drop out from beneath me—another fatal mistake often committed in scary movies. After several yards I realized that the fissure was trending downward.

I'm going deeper into the mountain. Not cool. Not cool at all.

Except for my penlight, the passage was totally dark, the kind of complete dark that crowds in on you. The air grew heavy. Oppressive.

No ventilation down here.

Though the temperature remained steady and moderate, I shivered continually. The weight bearing down on me seemed to grow heavier. I talked to myself in a whisper, fighting the sense of being buried alive. Then the passage widened a little and I reached its end.

I must have looked pretty stupid, just staring at the solid wall of jagged rock in front of me. I touched the wall with tentative fingers.

The passage just ends here?

Sure, a curious individual might have discovered the narrow hole behind the beam; they might, perhaps, have dared to squeeze through. But if they had followed the fissure and found themselves *here*, my bet was they would have shrugged and turned around. I think they would have believed the passage to be nothing more than a natural crack in the rocks—as I had.

But I hadn't come upon this passage by accident; *I had been directed here.*

When I consulted the map, it offered no help. The line on it just continued—as if the wall didn't exist. I began a careful, systematic examination of the wall with my flashlight.

I played my tiny light around the edges of the fissure's end and found nothing but the solid rock it appeared to be. Sighing, I leaned my back upon the wall and began to examine the sides of the fissure where it widened out.

Where one side jutted into the mountain, thus widening the passage, my dim light almost passed over something. Not sure of what I'd seen, I came close to the jagged wall and felt with my gloved fingers.

Ingenious, I acknowledged. *A wall in front of another wall, shielding passage to the next part of the tunnel.*

Yes, *tunnel.* For now I knew with certainty that, from this point on, the *rest* of the "fissure" was a manmade passage: A manmade continuation of something that began naturally; a creative extension made to fool the casual explorer.

The crack between the two walls was not much wider than the crack behind the beam. I turned sideways and slid along. It wound like an "s," a switchback, and I was glad when the new passage widened—until it ended only another six feet farther.

I stood before another rough iron door that, judging by its appearance, had likely kept uninterrupted vigil for decades. Just like the outside entrance, this door had no handle, no knob, and no lock—only a flat, riveted, reinforced surface.

Would I do the "left toe, right hand" thing I'd done outside to open this door? I consulted the map and instructions once more.

Look for a chalk mark on the floor to the right of the door.

I pointed my tiny light toward the base of the door and moved it right. The faintest mark appeared in the glow of my penlight.

Remove the mark.

I spit on the chalk and scuffed it with the toe of my boot. It dissolved as expected. I read the next line.

Feel for a lever in a crack just above the mark.

A shudder ran through me. *No way* was I inclined to "feel" for anything in a crack. Only God himself knew what kind of crawlers were in residence in the nooks and crannies of this tunnel! New Mexico boasts a super-sized centipede—and one disgusting bug from the spider family called a vinegaroon. That critter looks like the offspring of a scorpion and a giant cockroach. Ghastly.

I shuddered again, but I had my gloves on, so I resolutely bent to touch the floor where the chalk mark had been.

The stone floor was smooth to the touch through the leather of my gloves. The rock wall, however, was not. I walked my fingers up the uneven wall, examining ragged edges as I went.

Then I found it—between two rocks. The two rocks were smooth, different from the rest of the wall, like they didn't belong. Had they been hammered into a crack? Sandwiched between the two rocks was a narrow hole. Within the crack I felt a length of metal perhaps only a finger's width.

Feel for a lever.

The space between the rocks was only wide enough for the hidden metal bar.

That has to be the lever! I reported to myself.

Thank you, Captain Obvious.

You're welcome, Sergeant Sarcasm, I retorted.

I pressed down on the piece of metal. *Nothing.*

I tried to lift it. *It didn't move.*

Side-to-side. *Not even wiggle room.*

I could scarcely grasp the metal rod between my finger and thumb, so small was the hole. I pulled. Nothing!

Could you have made the opening any smaller? I whined.

I stood up and rubbed my eyes with my sleeve. *I pressed down. I lifted up. Wiggled and pulled. What remains?*

Ah. I knelt down and felt for the minuscule lever. This time I *pushed.*

The lever moved straight back, perhaps an inch. I heard a soft *snick* from the recessed lever—and then a click from the door.

The door, as corroded as it appeared, made not a sound as it swung open on greased hinges. I could see light not far off, but I hesitated. *This* door had no reassuring wheel and locking mechanism on its inside face. I felt all over its surface and could find no way to reopen the door once it closed behind me—I felt only the wide bolt that slid from the door's frame into the iron jamb.

Again, what if the door closed behind me and I couldn't open it from the other side? Fear of being sealed deep inside the mountain surged up from my stomach into my throat.

I walked back up the tunnel a few feet, fighting off the panic. *Go on,* I lectured my fearful self. *After all, if you weren't going to see this through, why did you come?*

I turned back. And had an idea.

I stripped off my left glove and slid it onto the fat bolt, then closed the door. As I'd hoped, it couldn't lock with the glove wedged between the door and the bolt hole. It was easy to pull the door open again.

Taking a deep, cleansing breath, I stepped through the ironclad door into yet another passageway carved out of the rock. I pulled the door closed, but with the glove over the bolt I could still open it.

I played my light on the wall to the left of the door and found a niche that mirrored the one on the other side. I felt inside. A similar lever.

All right, then.

I retrieved my glove and allowed the door to close naturally.

Somewhat relieved on that score, I looked down the passageway. The light ahead didn't seem far away, so I switched off my little penlight and went forward. The passage took an abrupt 90 degree left turn and narrowed. The ceiling dipped, too; I had to stoop to go on.

The light ahead grew brighter. I walked, bent over, for about five feet when the wall on my right ended and my next steps were out in the open. I straightened and found myself walking out into a domed room. I guess "cavern" is a better description, although I was certain it, too, had been manmade.

The ceiling of the cavern was about twenty feet high. Soft lights ensconced in the cavern walls lit the perimeter and fell upon a heap of chairs, desks, and equipment piled haphazardly against the cavern walls. I wended my way through the stacks of furniture, all of which carried a fine coat of dust, until I stood perhaps ten feet from where I'd entered the cavern.

I looked back to fix the location of the passage's entrance (my escape!) in my mind—and stopped to admire how well disguised that exit was. To the unschooled eye, it would have appeared that I had stepped right out of the cavern's wall. The crack or cleft from which I'd emerged was shielded, undetectable unless a person was close enough to discern the overlap between the rock walls.

I memorized the shape of the stones above my exit and the pieces of furniture strewn or stacked nearby. Then I moved toward the center of the cavern—not far away, really—where I could see equipment or machinery. No human activity made itself heard.

I walked straight toward the equipment until I stood on the perimeter of a small, but pristine laboratory setup: rows of workbenches, computers, monitors, equipment, and a tall glass structure.

"Hello, Gemma."

⌘⌘⌘⌘

CHAPTER 8

The words came from behind me, warmer and friendlier than I'd remembered. I turned.

"Hi, Dr. Bickel."

Neither of us spoke as I studied the scientist and he studied me. He appeared just as tired as he had the last time I'd seen him. He was pale, too, and thinner, perhaps. Maybe he seemed a bit more relaxed—he was certainly more relaxed than he'd been during the contentious exchange I'd witnessed between him, Dr. P, and General Cushing!

Complete silence reigned in the low-ceilinged cavern. It was eerie. Disquieting. I felt the need to break the silence.

"I followed your directions."

Well, of course you did. Splendid opening.

He nodded, his features softening further. "Yes, and I'm glad to see you looking well, Gemma. I've been, er, keeping an eye on you, a little afraid that they would do something, um, harmful to you."

I blinked, surprised. "To me?"

"Oh, yes. You do a masterful job with that innocent 'Why, I have no idea what you're talking about' air, but anyone with a brain who cared to look a little deeper would know it's an act—a well-played act, but an act nonetheless."

He sighed. "I know what you overheard that morning in the conference room after I stormed out. And I know you played dumb when General Cushing confronted you. So for a while I was concerned that they would see through your ruse and, um, *take steps* to silence you."

My head started to shake back and forth, just a little, denying the ominous significance of his words, but his low chuckle cut me off. It was a rich, unexpected sound. I decided that I liked it.

Well, this day is just filled with surprises.

Dr. Bickel took my hand and squeezed it. "Gemma, Gemma. You must have learned a long time ago—probably when you were a child—to make yourself less than obvious. You do it so well, so convincingly, that practically no one notices you!"

He grinned and squeezed my hand again. I hadn't seen Dr. Bickel grin before, either. It made his tired eyes all squishy, but in a nice way.

Still shaking my head, I found myself smiling with him. "I-I think you may be the only one who's ever noticed."

"My dear young lady, you should have been a spy or a professional poker player. *Or a politician.* I've watched you maintain the same give-nothing-away air indefinitely. You never stray from character; and, as far as I've seen, you have no 'tells' when you're bluffing or dissimulating."

Sheesh. Guess he has me pegged.

It was all *very* flattering.

It was practically embarrassing.

"Gemma, I think—no, I'm *convinced*—that, under the dull façade you so convincingly wear, you are a bright, intelligent woman. Oh, not, perhaps in a 'rocket scientist' kind of way, but rich in savvy. Yes, I've observed you, you know. You, in that conference room, ostensibly taking notes, all the while absorbing everything said and filing it away in that steel trap you carry around inside your head."

He paused and studied me. "You haven't been able to find a job, have you." It wasn't a question, just a bald statement.

I didn't blink, though. Not a micro-muscle in my face moved.

Dr. Bickel just nodded again, but his eyes were kind. Compassionate. "Cushing made sure you'd never get another security clearance."

This time I replied. "I figured."

He studied me for a few seconds more. "There you go again. Giving away nothing."

He looked out over the lab. "Well, then. I did invite you to come, so you're my guest. How would you like to see what I've been doing here?"

"Not yet, please."

The brows over his tired eyes lifted. "Ah, yes. You need to know how it is that I'm alive, am I right?"

"Yes. And why you've asked me here, considering that I broke about fifty laws along the way."

"Perfectly understandable. Let's see. I think you'd prefer the short answer first, long answer after, yes?"

I nodded again, still amazed at how very amiable Dr. Bickel was, still struggling to account for the marked change in his personality.

"All right," he agreed. "The short answer is: I'm alive because I knew what Prochanski and Cushing were planning and stayed ahead of it."

"How? How did you know?" I kept my expression neutral.

"My expertise is in mathematics, in three-dimensional modeling, and in the development and programming of complex algorithms. That's all done on computers. Along the way I became a bit of an adept, er, *hacker*."

I spotted a humorous gleam in his eyes.

Sure, pal. But enough to defeat Sandia's security? I said nothing, just kept looking at him.

He lifted one brow. "But I didn't need to hack a classified network, Gemma. I merely placed bugs where I needed them, to record what I needed to hear."

He'd done it again—answered a question I hadn't yet asked! "In the conference room, too?" *Totally against all DOE policy?* I sounded a bit incredulous.

Dr. Bickel smirked. "At last some real emotion. Again, I didn't need to. To be frank, dear girl, I used a Trojan horse of sorts to gain access to certain, ah, *conversations* to which I desired to be privy. To that end I planted a 'bug' on your laptop."

"On my laptop!" If I hadn't been so flummoxed I would have been outraged.

"Yes; not *in* it, but *on* it. Wherever you took your laptop, you took me. The bug was basically a flash memory recorder with a short-range transmitter. Voice activated. Flat, the diameter of a pencil eraser. It recorded everything said near it and transmitted the audio files to me. Your office was next to mine. That's all the range I needed to download the conversations."

He coughed. "By the by, I removed the bug the afternoon you were let go. When I came to say goodbye. Found another location for it after Security returned your laptop to IT."

I searched my memories, tracing them to that afternoon when he handed me his card—when I looked away as the Sandia security officer came through the door.

Had he leaned that far over my cubicle wall? And then, *But if he had my laptop bugged, that means—*

I tugged my thoughts into line. "So that's how you knew what General Cushing and Dr. P talked about in the conference room that morning? What they were planning to do to you? And what happened when they realized that I was still there?"

Other, more embarrassing ramifications started to sink in.

He knows. He knows I spied on him. I took my laptop to my weekly meetings with Dr. P. That means Dr. Bickel heard everything I reported to Dr. P.

I swallowed, fully expecting him to censure me for my deceitfulness.

Dr. Bickel merely nodded. I was positive he knew what I was thinking, yet he only responded to my questions. "Yes, I heard. The Pinterest board was a superb piece of deflection on your part, Gemma. Why, you almost convinced me."

His eyes twinkled as he said it. One corner of my mouth tipped up, then the other. We laughed.

Dr. Bickel sobered first. "It's good that you were so convincing or Cushing might not have insisted that you be sent packing. She might have, instead, had Prochanski keep you around and have him send you on an errand into the lab when the 'accident' was scheduled to occur."

I slipped on a vacant expression, but inside I shivered. "So how did Dr. P end up dead and you, um, didn't? How did you escape?"

"Oh, yes. That. Prochanski and Cushing's plan was for Rick, Tony, and me to perish together; however, I knew not only their timeline, but also their means." Dr. Bickel's voice roughened. A little anger was seeping through. "Quite the clever device, it was, too. It was designed and placed to point to human error—an error they intended to ascribe to *me*."

He turned red, and I thought his outrage a little comical, given the more serious intent of the plot. I kept that opinion to myself.

"Prochanski announced that we were to demonstrate one of our findings to a DOE bigwig. The detonation was set to take place fifteen minutes before the demonstration was scheduled—right when Prochanski knew the three of us, the intended targets, would be in the lab setting up the experiment. In reality, *there was no demonstration or DOE bigwig*. Prochanski just needed to ensure that the three of us—Rick, Tony, and I—would be in the lab when the explosion occurred.

"Unbeknownst to Prochanski and Cushing, I knew their schedule and I had located the device. I adjusted the time on the device they'd planted. I moved it *up* three hours. I sent Rick and Tony on an errand off base before the *real* detonation so that only Prochanski and I would be in the lab when it actually went off. I assured Prochanski that Rick and Tony would be back in plenty of time to set up for the 'demonstration.'

"Of course when the device *did* detonate, Rick and Tony were still off base and Prochanski thought he had three more hours to get out. He planned his exit accordingly."

Dr. Bickel made a "tsking" sound that was disturbing in its indifference. "They did try to kill *me*, after all."

I frowned. "But obviously *you* weren't in the lab when it, um, exploded and burned. And yet the media aired security footage of you and Dr. P entering the lab and never leaving. I watched footage of the two of you working on opposite sides of the lab right up until the explosion."

Over and over. Like a hundred times, I didn't add.

Dr. Bickel chuckled. "Yes; we were there, but someone altered the timestamp at the 'end' of the footage. Had to have been Cushing's doing—after her people did not discover my body in the wreckage.

"Cushing knew then that I'd foiled her plan and was on the run, so she had to convince everyone else that I was dead. If I were *dead* and she caught me, she could do whatever she liked with me."

His expression grew grim. "She had to 'prove' to the public that I was in the lab with Prochanski at the time of the explosion. If the real footage had been aired, it would have shown my quite-marked absence during the thirty minutes prior to the, er, *event*.

"In that hour before the detonation, I told Prochanski I was stepping out for a short break. I left the lab long before the base was engulfed in chaos."

"But-but how did you get on and off the base? It was shut down for twenty-four hours. They searched every vehicle and person leaving the base for days. And your car was still in the lot."

"I never left, Gemma."

I gave my face permission to ask the obvious question.

"I never intended to leave the base. Do you remember that I sent Rick and Tony on an errand? They were waiting for me in Rick's car at the base's golf course just off Pennsylvania, not far from the checkpoint through the PIDAS. When I left the lab, I got in my own car and drove to meet them.

"I got into Rick's passenger seat and we went through the PIDAS checkpoint together. He drove me to the munitions bunker that hid our western entrance, let me out, and drove back to the lab. In the meantime, Tony took my car back to the parking lot and left it there.

"Rick picked up Tony from the parking lot and drove them to get something to eat. A bit later the explosion occurred and the lab burned. My car was found in the parking lot where Tony left it, but I've been *here* the whole time."

I let my astonishment show for the first time. "Here? You've been here?"

"Yes."

"But . . . what is this place?"

Dr. Bickel grinned again and tugged his little beard. I was really warming to him by then. What he said next, put the icing on the cake.

"This, Gemma, is my notorious secret laboratory."

Dr. Bickel had a secret laboratory, carved into the foothills of the Manzano Mountains, accessed via the World War II tunnels? He'd been hiding in his secret lab for more than three months?

I liked it. I liked it a *lot*. I giggled; I laughed aloud.

"Well, come take a look." Dr. Bickel turned. He didn't call to me to follow him. He knew I would.

As we walked together through his lab, I took note of the three aisles of workbenches and their computers, monitors, and tools. I was familiar with some of the equipment, since I ordered most everything for the AMEMS lab. The setup wasn't much by Sandia's standards, though. The lab might even have been considered "sparse"—but it was still significant.

"How did you get all this stuff?" I was staring at a high-powered 3D laser microscope.

Dr. Bickel chuckled. "You know I'm a wealthy man, don't you, Gemma?"

I nodded, recalling some of the office gossip I'd overheard when Dr. Bickel first arrived. "Yeah. I heard something about that."

"Electronic purchasing and enough money can get you anything you want these days, Gemma. It was excruciatingly slow, but piece by piece, over the last year, Rick, Tony, and I assembled this tiny laboratory. Mind you, I'm not doing development or manufacturing here. I'm collecting and analyzing data more than anything else. Secret mountain laboratories have their limits, you know."

Ever practical, I asked, "How have you managed to live here? What have you done for food and water?"

"Rick, Tony, and I have been planning and executing our plan for a number of years now. We stocked this place well early on. I have an abundance of staples and canned goods on hand, and I have a minuscule but functional living space over there." He waved toward the side of the cavern opposite where I'd entered.

"So Rick and Tony were in on all of this? They helped you build this?"

"Yes, but they weren't the only ones. In the planning stages I had help from a select few "others"—all compartmentalized to keep them safe and our plan secret. It will take a while to bring you up to speed."

He waved his hand to encompass the roughly circular cavern. "Of course, we didn't have to build *this*. The military carved out this cave during the early Cold War. The project was deeply classified and therefore little known. See the stacks of furniture and equipment lying about? Very 1960s, don't you think? *Never used.* The government canceled the project for which this was excavated and furnished. They simply abandoned the site as it was. The entrances to this room were sealed off or concealed."

"Our tax dollars at work," I griped.

He snorted. "Indeed. An old but close colleague told me about this place many years back. He'd been assigned here and read into the project when it was still viable. He's been gone about ten years now, but in the months before he died he told me everything he could about it.

"You see, I've been planning for this contingency for more than fifteen years now. Even back then, I knew some pinhead in the military would decide to appropriate my research—probably just as it bore fruit. When I came close enough to achieving the results I hoped for, I maneuvered myself into a position with Sandia so I could fully prepare this place."

"I thought you hated your job with Sandia."

He made a face. "No. You mean I hated having to kowtow to that fool, Prochanski."

"Yes, I guess that's true." I grimaced: Dr. Bickel's disdain for Dr. P stung. I suppose I still harbored feelings for Dr. P, wounded and misplaced as they might be.

"It was necessary for me to debase myself for a time, as repellent as bowing and scraping to him was. I knew he was in cahoots with Cushing, too. However, the best means to keep abreast of their plans was to stick close to him. So I did what was necessary until we were forced to make our move."

"We?"

"Rick and Tony have worked with me for more than a decade. I brought them to Sandia with me when the government offered me a position there. Rick and Tony have known from the beginning where I was going with my work—and they agreed that we needed to protect it from exploitation. I trust them implicitly.

"We located old unclassified specs of the mountain, its tunnels, and storage plants. The three of us scoured them. Based on the *classified* information my deceased colleague provided, we drew in the location of this cavern and pored over the maps until we agreed upon the location of a new entrance. We didn't want to disturb the original entrance, you see, in case anyone in the military accessed the classified files and examined the original entrance to see if it had been disturbed after six decades."

"But how did you get access to the tunnels in the first place?"

He looked aside. "Getting inside the mountain requires a badge to clear the PIDAS checkpoint and a key to open one of the tunnel entrances. I have a key. I can't tell you who provided it, of course."

"But won't they know who went in and out of the checkpoint?"

"More than the mountain lies within the PIDAS, Gemma. NSA, DOE, and the military maintain classified facilities inside the fences."

He slanted his eyes toward me. "And the badge I used was real enough."

I nodded. "Real, but not *yours*, so it wouldn't point back to you and steer the search toward the mountain."

He shrugged. "Precisely. Anyway, we tunneled into this cave from the inside of an old storage closet inside the mountain. Nights and weekends—we spent a harrowing two months just getting into this room that first time. That was our initial, temporary entrance."

I thought about how beat Dr. Bickel often looked at work. Things were starting to make sense. "You said 'initial entrance.' You have more than one way in and out now?"

He nodded. "Yes. Here; let's sit down." He pointed to a couple of comfortable-looking chairs between the lab workbenches. The chairs looked like they belonged in the living room of somebody's grandmother, not in the middle of a lab in the middle of a cave in the middle of a mountain.

I sank onto the cushions of an old, overstuffed lounger, grateful to be off my feet. The chair was, surprisingly, still quite comfortable.

Dr. Bickel picked up the thread of our bizarre conversation. "Every part of our endeavor has been—and still is—fraught with the danger of discovery. We couldn't chance someone noting a disturbance in the storage closet and stumbling upon our entrance. It stood that the government would have other entrances into this room, entrances in addition to the primary one we knew of.

"Once we made it inside here, we found a second exit and followed it into one of the munitions bunkers. Very cleverly hidden, it is. That became our customary route in and out. We built my little living quarters around its opening. Then we *sealed up* our temporary entrance at the back of the closet."

"What about the way I came in?"

"Ah, yes. You came in the 'back door,' as we call it, the northern route." He gestured toward my entrance with his hand.

"We found the opening quite by accident when we were stacking all the furniture the government left here when they abandoned this room. It makes sense to me that the designers of this place would have kept an ace up their sleeve, a secret exit should it be needed.

"The northern entrance is cleverer than the route leading from the munitions bunker into this room. About six months ago, Rick decided to map the route as another escape route, should I need it.

"He explored the base's fence line from the open space and found the spot where you went under the fence. He made the cuts in the PIDAS, drew up the map and directions, and left them with me. It was to be *my* ace in the hole, if I needed another way out.

"As for the original, undisturbed entrance? We figured that if Cushing ever suspected I were hiding somewhere in this facility, she would request access to the specs of certain old, classified projects inside the mountain.

"If she *were* granted access to the classified maps, she would have no difficulty locating the original entrance to this room, what we now call the decoy door. We haven't touched that entrance from the outside; it has not been used in decades and is undisturbed. Ah, but from the opposite side? The inside?"

His eyes gleamed. "From the *inside*, we made the decoy entrance easy to breach, Gemma. And once inside the tunnel, just beyond the breach, we left evidence for Cushing's men to conclude that they had found the entrance I always use. We *made* it look that way—when, in point of fact, *I never use it.*"

"But why? Why make it easy for her?"

"Why trouble ourselves to 'make it easy'? Because if Cushing ever comes looking for me here, I need assurance that her attack will come from *that* direction, through *that* entrance."

He was almost gleeful. "We *booby-trapped* the tunnel leading from the decoy entrance to this cavern, Gemma! Not necessarily to harm anyone, mind you, but to, first of all, warn me of their approach and, second, to delay Cushing and her people. The warning and delay will allow me to do . . . what I need to do."

"Wait." I frowned. "At first you said 'we,' but now you keep saying 'me' and 'I.' 'Warn *me* of their approach; the door *I* use; time to do what *I* have to do.' I thought Rick and Tony were in on this?"

He shook his head. "No, not any more. Not since the incident in the AMEMS lab. Our plan called for Rick and Tony to disconnect themselves from me—absolutely—once I made my move, my escape.

"Once I fled here, I couldn't risk either of them being followed into the mountain. You see, I was certain Cushing would have them monitored until The Hot Place froze over—and I was right, by the way. And, of course, they couldn't come *with* me into this life of solitude— they both have families they love. They couldn't leave their wives and children, and neither would I allow them to put their families in danger by continuing to support me."

Dr. Bickel's voiced dropped. "You don't know Cushing, Gemma. You don't know what she's capable of."

I shivered. Dr. Bickel's narrative had taken five left turns in a matter of moments, but I *thought* I was still tracking with him. "So Rick and Tony helped you build this lab, but they haven't been here since before the, er, incident at the AMEMS lab."

"That's correct."

"Because General Cushing is having them watched?"

"She is."

"Because General Cushing knows you aren't dead."

Dr. Bickel inclined his head. "My body wasn't found in the wreckage. She went to great lengths to make the public believe it had been. Did you attend my memorial service?"

I nodded and shivered again. "And you think General Cushing has threatened Rick and Tony's families if they didn't tell her where you are?"

"I know she has."

"Because General Cushing still wants whatever it is you've got."

His whispered "yes" floated toward me.

"Rick and Tony. Cushing hasn't—?" I couldn't finish my sentence.

"Cushing has no proof they were involved with me outside of the regular workday. She will continue to watch them, however, and hope that they eventually lead her to me. She will watch them until she gets what she is after."

"And you've been here, alone, for three months."

He jerked his chin toward his chest once.

I stirred uneasily, the lounger no longer as comfortable as when I first sat in it. "So why did you reach out to me?"

Dr. Bickel sighed. "I considered every person I knew. It had to be an individual I trusted. Had to be someone nearby. *Someone Cushing wouldn't think of.* I need help, Gemma; I need help, and you were the only one I felt I could call on."

"Me?" That single word came out on a squeak. I cleared my throat and asked again, "Me? But-but why me? And how could I ever help you?" I watched Dr. Bickel carefully, and I thought his expression saddened—which did nothing to alleviate my anxiety.

"Gemma, as good as our planning was, some things require, shall we say, an *outside* source. I have my little quarters here. They are comfortable enough. I have an adequate bed and a little kitchen; I've even hacked satellite television and the Internet. I bring them down here by cable via the ventilation system."

"So what do you need me for?"

Unlike me, Dr. Bickel did not have the same ability to mask his emotions. He appeared a bit embarrassed and sat forward in his seat.

"I need someone to be my liaison with the real world. I own a safe house in Albuquerque—a residence I bought through a shell corporation I control. Quite untraceable, I assure you. The safe house is where we had the lab equipment sent when we were stocking this place.

"Occasionally I still require parts or supplies for the lab. Some supplies are quite vital to what I'm doing here. I can order what I need and have it sent to the safe house, but I need someone to pick up what I order and bring it to me."

Then I thought he looked embarrassed.

"And?"

I was right. He turned pink. "To be frank, I haven't had any fresh food since I went into hiding. The little frozen food I had is gone. All that remains is dried or canned. I-I need fresh meat, fruit, vegetables."

"You want me to grocery shop for you?" I was nonplussed.

He glanced down. "Three months without a steak, without a salad or an apple or yogurt is worse than I thought it would be."

I was amazed that he would put all he'd planned and worked for his entire life at risk—*for some greens and fruit*? But, maybe it was more.

"You must be lonely for another human's voice." The words slipped out of my mouth.

He studied the floor. "I knew you were more perceptive than people gave you credit for."

We were quiet for a few minutes. Then I asked the burning question. At least, it was burning to *me*.

"But . . ."

"But why *you*?"

"Yes. Why me, Dr. Bickel?"

"Because, dear Gemma, you don't have, er, *ties*. People living with you, making demands on you, inquiring after your activities."

"What you mean is I don't have a family." My throat squeezed on the words.

I was sure that Dr. Bickel's expression saddened a bit more. His "poochy" eyes seemed softer, moister.

"I'm sorry, Gemma. I don't mean to wound you."

I believed him. I truly did.

I sighed. "It's all right. What else?"

He nodded and looked away. "Thank you for understanding. It's just that, well, you haven't found suitable employment yet, and you already knew what we were doing in the lab—at least in generalities. And I will pay you well for your time. In cash."

I kept perfectly still as a palpable swell of relief rippled through me. I was grateful for my weekly unemployment checks, but they would stop in less than three months. Even *with* them, I was up against a wall.

Steak hasn't been on my menu lately, either, I reminded myself.

"Most of all," Dr. Bickel added softly, "I selected you because I knew I could trust you. You see, I know you saw things you could have reported to Prochanski, but you didn't."

I thought over his words for a moment. I was not innocent, not at all, but I had resisted *some* of Prochanski's demands.

"Maybe. I guess I did. Some."

His eyes glimmered. "And I believe we share a mutual, ah, *aversion* to General Cushing?"

"Her? I wouldn't believe her if she said my name was 'Gemma.'"

I'd trusted Dr. P, and that was bad enough, as it turned out.

Dr. Bickel's good humor returned with a wry smile. "Take a number; get in line! Imogene Cushing is intelligent, devious, and treacherous. She wants my work, Gemma, wants to take them—er, *it*—and use them—I mean *it*—to destroy every form of resistance to her twisted ideals of national security. Imogene Cushing actually views a near police state as our nation's most secure defense."

I composed my face in neutral lines again. "Obviously you know her better than I do." *And I'm sensing that your opinion is more than a little personal,* I added silently.

He eyed me. "Like I said, you are astute, Gemma. I've known Imogene since our early days at Virginia Tech. She was ROTC then. And we were, well, once upon a time we were, er, close."

Ah.

"So you've known her how long?"

"About thirty-five years. She's an engineer—did you know that? And quite a superb strategist. When she graduated VT, she went into the Army as an officer and we drifted apart. What I've always known about Imogene, though, is that, above all, she is ambitious. Ruthlessly, relentlessly ambitious."

He shifted in his chair. "I made the mistake of sharing my dreams with her back then. She never forgot. She knew that I would someday make a contribution to science that would change the world. She's dogged my career ever since—followed my research, read my publications, tracked my employment."

Dr. Bickel stared at me, imploring me to believe him. "I need to show you what I'm protecting here, Gemma. I need you to understand *why* General Cushing won't ever stop searching for me, why she had me declared dead after my body wasn't found in what was left of the AMEMS lab, and why I can never appear in the open—at least not until I am ready. Until *they* are ready. And until I have a means to keep them from being misused."

He stood up and gestured for me to follow him. We skirted the tables and headed for the corner of the lab closest to my entrance to the cavern.

While we walked, I looked around and asked, "How did you get power down here for all this?" My mind was still crunching the information Dr. Bickel fed me, sorting it, filing it, questioning it.

"The base provides electricity to the tunnels already. We tapped into it."

"But—"

"Yes, I know; my work uses a *lot* of power, and a spike in usage would raise the military's red flag." He chuckled. "So much is automated anymore, you know. I hacked into PNM's network. I programmed a little job to run after Kirtland's meters are read and fed into the system. Each month my program adjusts the mountain's usage in the system, capping it at what it was for the same month the previous year. The program then adds or subtracts a randomly selected one to three percent so the usage isn't *exactly* the same as last year. That, too, could raise eyebrows."

"But how do you account—"

"For the power the lab actually uses? My program distributes the excess usage across the remaining meters on the base. The meters themselves don't reflect the increase, of course, but once the metered amounts are in the system, my program adjusts them. Across the entire base, the added amount is incremental, hardly noticeable."

He looked pleased with himself, and I had to admit the level of planning and execution was simple yet staggering. Dr. Bickel stopped and I stopped beside him. He smiled and gazed up at a glass case, perhaps ten feet square.

I stared into the clear glass case. It could have been empty, but I soon perceived that it wasn't. I took a step backwards and scanned its interior.

I could hear . . . humming, clicking, buzzing. A faint haze inside the box shifted. Dissolved. Came back together. Reminded me of how mercury, when released on a plate, will flow and form new shapes. Only this, this *thing* was "flowing and forming" *in midair*.

"Do you see them?" Dr. Bickel asked. I turned toward him. He was beaming, I thought, as only a proud papa could beam.

"Them?" I was confused.

"I know you'll appreciate them, Gemma, when you see all they can do, when you know all that they *are*.

"Gemma, in this glass case is the fruition of my years of work: *Nanomites*—complete, fully functional robotic *systems* at the true nanometer level. Their program algorithms are the most complex, most sophisticated, most encompassing ever devised. Their systems—"

I tuned him out for a minute, my attention taken entirely by what was in the glass box. The humming/buzzing coming from the box creeped me out a little—but what the haze within the glass box did next creeped me out a lot.

My mouth opened to a stunned "o" as the silver haze resolved into blue letters.

H E L L O

Dr. Bickel hadn't pressed any buttons. Hadn't said anything. Hadn't gestured.

He grinned. "Ah. They've noticed you. They know they haven't seen you before."

⌘⌘⌘⌘

CHAPTER 9

"Well, I wish they *wouldn't* notice me!" I choked on the words, my eyes fixed on the glass case.

"You have nothing to fear from them, Gemma," Dr. Bickel reassured me. "They are hungry for information, not for people." He laughed at his joke.

I didn't appreciate the humor.

He launched into a longwinded description of the nanomites and their capabilities and I realized how much he craved, perhaps *needed*, someone to share this great achievement with him.

His tired eyes shone with pride. "The mites are invisible to the human eye, of course—but there are so *many* of them that they can sometimes be seen as a *nanocloud*. I smuggled the nanocloud out in two carryalls—customized satchels—when I fled the lab. It was close quarters, even for their tiny size.

"They have a need for space, you see, for room to move about and function, just as you and I do. And they did not appreciate being separated into two groups in the two carryalls. It was as disruptive to them as losing a leg would be to you or to me."

I kept my nervous eyes on the always-morphing, always-fluid—*nanocloud?*—in the glass case. The congregation of nanomites all but disappeared and then reappeared in a sparkling, shimmering mist. Within the mist, in contrasting blue, they again spelled out the word "hello."

"Raise your voice just a little and say, 'Nano, hello.'"

"What—I'm supposed to *talk* to them?" The skin on my arms went all goosebumpy.

"They already understand print English; I recently began teaching the mites *spoken* English, single words and short commands at this point. They don't have audio receptors of any kind; rather, they are able to receive and interpret sound waves."

He looked at me. "I've programmed them to recognize 'Nano' as the signal of direct address. When they hear you say 'Nano' they will pay attention to what you say directly after that."

He kept looking at me, waiting, so I cleared my throat and muttered, "Nano. Hello."

The mist (that's how I thought of them) glowed a little brighter, expanded to fill the case, then re-formed into the smaller haze.

It was all very interesting. I was even leaning toward "fascinating." Until the mites spelled,

N A M E ?

"Remarkable. They want to know your name. Well, I suppose that is to be expected since you are only the second person they have 'met' and they know *my* name. Well, Gemma, pronounce your name first and then spell it for them. Keep your tone uniform and your speaking pace steady. They don't yet know how to interpret verbal nuances."

"I'd rather not."

No, I'd rather not be on a first-name basis with them.

"Please, Gemma?" he asked again.

I could tell it meant a lot to him, so I—grudgingly—cleared my throat again and spoke out. "Nano. My name is Gemma. G. E. M. M. A."

Nothing happened. After about thirty seconds of waiting, I was relieved.

Until the cloud glowed brighter, shifted, flew apart, and re-formed. It began to spell. **G E M M A**

So now it knows my name, I mocked.

K E Y E S

It spelled my name again, my full name.

G E M M A K E Y E S

I felt sick.

"Astounding," Dr. Bickel breathed. "I made a copy of the training database from the AMEMS lab and brought it with me. The mites have full read rights to the database. They recognize your name and made the association on their own."

"I'm in the database?" I croaked. He had no idea how shaken I was.

"Well, of course. Everyone associated with the project has a profile in the database—including you. The sole purpose of developing the training database was to teach the nanomites, and I used every available piece of information associated with the lab as a means of introducing the concepts of human connections to them. I've spent my three months here doing nothing but teaching them and recording their progress."

Inside the glass case, the glowing letters of my name faded. I said nothing as I worked at processing the astounding revelations Dr. Bickel offered with such nonchalance.

"The nanomites are the first of their kind, Gemma, the first true *nano*electromechanical systems—NEMS—ever developed," he whispered.

"Why do you call them nanomites?"

"Because their 'built' size is roughly that of a dust mite—between ten and twenty nanometers."

The comparison curdled my milk, so to speak.

Yuck and double yuck!

Dr. Bickel didn't notice. "What should I tell you about them first? Where should I start? Well, I should say that between each other and among their tribes they share data and language acquisition (human, machine, and mathematical languages), and rule themselves cooperatively."

"Er, tribes?" Shaken or not, I was a bit intrigued.

"Ah, yes. *Tribes*. I suppose I need to explain the concept of roles."

"Roles?"

"Yes, *roles*, because the mites are not all the same. The nanocloud—the collective sum of the nanomites—performs optimally when the work of the sum is divided into five distinct roles, each role essential to the cloud's functional growth and well-being. Every mite is equipped to perform a *specific role* and, by virtue of performing that role, becomes a member of the 'tribe' that owns that role.

"And, oh! How they learn!" he enthused. "I encoded their system programming with, among others, adaptive population-based incremental learning algorithms based upon a multi-objective particle swarm optimization design."

I nodded. Slowly.

Everything he'd said after "And, oh! How they learn!" was like undercooked pasta hitting a wall. Did. Not. Stick.

"I gave the members of each tribe specialized hardware (in addition to their base hardware) and a complementary set of algorithms designed exclusively for that role. So the entirety of the nanocloud consists of a *very* large population of nanomites divided among just five tribes, with every mite performing the role assigned to its tribe for the overall good of the cloud."

Dr. Bickel warmed to his topic. "What the world has, until now, presumed to call 'nanobots' are no more than mere submicron 'dumb bots'—single functioning, unable to learn, and unable to adapt. They possessed no computing capabilities, while just *one* of my nanomites' integrated circuitry is as powerful as any personal computer on the market."

He may have realized that he was bragging a little. He coughed and, with a more modest air, asked, "Are you familiar with the concept of 'system on a chip,' Gemma?"

"Yes, roughly."

Meaning 'not at all.'

"A 'system on a chip' or an SoC, is an assemblage of integrated components built on the same platform that, *together*, comprise an entire functioning computer or other processing operation. Think of an SoC as an entire *computer on a chip.*

"Everyone uses SoCs without realizing they do—in 'smart' phones, tablets, and other mobile devices. Every year the functionality and processing speed of a single chip increases exponentially.

"Now envision a state-of-the-art SoC and a powerful NEMS device (a nano-sized robot)—manufactured *as one unit*. The resulting creature has all the mechanical functions of a complex NEMS device and all the processing power of a computer. Enter the first 'smart' nanomites, *one billionth* the size of a meter, one hundred thousand times smaller than the thickness of a piece of paper. Your DNA, Gemma, is 2.5 times *wider* than one of my nanomites!"

I nodded, but my skin itched and my stomach hurt.

Dr. Bickel raked his hands through his thinning hair. "Consider this, Gemma. We've been manufacturing integrated circuits—*computer chips*—on silicon, gallium, or other substrates for some time now by laying down a patterned layer and etching the channels and gates of the circuits out of the layer."

He huffed. "The process of stamping a mask onto a wafer and then etching out the circuitry must be repeated again and again, layer upon layer in a production line environment. To achieve a 'system on a chip' in this manner requires over two hundred layers! The process is tedious! Plodding! And fantastically expensive! Why—"

I had to interrupt his rant. "But isn't that how the MESA fabrication facilities work? Semiconductor manufacturing? Isn't that the direction of the MEMS lab?"

"Let them plod away," he barked. "Let them ignore and avoid the *real* question: How do we manufacture a NEMS device and its system circuitry together, as one? How do we *integrate* them in the manufacturing process? Conventional production line semiconductor processes will *never* be able to manufacture an integrated NEMS/SoC device. I knew this a decade ago! That was the real problem!"

He stared around, as though framing his thoughts for the next stage of his lecture. "You see, what was needed, Gemma, was a complete departure from 'production line manufacturing' and its limitations."

He slanted a sly look in my direction. I could tell he was ready to make the big announcement—and he was. "I determined that the solution was *additive manufacturing*—a process that adds only what is needed rather than etching away what is *not* needed."

He waited for me to respond, but I didn't get it.

"Digital, three-dimensional modeling and printing, Gemma! It's why we split off from the MEMS lab to form the AMEMS lab!"

I was more confused. *Printing* a nano-whatever device? I wasn't there yet.

He tried a different tack. "A computer-generated design incorporates all aspects of the device—all of the articulating mechanisms of the NEMS device *and* the system circuitry—into a single, perfect 3D model. The computer 'slices' the model into thin, horizontal layers so that the device can be built a layer at a time upon a 'backing,' a temporary foundation of sorts."

"All riiight."

He snorted. "Do you *know* what a 3D printer is?"

"Of course I do!" I frowned, still not making the leap.

"A *conventional* printer, one for printing documents, uses ink. *Three-dimensional* printers, in place of ink, use a more substantive material. The most rudimentary of 3D printers use a material such as plastic. In such a scenario, plastic filament is melted and fed into the printhead. The printhead extrudes the melted plastic filament as its 'ink.'"

Dr. Bickel's explanation took on a sing-song, rhythmic quality, as though he were recording a child's lecture. "The computer, following the design of the 'sliced' 3D model, directs the printhead to add fine lines of liquid plastic "ink" to the object's backing to make the first layer of the product.

"As the plastic cools, it hardens, yes? When the first layer is complete, the computer directs the printer to lay down the second layer. And so on. Like laying a complex pattern of, say, Legos.

"All these layers are built, one atop the other, in a single chamber. The printer adds only the material needed to make the object—rather than depositing an entire layer and etching away what is not needed.

"And if the printer needs a different color of plastic? The printhead is connected to multiple sources of plastic filament, each source a different color. The computer tells the printhead which source to draw upon for the correct color at just the right time."

He saw that my uncomprehending stare this time was *real* and patted my hand.

I slapped it away.

"Fine!" I snapped. "That gets us a multicolored plastic *ashtray*. How does that get us a 'smart' nanobot?"

"Very good, Gemma, very good," he soothed. "Let's take the next logical step. We are printing tiny objects now so, instead of liquid plastic, we require a different sort of 'ink.' What physical properties do we require of our ink?"

He answered his own question. "We require materials, such as a variety of liquid polymers, suitable for manufacturing a robotic device and all its moving parts: gears, pulleys, wheels, arms, tiny mechanisms, and tools. The idea is that, *whatever material is required to manufacture a functional electromechanical device,* is fed into the printhead and extruded at the correct time and in the correct place onto the backing.

"Remember how with our plastic example we needed different colors of the same liquid plastic to build our, er, *ashtray*? Because we are building circuitry *onto and into* the nano-mechanisms, the printhead also requires separate sources of conductive and nonconductive materials, primarily metals. We make several sources available, some doped with positive charges, others with negative charges."

I was intent on Dr. Bickel's words, a glimmer of perception out there on the horizon. The far horizon.

"The computerized design directs the printing, and the printhead adds *only* the material needed to produce the design; nothing is etched away and nothing is wasted. All this happens in a clean, sealed environment under vacuum. During printing the nanostructures are fused to the backing wafer for support. Then, when the printing is completed, the *many* nanomites built upon the same wafer at the same time are cut apart by a digitally controlled laser."

He paused to take a breath.

I paused to allow my brain's overheated circuits to cool, but he plowed on.

"During the last five years, I built three working prototypes of my 3D printer. All three moved me in the right direction with limited but encouraging results.

"Then eleven months ago, eight months before Prochanski and Cushing blew up the lab, we—Rick and Tony and I—completed development of my most recent 3D printer—and it was, at last, working at the level I wished.

"Since we were now printing at the nanometer level, materials had to be extruded through a *nanopore*, a membrane with a nano-sized hole. The printhead I designed had five thousand nanopore-sized extrusion points to accommodate the materials needed. We used a simple six-inch silicon wafer as our backing.

"The printer was functioning as I had designed it to. I manufactured a large batch of nanobots—mechanically functional, but not programmable.

"And then, I added one significant improvement: I replaced the existing printhead with a newer one."

He paused for effect. "This new printhead extrudes the desired materials in much smaller amounts."

I waited, holding my breath.

He watched for my reaction. "The new printhead prints," he dragged out each word, "one ion at a time."

"I'm sorry; come again?"

"My ion printhead allows me to print the nanomites *one ion at a time*. An ion is an atom or molecule with either a net positive or negative charge. The exactitude of such an approach is, without hyperbole, limitless. My nanomites," he gestured toward the glass case, "were precision printed *one atom at a time* using my ion printhead. They are as perfect as the digital renderings."

I was following, but it all seemed more than a little farfetched to me.

Dr. Bickel raised one brow and offered a knowing smile. "Do you recall the food replicator on *Star Trek, The Next Generation*? My breakthrough makes physical replication possible someday. Not today, but sometime in the near future. My 3D printer and its ion printhead is the first giant step toward *molecular manufacturing* and *Tea. Earl Grey. Hot.*"

I appreciated the Captain Picard reference but— "I don't think I understand how a 3D printer could make *them*," I pointed to the glass case shimmering not far from us and the *things* inside that had spelled out my name, "and make them seem so, so *alive*."

"The printer built their circuitry and hardware, Gemma, all their moving pieces and their system chips together. As one. In a single process. Next came my algorithms. My algorithms, programmed onto their system chips, brought them to life, so to speak, and enabled them to function independently and interdependently."

I nodded with what I hoped was appropriate reverence. "Then . . . this changes so much." I was grasping at the implications, stunned by the immensity of Dr. Bickel's developments.

"One more thing about their design, an elegant addition."

Only one?

"Each nanomite is equipped with a common connection type—*a nano-sized universal serial bus*. This is a 'group-technology' breakthrough that allows tribe members to connect, to piggyback atop each other—much like Lego blocks snap together—to amplify their functionality."

Perhaps I couldn't grasp every future implication of his several breakthroughs, but I was starting to sense why Cushing and Prochanski were so hot to steal Dr. Bickel's work—which brought on another slew of questions.

"But you did all this in the AMEMS laboratory. You documented your work, your inventions. You reported all your findings to Dr. Prochanski who reported them to General Cushing, so—"

"Not quite, Gemma. They didn't know *quite* all I'd done, nor did I give them access to *all* of my data before they made their move. Particularly, I did not give Cushing (via Prochanski) access to data on the ion printhead or my nanomites, and I'll explain why soon. Let's just say that what Cushing *wanted* and what she *got* were two different things."

He laughed, tickled at his own cleverness, and I was struck once more at how shrewd Dr. Bickel was proving to be.

He stood up to pace, waving his arms as he talked. "So! So Prochanski and Cushing planned from the beginning to 'requisition' the nanomites and the printer—but I knew of their plans. To keep them ignorant of the ion printhead and to prevent them from taking the nanomites, I was forced to come up with some, er, *creative*, um, *distractions*. Pay close attention now, Gemma.

"In our staff meetings you heard me report on the *nanobots*. On your last day you heard Prochanski and Cushing plot to steal the *nanobots* and get rid of me."

I nodded.

"From here forward, for the sake of clarity, you and I must distinguish between *nanobots* and *nanomites*. Because, you see, my dear girl, rather than my smart nanomites, the only bots I ever showed Cushing and Prochanski were my first, very crude nanoelectromechanical population—mere 'dumb' *nanobots*.

"As I said earlier, I printed the nanobots before I printed my population of nanomites. I printed the *dumb* nanobots using my last generation printhead. The nanobots possess no integrated circuitry: They cannot be programmed.

"Ah! But then I printed my *nanomites* using the ion printhead. Same printer—but very different 3D designs, employing two different printheads, and producing two very different outcomes."

He breathed in triumph. "We kept the two populations together in a glass case in the AMEMS lab, a case just like the one you see here."

"You hid the nanomites inside the case with the nanobots? You hid them in plain sight?"

"Yes, except, of course, one cannot see either population 'in plain sight.' Who was to say that two distinct populations coexisted, dumb nanobots and smart nanomites, or that the two populations were or were not within the glass case?"

He laughed, relishing his tale. "As I made progress with the nanomites, I attributed their headway to the nanobots. I presented Prochanski with solid data describing the nanobots' makeup and abilities, their performance metrics, and their steep learning curve.

"In short, I attributed every glowing advance of my nanomites to the nanobots, and I attributed the manufacture of the nanobots to my printer—which was very true. My printer did, indeed, print the nanobots. *However*, I kept Prochanski and Cushing completely unaware of my ion printhead and the existence of my nanomites."

I was stunned. "They believed the, er, *dumb* nanobots to be your *smart*, 'integrated system' mites and they intended to steal them," I murmured, finally beginning to catch up with him.

"And steal them they did. Prochanski had them removed from the lab just prior to the *incident*. Remember how I 'stepped out' of the lab before the device detonated? I told Prochanski I was going to lunch and would return in an hour. He had men with a duplicate glass case standing by. They removed the case with the nanobots as soon as I left the lab, and substituted an empty case."

His eyes glowed. "What Prochanski couldn't have known was that I had, the night before, *already removed my nanomites*."

"How? I mean, how were you able to separate the two populations?"

"I take your point; however, it wasn't that difficult. I connected a flexible hose to two specially constructed carryalls and placed a signal device in each of the bags. The devices 'called' the nanomites. They flowed into the carryalls in response to my signal. The nanobots, obviously, had no capacity to respond to anything other than a set of limited, pre-programmed commands. They did not hear or respond to the signal."

He frowned and then recalled where he'd left off. "As I said, I had removed my nanomites the night before. They were waiting for me in the two carryalls, locked in a subbasement closet, when I made my exit. I retrieved them and exited the building at the other end. To anyone who might have seen me, I was merely carrying two large briefcases."

I could hardly breathe—the complexity of Dr. Bickel's planning was astounding, and grew more so in the next part of his narrative.

"It took days for Cushing's military investigators to definitively rule that my body was *not* found among the ruins of the lab. What do you think, Gemma? What do you think she thought when Prochanski died and she found that I had escaped, eh?

"Prochanski assured her that he had all my data—including the performance data on the nanobots. He assured her that he had copied and removed my data to a safe location. And he assured her that he had the nanobots. Prochanski and Cushing had military scientists standing by to take over after my 'unfortunate demise,' yes?"

I nodded; I thought I knew what was coming.

"How long do you think it was before she began to suspect she'd been made a fool of, hey? How long for her scientists to examine the nanobots, compare their abilities to the glowing reports I'd tendered, and conclude that the nanobots were *not* the devices I'd reported on?"

He slapped his leg. "Ha-ha! *These are not the bots you are looking for!*"

Dr. Bickel roared with laughter. I did not. I was imagining General Cushing's black, bottomless eyes the moment she'd realized she'd been duped—and imagining it was bad enough. I wiped a shaking hand over my eyes.

Dr. Bickel tapped his chin. "Gemma, do you understand the nano-sized universal serial bus I described to you?"

I nodded again and made a little "uh-huh" sound in my throat. What else could I do?

"I told you how, at any time, members of a given tribe can piggyback with members of the same tribe to multiply their tribe's functionality and strength, yes? And yet, while the five tribes vary in their software and hardware, every tribe's hardware employs that same nanometer-scale universal serial bus. *Universal*, Gemma. And therein lies the power of this particular breakthrough.

"Any nanomite can, when needed, piggyback with a member of *another* tribe. This has two potential benefits: the ability to temporarily *share* roles which, theoretically, would temporarily increase the nanomites' computational power to an exponential level. The computational power of their joined systems will boggle the mind."

"Potentially? Theoretically?"

"Yes; I'm still exploring that realm of possibility."

Nanoelectricalmechanical . . . smart nanomites . . . nano-sized universal serial bus . . . piggyback with members of another tribe . . . exponential level . . . realm of possibility . . .

If my head had whirled off my neck just then I don't think Dr. Bickel would have noticed. He was too engrossed in his lecture. Fortunately for my spinning head, his lecture changed direction.

"Let me describe the tribes' diverse roles and why, then, the bus becomes important," he continued. "Some nanomites, for example, direct the collection, storage, and distribution of power for the nanocloud. The power management nanomites comprise what I call Beta Tribe."

"Power? Because they need electricity, right? To, um, do whatever it is that they do?"

Dr. Bickel chuckled. "Power? But of course they need power, Gemma. The nanomites need power or they will fail. The beauty of my design, however, is that the nanocloud can utilize power from *any* source of electrical current, including direct and indirect sunlight and organic or living things.

"The mites will conserve energy when they need to," Dr. Bickel added, "but, under pressing circumstances, they will employ whatever energy is available. Because their mechanical bodies contain the right mix of metals, the mites can generate power from citrus fruit if need be!"

Then he chuckled again and I demanded, "What's so funny?"

"I was thinking of some of my early experiments in the AMEMS lab. In one of them I provided the nanomites with a selection of citrus fruits and cut off the flow of electricity to the glass case. Scouts from Beta Tribe immediately investigated the fruits. Within minutes, the tribe swarmed the fruits and began generating power through them."

"From *fruit*?" I wasn't buying it.

"Gemma, most living things—including human beings—generate electricity. Without electricity our brains could not 'fire' and our nervous system could not communicate with the brain."

He shook his head as if he couldn't understand how my education had overlooked this vital concept. Well, my studies of *history* and *accounting* hadn't exactly concentrated on neuroscience.

"In a dire situation with no other power source, a single grapefruit could power a few of the mites for, say, an hour," he informed me. "The rest would agree to enter sleep mode until another source became available."

"What would happen if their power source was about to fail and they didn't have another one?"

He seemed unconcerned. "I'm not certain, Gemma, but they are amazingly resourceful. I'm sure they would come up with something."

He slipped his hands into his lab coat. "Now where were we? Oh, yes. Beta Tribe. Beta Tribe facilitates the appropriation and allocation of power. If necessary, the nanomites can pull power from whatever source is available to them. Every mite has its individual power storage capacity, of course, but Beta Tribe monitors, analyzes, and predicts need and suggests appropriate measures to optimize the cloud's supply."

"So some nanomites tell other nanomites what to do?"

"No. The nanocloud is not a dictatorship and no tribe has 'authority' or control over another. The nanomites are equally autonomous and decentralized: They are autonomous in that I do not control them, other than confining them to this case. They are decentralized in that they make decisions through tribal cooperation and consensus rather than via a central processing unit separate from them or hierarchically above them.

"Their decision-making is not hampered by human hubris or influenced by ego. The tribes report their findings to the other tribes and all the mites analyze the data. Then, through scenario-based decision trees, the mites prioritize possible actions and responses in terms of the nanocloud's well-being. The tribes then reach a cooperatively achieved consensus, usually within seconds, but sometimes longer."

Being naturally a glass-half-empty gal, I wondered how the nanomites "liked" being kept in a glass box. I wondered whether they might someday insist on being released "for the nanocloud's well-being." And should that "someday" arrive, I further wondered how Dr. Bickel would respond to the nanomites' "cooperatively achieved consensus."

I didn't mention my wonderings, though. I simply changed the subject: "How do they fly like that?"

"Oh, they aren't truly flying, at least not in the sense of birds or insects. They have no wings although each mite is aerodynamic in its shape. They navigate in a number of ways. In sunlight, they can use their mirrors to propel themselves short distances or—"

"They have *mirrors*?"

Dr. Bickel huffed, a little miffed that I'd interrupted. "Each mite has a tiny mirror that, when packed away, resembles a nano-sized slice of polished silicon. Those flashes and shimmers you see within the case? Those are their mirrors—which they employ for a number of purposes.

"This can be seen when, under the guidance of Beta Tribe, the nanomites deploy their mirrors in an optimal arrangement to take in power from solar rays. The nanocloud can then use the absorbed solar rays to power Delta Tribe's lasers to—"

"What? They have lasers, too?"

Dr. Bickel clucked his tongue. "Really, Gemma. It is proving difficult to provide you with a comprehensive overview of the nanomites when you insist on interrupting every five seconds."

I raised one eyebrow. "Well, *excuse me, Dr.* Bickel, but I don't have a Ph.D. in whatever it is that you have a Ph.D. in."

I waved my hand in the direction of the nanocloud. "This—*all of this*—is completely new territory for me and, if you'll forgive my saying so, your 'comprehensive overview' *presumes a lot*—like that I have a background in 'nanophysics.' Well, I *don't*. You know very well that I studied history and accounting. I didn't study *science*, thank you very much."

He was taken aback at my longwinded outburst. Maybe I was, too. At work I had never spoken my mind so emphatically, with such vehemence.

No, at work I'd been the dutiful, shrinking wallflower.

"I-I, uh-uh—" He actually stammered. "I-I, ah, must apologize, Gemma. I probably, no, I *do* sound like a-a puffed-up old windbag, prating on like this."

"Well . . ." I didn't want to tell him I agreed but, in fact, I did.

"It was quite, no, it was *very* inconsiderate of me." He looked down and ran a hand through his faded rusty hair. "I beg your pardon, Gemma."

Good heavens.

He was crushed.

I sighed. His apology rather melted my heart, to tell the truth.

"You know, Dr. Bickel, I'm very, um, jazzed by everything you're telling me, very engaged and intrigued in your many accomplishments." I tried to be soft, conciliatory.

He perked up at this and looked hopeful.

"If you could take my lack of technical knowledge into account and be patient when I need a little clarification, I would love to hear more."

He blinked and looked up at me, patently sorry.

I think, Dear Reader, that's when I really started liking Dr. Bickel.

"Perhaps I could list the five tribes? Tell you of their functions?"

"That would be great," I replied, "as long as I may occasionally ask questions. So I don't get lost."

"Yes, yes, of course. Thank you." His enthusiasm returned. "Well, as I said, Gemma, *five* tribes. Alpha Tribe holds the nanocloud's collective memories and learning. Think of them as being the library—the *historians*—of the nanocloud."

He preened, gratified to have validated my field of study.

I sniffed. *As if!*

"Beta Tribe, as I've already mentioned, manages the nanocloud's power needs. Gamma Tribe directs preventive and reparative maintenance—"

"I'm sorry—what kind of maintenance?"

He nodded and made an effort to be civil. "Maintenance is separated into two categories: work done on a regular basis to *prevent* equipment malfunction and work done to *repair* equipment malfunction."

"Preventive—like regular oil changes, stuff like that?"

"Exactly like that. Gamma Tribe maintains the nanomites or repairs them when they break down. Each mite is fabricated with a small bit of extra material for them to create or develop nano-scale *tools* as needed; Gamma Tribe either makes the tools they need for repairs or directs other mites to make them."

"Fascinating." I smothered a smile as I envisioned yellow 'mini-minions' running around with tiny tool belts slung about their girths.

"Yes, *quite*. Then, to answer your question of a few minutes ago, members of Delta Tribe each have a tiny laser. Only Delta Tribe."

"And they use their lasers to somehow propel the, uh, nanocloud, how?"

"Ah, yes. Delta Tribe aims their lasers at other nanomites' mirrors in coordinated bursts, generating short, dynamic spurts of propulsion. By focusing their lasers on the leading edge of the mirrors, they *push* the nanocloud in that direction, much as solar sails might. Delta Tribe directs the placement of the mirrors for their lasers to propel the cloud where joint consensus has determined it to go."

"Wow."

"Er, yes, *wow*! I appreciate your enthusiasm, Gemma, and that isn't the only use for their lasers."

"Do tell." I was hooked, I admit it.

"Defense, Gemma, defense."

He was smiling again and I grinned back, our little tiff behind us.

"The fifth tribe, Omega, directs the nanocloud's defenses. Delta Tribe's lasers are not the nanomites' only defense, but they are a powerful part of it. When connected to an uninterrupted energy source, the nanocloud can generate and direct a laser beam strong enough to cut through steel. It takes them a few moments to bring the laser up to power, but they are quite efficient."

My glance at the glass case was involuntary. Dr. Bickel followed my gaze.

"You question why they haven't freed themselves, don't you?" he whispered.

"Yes." I nodded at the same time.

"And I'm not entirely sure I can answer your question, Gemma, except to say that they haven't wanted to." Now he sighed, and I felt the weight of his concern.

The word to complete his sentence popped into my head, and I felt it had to be true.

Yet. They haven't wanted to free themselves yet.

"As I've been teaching them language, we've, well, I feel like we've rather *bonded*, the nanomites and I."

"Can you 'bond' with tiny machines?" I hadn't intended to sound so sharp, but there you have it.

He shook his head. "That was an unscientific assertion, wasn't it? And I am wrong, of course. The nanomites and I are learning together and I'm certain that my sense of 'bonding' is only a baseless human feeling I have. Perhaps the nanomites simply don't recognize a *data-driven* need to leave at this time. In any case, I have not, to date, seen them harness Delta Tribe's lasers in any manner other than to propel the cloud within the case."

We stared at them for long minutes. I had to marvel as they eddied and swirled behind the glass. It was hard to accept that I wasn't seeing *them* but the flash of their tiny mirrors—nor was I seeing them individually but in densely packed masses. With the little about them I had just learned, I acknowledged Dr. Bickel's pride over his success to be justified.

"How many of them are there?" I couldn't take my eyes off the morphing haze in the glass case.

"At present? I estimate the nanocloud at upward of several trillion nanomites."

I stared at Dr. Bickel. "At present?"

What did "at present" imply?

He looked away. "I smuggled fifty billion of the nanomites—our prototypes—out in the carryalls that day. However, while we were stocking this lab in the furious weeks running up to the 'incident,' I printed as many wafers as the printer's capacity could handle. We ran the printer day and night, each wafer yielding something on the order of *two hundred billion* nanomites. Rick and Tony loaded the printed wafers into protective clamshells and put them in Rick's car the morning of the incident. I could not allow the uncut nanomites to fall into Cushing's hands."

Something dawned on me. "The ion printhead! What became of it?"

Dr. Bickel sighed. "I had to let it go, Gemma. It and the printer went up with the lab in the explosion and fire. Cushing has the schematics for the *printer*, but she doesn't know about the ion printhead. I've stored *those* schematics in a secure remote server."

I slowly shook my head. "I wouldn't trust an encrypted account at some remote server farm," I objected. "You said Cushing is relentless. What if she discovers the location of your files? How secure are they, really, if the government wants them?"

"You're absolutely right, but don't worry. I assure you: anything I've hidden, Gemma, will remain hidden."

Now I sighed, not convinced, and swept my gaze over the lab. "So you brought the printed wafers for several trillion more of the nanomites here? You cut them apart and programmed them in the last few months?" I looked at the sparsely equipped lab. "Without the printer's digital laser cutter?"

Even I knew that to be an impossibility.

"Actually, I cut none of them." Dr. Bickel's sly smile reappeared.

Realization swept over me. "*They* did it?"

He was nodding, pulling at his scruffy beard, and beaming. "On a hunch, I placed five printed wafers into the case—one wafer of each tribe. I focused the 3D microscope on a sample and sent the feed of their activity to those monitors."

He pointed to an array of monitors lining a nearby workbench. "I recorded it all, of course, and it was most amazing. Emissaries of Gamma Tribe examined the wafers first. They seemed to hold a little confab—took about five minutes—before they arrived at consensus. After that they rejoined the nanocloud.

"Approximately fifteen minutes later, I observed contingents of all five tribes descend on the samples. Some began to cut and others to assemble the nanostructures in rows and ranks according to tribe—demonstrating that they recognized which mites belonged to which tribe.

"Gamma Tribe directed the operations, and Beta Tribe powered each mite as it came off the 'assembly line.' The last thing to occur was programming. Members of each tribe piggybacked with an unprogrammed mite of the same tribe and shared their programming with the newly cut nanomites. Within minutes, new nanomites were joining the nanocloud. I tell you, Gemma, it gave me chills!"

It gave *me* chills, too. "But what's to stop them from making more and more of them? Could they keep growing the, er, cloud?"

The idea that the nanomites might replicate themselves until *a trillion* was a *small* number for them was a scenario straight out of a horror movie.

"Oh, they haven't the parts to do so." Dr. Bickel was fiddling with the microscope's feed, obviously unconcerned with the implications of my question.

"They couldn't fabricate their own pieces and parts from raw materials?"

"Well, no. They don't have the polymers or the doped metals and they can't provide the atmospheric environment necessary for deposition. The mites cut apart the fabricated mites I gave them, powered them, and shared their common programming with them. That's all."

"All right . . ."

No, it *wasn't*, but I didn't know what else to say.

"Now, the mites can certainly *repair* each other, except in extreme circumstances," he went on, oblivious to my discomfort. "At the nano level, they can cut, weld, and glue—those terms being simplistic, of course."

"Of *course*."

Tone, Gemma, tone. My sarcasm was at the outer reaches of my control.

With that last announcement, he seemed to deflate. I imagined he had to be exhausted. I knew *I* was. Dr. Bickel broke off his lecture just before brain matter began leaking from my ears.

He glanced at his watch. "Goodness. Our midnight luncheon is quite past due. Care for something to eat before we continue?"

It had been a long night already and I *was* feeling hungry. "Um, yes, thank you."

He led the way past the aisles of laboratory tables and equipment over to the far side of the cavern. There, we entered his living area, built not entirely into the stone but also alongside of it.

I gawked around, amazed and a little delighted. The temperature in the cavern was pleasant and dry so the fact that his small dining area was out in the open was quaintly picturesque, in the manner of a sidewalk café.

All that's missing is a view of the Eiffel Tower.

His square table with chairs for two sat on a colorful carpet, but the "floor" beneath the carpet was stone. Two 40-inch monitors hung on the cavern's wall in view of the table. One screen displayed a live feed from a camera over the nanocloud. The second screen changed views every few seconds. As the image changed, I squinted at it—I was looking at an image of the wall that hid my entrance to the cavern.

No wonder he was waiting for me when I emerged from the tunnels!

Then the image changed. "I continually monitor the three entrances to this room," Dr. Bickel murmured.

Along the same wall, a few yards from his eating area, I saw a wide desk. A computer and several monitors sat on it. A tall bookshelf, spilling with volumes, completed his office area.

I followed Dr. Bickel through a doorway carved into the rock wall between his dining and office spaces—into a compact kitchen. The entire room was carved out of the rock and was fitted with cupboards, counters, and space-saving appliances. I was impressed.

"My sleeping quarters are through that doorway," Dr. Bickel motioned to the right as he lifted the lid on a crockpot.

I peeked into the room. It was more of a rock cell than a room. On the left of his bed was a chiseled platform topped with a mattress. Straight ahead another tunnel led away.

"That leads to my western escape route," Dr. Bickel said from the kitchen where he was slicing bread.

"One of the three entrances you spoke of?"

"Yes. You came in the back way, from the north. My bedroom route leads west, into one of the old munitions bunkers facing the base."

"And the third? The one you booby-trapped?"

"Ah. As I said, if Cushing comes looking for me under this mountain, we hope that she will 'stumble' upon that entrance. You can see where the tunnel comes in just over there." He waved a knife away from the lab, toward the wall opposite my entrance.

"Getting into the tunnel will be easy at first; however, I've made the remaining journey difficult for her by adding rock falls, false routes with dead ends, and other inventive distractions, so that I have enough time to take the nanomites and leave through either the western or northern routes."

He ladled soup into two bowls. "Would you take that plate of bread, Gemma?"

I lifted the plate and sniffed. The sliced bread was fresh-baked. A homemade, yeasty scent reached my nostrils.

Yum. My stomach grumbled in agreement.

We sat down together to a simple middle-of-the night lunch of soup, bread, and canned juice. "I hope you will forgive this plain fare, Gemma," he apologized.

"But it's delicious," I protested. "And this bread is wonderful. It's fresh, too—did you bake it yourself?"

He blushed, pleased that I'd noticed. "I like to cook, but as I said, I only have dry and canned goods left. I hope the next time you come I might offer you something better."

"The next time?"

He swirled his spoon in his soup. "As I alluded to earlier, I asked you here to offer you a job, Gemma."

If I hadn't been facing financial disaster, I wouldn't have let him make his pitch. I set my spoon down. "I'm listening."

"Did you find the trek onto the base and up the foothills into the tunnels too rigorous?"

I thought about it. "Not too."

Too rigorous? No. Unnerving and illegal? Yes. That.

"I would like you to make the trip on a regular basis, say once a week, bringing in things I need. I will pay you in cash for the items you bring me and pay you for each trip you make. What do you think?"

"I will need time to think about it." The prospect was scary—I thought about the three roads I'd crossed during my hike up the foothills. What if I were caught by a base patrol? What would the Air Force do with me? If I were apprehended and Shark Face heard about it, would she remember me and associate me with Dr. Bickel? I might be putting myself squarely into her sights.

I was quiet for a long while, lost in my thoughts, but my expression remained placid while I mulled over his proposition.

"The military doesn't patrol the mountain's perimeter often, Gemma."

My forehead creased. *How does he do that?*

"You know the draft folder in your email account, where unsent mail you've written is kept until you are ready to send it?"

"Yes." Where was he going with this?

"Check it regularly. We can communicate by placing unsent mail in that folder."

"You can access my email?"

He shrugged, embarrassed. "I hacked the power company's network, remember? I would have communicated with you through email left in your draft folder the first time, but I had no way of telling you to check it. However, if you agree to my proposal, I'd like to add some security to your account. Just to be safe."

I continued eating my soup and we finished the meal in silence. When we stood up, I gathered up my dishes.

"Leave them; I'll clean up, Gemma."

"All right. And I'll think about your proposal." I sighed. "So I just write an email and put it in my draft folder, and then you log in to my account, go to the draft folder, and read it?"

"Yes. And answer you in the same unsent email. Just be sure not to put anyone's email address in the 'To' field. That way it cannot accidentally be sent."

"All right."

Sounds like spy stuff.

We walked back toward the glass case on our way to my exit. It was the middle of the night by now, but I still felt quite awake.

"Would you like to hear more about the nanomites before you go, Gemma?"

125

"Very much, Dr. Bickel." I wasn't in a hurry to leave, and curiosity burned within me now.

"The best is still ahead," he assured me. "I think you'd be interested in how the nanomites learn, for instance."

When I nodded my assent, he went on. "Well, their core logic is *predictive*. That means I have programmed the nanomites to observe and to anticipate.

"They monitor and catalog the choices, behaviors, and actions of what or whom they are watching. Based on those observations, the mites anticipate the *future* choices, behaviors, and actions of the subject they are observing and prepare appropriate responses for those anticipated actions."

He must have interpreted my glassy-eyed expression as, "Huh?" which was a good choice, because that's what I meant my face to say.

He took a deep breath and pressed on. "A coarse example of predictive logic is how social media sites offer you new products based on your previous purchases, browsing history, 'likes,' and the groups you interact with. However, the nanomites' predictive behavior is much more sophisticated because they observe the world *directly* from their five tribal perspectives and share that information with the entire nanocloud."

"Tribal perspectives?"

Dr. Bickel's chest swelled. "Oh, yes. As part of its assigned role, each tribe is programmed to provide a unique but complementary perspective of behaviors, issues, actions, and dangers observed in the world around them. This is an impressive behavior, Gemma, because *gestalt*—the sum of the whole—is more powerful than the individual parts."

His eyes glowed. "And the mites' predictive logic leads to their greatest ability." He coughed. "I've been saving the best until last."

I smiled, my good humor restored by the meal.

"Do you know anything about quantum stealth technology, Gemma? Hyper-stealth technology? Passive adaptive camouflage?"

I smiled inwardly because Dr. Bickel wanted so badly for me to say, "No, not really. Can you explain?"

Pretty please?

I humored him. "No, I don't think so. What have those to do with the, um, nanomites?"

As I'd deduced, he was tickled that I'd asked. "So much, I assure you! Original stealth technology was about making an airplane undetectable by radar. When a radar antenna sends radio energy into the air and that energy strikes an object's surface, the signal bounces back to its source—which allows the antenna user to track the object's speed and location.

"The rounded and cylindrical shape of an airplane's body is very good at reflecting radar signals, so radar is how air traffic controllers track planes in flight. But what if you don't want an airplane to be tracked by radar?"

He waited a tick just to be certain that I wasn't going to try to answer his question. "Why, you redesign the plane so that it has only *flat surfaces* and *sharp edges*. In that way, the radar signal is deflected *away* from its source, rendering the plane undetectable. Another method is to treat the surfaces of a plane so that they absorb the radio waves instead of reflecting or deflecting them."

"But the nanomites aren't airplanes. What has that to do with them?"

He nodded sagely. "The same technology that tracks planes and satellites is also used to track weather phenomenon such as tornados and hurricanes and, with ground-penetrating radar, to find underground objects such as large fossils."

"Okaaaay . . ."

He chuckled. "But what has that to do with the mites, right?"

"Uh-huh."

"You already know that each mite carries its own mirror, and I've said that under the guidance of Beta Tribe, the mites deploy those mirrors to take in power from solar rays. Delta Tribe aims their lasers at other mites' mirrors to propel the nanocloud."

"You said that already—'like solar sails.' But I thought solar sails could only work in space?" I wanted him to know I wasn't a *complete* dunce.

Dr. Bickel chuckled; he slapped his knee and laughed. His wasn't a mean laugh—it was the laugh of a shared joke between friends.

All right, then. I laughed with him.

"Very good, Gemma! Very good. You are correct—and yet, at the nanometer level, the mites have found a way to make laser propulsion work. I hope to communicate with them someday on a level that will allow them to tell me *how* they get it to work, but we aren't there yet. When they do tell me, it will be a stunning new discovery.

"But, I digress. We were talking about quantum or optical stealth. The nanomites can employ their mirrors for yet another purpose: *to project what is around them*."

He waited for me to "get it," but I wasn't "getting it." I pulled on my "nothing" mask.

"I could reference the mathematics involved in quantum stealth technology, but that would only complicate it for you," he drawled, a little disappointed.

"If it's all *that* important to you, why don't you try it again the *simple* way," I countered, my tone chilly, expression indifferent. I didn't appreciate his revived superior attitude.

"I see." He fidgeted with a button on his lab coat as he, I hoped, was reforming his approach. "Gemma, do you recall how I described the mites' role division as tribes?"

"Sure."

He cleared his throat, ready to turn another corner in his lecture. "In nature, some creatures operate, innately, through what is called "hive" or "swarm" intellect. Ants, bees, birds, fish, and so on employ hive intellect: Ants march, bees swarm, birds flock, and fish school.

"Well, the nanomites also have a highly developed swarm mentality in which *the tribes* communicate, share information, and act in concert. They hold what I've termed "confabs" to share data, tribal perspectives, and possible solutions. Once a course of action is decided, the nanocloud—instantaneously—acts in a mutually agreed-upon manner."

"Yes, you said that already." I was following but, given his emphasis, I was starting to snap to new ramifications. "Are you saying that they *think*?"

He beamed. I was, again, a dull but at least satisfactory student. "Yes, in a very authentic way, they think. Of course, they are not capable of *independent* thought—each tribe's algorithms determine the range of its input into the nanocloud's decision making process. The nanocloud is dependent upon and limited by the advice and consensus of the whole of all the tribes' participation—but the nanocloud can arrive at that consensus and act upon it *in real time*."

"Wow."

"Yes, er, as you are quite fond of saying, *wow*." He ran his gnarled little hand through what bit of faded red hair remained on his head. I sensed he was near the apex of his discourse, close to the climax of his lecture.

He held up one finger. "Reflect for a moment on the nanocloud, on the *trillions* of nanomites, each armed with its own mirror. So trillions of mirrors, yes? *But* each mirror is more than a single, nano-sized slice of polished silicon. *Each mirror*, when fully deployed, has nine separate panels. The mites unfold their mirrors in three rows of three, multiplying the nanocloud's reflective capacity *by nine*."

He held up a second finger. "Next, consider that each of the nine panels is an independently articulating sheet. This means the mites can adjust the angle of every panel individually—any direction, any degree—to achieve maximum absorption *or reflective* effectiveness."

I watched his third finger go up. "Now think of each panel providing near-real-time reflections of the world around them and think of their joined computations approaching the speed of light."

He paused for effect. "Finally, think of them wanting to hide themselves."

We drew near the glass case containing the nanocloud, and still nothing came to me.

"I-I don't follow."

His face fell; he felt sorry for me—which didn't go down well.

"Just spill it, *Doctor* Bickel," I growled.

"Think, Gemma! Use that splendid, analytical mind of yours! The *reason* General Cushing wants the nanomites. *Why* she is obsessed with them."

I struggled to connect the dots.

Think of them wanting to hide themselves. Think of each of panel providing near-real-time reflections of the world around them.

"Are you saying they can sort of camouflage themselves?"

Dr. Bickel's expression read, *Come on; you can do it!*

Grrr!

"That they can use the, uh, reflections of their mirrors to . . . to . . . make it look like they aren't there? To make people see what is around them instead of seeing them?"

His eyes lit up. I *was* making connections, at last. I struggled on.

Why would Cushing want this 'quantum stealth' technology, this hyper-whatever-he-called-it thingy? What kind of military applications would it—

"Are you saying the nanomites can make *other things* invisible?" I was incredulous.

"It's optical invisibility, Gemma, optical invisibility. Also known as passive adaptive camouflage. The mites create optical invisibility by utilizing their mirrors to bend light and reflect the surfaces around them. *Nanostealth.*"

"But is that still invisible? They can make themselves and other things invisible?"

He didn't answer. Instead, he walked up to the case and shouted, "Nano! Hide."

The shimmering cloud flowing through the glass case paused. Froze in place.

And disappeared.

⌘⌘⌘⌘

CHAPTER 10

I stared into the case, searching for them. *Nothing.* The empty interior of the glass case stared back at me.

"The nanocloud is still in the case, right? I just can't see it?"

"You actually *can* see the cloud, Gemma, but the nanomites are reflecting a perfect 360 degree image of the environment around them, so that while you are looking *directly at them*, your brain believes the case to be empty."

My brain crunched the implications until, vaguely, I understood why Cushing wanted the nanomites, wanted their technology. "If Cushing were to get the nanomites, if she could replicate them on a large scale—"

"General Cushing doesn't merely want them for use in foreign wars against America's enemies, Gemma. She believes the only way to ensure national security is to monitor *everyone*, at all times, legally or not.

"At heart, Cushing doesn't want the best for a democratic nation; she wants control. She is evil and she is ambitious. She must never get the nanomites, Gemma. Never. Whatever it takes, I must ensure that they remain out of her hands."

"But-but if they are so dangerous in the wrong hands, if they can be used for evil, then why—?"

"Why build them in the first place? Why teach them?" Dr. Bickel stood a little taller. "Do you know how much suffering the nanomites could alleviate? How many diseases they could cure? All cancers could be overcome, quickly removed from a body by the mites' coordinated attack. Injuries and birth defects could be repaired without overtly invasive surgeries.

"Can you imagine the insect infestations that could be corrected, rebalanced without the use of harmful chemicals? Can you fathom the effect of the nanomites on food production worldwide? Starvation would become a thing of the past! The nanomites could predict weather patterns and facilitate rescue attempts under collapsed buildings! The list of good they could do is endless, Gemma."

His speech stirred me. I guess he knew it would.

"Will you help me, Gemma?"

I nodded. "I'll try it out, Dr. Bickel. See how it goes." I was committed now, but I felt oddly okay with it. And at least my money problems would be over for a time.

"And Dr. Prochanski did not help make the nanomites?" I asked in a whisper.

130

"That sham of a scientist? Not a chance."

Dr. Bickel's mood shifted. "The nanomites are purely *my* invention. I may not have invented three-dimensional printing, but the ion printhead? *Mine*. The nanometer universal serial bus? *Mine again*. Their intellectual attributes? All *mine*. I alone wrote the mathematical algorithms that allow them to function, to learn, to repair."

"Every move that buffoon, Prochanski, made in the last three years was aimed at bringing *my* R&D to fruition so that he could help Cushing steal it—and so that he could claim credit for my work." His eyes narrowed. "That's why he latched on to you, Gemma. He used you to spy on me, but the bugs I planted recorded everything."

I can safely say that Dr. Bickel launched into a bit of a tirade at this point. In a strident voice he rehearsed Dr. Prochanski's schemes and lies, his betrayal of our country, of Dr. Bickel himself, *and his manipulation of me*.

His rant didn't last long, and I figured he just needed to vent. He had been, after all, cooped up here alone for three months and had been forced to give up his entire life because of Prochanski and Cushing.

When he finished, he reddened, mortified by his outburst. He again stammered an apology. I said I understood. And I did. After all, who was I to judge?

I actually felt okay about Dr. Bickel. We'd weathered two or three short-lived spats and one embarrassing meltdown in the space of about six hours. That kind of transparency and resiliency was good for a healthy relationship. At least that's what Aunt Lucy had always said.

"Actually, Gemma, I need to retract a few things I said."

I cocked my head, waiting for him to speak.

"I said the nanomites were *my* invention, that it was all *my* doing."

I nodded.

"Except . . . every person is born with gifts, born with certain aptitudes and intelligences. Some are given more; some less. Yes, I have worked hard, but I can't take credit for what I've been, uh, *given*. I should have acknowledged that."

I thought it an interesting perspective. "So, 'given,' as in given by God? You believe in God?"

"Yes," he whispered, "but I confess I often feel very far from him."

I couldn't help him there, so I said nothing.

Dr. Bickel and I parted company with an awkward handshake an hour before dawn. He counted out eight hundred dollars in twenty-dollar bills into my hand before we parted and handed me a list of things he wished me to bring to him in a week's time. I stared at the cash in my hand.

I can pay my past-due utility bills and restock my kitchen.

I left Dr. Bickel's "lab under the mountain" before dawn with my mind spinning, my wallet full, and my heart a little troubled. I retraced my steps through the tunnels until I arrived at the door that led outside the mountain. I stepped outside, carefully closed the door behind me, and listened to the mechanism on the other side spin and slide home the bolts.

I peeked out from behind the rock outcropping and scanned for vehicles on the dirt road surrounding the mountain. By the position of the moon, night was almost spent. At least I had a little moonlight for my hike down the foothills.

I crept down to the three rocks that mark my PIDAS crossing, my "sentry boulders" as I'd started to think of them. I yawned. The next time I came, we had agreed that I would come just before dawn and stay until the sun set and shadows appeared on the foothills to help disguise my coming and going.

I waited and watched before starting across. I crouched and pushed through the cuts in the PIDAS fence and jogged away from the restricted area without incident. An hour later I arrived at my car.

The next week dragged on. "Real life" felt anticlimactic compared to all I'd learned and experienced on my trek up the foothills. I bought groceries, paid bills, and put the remainder of the cash Dr. Bickel had paid me into a coffee can in the freezer. And I planned my next trip into the mountain.

The downside of that first visit to Dr. Bickel's lab? His rant played on a continuous loop in my head. I fixated on his accusations of Dr. Prochanski, a man I had once admired and to whom I had given my trust. I began to process the extent of Dr. Prochanski's duplicity. As each piece of his deception came clear, the weight of his betrayal grew.

Dr. P didn't encourage me because he cared. He didn't suggest that I improve myself because he valued me. I thought he was a friend—or at least a trusted mentor.

But he didn't care. He manipulated me. Exploited me. He had a plan and he needed information. And who did he pick? He picked **me**—*someone he thought too naive and gullible to catch on to what he was doing. He picked me because I fit the bill: loyal, unquestioning, stupid. He used me and then he threw me away.*

I scrubbed at the moisture leaking from my eyes, angry with myself because I'd misjudged Dr. P so badly, because I *had* been naïve and gullible. Because I had been *deceived.* Made to look a fool.

Having been so deceived was the worst part. I'd been a victim before, but I had never thought of myself as a fool. It stung.

Sniffling and gritting my teeth, I vowed, "No one will ever take advantage of me like that again."

***

That week I bought a sturdy backpack at REI, one large enough to carry groceries but not, once packed, too heavy for me to carry on my trek up the foothills. Of course, the filled backpack also had to fit through the tight crack behind the beam in the main tunnel.

I filled the list Dr. Bickel gave me and, on the day we'd agreed, repeated my hike of the week before. I made the trip in the near-dawn darkness without any difficulties and arrived at the hidden entrance just as the sun cleared Sandia Crest.

Dr. Bickel "oohed" and "aahed" over the fresh foods I'd brought him. I was happy for him, and it gave me a little satisfaction to see his tired eyes light up.

Then he gave me a lecture on the strict "security protocols" he demanded I use: Absolute secrecy on my part and no Internet searches that could in any way attract attention. He presented me with a long list of keywords I was never to use in emails, social media, or search engines. The obvious ones were his name, General Cushing's name, and anything to do with MEMS technology.

"So I'm not supposed to look for work anymore?" I complained. "All of my adult work experience is in the MEMS and AMEMS labs at Sandia. *Of course* my résumé contains most of your keywords!"

"We can make an exception for that," he rushed to assure me, "although I do hope our arrangement is satisfactory?"

"It is, for now," I returned, "but how long do you plan to stay holed up here? When the nanomites are, er, *ready*, won't you want to reveal them—and yourself—to the world? Isn't that the surest way to keep the government from confiscating and, er, exploiting them?"

He thought for a moment. "I don't have those answers for you yet, Gemma."

I could tell he was troubled by my questions. Cushing had thrown a wrench into his intentions for the nanomites—even though he had foreseen and planned for possible government interference. I was convinced that Dr. Bickel had schemes he was unwilling to disclose yet.

I folded my arms. "Well, I can't take money from you and still claim unemployment."

"I would prefer that you did, since I'm paying you in cash. It would be safer for me."

His face was growing a little red. I stood my ground.

"No, Dr. Bickel. I won't cheat. I can't keep claiming unemployment if you are paying me."

Dr. Bickel stroked his beard and considered my ultimatum. He gave his scraggly beard a last tug as if coming to a decision. "Very well. We will consider you an independent contractor and your work for me a contract position. At the end of the year, I will provide you with a legitimate 1099-MISC, one that will pass muster with the IRS. The money you receive from me will be legitimate self-employment earnings you can report to the unemployment office. You won't need to claim unemployment benefits as long as you work for me."

"How will you do that?" My frown deepened. "Will it be legal?"

"Yes, quite. Leave that to me. I have avenues," was all he would say.

I left late that day, conflicted and tussling within myself. On one hand, I had money in my pocket that would allow me to sleep at night instead of worrying that my electricity would be turned off. On the other hand, I wondered if I'd made a terrible mistake by agreeing to help Dr. Bickel. I wondered if opening up that email hadn't been the biggest misstep of my life.

I will have to get a real job again someday—and Dr. Bickel isn't exactly in a position to write me a glowing recommendation, what with the whole being "dead" thing and all.

I had another idea.

I can keep looking for work while helping Dr. Bickel and, when another job comes up, I will take it. If I make trips for him after that, I won't take any money for them.

***

I spent July Fourth with Abe. He cooked brats in his backyard and I brought a salad and a dessert. When it grew dark we saw some of the fireworks from Kirtland and, closer, from people in the streets around us who insisted on defying the law against aerials.

I'd been so preoccupied with the whole "Dr. Bickel" thing that I hadn't thought about Zander in days—until he showed up on my doorstep two days after the Fourth.

"Hey. I was in the neighborhood and thought I'd stop in and say hi."

"Hi, yourself."

"Meet me in the backyard?" Zander's voice was playful, and his gray eyes crinkled in that way I liked.

"Lemonade or tea?" I arched my brows in a mock-serious manner, the rest of my face expressionless.

He sighed. "Oh, wow. That's a tough one."

I frowned. "Well, you should have come prepared."

We stayed in character, both of us severe and serious, until he cracked. I, of course, knew that I would win. I could keep a straight face forever.

"I'll leave it to you then," he grinned, and we laughed together.

I went to see what I had in the fridge while he loped around the house. He was waiting for me on the steps when I came out with ice-filled glasses and raspberry iced tea.

"Good choice," he murmured after downing his first glass.

We talked for an hour or more, I think. He managed to pry most of my history from me that day. He was good like that, letting me talk and actually listening.

"So your twin sister—Genie? She's an identical twin?"

"Technically, yes, but we don't really look like each other. We're not alike in any way, actually."

"So what's she like, this lawyer sister of yours? And if you're identical twins, you must look *something* like her," he insisted.

I shuddered inside. "Well, she's quite pretty, actually; she's very stylish and can be witty and vivacious. But I'm like a twentieth-generation photocopy of her. A really bad copy."

Zander looked at me then, puzzled. "Then she must be drop-dead gorgeous."

Now I was confused. "Wha-what do you mean?"

"Are you fishing for a compliment, Gemma Keyes?" Zander demanded.

I was surprised into blushing. "No. Of course not. Never mind."

His brow wrinkled. "You'd think you didn't own a mirror, Gemma. You are a lovely woman. I like that your loveliness is natural, too, that it isn't painted on. I can't imagine Genie being prettier than you are. Maybe *as* pretty, but not prettier."

I was shocked and didn't say anything. *I* was the dull, drab one of the two of us. At least according to Genie.

At least according to Genie. A tiny, improbable suspicion bloomed in my mind, but I had to put off exploring that suspicion to respond to Zander's next question.

"And you said you and she weren't alike in any way. What did you mean by that?"

Careful, Gemma. I had to caution myself when it came to Genie. A lifetime of caution is a hard habit to break.

"She's, uh, we, well, we have different personalities." It was a weak reply and I closed myself up tight after I'd said it.

I didn't realize I'd "gone away" for a few minutes or notice how quiet Zander had become. When I snapped out of it he turned his eyes away, but I guessed he'd been watching me while I zoned out.

Not to worry, I told myself. *I didn't give anything away.*

Maybe, but his next question was penetrating. I wasn't ready for it.

"Gemma, are you frightened of Genie?"

My hands, suddenly sweaty, clenched and unclenched on my thighs. "Of course not."

"I think you are." It was gently said, but Zander sounded convinced. "I don't know what the issue is between you sisters, but I can see that it's painful to you. I'm sorry I butted in. Sorry I caused you discomfort."

My childhood had tutored me in the art of hypervigilance. I'd learned to watch, to observe while not being observed, to school my emotions, and to weigh my options before acting. In short, I'd learned to survive.

I nodded, and I kept how undone I was feeling hidden from him.

After Zander left I stood over the counter in my kitchen, thinking. A line of tiny "sugar" ants trailed across the floor and up onto the counter. I observed their purposeful progress, their unfaltering determination to cart away whatever edibles they found. Aunt Lucy had hated the "little buzzards" with long-suffering fervor.

Nothing she tried had deterred the ants from their objectives for long: not sprays or powders or baits, so she obsessively wiped counters clean and swept floors of crumbs. When I asked why she didn't hire an exterminator, she answered that she had, several times, but the ants always returned.

"The exterminator says there's a crack in the house's foundation," Lu explained. "The ants live in the ground below the crack where he can't reach. He said he would never be able to kill the colony, because the ants we see are only a tiny part of what's below ground."

The idea of a crack in the cement slab under the house stuck with vivid glue. I don't recall when I first started applying it as a metaphor to my sister, but sometime in my early teen years I came to grips with how deeply the crack in Genie's foundation ran.

I'd never looked at a trail of ants the same after that; instead I studied them for some clue so as how to understand my sister . . . and what must lie "below ground" in her heart.

Until today, no one had guessed at the truths I covered so well. And yet, in the space of minutes, Zander had come close to penetrating my walls of secrecy and self-defense.

I would have to be more careful in the future.

***

I trekked up the foothills to bring Dr. Bickel supplies before dawn the next morning. We had agreed on an eight-day cycle for my visits so that hikers and mountain bikers who were regulars on the trails would be less likely to remember me. After that, we settled into a comfortable routine.

I stopped filing for unemployment, but kept searching for work and I applied when I found something. Nothing seemed to be a good fit for me, though, other than government or government contractor jobs—and I knew I wouldn't be getting a call for one of those.

When the job search grew discouraging, it comforted me to think of the small but growing stash hidden in my freezer. Yes, the money was good because Dr. Bickel was generous. On the flip side, I'm sure he felt he had to be liberal—given the risks I took.

Each time I saw him he gave me a shopping list for the next time—and paid ahead for the groceries and my efforts. I varied the grocery stores where I shopped for Dr. Bickel, picking stores I hadn't shopped in before, stores not near my home. Twice I went to his "safe house" as he called it and picked up orders he had purchased over the Internet and had shipped to the house.

Dr. Bickel had a locked mailbox at the safe house, and the orders I picked up were small parts for lab equipment. I didn't want to think about what might happen if something big and vital to his work went out and needed to be replaced. Something that wouldn't fit in the mailbox. Well, the situation hadn't occurred yet, so I put it out of my mind.

As far as food went, Dr. Bickel had enough staples in his kitchen's pantry to last years: pasta, rice, peanut butter, dehydrated potatoes and fruit, and racks of canned goods. However, I totally understood how hard it would be to go without anything fresh.

Once in a while Dr. Bickel developed a "hankering" for something exotic (like crab), but most times I bought pretty much the same things: steaks, chicken, salad greens, eggs, half-and-half, butter, English muffins, fresh fruit, and a few in-season veggies like broccoli or asparagus.

I laughed when I found out that he was fond of Gummi Bears! Every shopping list included a bag of the chewy candies. One of the smartest mathematical minds in America or maybe the world? Go figure. He was human after all.

And Dr. Bickel seemed genuinely happy to see me when I made the hike into the tunnels and to his lab. Yes, he paid me to fetch his groceries, and I received the money gladly, but perhaps I wasn't just a means to an end for him. Perhaps our deal was not just a mutually beneficial arrangement.

The truth was, I had by now realized that Dr. Bickel's gruff and touchy manner back in the AMEMS lab had been nothing more than a smokescreen he'd put up to keep people (other than Rick and Tony) at a safe distance. I think it was a facade he'd used from the early days of his career to keep those who would exploit his work at bay. I came to understand that he'd presented a false front to the world most of his life.

Yes, we had some things in common.

***

I glanced at my cell; the caller ID read simply, "Roanoke, VA." I already knew from the ringtone who it was. I'd made the tone especially for her.

The phone "rang" again, belting out the "Flying Monkeys Theme" from *The Wizard of Oz*.

Dun-duhdada-dundun; Dun-duhdada-dundun.

Genie.

She called every six months or so. We never exchanged meaningful news—the call was her way of ensuring that the inferior planets circumnavigating her Sun stayed in their proper alignments. If I answered the phone, her part of the conversation would consist of a couched interrogation. And if she didn't like the answer to a question she would dig until she got the one she wanted.

If I *didn't* pick up, she'd just call again. And again.

Not much of a choice, huh? You don't know how often I'd fantasized about blocking her number.

"Hello."

"Hi, Gemma. Just checking in."

Right.

"How are you, Genie?"

Deflect, deflect!

"Oh, doing well. I've been offered a partnership in my firm."

"That's wonderful. Do you have to buy into it?"

Keep her busy answering my questions.

"Of course. But I called to check on *you*. How is your job going? I heard there was an accident at Sandia back in March. Nothing near you, I hope?"

I skirted the first question by answering the second. "Actually, the incident involved two of my coworkers."

Artfully done, Gemma.

"Oh, dear! They weren't injured, were they?"

See, I understood that she already knew the answer to her question. "I'm afraid they were both killed. It was horrible. I'm still grieving."

True enough.

She was silent and I swallowed. Silence from Genie was ominous.

"But Gemma, are you being completely candid with me? Are you still working at Sandia?"

Aha! She *did* know the answer. "I'm sorry—did I say I was? Please don't concern yourself, Genie. I'm working on a contract at present, until a more permanent position opens up."

That was true, too. Dr. Bickel had promised a legitimate 1099.

"Really? With whom?"

Drat. I should have anticipated that question.

"Just another research facility. How did you know I wasn't at Sandia anymore?"

I had my suspicions. Genie and Belicia Calderón had too much nastiness in common not to share the wealth.

"Oh, Gemma. So defensive! If you must know, Mrs. Calderón has expressed some concern for you. She feels that you might not be able to make your mortgage payment. Like a good sister, I'm just making sure you're *all right.*"

But without an offer to help, right?

I had to bite my tongue. "Please tell Mrs. Calderón that my finances are in good shape. You might also tell her that my finances are none of her business."

"I'm sure you can tell her yourself, Gemma." Once she had succeeded at putting me on the defensive, Genie no longer needed to keep me on the phone. Mission accomplished.

"Talk to you later, Gemma." The line went dead.

Zander came by occasionally through the heat of the summer. He was out of town helping with youth camp late July into August but, usually when I didn't expect him, he'd drop by.

It was the same thing each time. We'd sit on the back porch drinking tea or lemonade, talking about my garden. I sent tomatoes home with him in August, but I was sending tomatoes to everyone in the neighborhood by then. My tomatoes were really "coming on" in the late summer heat. Abe and the Floreses especially appreciated them.

Zander and I laughed over some of the young "characters" he'd encountered at camp. His descriptions were rich and vivid, always good-humored. Even though I could tell that he worried over a few of the boys he interacted with, I could also sense a love or compassion for them.

"Where's that hideous cat of yours?" Zander asked one morning. "He's usually crawling up in my lap by now."

I laughed. "Thank you for admitting he's ugly! Aunt Lucy wouldn't allow me to call him names, but you'd have to be blind not to see that Jake is one of the sorriest feline specimens ever born."

"And that's putting it mildly," Zander muttered from behind his hand.

I burst into giggles. I couldn't help it. Then we were laughing.

"You know that cat hates me, don't you? He only cozies up to you to spite me," I finally managed. I wiped my eyes with the corner of my t-shirt.

"Is it 'cause you're so charming?"

I knew he was teasing, so it didn't sting. Instead it felt, well, comfortable, like all our conversations. "Yeah. My charm is legendary."

I waggled my eyebrows and he grinned. And then I asked something I'd been thinking about. Thinking about a lot. I hadn't planned on asking today, but, well, it just came out.

"Zander, can I ask you a question?"

"Sure." He swirled the last two ice cubes in his glass.

"How did you choose to be a pastor? I mean, I guess you don't seem the, um, type to me."

He just nodded, still swirling the ice. "That's a great question, Gemma. It might take a minute to explain. Is that all right?"

"Let me check my busy schedule." I examined the palm of my hand. "Hmm. Looks like I have a minute between my mani-pedi and my standing massage appointment."

He grabbed my hand and scrutinized my nails—my ragged, dirt-filled nails. "Miss, you'd better call and schedule extra time on that manicure."

We laughed again. Then Zander's face softened, became almost a little sad.

"When I told you about my family, Gemma, I didn't really say much about me. The fact is, I left out a lot. The details aren't important except to say this: Until about eight years ago I was involved in a gang. Had been since high school."

The blood drained from my head and rushed to my feet. I felt it tingling in my toes as it arrived there. "A gang. Like Mateo?"

He didn't look at me. Instead he stared over my garden. "Yes. And worse, possibly."

I could see his jaw working, his lips thin and taut. My mind was having trouble wrapping itself around what I was hearing.

"I ran with a bad crew down in Las Cruces, Gemma. I dealt drugs. I drank and caroused. I was violent. I . . . misused women."

No. No! I protested, horrified.

He glanced at me and I knew what he saw on my face pained him. "I'm sorry, Gemma, but I want to be truthful with you."

I was frozen; I couldn't move.

"I would still be that man today," he whispered, "if not for the God of grace."

We were silent while, inside, my image of Zander was shattering.

He broke the silence at last. "About eight years ago I was living in Phoenix. I was minding my territory one evening, just taking care of business. A rugged old guy wandered up to me. I thought he was buying. Instead he looked me over and said in a gruff way, 'Son, I was where you are twenty years ago. Different town, same drugs. Different corner, same grave just waiting for me to fall into it.'

"He came closer and said, 'How many years or months do you think you have left before someone puts a round in your head or slides a shiv between your ribs? Jesus would like to set you free from the grave you've dug for yourself before that happens.'

"Of course, I told him to get the *blank* away from me before I shanked *him*. He smiled, though, and replied, 'Kid, there isn't anything you can do to hurt me hasn't been done before. I've been shot four times, knifed twice, run down by a truck, had a needle broke off in my arm, and been beaten more times than I can recall. I still care what happens to you.'

"He asked me, 'Can I just tell you one more thing? And then I'll leave you be.' I wanted to curse him, make him shut the *blank* up and get out of my face, but I couldn't get my mouth to work. He just nodded this *knowing nod* and said, 'All I want to tell you is this: Jesus loves you, boy. And he has the *power* to change you, inside and out. The Good News is about change. About transformation—a transformation of the heart and soul. It's about letting God peel off the old, ugly, scarred man and letting him give you a new life, a life Jesus died to give you.'

"And then he asked me, 'Do you like this life? Or do you want a new one?'"

Zander heaved a deep sigh. "I was raised to know right from wrong, Gemma, but up to that *very moment* I actually believed I was fine—happy and content with my life of money, power, drugs, alcohol, violence, and women. But in less than two minutes that old guy's words rocked me to my core and ripped away the lies I'd fed myself."

I thought I saw moisture in the corners of Zander's eyes. I was embarrassed for him and looked away. He didn't seem to mind.

"I followed that man away from the corner I was working and got into his car. He started driving and we didn't stop until we reached Albuquerque. He knew I had to leave Phoenix right then if I was going to get away from the gang—they don't let you leave alive, you know."

I swallowed. "What, um, what did you do then?"

"What did I do? I stuck to that old man like puncture vine sticks to the bottom of a shoe. Everywhere he went, I went. Where he slept, I slept. No one knew where I was, not my old gang, not my so-called friends, not my family.

"He read the Bible to me every chance we got. I went with him when he went out on the streets to talk about Jesus. I soaked in a lot of what he had to offer.

"Then one day he says to me, 'Kid, you need to go to Bible school.' He took me to see a pastor *who took me into his home*. Gemma, that man and his wife just brought me into their home and treated me like their own. They helped me to apply to Bible school. Helped me get the money together. Prayed over me, wept with me, loved me."

Zander's voice dropped to a whisper. "I spent two years at Bible school. Never went home between terms, just stayed there and worked to earn my keep and my tuition. Two weeks before I graduated, I called my folks and invited my family to come see me.

"We talked for a long time. I apologized for the grief I'd put them through when I'd been involved in the gang and their criminal activities. I shared what Jesus had done for me.

"That was more than six years ago. I still take each day as it comes: another day to be thankful for; another day to share God's love."

We didn't say much more. After a bit he said he had to get going.

I hadn't commented further on his story, and I was sure that was the last time I'd see him.

⌘⌘⌘⌘

CHAPTER 11

I wrote earlier that Dr. Bickel and I had agreed on an eight-day cycle for my visits. We also agreed that I should arrive and leave in the dark, or close to it, to lessen the possibility of detection. I preferred coming before dawn and leaving after dark. That meant I would be spending a very long day with Dr. Bickel each trip.

At first, I thought it would feel awkward being with him for hours on end (but less awkward than my spending the night in the lab!) or that he would go off and work with his nanomites and leave me to be killed by boredom. What did happen, the little routine we fell into, turned into some of my happiest moments since Aunt Lucy died.

On the day scheduled for me to tote in the new supplies, I would leave home hours before dawn so that I entered the tunnels while the foothills were still in the dark. Dr. Bickel would greet me with a hot breakfast and I would unload my backpack. The pitifully few items I actually brought seemed like a lot when I was carrying them, pushing them ahead of me under the fence and through a few other chokepoints. But when I unpacked and stacked them on his kitchen counters, I always wished I had brought more.

Following breakfast, Dr. Bickel would go off and work for a few hours. I would sit back on one of his comfortable circa-1960s chairs and enjoy a book. He had an eclectic taste in novels, and I discovered Brad Thor and James Rollins during those visits. After I had become fans of their writing, I mined my local library to read everything else they'd written.

Then, to celebrate my visit, my new friend—the talented but socially awkward scientist—would serve a truly remarkable midday dinner. He was (as it turned out) quite as good a cook as he'd said he was, and I began to look forward to such treats as freshly baked breads, a small assortment of fanciful appetizers, a main course accompanied by all the trimmings, and a totally *awesome* dessert.

Dr. Bickel had this little trick he liked to play: He would keep the dessert hidden away until time to serve it, then he would bring it out with a mix of flourish, pride, and embarrassment. I loved taking pictures of his sweet creations with my phone and raving over his inventiveness, especially given the limits to his supplies.

When, at the end of the day, he handed me his shopping list for my next visit, I would try to decipher from the list of ingredients what fun or fabulous confection he was already conjuring ahead of time. Still he managed to surprise me, and I loved that.

Yes, my funny friend was a bit unpredictable—some might say eccentric, bordering on mad. That was the paradox of Dr. Bickel: unexpectedly tender and whimsical one moment; paranoid and given to garrulous rants the next; yet somehow brilliant and insightful. And while he might be perceptive on many levels, he was utterly blind toward his own shortcomings. Certain topics (like corrupt generals and unscrupulous government bureaucrats) just set him off, so I learned to avoid those areas.

Sigh.

I miss him and his desserts. I miss how he flushed with pleasure when I praised each delectable offering. I even miss the tirades—and the embarrassment and apologies that inevitably followed.

After dinner, we would clean up together and sit down to a game of Canasta. Aunt Lu and Genie and I used to play Canasta, so one day I brought up a double deck of cards and insisted on teaching Dr. Bickel how to play.

"I've never played cards," he grumbled, struggling to hold fifteen or more cards in his hand.

"Good. Then I have a chance of winning."

At first, while learning how to hold and manage his cards, he would fumble and drop a few (or a bunch) from his hand *and pitch a fit.* On those instances, he would explode in frustration and, more than once, he threw his hand on the table vowing, "I'm done with this stupid, mindless game!"

I didn't let him quit, though, and didn't let his conniption fit go unchallenged.

"Really? The *inspired Dr. Bickel,* one of the world's most *exceptional* and *accomplished* minds, can't master a simple card game? Can't beat my small, limited intellect?"

His eyes would narrow and, without a word, he'd shake the cramp out of his hand, pick up and sort his cards, and rejoin the game.

Oh, I ribbed him mercilessly. It was good for him—and fun for me. I decided that too much cerebral activity as a child and a young adult had robbed my Dr. Bickel of a normal coming of age. I doubted that he had enjoyed the little joys of family life while growing up. I'm glad to think that in his last days he experienced some of life's simple pleasures.

As summer wore on, we laughed and vied for supremacy over those card games. He rarely won—a surprise and a huge blow to his ego—but then *he* didn't grow up playing cutthroat Canasta with Aunt Lu and ego-freak Genie. As soon as Dr. Bickel had learned Canasta, though, and was starting to gain on me, I added a third deck and taught him Samba, a more complex variation on Canasta.

I had no idea that our arrangement and those idyllic days would come to a crashing end.

Soon.

***

It was late in August and night had fully fallen when I left the tunnels after another visit. I descended the steepest part of my climb and was not far down the slope from the outcropping that screened the door to the tunnels. I was approaching the road that banded the mountain when I heard the roar of an engine.

Headlights rounded a curve, and I panicked. Instead of dropping to the ground, I scrambled back up the slope toward the tall rocks. The lights of the vehicle briefly illuminated me.

By the time reason overcame my stupidity, a base patrol vehicle had screeched to a stop just downhill from me. I slithered between two rocks where I was screened from view.

I heard the two airmen on the road yelling back and forth, heard them on the radio raising the alarm. One of them scanned the hillside with binoculars. I wondered if they were the night vision kind.

If I stay here, they will find me.

I glanced above. I could get back to the door if I moved quietly.

I stayed low and crept back up the hill. My legs and back burned from the effort to climb in a crouched posture. I kept an ear tuned on the two airmen but concentrated on staying close to the ground.

When I reached the outcropping and slid behind one of the first rocks, my heart was pounding. My legs quivered like rubber, more from fear than from exertion.

I moved farther into the rocks, knowing the airmen could not see me. Then I peeked between two boulders to see what they were doing.

They were waiting.

Ten minutes later, two other vehicles arrived and several SPOs— armed DOE security police officers—jumped out. One of the vehicles maneuvered sideways on the road until its headlights lit up the hillside. I watched as five SPOs with flashlights formed a line and began climbing the hill.

I swallowed hard. *If I had remained where I was, if I hadn't climbed back up here, I would have been trapped.*

"The guy was about where you are," one of the airmen yelled.

"Are you sure? I don't see anyone," a SPO answered. He moved his light across the rocky slope.

The two airmen were talking to each other, but they seemed to disagree. The one who had yelled to the SPOs insisted, "I know what I saw!"

The SPOs were only yards below me. If they kept coming, I would have to retreat back into the tunnels and pray they did not venture into the rock maze and find the door.

As they neared the base of the outcropping, one of the SPOs called a halt. "Turn back, spread out, and sweep the hillside again."

They are turning back!

I shook with relief.

Twenty minutes later, the airmen and SPOs loaded into their vehicles. The airmen continued on their patrol; the SPOs returned to wherever they'd come from.

I didn't care where they'd gone; I was just happy they *were* gone, and I was relieved to have escaped detection and capture.

By the time I made it back to my car, it was close to midnight and I was exhausted, physically and emotionally. But when I got home I couldn't quite calm down, so I took a few minutes to write an email to Dr. Bickel and leave it in my draft folder in a message with the subject line, "Position Description."

I made my next trip into the mountain the Tuesday after Labor Day. It was uneventful, but I think Dr. Bickel and I were preoccupied with our own thoughts that afternoon. During our midday meal, I rehearsed the incident to him again and answered his questions.

"I have concerns about General Cushing," he admitted. "It's just a feeling, but I have this sense that she's closing in."

"How could she be? How would she find you?" I didn't want to hear what he was saying. "Are you basing your concerns on anything other than this *feeling*?"

"You're probably right, Gemma. I'm sure everything's fine," he murmured when we'd talked the event to death. I could tell he was troubled, though, especially when he added, "Still, we should take additional precautions"

"Such as?" I demanded.

He thought for a while before he replied. "I have a cell phone I want you to take with you. It's what they call a 'burner.' Untraceable. Plug it in and keep it charged, but don't use it except in the direst of circumstances."

He dug in his desk drawer, removed a phone and its charger, and handed them to me. "Only the direst of circumstances," he repeated.

I tucked the phone and charger into my backpack, the words "direst of circumstances" digging a hole in my gut. We sat down to play cards, but I could not seem to relax. For the first time ever, he beat me at Samba.

***

Zander called the Friday after Labor Day weekend. "I thought I'd give you a call instead of randomly showing up at your house."

"That's considerate," I laughed.

I'd thought a lot about what he'd told me, about his past with a gang. It still bothered me, but maybe not as much as it had when he'd first told me.

"I can manage 'considerate' once in a while," he replied.

We were joking with each other, completely at ease again. I was surprised—but glad.

"So, listen, a group of us from church are doing a barbecue tomorrow at a park where we know a lot of homeless people hang out. We posted signs letting them know about the food and when we'd be there. I thought you might like to come and help?"

"You're going to barbecue for the homeless?"

"Yup. We'll have burgers, dogs, potato salad, and baked beans. We'll also be giving away bottled water, wipes, socks, things like that."

"And you want me to help." Derision had leaked into my voice. "You mean no one at Downtown Community warned you about me? I developed quite a reputation for being a troublemaker back in the day. They even asked Aunt Lu not to bring me to kids' Sunday school anymore. I had to sit in her class with adults."

"Oh, *please*." He was just as sarcastic right back at me. "I've heard those tales. Whatever they still say about you, I know better."

He waited a tick; his timing was dead-on. "I know you're *much* worse than that." He snarled, winked, and added, "*You rabble-rouser, you.*"

It was just the right touch of edgy, dry humor. I snickered.

He asked again. "So what do you say? Barbecue for the homeless?"

I sighed (in keeping with our little charade), but I was intrigued. "Yes, all right. What do you want me to do?"

"Just dress casually—you know, nothing you are afraid to get dirty—and be willing to work. I'll pick you up around four tomorrow. Probably have you home by dark."

"All right."

We hung up and I thought about his offer again. Was it a date? Or was it just an attempt to get me involved with his church?

I sighed. *Neither one of those scenarios will work*, I warned myself. *I'm not ever going to "get involved" with his church, and he can't "get involved" with someone like me.*

The "someone like me" stuck in my craw. *Someone who doesn't believe the way he does,* I amended.

He picked me up the next day and as I got into the passenger seat, I was surprised to see another woman sitting in the back. I stared at her, my face a perfect blank slate.

"Gemma, this is my little sister, Isabelle."

Sister?

"Don't ever call me Isabelle," she scowled. "It's Izzie." Then she flashed a smile and grabbed my hand. "Nice to meet you, Gemma. Zander's told me about you."

I managed a smile in return. "Nice to meet you, too, Izzie."

The ride to the park took about ten minutes. The whole time, Izzie and Zander cracked jokes and teased each other. I stayed silent but smiled along with them. It was fun listening to siblings get along. I didn't know much about that.

When we got to the park, a crowd of about twenty young men and women were unloading two pickup trucks and hauling grills, tables, chairs, ice chests, and boxes to the center of the park. The park was one of Albuquerque's older ones; it boasted a wealth of stately cottonwoods and lots of shade. It was also rundown.

If Zander's church was looking to attract the homeless, they'd come to the right place.

Setting up for the barbecue was chaos, but light-hearted chaos. I pitched in with the others and followed the orders of the couple who seemed to be in charge. I noticed that Zander did, too.

An hour later the mouth-watering aroma of grilling hamburgers and hotdogs filled the park. Maybe a hundred or more people were gathering for the food. Call me clueless, but I was a little dumbfounded at how many of the homeless adults had their kids with them.

Kids are homeless, too?

I had no idea.

Izzie must have guessed what I was thinking. "Lots of people are only a paycheck away from disaster, Gemma."

My tongue felt stuck. I'd come too close to disaster myself to hazard a reply.

Izzie and I manned the potato salad and baked beans table. I was quiet as I spooned beans onto paper plates; Izzie was anything but.

"Hey, Sweetie! You like potato salad? How hungry are you? I'll give you extra if you give me a smile," and, "You look like you're a growing boy. You need to carb-load, Hon. Gemma, give this good-looking young man some baked beans. No; give him more than that. He's gotta keep his strength up."

With every interaction she added, "And I want you to know how much Jesus loves you, *Chica*," or "Jesus loves your smile, Baby." Something along those lines. It was kinda sweet.

The men we served were the hardest for me to handle—guys who were in their thirties or forties but who looked so much older, their skin weathered by the outdoors, their hearts and eyes worn by hard living. They were mostly quiet and nodded their thanks.

I needed something to drink. I turned away to take sips from a bottle of water. I didn't think I could take much more of this.

At another table I saw Zander and a few other men filling plastic grocery bags with bottles of water and sundry items. People lined up for those meager supplies, too.

When the food was gone (every last bite of it) Zander climbed up on a little wooden platform under a tree and started speaking. He didn't have a microphone and he didn't speak loudly. What was interesting was that the crowd in the park quieted and some of them came in close to listen.

So did I. Zander's voice carried well to where I leaned against a tree.

"Folks, I hope the little bit we brought this afternoon encourages you. I use the word 'encourages' because I think it takes real courage to live today. Times are hard and courage is not always easy to come by."

He smiled and reached out with that smile to draw his listeners closer. "A long time ago, about five thousand people walked for days to listen to a man they hoped could give them courage. If you think times are hard today, it was a lot harder back then. These people and their kids were out of food, and there weren't any stores around to buy more, no McDonald's on the corner. The man they'd been following was Jesus, and all he had was five little buns and some dried fish. Still, he told his friends, 'Give these people something to eat.'

"His friends fed all five thousand people that day, five thousand people who had walked three days to hear what Jesus had to say. As I said, just bread and dried fish—but everybody ate until they were full and there was *still* food left over! *It was a miracle.*

"Today's barbecue isn't a miracle, but it is offered in love. And I'd like to share the other kind of food Jesus came to give the people, the kind that those folks were willing to walk three days to get.

"To one woman Jesus once said, *Those who drink the water I give will never be thirsty again. The water I give them becomes a fresh, bubbling spring within them, giving them eternal life.*

"To a different crowd Jesus said, *The thief's purpose is to steal and kill and destroy. My purpose is to give you a rich and satisfying life. I am the good shepherd. The good shepherd sacrifices his life for the sheep.*

Zander smiled. "Today we gave you a little something to eat and a few things to take with you. We hope you'll go away knowing that you are not alone in this world. More than that, we want you to know that Jesus, the good shepherd, still offers living water. He still wants you to be free inside, free from the thief that steals, kills, and destroys, free to have a full, satisfying life.

"If you would like to know more about the life Jesus offers to you, please meet me under that tree over there and we'll talk. I would be happy to talk with anyone and pray with you, too."

He walked over to the tree he'd pointed at and a few people made their way toward him. I was shaken. I took a deep breath and let it out.

Hard-core. He's a hard-core Christian. It wasn't that I hadn't already known it, but knowing it and seeing it in action were two different things. I needed to get away. I couldn't keep seeing Zander anymore.

I looked around. "Hey, Izzie." I walked up to where she was boxing up tablecloths.

"Hey, Gemma!" She smiled at me.

"So, um, listen. I'm going to take off now. Thanks for inviting me."

She saw me then, fiddling with my shirttail and not making eye contact. Her smile faded. "How will you get home, Gemma?"

"Oh, I'll just walk."

"Are you sure?" I think she was asking me more than one question.

"Yeah. I'm sure."

Zander called that evening. I was expecting him to. I hoped I was ready.

"Ah, how's your garden going?"

"It's okay. I have lots more tomatoes and peppers coming on."

"Well, I just wanted to see if you were all right."

"I'm fine."

Awkward silence.

For the first time, conversation was uncomfortable between us. Neither one of us wanted to bring up why I'd bailed on him and Izzie at the barbecue. We knew anyway.

The next day Zander knocked on the door but I pretended I wasn't home.

It's better this way, I rationalized.

I peeked through the curtain, expecting to see him leave. But before he got in his car, he walked across the road to Emilio's perch on the curb. Again.

Zander had a *Blake's Lotaburger* bag in one hand, something else in the other, and a Powerade bottle under each arm. Zander sat on the curb next to Emilio, his long legs sticking out into the street far past the boy's legs.

Zander deposited the bag and Powerade bottles between the two of them before offering what he had in his other hand to Emilio. Emilio took whatever it was and turned it over in his hands.

I thought it looked like a block of wood.

I guess that makes sense, what with Emilio's fetish for carving.

Zander pointed at the chunk of wood and made some gesture. Emilio nodded and handed his knife to Zander, who examined it.

"That kid's likely to turn that blade on me the next time he breaks into my house," I sniffed.

As those words dropped out of my mouth, I was dismayed to hear how calloused I sounded. I shook my head and gnawed on the inside of my cheek, upset with myself—and angry with Zander, yet unable to tell myself why.

Zander handed back the knife, patted Emilio on the shoulder, and then, as though he'd forgotten it, reached for the *Blake's* bag. He looked inside and said something to Emilio, who shrugged.

Zander pulled out two wrapped burgers. He handed one to Emilio. Then he reached inside and retrieved a paper sleeve brimming with fries. He handed that to Emilio, too.

The kid placed the paper wrapping for his burger in the concrete gutter and poured the fries out. He'd already stuffed half of the burger into his mouth; he tossed back a handful of fries, too.

Zander had taken only two bites by the time Emilio had polished off his burger. The kid was devouring fries with both hands.

Quite casually, Zander dumped half of his fries onto Emilio's burger wrapper, where they disappeared before Zander finished his burger. He cracked the lid on one of the drink bottles and set it on the paper near Emilio's vanishing fries.

When Zander cleaned up the trash from their meal, he left the second Powerade on the curb and slapped Emilio gently on the back. I was surprised—no, astounded—when Emilio flashed Zander a smile.

⌘⌘⌘⌘

CHAPTER 12

Zander called a few times and came by twice more, but I didn't answer the door or pick up his calls. I didn't hear from him after that and, while it smarted a little, I was also relieved. I turned my attention to my job instead.

I was late getting going the day of my next scheduled visit. Dawn was much too near when I packed groceries into my backpack and carried it out to my car. Emilio sat on *my* curb, his small blade carving through another scrap of wood.

"You goin' hiking again?"

I was so surprised by his unexpected question that I nearly dropped the backpack—which would have been rough on the eggs.

I turned toward him, face placid, framing an answer. "Yeah. I try to get out for the whole day, couple of times a month." It wasn't exactly a lie. Not exactly.

Emilio had never spoken to me. He'd rebuffed every greeting I'd offered when he'd moved in with his uncle, so I'd stopped trying a while ago. And our last encounter had been, after all, in my kitchen over a sack of pilfered food.

"That guy go with you?"

By "that guy," I assumed he meant Zander.

"No."

"He coming 'round soon?"

I sighed. "No. I'm sorry; I don't think he's coming to see me anymore."

He mumbled something, a curse word, I thought. I couldn't see his face. He was turned away from me and it was still dark.

"Where you go?" he asked finally. His eyes never left the chunk of wood in his hand or the blade he plied to it.

"Just up in the foothills." My response sounded natural enough to my own ears, but my heart thudded in my chest. "Lots of trails to explore up there."

"Yeah. I'd like to do that. Sometime."

I placed the backpack on the floor of my back seat and closed the door. I was considering what he'd said, looking at it through my observations of his home life. The conclusions were distressing.

"Well, why don't you go, then?"

He mumbled a few more words under his breath. I was certain he was cussing this time.

His response confirmed what I'd guessed: He had no one to take him. His uncle would be more inclined to teach him how to cook meth than take him—God forbid—*on a hike.*

From everything I'd seen, Mateo didn't allow Emilio to leave the block, which would partly explain why the kid was always perched on the edge of the sidewalk. Come to think of it, I'd never seen Mateo's girlfriend Corazón leave the house either, except to walk to the little grocery a few blocks away—unless, of course, Mateo took her somewhere else. Yeah, from what I'd seen, Mateo ruled Corazón and Emilio's every move, and he did so with an iron fist.

I shocked myself. "Want to go with me sometime?"

I wasn't offering to take him today, of course, but he and I could go any day I wasn't headed up to the tunnels. Not that I thought we'd ever go; I was certain he would turn me down. I was just checking.

"Naw." His face flamed red as he mumbled the one-word reply.

"Because Mateo won't let you go?"

I was pushing the boundaries of common sense and caution now— but there you go. I do that sometimes. Because I *really* don't like people who control others through fear and intimidation.

Emilio's black eyes turned toward mine and stuck there. I didn't blink and I didn't look away. I kept my expression impassive.

He broke first.

"What you care?" he spat at me. With an angry snarl, he stood up and stomped away toward his uncle's house.

Leave it alone, Gemma, my inner voice warned. *Just leave it alone.*

Nodding in agreement, I got behind the wheel and headed for the foothills.

I parked on a street I hadn't used before, along a sidewalk and under the branches of a spreading tree. The tree's branches brushed the roof of my car. I climbed out, shouldered my backpack, and headed toward the trailhead.

My hike up to the tunnels was uneventful, the climb quite enjoyable, really. I came at the PIDAS from a little different direction today, to prevent wearing a path to the cuts in the fence. I didn't mind the extra climbing. In fact, I was in better shape for the several hikes I took each month.

"Bonus!" I said aloud and laughed.

***

Dear Reader,

I have spun this tale full circle now. We have arrived back at that mid-September day, the day of Cushing's attack on Dr. Bickel's lab under the mountain.

Oh, I miss him. I do.

I apologize for the soppy tone. I've been isolated for a couple of weeks myself now and, well, I guess I understand how alone Dr. Bickel must have felt, by himself under the mountain.

Anyway, on that last day, Dr. Bickel made another great midday meal for us: salad; pasta and pesto sauce with chicken and artichoke hearts; and fresh-baked garlic bread. It was so good!

We were too full to eat dessert right away, but Dr. Bickel showed me the two beautiful frozen parfaits he'd made. They were simple, really, just colorful sliced fruits and flavored ices, but elegant and sweet. Perfect for summer. We decided to save them for later.

I'm looking at a picture of them on my phone right now, the shimmering strawberry and kiwi slices peering through the tall glasses. We didn't get to enjoy them. We were into our card game and I was up by 1,500 points when the first explosion blew our world apart.

You know what happened right after that. If you've forgotten, you can re-read the first entry in this account.

I can't bring myself to write about it twice.

⌘⌘⌘⌘

PART 2:
STEALTHY STEPS

CHAPTER 13
THE MORNING AFTER

Do you remember my saying I had to talk myself off the crazy ledge before I could drive myself home? Yeah, *that* was a noteworthy moment!

My memories are a bit hazy after I pulled off the freeway and had my little nervous breakdown. Eventually I guess I just set the car in motion and let it find its own way home. I don't remember checking for traffic while getting back onto the freeway, so I'm grateful that we, my trusty Toyota and I, weren't flattened by a semi when we merged back onto I-40.

Then, somehow, I was back in my own neighborhood and sort of snapped out of it.

I kept my speed under 15 miles per hour the last block before my house. My engine made less noise at that speed. I came around the curve, passed by Abe's house, and entered the cul-de-sac. Then I stepped off the gas and let forward momentum carry the car over the curb and down the driveway to my garage door.

I sat with the engine still running, breathing hard and scared out of my mind. I wanted to bolt, to tear up the steps and into the safety of my house, but I was frozen in place. Getting inside presented a challenge, the first in a line of challenges I would face that morning.

I've told you how the folks in my neighborhood watch out for each other? So when I came home *that morning*—the morning after the attack on Dr. Bickel's lab—it had to have been after 6:30 a.m., and I knew curious or prying eyes were likely to be watching. I had to be careful.

These old houses don't have attached garages—just tiny, detached ones toward the back of the lot. My old Corolla fit inside my garage (just barely), so I never left it in the driveway. (Not the best neighborhood, right?) The problem was, I didn't have an electric opener on my garage door, so I had to get out of my car to raise the door.

I also described the two break-ins to my garage earlier. Do you remember the humongous screwdriver I stuck through the door's track just above one of the wheels? Well, the screwdriver guaranteed that no one could open the garage door from the outside—and "no one" included me. That meant I had to enter the garage by the side door.

Once in the garage, I would remove the screwdriver and lift the door. Then I would drive into the garage and park, get out and pull down the door, and stick the screwdriver through the door's track again.

I would leave the garage by the side door, locking it behind me, and go inside my house via the kitchen door. (For that reason, I almost never used my front door.) And my kitchen door is diagonally opposite the garage's side door—in plain view of the neighborhood.

Have I painted a clear enough picture? In my mind, the whole world could see me come and go. Except they would *not* see me.

Anyway, my car rolled up to the garage door that mid-September morning and stopped. Before turning off the engine and opening the car door, I paused and looked around for my neighbors. I wondered if any of them were out and about so early.

Mr. and Mrs. Flores were retired. They often walked their little dog, Pepé, as soon as it was light enough. I was relieved not to see the sweet old couple, but I figured they could pop out any time.

You've met Mrs. Calderón, our mean-spirited gossip. She slept late, so I wasn't as concerned about her. Not this early at least.

I wasn't worried about Abe, either. Although I considered him a real friend, that didn't mean he wouldn't freak out about *this*. But, like I said, since Abe was not out on his porch, I wasn't worried about him.

I was, however, on the lookout for Emilio.

So I stayed put, scanning for "watchers." And there he was, perched on the curb in front of his uncle's house—kitty-corner to the right of my driveway *at the crack of dawn*—whittling on a stick of wood, scowling, and shooting daggers at my car from under his bunched brows.

How was I going to run that Keystone Kops fire drill—get in the garage's side door, lift the garage's car door, get the car into the garage, close the door, and jet out the side door into the house—all without Emilio noticing . . . that I wasn't exactly *myself*?

I scowled back at Emilio.

Fat lot of good that did.

I was angry. More than that, I was scared. Scared because I didn't understand what had happened to me. All I wanted was to crawl into my bed and fall into a dreamless sleep—from which I would eventually awake *back in the real world*.

But to do that, I first needed to get into my house.

Unseen.

And that's the joke, Dear Reader, the ridiculous joke. Because as far as I could tell, I already *was* "unseen."

I stared at my hands on the steering wheel. I knew they were there. To prove my point, I used my right hand to turn on the radio. Music filled my car.

I pushed the knob off and again wrapped my shaking fingers around the steering wheel. I could see the steering wheel just fine. I just couldn't see my hands on the wheel. Or my arms.

I pulled the rearview mirror toward my face—for the umpteenth time—and got the same view of the back seat, said view apparently *right through my head*. I gagged and thought I would throw up, but I had nothing left in my stomach.

At the reminder, a raging thirst revived. I had thrown up hours ago. How long had it been since I'd had anything to drink? I licked my lips; they were as dry as tissue paper.

Hot, frustrated tears dripped from my face. I knew they dripped, because I *felt* them—not that I could *see* them in the mirror, because I couldn't!

Movement in my rear-view mirror recaptured my attention. Emilio, across the street, rose to his feet. He glared at my Toyota, distrust oozing from every pore. He had to be wondering why I was just sitting there, why I hadn't gotten out to open the garage door.

Great. Just great! Now I've attracted his attention!

He cocked his head, but kept staring toward me. Except I knew he couldn't see me. He should have been able to see my form in the driver's seat but—

He frowned and looked around as though thinking, trying to make up his mind.

What do I do if he starts walking toward me?

Which is exactly what he did.

I panicked. He was in the middle of the street, headed my way, when I, without a conscious decision, locked all my doors and shut off the engine.

He stopped, right in the middle of the cul-de-sac, and stared. Puzzlement flitted across his face.

If I'm really invisible, I reasoned, *then he can't see me sitting here. All I have to do is be still and wait him out. He can't watch forever.*

I looked down and freaked: My keys were still in the ignition. I yanked them out and threw them into my car's litter bag where they'd be out of sight.

Emilio stepped up on the sidewalk next to my driveway and paused. He folded and pocketed his knife and held up the piece of wood he'd been whittling, making a show of examining it. At the same time, he was checking out my car and scoping the neighborhood to see if anyone else was paying attention.

Oh, you're good, I sneered.

Showing no hurry, he sauntered up the drive to my car and stopped next to my door. He stared into my eyes and I, wide-eyed and hyperventilating, stared back. Sweat ran down my neck but I didn't move a muscle.

It was a weird, curious experience. I could see him, of course, but it was obvious that he could not see me, and that was the curious part: I was, I realized, privy to his unguarded expressions and movements. I felt like a spy or (*yuck*) a voyeur.

It was creepy.

It was intriguing.

It might have been entertaining if I hadn't been so parched, so anxious.

Emilio shot another covert glance around him before he tried my car door but, of course, it was locked. He glanced into the back seat, and then turned and studied my house's kitchen door, the one I always used.

I was glad right then for the barred and *locked* security door.

Emilio turned in a circle, apparently scanning for me and chewing his bottom lip. I'd seen the lip-chewing thing before, usually accompanied by a scowl of disdain, but I hadn't seen him do *this* before: He wrapped arms around his middle and hugged himself. Hard.

Whoa! This kid is really skinny.

Then it hit me: *Emilio is hungry.*

If I could have seen my own face, I would have slapped it.

How could I have been so dense? In a blinding flash of genius (*duh!*) so much made sense, and I felt a bit ashamed. Except for school and nighttime (and where did he crawl off to then?), this kid had sat on the curb across the street for a year, dodging Mateo's fists and likely going hungry.

Aunt Lucy would have realized. Aunt Lucy would have seen, my conscience informed me. *Aunt Lucy would have done something.*

Emilio wheeled and set off toward his house. I grabbed my keys and, as soon as he was about halfway across the street, I eased my car door open. As it had in the foothills, it creaked—and I froze. Emilio must not have heard it, though, because he kept walking.

I got out, pressed down the lock, pushed the door, and used my rump to make it latch. Quietly.

Emilio kept walking, but he was almost to "his" curb. I sped up the steps to my kitchen door, unlocked it, and bounded inside.

At the last moment, I remembered how the security door swung all the way out on its own and that I had to pull it shut. I reached back and grabbed it, yanking it toward me. It slammed closed with a *bang*.

I flinched a little then turned the deadbolt latch and closed and locked the inside door.

Home!

I cannot express the relief I felt at that moment. I went through the kitchen touching every dear object but stopped short at the sink—*water!*

I grabbed a glass and filled it, letting the tap run while I gulped down several glassfuls. When I was sated, I filled the kettle and set it to heat some tea water. I took another half-full glass to my little table overlooking the neighborhood and flopped into my chair.

Emilio had crossed back to my house.

From the foot of my driveway, his eyes darted from my back door to my front door. He strode down the sidewalk, scanning my windows, his jaw hanging partway open.

He had to have seen the side security door swing wide and then close on its own.

Ooops.

I swallowed again. *Well, what if you did?* I demanded silently. *Just what can you do about it, you little monster?* I stared back at him, but it was apparent that he could not see me.

Little monster? My conscience reminded me how thin Emilio had grown in the last year and how I hadn't noticed. Had I also misjudged the budding juvenile delinquent's motives? I could almost hear Aunt Lucy clucking her tongue and planning some do-good Christian intervention. I cut her off.

You have your own problems, Gemma, I lectured. *You aren't responsible for that kid.*

I squashed Aunt Lucy's reproving voice and returned my attention to my own issues. Now that I was inside my home and feeling safer, I could relax my vigilance, at least a little.

As soon as I did, my body started complaining again. That dull, persistent ache throbbed everywhere—in my neck, my back, my hands, and my joints. Even my skin pulsated.

I'm running a fever. I have to be—it hurts so much.

And I felt drained, more so than just missing a night's sleep: My very bones felt weak. Rubbery. I dug around in the kitchen junk drawer and pulled out a bottle of ibuprofen. I swallowed two pills and hoped they would work fast.

Now that I had slaked my thirst, other concerns raced around in my head, bumping and colliding. Every new thought I formed only generated more questions. The kettle whistled and I took it off the burner, but questions—so many questions!—pounded in rhythm with my aching joints. My questions demanded answers, answers I couldn't seem to produce.

Why can't I remember?
Why was I up in the foothills?
And why was I up there at night?
What happened to me?
Why can't I remember anything?
Why, why, why?

And the most important question was, *Why am I invisible?*

It was the first time I'd allowed myself to frame the word and I shook my head in denial. I'm not a whimsical person; I'm not given to daydreaming or fantasy. "Invisible" is *not* a word that belongs in *real life.*

I must have made the tea on autopilot because when I came to my senses I was again sitting at the table in front of the window, greedily sipping the sweet brew. I glanced up.

Emilio was still standing on the sidewalk in front of my house, *in front of my window,* his eyes agog. I looked down and saw my mug hanging—just *hanging*—by itself in midair!

"Oh, crud." I slammed the mug onto the table, sloshing tea on the tablecloth, and checked Emilio's reaction.

Frankly, it was comical, totally like something out of a cartoon: His expression was pure incredulity. He actually shook his head *and* rubbed his eyes.

I laughed.

I had to.

What else could I do?

⌘⌘⌘⌘

CHAPTER 14

I couldn't stop the laughter bubbling up in my throat. It kept coming and coming and it grew and grew until it was wild. Hysterical.

My body hurt with every spasm, and I couldn't curb it, the hysteria. I laughed until I felt my head was going to launch right off my neck and roll on the floor. All the while, Emilio stood out front, his face radiating confusion and doubt.

When the hysteria tapered off, I sighed and glanced down—down to where I *knew* my arms and hands were wrapped around my mug of tea— but I could only see the mug and my little table. I wiggled my fingers. No change. I clasped my hands together. Nothing. I knew I was "there," but I couldn't see myself.

A sob, the tail end of the hysterical laughter, jumped out of my chest, and a rain of tears followed. I tried to smother them, squeeze them back, but they leaked out anyway.

I dug the heels of my hands into my eyes and smeared the salty water over my face. When I looked up, Emilio was *still* there. He was scanning my house, his eyes jerking back and forth, looking for any sign of movement. I could see his puzzlement changing to wariness.

He looked terrified, too.

"You think *you're* scared?" I hiccupped over another sob. "*I'm* the the invisible freak!"

Invisible? Like I said, *people can't be invisible!* Not in the real world.

The mad laughter rose again in my throat—and just as quickly gave way to sobs. I buried my face in my hands. More crying. More sobbing.

"What am I going to do?" I wept aloud. "*What am I going to do?*"

My whole body throbbed and pounded. I can't overstate how intense the pain was! And a low hum, a tiny hiss, kept popping up somewhere behind the pain, like static behind or underneath a song track. I shook my head to rid myself of it.

That wasn't a good idea. I was already bone tired and sick—*so sick.* Shaking my head made the room spin and aggravated the headache.

I need to sleep! My body insisted on it, but I couldn't. Not just yet. I had too much adrenaline pumping through my blood and too many questions caroming around in my brain.

I slumped in the chair and leaned my elbows on the table. As I did, a tiny movement caught my eye.

The cushioned vinyl tablecloth "gave" just a little where I rested my elbows.

I lifted my right elbow and placed it on the cloth again, watching the cloth depress and form around my elbow—except then the depression disappeared!

I lifted my elbow and, this time, poked the tablecloth with a finger. *There.*

But as quickly as I'd seen the shallow depression, it was gone.

"What?" I was puzzled and amazed. I swallowed down the thrum of fear rising from the pit of my stomach.

The humming that had plagued me on my way down the flanks of the foothills grew louder and nearer. I tried to ignore it, but it rose in volume until my head was beating out a rhythm in tune with the chittering buzz.

I couldn't take the pain any longer.

I jumped up from the table. "Stop! Stop it!" I screamed as loud as I could and squeezed my temples. "Stop it!"

Movement through the window—Emilio again, cocking his head as though listening. Had he heard my shrieks? I clutched my head and held my breath. He appeared uncertain, perhaps concerned, but made no move toward my house.

"Oh, it hurts!" I moaned, concerned at how deep the fatigue ran, how tired and wrung out I was. To my grateful amazement, the clicking/buzzing softened and retreated until it petered out. As the chittering diminished, my thudding headache softened, too.

It had to have been the lack of sleep that made me a little dizzy, right? I sat down and my attention wandered back to the tablecloth phenomenon.

I need to understand what is happening, I told myself. I poked the cloth, saw the depression, and watched it disappear.

I poked again. Same thing: I'd see the slight depression in the cloth and then it would smooth out and look as if I *weren't* still poking it. I started poking with fingers from both hands. Same result each time.

Something else made me pause: a faint shimmering around my finger that appeared for the *briefest moment* and was gone.

I poked the cloth, slower this time. The "poked" spot wavered for a fraction of a second and disappeared.

"What is going on?"

I started jabbing my fingers into the tablecloth as fast as I could, but it seemed to me that as fast as I poked, the shimmering/disappearing grew faster, too, until I could no longer see the phenomenon. It was as though *whatever was happening*, was happening as fast as I could move—faster than my eyes could register it!

The word *predictive* popped into my head.

Where have I heard that word?

I sat back, concentrating, desperate to pull my scrambled thoughts together. My thoughts kept jumping to fragments of what happened in the foothills. Bits of memories floated in and out of focus—near, but frustratingly elusive. I could not seem to grab hold of those bits and string them together into something concrete.

I need some way to catch those pieces so I can look at them objectively.

Exasperated, I got up and stalked into the living room. I went to a bookshelf and grabbed a spiral notebook and pen. I returned to the kitchen table and sat down. I put the pen on the notebook and closed my eyes.

I will just let my thoughts float, I told myself, *and will write down whatever comes into my head—without thinking about it or trying to make sense of it or trying to connect it to anything else. Just write whatever comes.*

For a while, I allowed the chaos in my head to reign without attempting to impose any order on it—and it was hard, let me tell you. I was sick and worn, but I willed my pen to take on a life of its own while I gave free rein to the random pieces floating through my mind.

I must have fallen asleep. I must have relaxed until the exhaustion of the sleepless night kicked in. My head rested on my left arm and I'd slobbered on it a little.

Ick.

I sat up, wiping my face and then my arm, easing the crick out of my neck. My thoughts were fuzzy and I guess I'd forgotten that I was *invisible*, because when I saw the pen move by itself I about had a heart attack. Then I realized that I was *holding* the pen. I had moved my invisible hand and the pen had moved with it.

I glanced down and drew in a breath. The notebook was covered in a mish-mash of writing. Toward the end of the page, the writing had become larger and less legible until it flowed off the page and onto the vinyl tablecloth. Ink covered the cloth in roughly a foot square. Words and phrases were scrawled in several directions, overlapping each other.

My hands shook when I picked up the notebook. The writing on it was scribbled and disjointed—as disjointed as my thoughts about last night were—but, together, on the same page? Now I could see the bits and pieces holistically, could maybe make some sense of them.

DrBickel DrBickel

"Dr. Bickel?" My brow creased. "Why am I writing about him? He's-he's *dead*." I frowned again, because my whispered words carried a hollow, uncertain ring.

DrBickel
nice he's nice
Dr. P no not no

The writing here was indecipherable. I'd written over it and over it until the ink had soaked the paper and torn through it.

tunnels tunnels tunnels door door lever find lever find lever
cave big cave lights lights—something more that, try as I might, I couldn't read.

"Tunnels? Cave?" The words fell from my mouth with a vague sense of familiarity.

A few lines down, I made out *glass box glass glass mites mites mites cloud nanocloud*

hello (something, something)
hello
hello Gemma

"Hello, Gemma!" The image snapped into focus.

"I was with Dr. Bickel! He's *alive!* We were somewhere inside the mountain, in the Manzano weapons storage facility. In the tunnels?"

From there, I pulled more fragmented thoughts together. "He, Dr. Bickel, constructed a little laboratory off the tunnels inside the mountain! He had a glass . . . box. A glass *case*. Filled with *nanomites*! Billions of them. No. Trillions."

The nanocloud formed before my mind's eye: Their hazy, ephemeral gray, shot with flecks and flickers of color, moved and morphed like thick liquid. The cloud's metallic shimmer reminded me of gasoline on water, while in the background Dr. Bickel explained what they were, how they worked, what he had accomplished with them.

Yes.

I was beginning to remember. I turned my attention back to the notebook.

The writing was increasingly difficult to follow. It grew larger and sloped away from the lines and off the page. I stood with the notebook in hand and laid it this way and that on the table, turning it until it was lined up exactly where the writing ran off the page and onto the tablecloth.

As illegible and disjointed as the scribbled words on the notebook were, the writing on the table was worse. I'd written and then written over what I'd written several times before sleep had claimed me.

Standing above the inky jumble, certain words began to emerge from the chaos. I grasped a thread and, like untangling a knot—

I grabbed the notebook, flipped it over, and wrote down what I could make out.

men
gun
gun
guns
shoutshoutshout
men
guns
fraid
cush
cush
cushi
bat
bat

Cushing! General Cushing? Was she there? In my fuzzy memory, I could hear shouting, soldiers shouting, but could not make out the words—I could only see Dr. Bickel's face, etched in horror.

Bat?

I saw light glint off a metal baseball bat as he swung it toward the glass case—and connected. The corner seam in the case split apart and, as though a great blockage had dissolved, my mind cleared.

I remembered everything.

I knew that my eyes were wide open, staring across my little front yard, but they saw only what my mind replayed: Dr. Bickel smashing the giant glass case. Dr. Bickel waving his arms at the nanomites and screaming "Nano, hide! Hide!"

Dr. Bickel turning, seeing me as if he hadn't known or remembered my being there; Dr. Bickel shoving me toward the door into the tunnels.

I fixated on that moment, the expression of anxiety on his face, the worry in his voice. His protest, his cry—everything good I had come to believe about this man: Compassion, care, concern.

For me.

From where we huddled behind the last line of lab tables we saw men—dozens of soldiers in battle gear with weapons drawn—burst from the front entrance tunnel, flood the cavern, and spread.

"Go, Gemma!"

Heeding him, I ran.

We can still reach the back wall! I told myself. *We can!*

I remembered thinking, *If we can reach the back wall of the cavern without being intercepted, we will be safe!*

My breath caught. Dr. Bickel hadn't followed me. I remembered hearing him shout, "Hide! Hide, Gemma!" But he hadn't followed me!

I was going to go back for him when I heard gunfire—and something struck me in between my shoulders, knocked me down. Had I been shot? So much pain! I couldn't catch my breath!

I stared straight ahead and replayed Dr. Bickel's last words. "Hide! *Hide,* Gemma!"

Or had he said, "Hide! *Hide Gemma!*" . . . to *them*?

The awful truth was dancing around the edges, forcing itself into my conscious mind: It didn't matter which way he'd said it or which way he'd meant it. Only how the nanomites interpreted what he said mattered. Only what the mites *believed he'd meant* mattered.

I relived the moment when the corner joints of the glass case had given way, how the nanocloud had flowed out, how they had bunched and rocketed toward the ceiling of the cavern. In response to Dr. Bickel's urging I'd run toward the back of the cavern, toward my exit—until something had slammed into my back and knocked me to my knees.

I hadn't been shot.

They had swarmed me. *The nanomites had swarmed me.*

I felt again the stunning impact followed by the stinging pricks of their entry into every part of my body. My skin burned; it was on fire! I was choking, suffocating, as they rushed down my throat. The memory of their clicking and buzzing sickened me. I dropped my head on the table and tried not to scream, but I was terrified.

They are inside of me! The nanomites are in me!

I couldn't wrap my mind around it.

It's why I am so sick, I realized. *They are making me sick!*

"Get out! Get out of me!" I moaned.

I heard only a few isolated *clicks* and then silence.

I lay with my fevered face on the table, thinking about Dr. Bickel, sorting through the impossible facts, trying to make sense of them.

Two hours later, I was no closer to figuring out what to do next. I rubbed my gritty, sleep-deprived eyes. I was weaker now than when I'd come home.

"I need to sleep," I whispered. I left the table a mess and dragged myself toward my bedroom. The sight of my bed had never been so welcome.

I'll be safe while I sleep, I told myself. *I can think this all through later, when I have a functioning brain.*

As beat as I was, I decided that Emilio did not pose an immediate threat.

Who's going to believe a skinny, ten-year-old brat when he says he saw a coffee mug floating in the air from twenty feet away?

I ripped off my torn, grimy clothes and dropped them to the floor. I paused and stared. As each item of clothing left my hands and hit the floor, it became visible.

"That has to mean something," I mumbled, but my strength was draining away. I didn't care that I was putting my equally filthy body into a clean bed. Spending what little energy I had left, I crawled beneath the covers.

I should have succumbed to sleep right away, but my mind, exhausted as it was, refused to shut down. Paranoia ran its fingers up and down my spine, tapping out a warning.

General Cushing has to be—she must be!—looking for the nanomites. How long before she sends someone to question me? Except they won't be able to find me! How long before someone figures out that the mites—

I was not ready to put into concrete terms what had happened. I was not ready to slap a label on *The Event*. I was like an obstinate Scarlett O'Hara: *I will think about that tomorrow.*

Or whenever I woke up.

My body surrendered then, and my last conscious thought was, *It's not fair. I never asked for this to happen to me! Now I'm in this mess and look what they did to Dr. Bickel! They killed him! Oh, Dr. Bickel!*

Before I slept, the rational, organized part of my brain reasserted itself. To the panic caroming off the walls of my brain it spoke calmly. Logically.

I will find a way to deal with this, somehow. I will figure out something. I have to, because I can't afford to attract attention to myself.

I am certain my life depends on it.

⌘⌘⌘⌘

CHAPTER 15

Dear Reader,

I have now related the whole chain of events up to and including the first entry of this account. Now you know what happened to me and how it happened.

The following morning, after I made it home and after I remembered being in the lab with Dr. Bickel, I finally went to bed. I fell asleep around midmorning. I hadn't slept at all the night before.

Do you remember how sick I'd felt when I fell into my bed? How drained?

I almost didn't wake up. As in *ever*. I still shiver when I think of how close I came to dying in my sleep. In my own bed.

Toward evening, after I'd slept in exhaustion for maybe seven or eight hours, my right hand began to hurt. I mean, *really* hurt. It stung and burned as though it were on fire.

I squirmed in pain, but I couldn't seem to wake myself up. The sound of chipping and buzzing grew so loud in my head, though, that I, at last, began to stir.

I swung my legs over the side of my bed and started to stand—but I couldn't. I couldn't hold myself on the edge of the bed either, and I tumbled off the mattress onto the floor.

I was awake but so weak! My hand had stopped stinging and the noises had faded, but I was alarmed at how little strength I had.

My body was like water, poured out on the floor, spreading, soaking into the carpet, dissipating . . . My arms and legs no longer felt attached to my nervous system. They refused to respond with more than a twitch.

As life seeped from my bones, fear settled in its place. This weakness was unnatural, caused, no doubt, by *them*, by *what they were doing to my body*.

My bedroom windows were shaded and the room was shrouded in twilight. I lay alone, frightened, unmoving, in the near-darkness.

I rested for a while and then that spot on my hand began to burn again, as though someone were sticking it with a hot pin. I gritted my teeth and turned my head until I could see my bedroom door. By sheer determination, I managed to inch on my stomach to the door and grasp the jamb. Bit by bit, I pulled myself up onto my knees.

It was hard, exhausting work. I clung to the jamb, sweating and fearful I would fall backwards if I let go.

After a few minutes of heavy breathing, I reached feeble fingers toward the light switch. As I inched my hand closer, a trail of warmth ran from my shoulder, shot up my arm, and stretched and strengthened my hand—

The instant my fingers encountered the switch, my palm flattened and fastened to the switch plate. My palm was glued to the plate as though tendrils had emerged from my hand and sunk into the plastic. Electric current rolled from the outlet into my hand.

The switch plate under my palm grew hot from the current passing through it, but not hot enough to burn me. The warm flow of the current traveled up my arm, flowed into my chest, and ran down the other arm, down my legs. A shrill, excited thrumming played in my head.

Power? But of course they need power, Gemma. The nanomites need power or they will fail. The beauty of my design, however, is that the nanocloud can utilize power from any source of electrical current including direct and indirect sunlight and organic or living things.

The tendrils binding my hand to the light switch released their hold, and my hand flopped to the floor. All was silent.

I sniffed. My nose was dripping. I climbed to my feet and reached for a tissue box on my nightstand. I saw the tissue as I raised it to my face. I was still blowing my drippy nose when I realized that I was standing up under my own steam. I felt stronger. Less achy. Less sick.

I thought again about how Dr. Bickel had described the nanomites' power needs and how they derived the energy they needed: *Organic or living things.*

"Living" things as in people? My logical mind produced the question.

I tossed the used tissue into the wastebasket next to the nightstand. As it left my fingers, a bright stain bloomed on it. I leaned over and inspected the tissue now lying at the bottom of the wastebasket. I stooped and picked it up by one corner. It was stained with blood. Bright, fresh, red blood.

My blood.

I shivered and swiped at my still drippy nose with the back of my hand. I looked at my hand. No blood.

Hmm.

I drew another tissue from the box and blew into it. When I pulled the tissue away, it appeared unchanged—but a moment later a bloody smear appeared—not as much blood as the first tissue, but blood nonetheless.

I sighed, tossed the tissues into the wastebasket, and wandered into the living room, captive to my worried thoughts.

Too many questions. Too many questions with really scary, impossible answers.

I turned on the lamp hanging over my favorite reading spot, the corner of my sofa, but I didn't sit down. I stood there, puzzling over my experience of the last few minutes.

"The nanomites need power or they will fail," I quoted Dr. Bickel aloud. "What can I deduce from that?"

A snort of irony followed my question. "I think I can safely say that *they* just got a much-needed *power bump*," I grunted, "and *their* getting a dose of electricity seems to have made *me* feel better, too."

I did feel better—stronger—since the mites received their dose of electricity. On the other hand, my bones and skin still ached with fever. And why was my nose bleeding?

That can't be a good sign.

I frowned as I pondered the two tissues laying in my bedroom wastebasket and my drippy nose. "I have a nosebleed—and I am a little scared to consider *why* my nose is bleeding."

It would have been easy to drive myself nuts brooding over the damage the mites were likely doing to my insides. I turned my speculations away from that line of thinking and onto a related puzzle piece.

Why does blood show up on the tissues but not on the back of my hand? I was intrigued—in a macabre kind of way. Some possibilities suggested themselves.

"As long as the blood is *in* or *on* me, it is as invisible as I am?" I wondered aloud.

It didn't make sense, and I shook my head, frustrated—and then recalled taking off my soiled clothes before collapsing into bed. As soon as I'd peeled them off and dropped them on the floor, I could see them.

Same thing.

"Yes," I added, "It is the same thing! *I* am invisible and so are the things in me and on me—but as soon as something is apart from me it becomes visible? All right, but why? What about the mites makes things invisible or not invisible in the first place? How do they do it?"

That whole line of questions stumped me. I circled back to the "power" issue.

"They got 'fed' from the light switch and that made me feel better, but not completely better. So if I feel *somewhat* better now that they have gotten some power, just which part of me is it that feels better?" I asked. "And why?"

I'd been incredibly weak when I woke up, too weak to stand. Then the nanomites got their electrical boost.

A horrifying conclusion began to form.

I sank into my corner of the sofa, distressed by the wave of revelation washing over me: From the time the nanomites left their glass case, they had been without their normal power supply.

The mites will conserve energy when they need to, Dr. Bickel had said, *but, under pressing circumstances, they will use whatever energy is available.*

What happens if their power source is about to fail and they don't have another one? I had asked him.

I'm not certain, Gemma, but they are amazingly resourceful. I'm sure they would come up with something.

"They-they almost drained me dry," I whispered. "They needed my energy and I went to sleep, because I was so tired—*because they had used up almost all my body's electrical energy! They almost drained me dry!*"

I rubbed my right hand. The stinging, stabbing pain had not returned, the stinging, stabbing pain that had awakened me—the buzzing, clicking noises and the pain in my right hand that had stirred me out of a dead sleep.

A dead sleep.

I went cold all over.

The nanomites awakened me because, because I was almost used up?

That insight was followed by a more obvious, scarier one: *If I had not awakened when I did—if **they** hadn't awakened me—I would have died! Died in my sleep!*

I leaned back against the sofa's cushions, breathing rapidly.

"Why didn't they just swarm and propel themselves to the light switch on their own?"

*But they **didn't** swarm and leave my body. Instead, they stung my hand until I woke up. They could have reached the power on their own—but for some reason they awakened me.*

"They don't have feelings. It can't have been altruism on their part—they only follow their program algorithms."

More thoughts tumbled through my head.

*Do they, for some reason, think that they need **me** to give them access to electricity instead of getting it themselves?*

The list of half-baked deductions about the nanomites was growing, but each possible insight generated another round of questions.

All right. Say they do need me—but why? Why do they need me?

I stared at the wall for a while, recalling Cushing's attack on Dr. Bickel's lab, and allowing more conclusions to form.

Hide! Hide Gemma!

"Is it because they are *obligated* to hide me? To *keep on* hiding me?" I whispered those queries into the twilight shadows lengthening in my living room.

"If they believe Dr. Bickel ordered them to hide me, and he isn't here to tell them to stop, then what?"

It was crazy. I didn't want to believe it. I didn't want to, but . . . but it made a weirdly logical sense. Almost.

My stomach turned over. I hadn't eaten in more than twenty-four hours—not since the meal Dr. Bickel had prepared for us in the cavern prior to Cushing's attack. My belly rumbled again. I ignored it and returned to the on-again, off-again invisibility issue.

"How are they doing it? How are the mites making me invisible?"

When my stomach protested a third time, the chittering/buzzing started up—and the now-familiar stabbing pains in my head kicked in.

"All right, all right. I'll get something to eat."

The September sun sets around 7 p.m. in Albuquerque; after that it grows dark quickly. The living room's lamplight emphasized how dim the rest of the house had grown. I padded on bare feet into the kitchen, flipping on a few lights as I went. As I walked past my kitchen table, I glanced out the window into the deepening twilight, but I really couldn't see anything.

Was Emilio back to sitting on his curb across the cul-de-sac? Or, after my return home and the freaky things he had seen, was he still watching my house?

I pulled the blinds closed over the window that looked out on my neighborhood.

I may have to live with my blinds closed like Abe. The thought popped into my head and I didn't like it.

I was very thirsty again. After a long drink of water from the tap, I put the kettle on for tea and started heating some oil to stir-fry some chicken and vegetables. At the smell of the oil heating, my stomach lurched. I was famished! While I chopped vegetables and cut up a chicken breast, I chewed on the unanswered questions plaguing me.

"*How* are they hiding me?" This was the question that bothered me the most.

Do you know anything about stealth technology, Gemma?

Dr. Bickel's words popped into my head. The knife I was using to chop vegetables poised motionless above my cutting board while I considered it.

"Oh, wow." I scrunched up my face and tried to recall what he'd told me.

It's optical invisibility, Gemma, optical invisibility. Also known as passive adaptive camouflage. The mites create optical invisibility by utilizing their mirrors to bend light and reflect the surfaces around them. Nanostealth.

Were the nanomites only camouflaging me and making it *seem* that I was invisible?

"That would mean I'm not truly invisible; I only appear to be invisible."

What difference would that make? For all intents and purposes, I'm still invisible!

A faint scratching near the back door interrupted my reverie. Jake bounded into the room via the cat door. Tail in the air, he went directly to his bowl next to the stove and sank his fat mug into his dry food.

I said nothing to him as he ate. Our relationship didn't include pleasantries or chitchat. I finished my dinner preparations and sat down at the table to enjoy the savory chicken and vegetables. I relished each bite—I don't think anything had tasted so good in a long time.

I wasn't prepared when Jake jumped into my lap. He must have smelled the warm chicken on the table—however, he had not seen me in the chair.

I uttered a surprised shriek and jumped.

Jake jumped higher.

Have you watched a cat lose its mind?

Jake scrabbled and ran in six directions at once. Chicken stir-fry flew everywhere. When Jake finally gained traction, it was on me. He clawed his way up my front side and launched himself from the top of my head.

The pompous, unflappable Jake, the "I-do-not-deign-to-notice-you" King of Keyes Castle, streaked across the living room, sling-shot around an arm chair, and catapulted over the couch, caterwauling as he went.

It was an epic moment in the ongoing saga of *Jake vs. Gemma*. It was an unplanned triumph—but I was willing to take it.

I laughed until I cried. I was still laughing as I cleaned the remnants of my dinner from the table and floor.

⌘⌘⌘⌘

CHAPTER 16

What I salvaged and actually ate of the chicken stir-fry made me feel better. I felt less feverish, less achy afterward, and my bloody nose seemed to have dried up. My thinking seemed less muddled, more cohesive.

It was time to get a handle on things. I drew the spiral notebook toward me, turned to a fresh page, and started a list.

"Number 1," I murmured. And, for the first time, I penned the revolting, impossible truth: *Number 1: I have several trillion—give or take a few hundred billion—of Dr. Bickel's nanomites "living" inside me. My body's immune system must be on the offensive. That would explain the fever and aching.*

Looking at the dry, matter-of-fact statement on paper made my situation much too real. That moment—the horrifying moment when the nanocloud ploughed into my back and knocked me to my knees—came rushing back. I relived the stinging, fiery pain of their combined *trillions* drilling and burrowing into my skin, felt the suffocating flow of them flooding my mouth and nostrils and forcing their way down my throat.

Nausea almost brought the chicken stir-fry back up. I swallowed it down and, with a shaking hand, forced myself to scratch, *Number 2: "They" (the nanomites) think Dr. Bickel ordered them to hide me.*

Had he? Had he ordered them to hide me, to save me from General Cushing and her stormtroopers?

Hide! Hide Gemma!

Or had he screamed, "Hide! Hide, Gemma!" to *me* and *not* to the nanomites?

Would I ever know what his command had meant, which way he had intended it?

Except what he'd meant or intended didn't matter. Only what the mites *believed* he'd intended mattered. And if they believed Dr. Bickel ordered them to hide me, then—

I shook my head and went back to how the mites were doing it, how they were using their mirrors to render me "optically invisible" to the world. Under my breath I murmured, "The mites must be *in* me but they must also be *on* me, on the surface of my skin, if they are using their mirrors to hide me." That was a new detail. I added it as a note under Number 1.

I heard my cell phone ringing from somewhere in the back of the house, likely my bedroom.

My first panicked response was, *I can't answer it!* I pattered down the hall and found my phone in the pocket of my grungy jeans still lying on my bedroom floor.

I checked the Caller ID.

Zander!

I couldn't decide how to handle the call, so I let it go to voicemail. When the phone vibrated that I had a new voicemail, I put it on speaker and listened to it.

"Hey, Gemma. I came by around lunchtime and saw your car in the drive, but I couldn't find you. Just wanted to say 'hi.' I'll catch you later. Have a blessed day!"

He came by while I was sleeping, I realized. I was going to have to keep him away from me somehow. His voicemail reminded me that my car was still in the driveway—one more detail I needed to handle.

And his 'have a blessed day'?

He had no earthly idea.

I sat down and poked the cushioned tablecloth with an index finger, looking for the expected indentation. Nothing. I poked again. As closely as I watched, I never saw one. I poked with both hands, alternating them and, one time only, glimpsed a shimmer as the nanomites "removed" the indentation.

Of course, I now understood that they were not *removing* the indentation; they were only camouflaging my fingers *and* the indentations they made in the tablecloth.

"You little buzzards are fast learners," I snarled. A couple of "clicks" echoed from the back of my head. Under Number 2 I scrawled, *The mites learn quickly. Dr. Bickel said he programmed them for "predictive" learning, which means they remember that I poked the tablecloth earlier today and so they were ready for it when I did it again just now.*

"Number 3," I whispered and wrote, *The mites need power to survive.* "And now, so do I," I added.

I scratched an outline beneath the third statement:

a) Dr. Bickel designed the nanomites to draw power from multiple sources—including me if I'm not careful! BE CAREFUL, I added in all caps. I underlined it a couple of times, too.

b) When they use me as a power source, I grow weak.

*c) Therefore, as long as they are inside of me, I will need to provide them with power—so that they **don't** use me.*

d) They have proven that they can draw what they need when I touch a light switch.

"How often do you need to 'recharge?'" I fretted. "How long after getting power until you start draining me again?" I didn't like where that line of thinking was headed. Not at all.

I strode to the nearest light switch and placed my hand on it. Like before, my hand seemed to fuse to the plate and warmth overspread me as the mites drew power from the switchbox. A few minutes later, my hand released.

When my hand dropped, I felt oddly—*unnaturally*—refreshed.

"Interesting."

I returned to my list and added, e*) I need to figure out a way for them to be "plugged in" all the time.*

It was fully night now, but I wondered about tomorrow and what would happen if I went outside into the sunshine. Would the mites automatically convert sunshine to solar power?

Suddenly, my house felt close and stuffy, and I had the urge to be *outside*, breathing fresh air. I was jumpy. Antsy. Needed to blow off steam.

Was my newfound vigor the result of the mites taking in power from the light switch? Did their action recharge me, too?

I turned off the dining room and kitchen lights. Standing in my darkened kitchen, I cracked open the side door. I drew it toward me and stood looking through the security door's screen. All seemed dark and still between my house and Mrs. Calderón's.

Across the cul-de-sac the atmosphere was very different. Shouts and raucous voices drifted from Mateo's house: He and his crew were having another wild party.

I wondered whether Abe would be sitting watch on his front porch, and I had a strong desire to see him. I couldn't divulge to him what had happened to me, I decided—he was an old man, after all, and just might keel over!—but I longed just to see his familiar, kind face.

After a moment I opened the security door and descended the steps. The air, warm and dry, felt good on my skin. I closed the security door behind me and stood in the shadows a few minutes longer, just watching. Listening.

Mrs. Calderón stayed up late most nights but, true to form, her blinds were drawn. I could hear the faint sounds of a television coming from her house.

I stepped out of the shadow of my house. Yes, I could see well enough by the street light glowing dully on the mouth of the cul-de-sac. I extended my left hand and glanced down at it. Nothing. I lifted a foot out in front of me. Nothing.

I put my foot back on the ground and looked toward my toes. Nothing. I turned this way and that and saw only the paving-stone walkway to the garage and the grass down the side of my house.

*If the mites are using the optical invisibility thingy Dr. Bickel described, then I'm not really seeing **through** my toes, I'm seeing a reflected image of what lies **beneath** my toes.*

It was weird.

It was beyond weird.

I tiptoed, barefooted, down my drive to the sidewalk and turned right. Mr. and Mrs. Flores' house was dark except for a dim yellow light over their door, while Mateo's house was lit up like a Christmas tree. Six or seven vehicles, pimped out with custom wheels and paint, filled his drive and lined the curbs.

I listened for my footsteps as I walked, listening for what someone else might hear, but my bare feet made little sound on the smooth concrete. As I drew near the cars parked in front of Mateo's house I became more cautious. A gang member might be sitting guard in one of the cars.

I was almost past Mateo's house and the clutch of cars parked in front when I heard something close by. I froze, my heart thudding in my ears.

It was the strangest feeling. Here I was, basically invisible to the naked eye, "sneaking" around the cul-de-sac, *and yet*, because I wasn't used to being "invisible," I had to squelch the urge to hide between cars.

Again, really weird.

Huh! I don't need to hide in order to "sneak" around. My astute brain produced that dazzling conclusion all on its own, but the next thought really got my attention.

If no one can see me, then . . . maybe I could do some unusual things.

I decided *that* idea deserved further consideration.

I was still standing there, wondering what I'd heard, what had alerted me, when I caught the sound again—from near the overgrown juniper shrubs between Mateo and Abe's houses. (Technically, the shrubs were only overgrown on Mateo's side; Abe kept *his* side trimmed at precise, ninety degree angles.)

There it was again. It sounded like a sniff. A wet, watery sniff.

I was, naturally, a little curious.

No one can see me. No one can see me, I repeated to assure myself. I crept closer, listening for the sound, until I saw him.

Emilio.

He was sitting on his haunches, scrunched under wild-growing juniper branches, as far back in the bushes as he could go, pretty much hidden from the lights of Mateo's house. I stepped a little closer and heard a sob. Bent down and peered into the bushes. Saw him swipe at his eyes.

I had to look away. It felt wrong to be privy to his unguarded emotions, but I couldn't prevent my heart from producing lots of reasons for his sorrow.

What must life be like for this kid? I glanced at Mateo's brightly lit windows. Raucous music and the roars and shouts of drunken laughter filled the air.

The kid is always hiding. Always trying to stay out from underfoot. I wonder if he ever feels safe.

I understood not feeling safe. I had never felt safe as a child, but at least I'd had Dad and Mom and, later, Aunt Lucy to protect me, sometimes even when they didn't understand *how* they were protecting me.

I think Dad might have realized, before he died, what was going on. I think he had at least begun to suspect, because he had taken to watching more closely. Or at least I thought he had. A myriad of painful memories flitted through my mind in the few, brief seconds before my attention circled back to Emilio.

He is alone. Terrified. Probably hungry.

I pondered Emilio's situation, many empathetic feelings grappling with my new circumstances and well-founded caution. I glanced toward him again. Aunt Lucy's voice rang in my head as I studied the boy.

We show our gratitude to God for all we have by sharing with those who are not as blessed, those who might be far from Him, she had always insisted. *When we give kindness in His name, we show God's love.*

Genie had sneered at Aunt Lu behind her back. I hadn't, not because I agreed, but because I respected Aunt Lu. Still, I hadn't believed what she said any more than Genie had.

I grimaced, saddened that Aunt Lucy wasn't here, that she wasn't around to tell me what to do. Then shame washed over me.

As if I need her to tell me what to do! I already know what she would have done. She wouldn't have hesitated, not for a heartbeat.

I backed away from Emilio. A few feet distant from him, I turned and sprinted back to my house.

Ten minutes later I returned. A brown plastic grocery sack bulged under my shirt, but as far as I could tell, looking down, the sack was as invisible as I was.

"Thanks," I whispered, surprising myself. I wondered who I was thanking—the nanomites?

The trick would be getting the sack to Emilio without revealing my, er, *unique condition* and/or causing the kid a mental collapse.

He has enough problems as it is.

I tiptoed past where I'd seen Emilio crouched in the bushes then turned back. The shrubs screened me as I slipped forward. When my eyes adjusted to the shadows I made him out, head down on his knees.

Good. He isn't looking up, I thought.

I backed away a few yards and pulled the sack out from under my shirt, trying not to make any noise. Holding the bag by its plastic handles, I crept forward again. Emilio's head was still down on his knees.

Perfect.

From a height of maybe four inches, I dropped the sack onto the sidewalk. As it landed on the cement, it made a soft "thunk." I drew back, unseen and unheard. I circled one of the gang's cars until I was between it and the next one.

From between the two cars I had an unimpeded view of Emilio. His head was up. He remained unnaturally still.

He had to have heard the sack hit the sidewalk.

I could see the only part of him that did move—his eyes—jumping nervously back and forth, searching for the source of the unexpected noise.

I saw the exact moment his eyes lit on the plastic sack. If possible, he drew farther back into his hiding place, making himself smaller. When a few minutes passed and no one had appeared to harass him, Emilio studied the sack. Mistrust radiated from him.

I guessed that another ten minutes had gone by. My bare feet, unused to standing on the rough asphalt, were becoming a little tender. However, I wasn't going to leave until I'd seen Emilio *pick up that sack.*

I glanced toward Abe's house. He usually sat and rocked within the shadows of his deep, covered porch. I couldn't tell if he was there or not. When I turned my attention back to Emilio, the sack was gone.

Wow. He's quick! But then I'd already known that, the way he'd lit out my front door the afternoon I found him ransacking my kitchen.

I could make him out, back in his little hidey-hole, exploring the sack's contents. When I heard the *pop* and fizz of a can opening, I smiled. I'd packed two peanut butter and jelly sandwiches, a baggie of celery and carrot sticks, an apple, and two cans of soda into the grocery bag. I hoped it would make a difference.

I walked back home, a little lighter of heart.

Though I'd slept part of the day away (almost dying in the process), I was feeling fatigued again, ready to sleep. I was a bit nervous about climbing back into bed, so I "fed" the nanomites from the light switch first. Then I decided to take a long, hot shower, thinking I'd "top off" the nanomites afterward.

I hadn't considered how *they* might feel about a shower.

When the hot spray hit my body, the noise in my head exploded. The mites' chipping, buzzing, and clicking rose to painful, deafening levels. Yeah, I don't know what *they* thought, but *I* was furious.

"*Ow!* Stop it!" I shouted.

My demand went unheeded. I turned up the hot water and stuck my head under the shower nozzle, hoping I could wash them all away. No such luck. The hum-and-scree behind my eyes (like squealing chalk on a blackboard) intensified.

I'm stubborn. I soaped myself down and shampooed, sponging off the layer of grime I'd picked up in the foothills. All while my head pounded like a jackhammer.

I was rinsing conditioner from my hair when I remembered something. Something pretty important.

Raise your voice just a little and say, "Nano, hello."

What—I'm supposed to talk to them?

I've programmed them to recognize "Nano" as the signal of direct address. When they hear you say "Nano" they will pay attention to what you say directly after that.

I pulled my head out from under the showerhead and shouted, "Nano! Stop it!"

The dissonant squeal in my brain ground to a screeching halt.

"Well!"

I was jubilant! For about five seconds.

The crazy-making cacophony kicked in again.

Irked and near-blind with pain, I continued rinsing my hair, but my mind wasn't on my task.

Dr. Bickel said that he taught them some single words and some short commands. I know that they understand "hello" and "hide." Maybe they don't know "stop it." Maybe I need to use a different word to make them shut up.

Cheered, I called out, "Nano!"

Again, the noise ceased.

Ah ha! They are listening! Listening for the command!

"Nano. Quiet."

They were attentive for a few seconds and then the reverberating racket resounding in my head recommenced.

"Nano!"

They listened.

"Silence!"

And silence reigned.

My brows shot up. I waited a minute. I finished rinsing my hair. The noise did not return. I climbed out of the shower and toweled off.

Oh, blessed peace and quiet!

I pulled on a nightgown and turned on the hair dryer. The mites were quiet—until I turned the heated air on my head.

They didn't like that. Apparently, they *really* didn't like that.

"Ouch!" I dropped the dryer and pulled my injured hand to my chest. They had stung my hand!

"You rotten little beasts!" I screeched.

I couldn't very well go to bed with wet hair. I picked up the dryer and turned it on again. "Nano! No!" I turned the hot air to my head. I looked into the mirror above the sink where the dryer was blowing on—supposedly—my invisible hair.

They stung me again.

"Nano! No, no, no!"

I shouted. I scolded. I cajoled. I begged. I was a harassed mother engaged in battle with a three-year-old—and I was not about to let the three-year-old win.

I turned the dryer on and held it away from my head while I considered word choices. "Nano. No hurt! No sting!"

I waved the dryer over my head to emphasize my point.

If I were to describe or characterize what happened next, I would call it verbal mutiny. Have you heard griping and complaining described as "chipping your teeth?" Well, that's what they did.

They chipped, they chittered, they chattered. At a dreadful, high-pitched level, they let me know how *very much* they disliked the dryer's hot air directed at them. Except the hot air wasn't directed at *them*, it was directed at *me*—and I refused to abdicate my own body to *them*—not now and not ever.

It was a war of wills.

A contest for control.

You will lose, I vowed.

I flipped the dryer's switch on high and aimed the blast of warm air toward my hair. I clenched my teeth against the dissonance in my head. I set my jaw against the pain the mites' protests were producing.

I wielded the dryer and hairbrush until my hair was dry. Only when I was good and satisfied did I switch off the dryer and put it away.

The mites' griping petered to a close, leaving me dizzy and relieved.

"Bad Nano!" I grumbled, weaving on unsteady feet into my bedroom. I popped two ibuprofen and rubbed my eyes.

Tomorrow we are going to set a few ground rules around here. If Dr. Bickel could teach them simple commands, so can I.

I slapped my hand (with more force than necessary) onto the light plate and let the nanomites jack up my electricity bill. When they were done, I fell into bed and into an exhausted sleep.

⌘⌘⌘⌘

CHAPTER 17

Getting up early is a singular pleasure: I love watching the night give way to dawn and I like getting a jump on the new day. I usually set the pot on a timer each evening so the coffee will be ready when I get up the following morning—because the aroma of fresh-brewed coffee really *is* the best part of waking up.

When I bounded out of bed the next morning, I exulted over how much better I felt. I hummed as I climbed out from under my covers. I placed my hand on the switch plate to give the nanomites their "breakfast" and skipped into the kitchen to grab my first cup of java.

I sat at the old kitchen table sipping on my coffee and watching sunlight creep over Sandia Crest.

No feverish, achy feeling, I realized. *No drippy nose.* It was undeniable: I was feeling better. I took another blissful sip. *Is my body adjusting to the mites? Is it healing in spite of their presence?*

And I wasn't fatigued. In fact . . . I actually seemed to have energy to burn.

I plunked my mug onto the table; I almost spewed coffee.

What is he doing up this early in the morning?

Emilio, his skinny arms folded across his chest, glared into my window from the sidewalk. I glared back.

The kid's eyes flickered from window to window. The blinds were closed on all rooms but the dining room. His gaze swept over my car, still parked in the driveway, and then returned to my front window, uncertainty on his face.

He doesn't see me. Does. Not. See. Me.

But did he see my magic, floating coffee mug again?

I really have to stop sitting here in the open while I'm drinking my coffee or tea.

He was wearing the same soiled clothes he'd been wearing yesterday. Had he slept in them? Had he slept in the bushes or had he snuck inside to sleep after his uncle's drunken crew had passed out?

Emilio's stubbly shaved hair did him no favors, either—it accentuated the uneven shape of his head and left his ears sticking out. Worse, his shaved head made him look like a gangster-in-training, a chip off the old Uncle Mateo block. And that, for many reasons, was just wrong.

What really did it, what especially marked him as a "mini-me" gangster, was Emilio's hard, closed, expression—that "I'm tough; don't mess with me" look.

I'd seen more than that from him, though, hadn't I? I'd seen Emilio puzzled, scared, maybe completely freaked out. And I'd heard him sob when he thought no one was listening.

So we stared at each other, although I was certain he could not see me.

He looked away for a few ticks, as though coming to a decision. When he looked back, he stared at me, *directly* at me. And gave a little bob of his chin. Like, "well, all right, then."

What?

Emilio placed something on the sidewalk and turned on his heel. As he sauntered away, I tried to figure out what he'd left there, but I couldn't make it out.

Of course, it intrigued me. And it bugged me, because I couldn't just go out and get it.

Well played, kid, but no dice. Not gonna take the bait.

I fetched Aunt Lucy's old binoculars from the hall closet. Standing far enough back from the window where outside eyes could not penetrate, I pointed the binoculars to the sidewalk and dialed in the focus.

A small cross, perhaps two inches in length, lay on the cement. Through the binoculars, I could see that it was carved from wood and had been rubbed until it glowed.

A peace offering? A "thank you"? Had he decided that he knew who'd fed him last night? I couldn't answer those questions, but I had to leave the cross where he'd left it, didn't I?

I went to put the binoculars back in the closet and thought better of it. I might need them again. I hung them over a kitchen chair, where they'd be within reach.

I stayed indoors the next three days, not wanting to raise any suspicions or take the chance that someone might see a door opening on its own or a shimmering movement where one did not belong. Then my caution reversed course: Wouldn't my neighbors get just as suspicious if they stopped seeing my normal routine?

I was being paranoid—but with good reason, right? Yes, I was invisible, but I wasn't confident in my new "skin," so to speak, and my feelings flip-flopped all over the place.

At least I used those three days well.

Through experimentation, I found that I could hold an extension cord and the mites would feed from it as well as from a light switch. As soon as I picked the cord up (as long as it was plugged in), the mites would "fasten" to it and take what they needed.

If the mites had been disconnected for a while, I could feel them drawing a lot from the cord. If they just needed to be "topped off,' they fed slowly, and I felt something like a low, rumbly vibration moving through me.

Soon I was going about my business with my longest extension cord looped over my belt, touching the skin under my shirt. The mites took care of the rest. Other than getting used to the cord's twelve-foot range restriction, the arrangement was a big improvement—because before that I'd sometimes reach to turn on a lamp or a light switch and be unexpectedly glued to it for twenty minutes at a stretch.

No bueno.

At least I wasn't terrified that I'd die in my sleep anymore. I had that aspect fixed, too: Before I climbed into bed I tied the extension cord to my wrist and the mites fed continuously all night. Still, the arrangement was awkward, and if the relationship were a symbiotic one, I sure hadn't realized any benefits on my end yet.

What else did I do those three days? A big, fruitless chunk of time was spent trying to find the right command that would tell the nanomites they didn't need to hide me anymore.

"Nano! No hide! No hide Gemma!"

"Nano! Unhide Gemma!"

"Nano! Abort command, 'Hide Gemma'!"

"Nano! End 'Hide Gemma'!"

"Nano! Stop hiding Gemma!"

"Nano! Dr. Bickel says 'Don't hide Gemma!'"

"Nano! Red rover, red rover, send nanomites to Dover!"

"Nano! Go away!"

"Nano! Discontinue stealth mode!"

"Get out! Get out, you nasty *freaks*!"

Grrrr!

Meanwhile, the range of *responses* to my ineffective commands swung from comical to the macabre—depending upon whether or not your sense of humor has been completely skewed out of norm by an infestation of nanomites.

"Nano!" always produced instant silence, an alert attentiveness— something that felt akin to a German shepherd poised to attack—which was disconcerting.

After I said "Nano!" and the mites came to attention, the next words or phrases I used produced a wide pattern of responses in clicks, chirps, buzzes, or hums. I didn't know what to make of them and I can't replicate them—but I do possess a vivid imagination that supplied a kind of "reply and ranking system."

"Nano! No hide! No hide Gemma!"

Click, clickity, click. Minus three points for talking down to us.

"Nano! Unhide Gemma!"

Buzzzzzzzzzzzzzz. Six points for precise diction; null score for 'wrong command.'

"Nano! Abort command, 'Hide Gemma'!"

Five points for originality. Still wrong command. And we haven't forgotten the hair dryer business. Not even.

"Nano! End 'Hide Gemma'!"

Negative two points for poor grammar. So much for today's college education.

"Nano! Stop hiding Gemma!"

*Hide and seek? Yes, yes, yes! We'd love to. **You hide first**.*

"Nano! Dr. Bickel says 'Don't hide Gemma!'"

Dr. Who? Goodie! Where's the tardis?

"Nano! Red rover, red rover, send nanomites to Dover!"

Been there. Boring.

"Nano! Go away!"

Pffffttttt!

"Nano! Discontinue stealth mode!"

*Resistance is futile. You **will** be assimilated.*

"Get out! Get out, you nasty nanomites, *you freaks!*"

The Russian judges award straight 10s but are being investigated by the Olympic committee for cronyism. The athlete has been disqualified and banned from future participation.

Sigh.

As you might presume, I abandoned this amusing but unproductive pastime to try other approaches. Dr. Bickel had said that the mites understood print language, so I opened my laptop and typed a long communiqué to them, complete with salutation, social niceties, and closing cordialities. I got nowhere—even after pointing to the screen and practically screaming, "Nano! Nano!" to get their attention.

Reruns of Mork and Mindy, anyone?

Next I used the laptop to first type and then read aloud simple words and phrases, hoping to teach the mites new commands.

My favorites were "roll over" and "play dead."

We got on famously.

Note to self: I am now convinced that Dr. Bickel quite exaggerated the mites' intelligence.

I took a break from my attempts to evict the mites to focus on the logistics of my situation. You know, the whole, "Oh, wow! Now that I'm invisible, how am I going to pay my bills?" And that pesky, "How will I survive as an invisible person in a visible world—whether or not General Cushing ever comes looking for me?" question.

I'm not what they call a "prepper." I usually buy and eat fresh and raw foods as I need them.

With admirable courage and dignity, I faced the stark reality that two cans of tuna, a canister of wild rice, and a jar of peanut butter were all that stood between me and an ignoble demise via starvation.

Yes, I'm being facetious.

I did what I always did: I sat down and took stock of my options. For three months I'd earned a generous cash income from Dr. Bickel—self-employment, he'd called it. That job was over now, but I had a few months of unemployment benefits I could reapply for—benefits I could activate either over the phone or online.

As long as I kept applying for jobs and no one actually invited me to an interview, I would have a meager income for a few more months. My savings account contained a little (very little) money—and I still had a half-filled can of cash stashed away in the freezer. I counted out the cold cash from the coffee can: $1,100.

Do any Albuquerque grocers deliver?

I typed "Albuquerque grocery delivery" into a search engine and got a long list of returns.

Aaaaand apparently grocery delivery isn't a sustainable business. Link after link led nowhere. Some links were dead, some businesses were closed; the rest of the listings were for frozen or takeout foods. Even Walmart let me down.

Then I found Amazon's Grocery & Gourmet Food page. If I didn't mind salad or fresh fruit never passing my lips again, Amazon was the answer.

Soon I will know exactly how Dr. Bickel felt, I snarked.

Well, to be fair, I really could get much of what I needed online, and I certainly would *not* starve anytime in the near future. I would just have to figure things out as I went along.

"Figure things out" became my new mantra. I spent the next hour trying to "figure things out" and gave my brain a cramp. What did people who couldn't go out in public do, anyway? For heaven's sake, what did bank robbers "on the lam" do? OD on pizza delivery?

A life of crime never sounded so unappealing, so unromantic.

Besides that, no criminal had *my* problem. In fact, no one had *ever* had my specific problem. I was the world's first "invisible" woman— and my condition did not come with instructions.

*Hold on jest a cotton pickin' minute, Junior. Ah said, ah **said**, hold on there.*

I was still on Amazon. I switched from groceries to books and typed "invisible man."

Ralph Ellison's *Invisible Man* came up first. I read the description: The story wasn't about a literal invisible man, and the reflections of a black man growing up in a world in which he *felt* invisible would not help me in my pressing circumstances, as compelling as the story might be.

H.G. Wells' *The Invisible Man* was next on the list. Although fiction, perhaps I could glean some ideas from this book. And one version was free on Kindle! I pointed my cursor at "Buy now with 1-Click"—

Wait.

Life-long hypervigilance—my habit of scrutinizing options before acting—warned me to wait and think before I clicked.

I dabbled my toes in the Paranoia Pool: No Feds had come knocking on my door. *Yet.*

Shark Face had the unlimited resources of the federal government behind her—but did she know about the nanomites' stealth capabilities? If she did, it would be nothing for her IT lackeys to scan Internet traffic for certain search terms or patterns. Or *purchases.*

If they were searching on the word "invisible," her stormtroopers could scoop me up in, well, a nanosecond.

You're such a clever punster, Gemma.

I had come within a hairsbreadth of buying the book and felt ill from anxiety. I went to close the browser and paused again. I returned to the list of books and scanned farther down the page. I was looking for a similar title.

There it was: H.F. Saint. *Memoirs of an Invisible Man.* That was the book I'd been searching for, the one I hoped would be most helpful. Except I would need to get it in a different way—and I already knew who had an old copy.

Again, the "how" was going to take some "figuring it out."

Those three days dragged by and I fell into some semblance of routine. In the mornings I searched for work and rewrote my résumé and cover letter: I rewrote them so that mine would be the first application *tossed out.* I added little spelling errors and gaffes. I made my cover letter read like it was written by a high school dropout.

I'd never worked so hard *not* to get a job! But every application added to the list of job searches needed to keep those unemployment checks coming.

In the afternoons I worked on the mites' language training (a complete waste as far as I could tell) and made lists of things I should *figure out*.

What does a list of "things I should figure out" look like? You'd be surprised.

For starters, I was very worried about my PNM bill. PNM is the local electric company. What if my bill doubled or tripled as the mites fed? How would I pay it? What if my bill was higher than triple? What if the amount of electricity the mites imbibed was astronomical? How would I explain it? Would PNM come looking for a "leak" in my meter?

I believe I confessed earlier to not being scientific?

Anyway, my electric bill topped the "figure it out" list. Other items on the list included fresh food (I ran out of fruit and salad makings on the second day), nosy neighbors, and curious kids. And what I would do when my unemployment and savings ran out.

That third night, when darkness became my friend, I slipped outdoors. I stopped and peered down at the cross Emilio had left on the sidewalk. It was plain and yet elegant in a simple way, and the polished wood glowed. He'd done a nice job, but I still needed to leave it where it lay.

So, while the rest of the world was tucked up indoors, I walked the neighborhood. I reveled in the fresh air and the sense of freedom I felt in the night.

Which is strange, right? Since I was invisible and all? I know, but I was still adjusting, still trying to "figure it out."

***

As the next day dawned, I sipped my coffee at the kitchen table, careful now to keep my mug from view of the window. I watched Emilio, head down, trudge off to catch his school bus. I saw old Mr. Flores take a broom out into the cul-de-sac and sweep up the broken glass and trash left by Mateo's crew. Mr. Flores did that, cleaned up after the gang parties every few days.

It made me spitting mad, but I understood: Mr. Flores wasn't ready to surrender our little neighborhood to the gangs.

The day dragged on, and I grew anxious. Itchy. Restless. By the time late afternoon arrived, I was going stir-crazy—and reckless. My thinking jumped about in wild tangents.

If I'm basically invisible, why am I afraid to go outside? Who's going to see me? Why don't I just figure out how to sneak around? If I make a little boo-boo, who's going to believe what they see? Er, don't see. Right?

That "figure it out" list I was making? I started a new "figure it out" list—a list of what I needed so I could go where I wanted to go and do what I wanted to do *while I was invisible.* At the top of the list? A pair of lightweight, ultra-quiet shoes. I got crackin' on the Internet, looking for the right pair.

A few afternoons later I had the scare of my life: The front doorbell rang.

I freaked out. I really did. I was convinced it was Cushing and her army. I tried to run, but I couldn't get my legs to work. And where would I go anyway? I was sure they had my house surrounded.

The bell rang again and a voice called out at the same time. "Gemma? You in there? Girl, I ain't seen you in days. You okay? Gemma!"

Abe! I clutched my chest and tried to cram my thundering heart back inside. I didn't know what to do. Should I pretend I wasn't home?

I opened my mouth to answer and the nanomites went nuts. Apparently the mites were voting for silence.

Over the riot in my head I heard Abe add, "Gemma? Your car's been settin' in the drive for days. That ain't like you. You need to answer me now, hear? Or I'll get the police to come do one of those wellness checks on you."

I walked up to the door and made a horrible coughing sound. It wasn't as hard to fake as you might think, because the mites had flooded my throat until I gagged.

"I'm just sick, Abe," I croaked. "I've, uh, caught a bad bug."

And the puns just keep coming. Unbelievable!

I smacked myself on the forehead, but at least the mites had stopped trying to choke me. They just wouldn't shut up about it and were warning me in their inimitable way to keep quiet.

Well, if their Prime Directive was "Hide Gemma," they were doing their job, but they gibbered so loud I couldn't hear myself think!

"Nano! Silence!" I choked.

Abe knocked again. "Gemma? Someone in there with you?"

Cough. "No."

"Thought I heard you talking to someone. You sure you're okay?"

Cough. Hack. "I think I'll be fine in a few days. Just need to rest."

"Well, do you need anything? And I found this cross out on the walk. It yours?"

I coughed (badly) a few more times. "Um, yeah, it is. Guess I dropped it."

"Well, open up so's I can give it to you."

(Panic!) "Oh, no, Abe," *cough, cough,* "I don't think that's a good idea. I, um, don't want you to catch what I have." (*That* was true.) "Maybe just put it under the mat, okay? I'll, um, get it later."

I heard some shuffling outside the door and the thump of the mat as Abe dropped it. "All right, Gemma. But I think you need some of your Aunt Lu's chicken soup."

My throat closed up for reals when Abe said that. I didn't have to pretend when I croaked, "It could fix anything, couldn't it?"

"Yup, it could at that," he whispered. I almost didn't hear him.

"Thank you for coming to check on me, Abe." I meant it.

"You call me if you need something, you hear?"

But I did need something—and it was something he could get for me. "Abe? I could use a good book."

He guffawed. "Thought you had all them Kindle books on that electronic gizmo."

Think quick! I coughed to give myself a moment.

"I, um, was hankering for an old book, something I read a long time ago. I don't think it's available on Kindle. That *Memoirs of an Invisible Man?*"

"That old thing? Only halfway good. Movie not much better. You sure you want it?"

"Yes, please." *Cough.*

"I'll fetch it for you—and I don't need it back."

He shuffled off the porch and I peeked through the curtains to watch him. Darned if Emilio wasn't *right there* on the sidewalk again!

"Kid, you are standing on my last nerve," I scowled through clenched teeth.

He had noticed the curtain move and was all eyes and steely watchfulness. Abe nodded to him as he passed. Emilio was still waiting, watching, when Abe came back.

"You need something, young man?" Abe inquired.

"Nah. Just wondering . . ." Emilio's response trailed off.

"Gemma's got herself a bad cold. I'm bringing her this book."

Abe stood there, waiting for Emilio to move on, until the kid shrugged his shoulders and turned toward his uncle's house. I watched their short exchange. As Emilio marched away, I watched him glance over his shoulder, his black brows drawn down over wary dark eyes.

I wasn't fooling him a bit.

⌘⌘⌘⌘

CHAPTER 18

As big a pain in my backside as Emilio was, I was touched by the kid's gift. I strung the cross on a chain and hung it around my neck, then spent the evening reading the first chapters of *Memoirs of an Invisible Man*.

Just to recap, for those who may not be familiar with this novel, the book's main character is Nick Halloway. Nick was unfortunate enough to be inside a building that housed a research laboratory when an explosion (an experiment gone awry) occurred.

The explosion didn't demolish the building, however. Instead, the experiment-gone-wrong turned Nick, the building, everything *in* the building, and the entire area *around* the explosion, right down into the ground, *invisible*.

I was drawn to the fictional account because the author had been so inventive in his description of how Nick survived as an invisible man—how he got around, how he kept his condition secret (more or less), how he provided for himself, and how he eluded capture. Nick's emotional state during his adjustment sounded a lot like mine, and I was able to apply several of the practical aspects of Nick's survival to my own situation, although our conditions and problems were somewhat different.

How were they different? Well, Nick had to deal with the problem of clothing. Only things that had been affected by the explosion were unseen, so the suit he'd been wearing when the event occurred was invisible; however, anything else he put on (or in his pockets) was *not* invisible! This limited him to only one set of clothes, which presented another whole set of problems—like the time when he undressed, set his clothes down somewhere, and couldn't find them again.

Nick also had an issue with eating: *Everything he ate was visible.* I laughed over his account of watching himself in a mirror as he chewed and swallowed food and then observed and timed his digestive process until the food disappeared.

Observed his digestive process. Ick.

Nick and I actually were in quite different circumstances: He truly was invisible; I was "only" optically invisible. Those differences didn't mean my life was any less strange or difficult, in the practical sense, but my form of invisibility had certain, rather huge advantages.

The most significant advantage was how the mites covered any clothing I donned. It was as though they "guarded my perimeter" by hiding whatever fell within that perimeter—including my digestion.

And after a short learning curve, the mites also camouflaged the physical impressions my movements made—like how they hid the small indentations of my fingers when I pressed them into my padded tablecloth.

Nick really struggled with that situation. People could "see" the temporary indentations his feet left on a carpet, as an example.

I don't have half of his problems, I admitted.

Still, I admired Nick's ingenuity. I pondered his fearless attitude about running around in visible society. In contrast, I was terrified of being noticed. Of course, part of Nick's fearlessness grew out of necessity, because some very tenacious government people were hunting him.

That was the other thing we had in common: an enemy.

Nick's nemesis, *Jenkins*, had known of Nick right from the beginning, had known who he was and how he'd become invisible. Jenkins' pursuit was relentless. He figured out Nick's vulnerabilities and used them against him.

Yes, Nick was on the run from the get-go, whereas I, to date, was not.

My throat dried up as I appreciated how quickly my circumstances could change. For the first time in days, I thought about General Cushing. *Shark Face.* I knew *exactly* what kind of person she was—how tenacious and determined, how devoid of scruples, how without mercy.

Just how badly did she want the nanomites? Badly enough that she approved and planned Dr. Bickel's murder.

I tried to swallow but couldn't. As I considered Dr. Bickel's death, my heart ached afresh with the knowledge that I'd never see my funny/accomplished scientist friend again.

No more gourmet lunches followed by "surprise desserts" with all the fun and fanfare. No more competitive games of Canasta or Samba. No more shared jokes and teasing laughter.

I resolutely turned from my grief and focused my energy on more pressing problems. I knew that Cushing would upend every rock, scrutinize every byte of Dr. Bickel's data, and hunt down all leads in her pursuit of the nanocloud. Had she any idea where the mites had gone? Where they had hidden? More importantly, did she suspect anyone of helping Dr. Bickel during his sojourn in the mountain lab?

I grappled with unpleasant possibilities: Was I on her radar? Was she observing me *right now*, watching my daily activities?

Was she, too, at this moment, "figuring things out"?

Licking my lips, I came to some initial conclusions. *Just in case she is studying me, I can't do anything out of the ordinary, anything that would raise a red flag, like withdrawing a large sum of cash or going "silent" on the Internet.*

The importance of "normalcy" registered with me. *If I abandon my regular routines, my absence will attract attention, too. I must keep up my Facebook and Pinterest posts, keep applying for jobs, keep my life as normal as possible.*

But if I did all that and she came for me anyway, was I in any way prepared to run, to elude her? Would I be able to survive as well as Nick had?

The specter of my life, should Cushing capture me, was ominous: Knowing her, I would spend the rest of my days as a guinea pig in a secret government prison.

*It's not a matter of **if**, but of **when**. Someday, whether it's the government or others, someone will stumble upon the truth. When that happens, I will need to go,* I thought. *To do so, I will need basic necessities and cash in hand. I won't have access to my bank anymore.*

And yet, no big cash withdrawals.

The more I pondered my situation, the more I saw how unprepared I was. I realized how vital the cash in my freezer might prove to be, too. I kept thinking of Nick Holloway and what I'd learned from *Memoirs of an Invisible Man*. I began rereading it, marking it up, referencing it as a "play book."

At the very least, I need an escape plan, I told myself, a*nd I'll need to pack a "bug-out bag,"* something I'd overheard Rick and Tony, both ex-military, describe once. I couldn't find the backpack I'd hauled Dr. Bickel's supplies in, so I rummaged through my closet and found an old duffle bag.

It's pretty large, I mused. *If I overpack it, I won't be able to carry it very far.* And then I asked myself, *Just what will I need?*

I needed to make a list of the basics I'd require if I had to leave my house in a hurry. Right then, though, I crammed the duffle bag full of clothes to see how it might work.

I slung the packed duffle bag crosswise over my shoulder so it hung down on my left side and left my hands free. It was a long bag, and it stuck out in front and behind me. The mites clicked and hummed, and the front end of the bag started to disappear as the mites did their work.

I strode around my room with the bag, feeling its size, mentally listing what I would actually pack in it, and visualizing my running with its weight and bulk. I was startled out of my thoughts by unexpected movement in the closet mirror. I pivoted so I could see over my shoulder: The back end of the duffle bag hung by itself in midair!

"Nano!" I was shocked. Alarmed.

Immediately, the mites' chatter picked up. They sounded a little harried.

As I stared, the visible back end of the bag became smaller, until it disappeared. I sighed, relieved. Then I pirouetted before the mirror and—

"Nano!"

The front end had reappeared!

"No, no, no!" *What is their problem?*

The mites chittered and hummed, louder now, and I watched them re-cover the front of the bag. It was fascinating, really.

Until the back end popped into view.

"What? Nano!" I was growing a little concerned, but the nanomites kept working at it, their noises a frenzied buzz.

Soon the back end of the duffle bag disappeared—only for part of the front to pop out. Again.

Over the next five minutes, the mites buzzed and chipped and worked with furious resolve, but the front and back ends of the duffle bag swapped visibility back and forth. If the front end vanished, the back end materialized. If the back disappeared, the front appeared.

When Genie and I were in middle school, Aunt Lu had taken us on a picnic behind Sandia Crest. We'd fed unshelled peanuts to a chipmunk that day. He had stuffed nuts into both of the pouches in his mouth until they were so full that nothing more would fit in.

The chipmunk looked like he had a bad case of the mumps! But was he satisfied to take his bounty home and store it? No. As long as nuts remained on the ground, he wanted *more of them*.

So, with both sides of his face bulging, the cute little critter had tried to cram *one more* peanut into his mouth. Except when he shoved it over on the left side, a nut from the right side popped out. And when he tried to push that nut back where it came from, a peanut on the left flew out. We laughed and laughed at the chipmunk's comic attempts, but try as he might, he could not fit another single nut into his mouth.

The mites, like that chipmunk, kept trying and trying, and I could hear their frustration mounting. They managed, at last, to cover all of the bag, but I shook my head.

It was the first time I'd seen the mites struggle to hide something on me—and it was disconcerting to see that they *did* have limitations. Their struggle to hide all of the bag made me question how well they could maintain such tenuous coverage.

"This duffle bag isn't going to work—not if it's going to take you ten minutes to hide it!" I grumbled.

Are they limited in how much surface area they can cover?

Genie had learned about "surface area" the hard way.

Aunt Lu had insisted that Genie and I help her paint the kitchen one summer. Genie had immediately claimed the pantry to paint while Lu had started on the walls in one corner and I in the opposite corner.

When Lu wasn't looking, Genie stuck her tongue out at me and snarked, "I'll be done long before you are!"

My sister thought she was getting away with the least amount of work, but she hadn't counted on the pantry's six shelves (top sides, undersides, and edges), the pantry's ceiling, the four walls, and the inside of the door and its jambs—almost all of which had to be painted with a brush rather than a roller.

Two hours later, Lu and I were finished. Genie, complaining under her breath, toiled away for another hour before the pantry was done. Genie had been livid over her mistake.

I snickered at the memory of the furious tantrum she'd thrown afterward.

*Surface area. The more edges and planes I attach to my body, the more surface area the mites have to cover. Or perhaps the difficulty is the **speed** at which they can cover that area? Or is it both?* I pursed my lips. *I need them to be fast. Maybe I should use something more compact, something that hugs my body?*

That last thought gave me an idea. I went to the kitchen and pulled out a lightweight fabric grocery sack. I filled the sack with clothes from the duffle bag, then slung the sack over my shoulder.

The handles were too short to be used as shoulder straps (the bag hung just below my armpit), but with a few alterations? I revolved in front of the mirror and saw that the mites were able to cover the sack, although it still took them a few moments.

"Not fast enough," I chided them.

They chipped a protest in return.

"Too bad. If you don't like it, hit the road."

But one sack wouldn't hold all of my bug-out supplies, either.

Testing the mites further, I hung a second sack from my other shoulder. Again, it took the mites a few moments to adjust their coverage.

New items to hide? Different kinds of items? I mulled over how the mites had to "learn" to hide the tablecloth when I poked it. How, when they had figured it out, they had hidden my movements quickly—but the learning had taken time.

Would their predictive ability work faster if they were always dealing with the same surface type, a surface they were already familiar with, like the tablecloth?

I frowned. "What if I could reduce the actual surface area the mites have to cover? Like painting a wall instead of a pantry? What if the surface area were the same and only what was *under* it changed?"

I went looking for a loose shirt to cover the sacks. I dug through an old box and came up with one of Uncle Eduardo's baggy (*huge*, actually) old t-shirts. Apparently he'd been a big, barrel-chested man.

All right!

I threw the shirt on over the grocery sacks. As it settled, it disappeared—and so did the sacks beneath it.

"Much faster," I breathed. Fully loaded, the sacks would bulge, but the bulging wouldn't matter as long as the mites cloaked the t-shirt, thus cloaking the sacks.

These sacks will work, I decided, *with a few adjustments.*

I pulled off the shirt and sacks and laid them aside. Then I sat down to start a list of what I would actually need if, indeed, I had to run. I listed the cash from my freezer at the top and added some changes of clothes and toiletries.

What else will I need? Well, I can always get what I need later.

Yes, I had certain advantages over the fictional Nick Holloway, but I hadn't considered what had to be the greatest plus of all: *technology.* The Internet hadn't existed back in Nick's time.

It's simple for me to find and buy what I need online.

Then it dawned on me: I wouldn't be able to take my smart phone when I ran. Not my phone, not my laptop, and not any of my online accounts. I would have no credit cards. Gemma Keyes would tangibly— and *virtually*—disappear from the world.

My situation wouldn't be hopeless, but it would certainly be more difficult.

***

Late in the evening a couple of nights later, when I thought no one would be paying attention, I decided to put my car in the garage. Yes, it was a risk to move it, but leaving it in the drive, attracting unwanted attention, was a bigger one.

I went out the side door—and then did something unplanned, something completely spontaneous—something not just a little reckless but *really* reckless.

I climbed into my Corolla, turned the key (which turned out the interior light that had gone on the instant I'd opened the car door), and backed out of the drive. I kept the headlights off until I left the cul-de-sac.

Then I turned them on and drove.

I can't tell you how good it felt! How liberating! How ridiculously wonderful.

My dash clock read a little past ten, not terribly late yet. I drove to the nearest Walmart Supercenter.

The 24-hour store had few shoppers that time of the evening, and the huge lot gave me plenty of parking options. I drove far out in the lot and pulled in next to a Ford pickup—a big one that would provide plenty of "screen." I got out of my car quickly—before I lost my nerve.

I scanned around. No one was near me, no one who might notice that my car had no driver and that when the door opened no one got out. I shrugged and jogged toward the store entrance.

As I came up to the Walmart entrance, the mites grew uneasy and communicated their unrest with a variety of clicks and whistles. I ignored them. I told myself I was only going to walk around. Reconnoiter. See what interacting in a crowd was like.

It was almost too easy. I waited until a customer coming out of the store activated the automatic door. I walked inside while the door was still open. And I was being careful! I paid attention to what people were doing and kept out of their way.

As I said, the store didn't have many shoppers. Still, whenever my path came within spitting distance of anyone else's, the mites elevated their DEFCON status—which hurt. A lot.

I wanted to rip my brain out. That's how annoying the racket was.

Under my breath, I hissed, "Nano! *Shut it.*"

They didn't immediately calm down; however, after I'd navigated enough close encounters without drawing attention to my "InvisiGirl" state, the mites grudgingly conceded that I wasn't going to give myself away. They finally shut up and settled down.

I sighed and rubbed my eyes.

I need a couple ibuprofen.

Instead, I gravitated toward the produce and my mouth watered. Had I been without salad and fruit for only a few days?

More like nine or ten days, I calculated.

For a brief moment, I considered filling a sack and stuffing it up under my shirt. The produce would be as invisible as I was.

No. It was Aunt Lu's voice resounding in my heart.

I nodded, agreeing. No, I was not a thief, nor would I become one today; she had raised me better than that. Whatever I needed I would pay for—which meant I wouldn't be taking anything home tonight since I didn't have any money with me.

So I wandered the store, feeling almost part of the human race again. Almost. A teen girl and her boyfriend, giggling and tearing down the aisle, nearly ran me down.

Nearly. While the mites were having a conniption fit, I stepped out of the teens' way. With time to spare.

Time. The word resonated with me. All I needed was *time and experience* before I would be able to go about in the world, confident and unafraid. I liked that picture: Me, navigating through everyday life without fear, without worry.

Speaking of experience . . .

I went to the front of the store and watched a woman use the self-checkout lane. The tricky part for me would be the fruits and vegetables—items without barcodes. I didn't exactly breathe down the lady's neck, but she did look around toward me once, with a puzzled expression.

I stuffed a fist in my mouth and stifled the snort-laugh that had almost jumped out.

I recovered and moved to an idle self-checkout machine and started to fiddle with it, looking for the instructions on how to pay for produce. The woman on the other self-checkout machine glanced at the machine I was playing with. She blinked, still a little confused, and then shrugged and returned to her purchases.

Being invisible had its plus side. I grinned and went back to studying the checkout options.

On the ride home I felt strangely settled. Comforted. I stopped in the driveway, got out and opened the side garage door, drove my car inside, closed the garage door behind me, and slid out the side door. I looked around to see if anyone was watching, but I wasn't feeling terribly paranoid about it. I was actually feeling a little proud.

I guess you can get used to anything eventually.

Before I retired for the night I added two items to my list of things to make life as an invisible woman easier: *Order electric garage door opener. Figure out how to turn off the interior light in my car.*

***

The next morning I phoned up a local company that installed garage door openers.

"Listen, I'd like an opener installed, but can't be home during the day. Will your installer come out, look over the job, email me a bid, and then install the opener when I'm not at home?"

"Sure thing. We do that all the time. After you approve the estimate, we'll take your payment by credit card over the phone and schedule the installation. How's next week look for you?"

I made arrangements for the estimate and then went in search of my car's manual. With only cursory glances to see if anyone was looking my way, I went out the side door and into the garage via its side door. I found the car's dog-eared manual in the glove box.

"A switch? I didn't know there was a switch," I mumbled. "Too easy."

I found the switch on the dome light and flipped it off. I was cramming the manual back into the glove box when I realized it, too, had a light. A few seconds later, I'd popped the bulb out.

I glanced at the dome light again. I pried the dome light cover off and removed that bulb, also.

"Just to be sure."

The whole process took less than five minutes and then the inside of my car was "light free," even when I opened my glove box.

That night, same time as the night before, I made a second run to Walmart. I wore one of Uncle Eddy's old shirts. This one buttoned up the front. Under the shirt hung my two fabric grocery sacks crisscrossed over opposite shoulders.

Like bandoliers, I giggled. *Lookit me. I'm Yosemite Sam!*

I'd spent part of the day cutting and sewing long straps to the grocery sacks so they wouldn't strangle me. With the added strap length, the sacks hung down to my waist.

Then I pulled the baggy shirt over my head and down around the sacks and practiced filling the bags with groceries from my kitchen, checking to make sure that what I put in them stayed "invisible" during the whole process.

The mites made various comments during my experiments. I don't know if they were expressing—ahead of time—their concerns about my plans or if they resented the extra work of covering the large shirt and all that I stuffed under it. If they resented the extra work or all the trial and error practices, I was unmoved.

"Nano! Do me a favor and get lost," I grumbled. As far as I was concerned, they owed me. Big time.

Symbiotic relationship, my left foot.

I drove to Walmart and got out, pleased that my car's interior lights could no longer illuminate my *absence*. Once in the store, I browsed the aisles and covertly filled the sacks with what I needed or fancied. I kept one of my baggy shirt's buttons undone. It made slipping items into the sacks easier.

It also made it tricky for the mites, who hummed and buzzed over the addition of each item. More than once I saw a shimmer as they struggled to accommodate my added baggage. I was tempted to bust into a malicious chuckle—but I digress.

Besides, after I'd added a few items to the sack, the mites had already figured it out. No more shimmer.

I don't need to coddle you, I sneered.

When I had what I wanted stowed under the shirt, I had to hang around awhile until the self-checkout lanes were empty. Then, as fast as I could, I pulled the items out one at a time, ran them through the scanner or used the produce option until the sacks on the side of the scanner were full and I was done.

I had cash with me and I had just finished paying when a Walmart checker wandered over. His name tag read, "Gary Vigil." He noticed the two sacks of groceries on the side. He checked the readout and saw they'd been paid for. He frowned and looked around for the groceries' owner.

I tried to be patient, but I was getting a little anxious. If he took the items away to restock them, I'd have to start over, and I didn't want to do that.

Then the strangest thing happened. I'm not joking. I'm still chewing on it and considering its implications.

The music coming over the PA system cut out and a mechanical voice intoned, "Gary Vigil. Gary Vigil. Report immediately."

Except the mechanical voice pronounced "Vigil" with a soft "g" (like *gee* whiz) making Gary's name "vigil" (as in "candlelight vigil") instead of using the Hispanic pronunciation, "Vee-hill."

"Report? Report where?" He grumbled something uncomplimentary before striding away.

I stood there blinking, wondering if what I *thought* had happened actually *had* happened. Could the mites really have—

Honestly, I'd only stood there *three seconds* before the nanomites stung my hand.

"Okay, okay! I'm on it. Sheesh. My hand is gonna have a callus at the rate we're going," I complained. I grabbed the sacks and pulled them to the side of the scanning station. I was, for the second time, about to move the items one-by-one into the sacks under my shirt when I had a better idea.

No one was nearby except the checkers in other lanes. I got down, sitting on my heels, lifted my shirt, and stuffed each plastic grocery bag into the fabric sacks hanging over my shoulders.

I was done in five seconds and out the door in another five. The rest of the trip home was uneventful, but it left me with a lot to think about.

In the meantime, do you remember that reckless, "I-don't-care" feeling I mentioned earlier?

It got worse.

That rash, careless attitude did a slow burn deep down inside. Agitated and restless, I found myself holding heated conversations—*with myself*—that went something along these lines:

My whole childhood was spent hiding. If I didn't keep out of Genie's way, she would make me pay. I had to be quiet or she would make me wish I had been.

Not one person saw what she was doing or what she was really like. I was always afraid of running afoul of her and her temper, so I kept quiet, kept to myself, stayed in the background, stayed in the shadows.

No one helped me! No one saw through her lies!

*No, **she** was always the pretty, vivacious one, the one everyone noticed—while **I** was the plain, ordinary one—the stupid twin sister that people scarcely realized existed—except when I got in trouble. I was too afraid of Genie to speak up, to compete with her or tell the truth about her.*

As the twig is bent, so grows the tree! Even after she left for college, I knew I would always be ordinary and plain. No one special. A woman no one noticed.

*Well, it wasn't fair! It wasn't right! But then, life **isn't** fair, is it?*

*Still, when she finally went away, I started to hope again. I worked hard and I had dreams that my life was actually going somewhere. I had a great job and, at last, people were starting to value my work, starting to value **me**.*

The anger swirling around in me sizzled a little hotter.

*Now everything I worked for is gone. Gone! Ruined! Because of these stinking nanomites! What did I do to deserve these, these **things** living in me, controlling my life?*

*It wasn't bad enough that I lived in the shadows all my childhood, **practically** invisible? Now I have to live out the rest of my life **literally** invisible?*

Now I'm nothing more than a freak!

A long-simmering rage bubbled to the surface and with it, a new determination. Maybe it had more to do with Genie than I recognized, but I was *done*. I was through being passive. Finished taking the blame for *her* actions. Done trying to please, trying to fit in—trying to hide my true self. And done letting the nanomites try to control me.

Just *done*.

***

Okay, well, maybe "done" didn't fit *all* situations.

Zander came to the door late Sunday afternoon. He knocked, rang the bell, and called to me through the closed and locked door.

"Gemma? Gemma, I know you're in there. Listen, Abe is really worried about you. I am, too. Please, can we just talk?"

Jake, on hearing Zander's voice, rubbed up against the door and yowled as if I'd neglected to feed him for a week.

Traitor! Ingrate! I nudged him away from the door with my foot which, of course, freaked him out. He screeched and attempted to scatter to the four winds—meaning his feet were moving in all directions but going nowhere until his claws got some purchase in the carpet and he bolted from the room.

"Gemma? Is Jake okay? Are *you* okay?"

I stared at the floor and shook my head. Maybe I needed to call him and call Abe, feed them the same plausible line, something that would put them off a while longer. But suppose I did? Sooner or later someone was going to pull the trigger on a wellness check by the police—and I was not ready for it to be "sooner."

My thoughts returned to Zander. *What would I say to him if I called him?* I asked myself. *What story do I tell him? And Abe? He knows me too well. He will know I'm telling a tall tale.*

I just kept silent.

"Gemma, this isn't over. You need to let us see you so we know you're all right."

Zander's steps clattered down the porch and away from my door. I chanced a peek through the curtains. He was headed across the cul-de-sac toward Abe's house. I slid out my side door and followed behind. The sky was hazy, my shadow negligible.

He almost missed Emilio. Almost. The kid was tucked inside the little hidey-hole he'd formed by pushing into the bushes so often.

Zander stooped down in front of Emilio's spot and talked with him for a few minutes. When he stood up, his face was flushed, his mouth turned down.

Wow. I think he's angry! I've never seen Zander angry, I realized. I was astonished. Christians weren't supposed to get angry, were they? And ministers? Didn't the "not supposed to get angry" rule apply double?

Instead of continuing on to Abe's house, Zander strode to his car and tore away from the curb. Fifteen minutes later he returned. I was standing on the sidewalk far enough from Emilio to feel comfortable.

Zander had a little rectangular box from a chicken place out on Central. He called Emilio out and gave it to him. They sat on the curb and I hung back as Emilio tore into the chicken and whatever else was in the box, but Zander kept him talking. After a few minutes it dawned on me that they were talking about *me*.

Not good! No, not good at all. I edged just a little closer.

Emilio actually waved his hand in my direction just then—and I froze. Then I realized he was pointing at my house, not at me. He said something that made Zander's gray eyes squint, and I could tell he was confused.

Good. Confused is good! Better than believing the yarn Emilio is likely feeding him.

I moved up onto Mateo's "lawn" (not much more than neglected weeds and snake grass) so I wouldn't be between my house and Emilio's pointing fingers. I was, however, between them and Mateo's house.

Uh-oh.

I hadn't yet gotten close enough to overhear exactly what Emilio and Zander were talking about—but I couldn't miss when Mateo stormed out his front door behind me. Zander and Emilio had their backs to Mateo and neither noticed his approach.

I didn't know what to do. Should I cough or make a noise? I picked up a pebble instead and tossed it toward Zander. It smacked him on the shoulder and he glanced up—and caught Mateo's advance.

In case you haven't figured it out, Mateo isn't the shy and retiring type.

"Hey, you *blank*! (Insert pejorative term of your choice.) What the *blank blank* do you think you're doing?"

Zander stood up and folded his arms across his chest. Emilio jumped to his feet, too, and huddled behind Zander's back.

"We're just talking."

"What's that?" Mateo got in Zander's face and pointed at the KFC box.

"I was just sharing a meal with your nephew. No need to get upset."

"Get over here," Mateo yelled at Emilio.

The kid, his expression fearful, crawled out from behind Zander. As soon as he was within reach, Mateo's hand lashed out, striking Emilio full in the face. The kid stumbled and fell to the ground. Then he was up again, and moved out of Mateo's range.

No sooner had Mateo's palm connected with Emilio's cheek than Zander's hand snaked out and caught Mateo's wrist. Zander yanked Mateo closer, and Mateo struggled against Zander's grip.

Zander and Mateo's faces were inches apart when Zander snarled, "Jesus saved me out of the gang life, but that doesn't mean I don't remember what I *was* or how I used to deal with a *pandillero* like you. *Now back off.*"

He released Mateo's wrist, at the same time shoving him backwards and off balance.

I was staring dumbstruck at a very different Zander, a man who was as familiar with violence as Emilio's uncle was. Zander's eyes glittered with fearsome fury and I skittered away, shaking my head, trying to reconcile the man in front of me with the kind associate pastor I knew. The pieces did not fit.

Mateo must have seen something in Zander's face that he didn't like, either, because he stood his ground but did not retaliate. "This is my turf, you *blank*. I don't care who you are. If you want to keep your pretty-boy looks, you'd best get the *blank* out of here."

The encounter had taken mere seconds, but Emilio had used the precious moments to snatch up the chicken box and vanish. Maybe those seconds were exactly what Zander had hoped to buy.

Zander's features smoothed. "Like I said," he repeated, "I was just sharing a meal with your nephew. No need to get upset."

He nodded to Mateo and stepped away toward Abe's house. I followed at a distance, but I kept looking over my shoulder. Mateo, arms folded, face set in grim lines, watched and then stalked back to his house.

I shook my head, hoping to clear it. I didn't like how much Mateo's angry expression reminded me of Emilio. I didn't like thinking of Emilio growing up to be like his uncle. I steered away from thinking about the Zander I'd just witnessed in action.

That was worse.

As I drew abreast of Abe's house, my old friend stepped out of the shadows of his porch and greeted Zander. "That was a close one, son," he said softly.

Zander climbed the steps and the two of them sat down together. I sat on the steps and listened in.

"Yeah, but I can hold my own," Zander replied. He was, I thought, still angry—but trying very hard not to let it come out in his tone.

"So did you see my girl Gemma?"

"Nope. But I'm pretty sure she's in there." Then Zander snickered. "Jake's in there and you know how Gemma isn't exactly his favorite person?"

"Whoo-ee! That's an understatement, pastor!"

207

Zander snickered again. "Well, Jake sounded happy to hear my voice but tore away from the door just like he does whenever Gemma gets too close."

"Ha! I do b'lieve Jake thinks Lu left that house to him and not to Gemma! They been feudin' over it ever since. Like cats an' dogs, like cats an' dogs!"

Abe and Zander then had a good laugh at my expense while I fumed on the steps below them.

Finally Zander added, "So yeah, I'm pretty sure she's in there. I just don't understand what she's hiding."

The swing where they were sitting swung back and forth for a few minutes. Then Abe laughed softly.

"Once my Alice colored her hair," he reminisced. "Don't know 'zactly what went wrong, but the solution fried her hair something awful. Most of it fell out—left her nearwise bald. Never will forget it—nor the smell of all that fried hair."

"You think Gemma fried her hair?" Zander was as dubious as I was insulted.

"Never know. Alice, though? She din't go to church for three weeks. Had me cut off the parts that din't fall off, make it more even-like. Wore a hat, she did, ever'where she went, for months after that."

I'd heard enough. I stormed across the cul-de-sac and in my side door, slamming it behind me. Abe and Zander were still chuckling when I left.

***

Nothing Zander had done fixed Emilio's situation one bit. A box of fried chicken wouldn't mend the pain of abuse Emilio dealt with daily—pain I could relate to all too well. The next morning I watched Emilio march to the bus stop, shoulders slumped, head down.

"Yeah, I feel ya, kid," I whispered. The anger boiling around inside of me scooted over and made room for resentment toward Mateo for his treatment of Emilio. I knew the school would feed the boy a hot breakfast when he got there, but that just made me madder.

He shouldn't have to depend upon the school to feed him, I seethed. *That's Mateo's responsibility.*

I pulled on shoes and a hoodie and ducked out the kitchen door. I jogged across the street to Mateo's house. Bottles and cans littered the sidewalk and his lawn. Mateo's car was the only vehicle parked in the driveway, but last night the cul-de-sac had been lined with his crew's cars for another wild party.

This morning Mateo's house was still. How hard could it be to walk inside and take a look around? His house had the same floorplan as mine, so I was familiar with the layout. If I saw what I expected, I could phone in an anonymous tip to Children, Youth, and Family.

Why not?

Turns out Mateo and his girlfriend were still sleeping, but their side door was unlocked.

So Emilio gets himself up and out of the house for school on his own? I pondered that realization as I snooped through their kitchen.

It was worse than I had imagined. Mateo's crew had left ample evidence of their self-indulgence: The counters and floor were filthy. Dirty dishes and empty bottles were piled everywhere. The trash overflowed.

I eased open a cupboard door and then another and another until I'd looked in all of them. I tried the fridge. I found nothing more than coffee, condiments, and a lone box of cheap wine.

Do these people ever buy food? No wonder the kid's starving. The growling in his stomach is prolly what wakes him up in the morning, gets him going.

That careless, almost reckless thing in my belly glowed a little hotter.

I heard stirring noises from the other side of the house and the sound of a toilet flushing. I moved into the dining room, behind the table, where I could watch and not be in the way.

I glanced down at the tabletop.

Interesting.

Corazón wandered into view.

She looks terrible, was my first thought. Her hair was dirty and matted. Dark circles hung under her eyes. I remembered how lovely the girl had been when she and Mateo had moved in a couple of years back.

"Lovely" seemed miles back in the rearview mirror for Corazón.

She set to work making coffee. As soon as she flipped the switch on the pot, she took out the trash, ran a sink of hot soapy water, and started making inroads in the piles of dirty dishes.

The distant toilet flushed again and Corazón flinched.

A moment later a shirtless Mateo sauntered into view, his gut hanging over a pair of pajama bottoms, his feet scuffing along in old slippers. I had a good look at him, probably the closest I'd ever had. His dark eyes were bloodshot, his face lined and puffy. The man was not old—maybe in his late twenties—but he was already running to fat.

Yeah, a steady diet of alcohol will do that for you, meathead.

Mateo's head was shaved like Emilio's and his left hand, arm, shoulder, and neck were covered in swirling ink. I didn't know gang signs but I would have bet money he bore his gang's emblems in his body art.

He had scarcely plopped into a chair when he demanded, "Where's my *blank* coffee?"

"I have it, Baby." Corazón set it in front of him and stepped back. Quickly.

Mateo grunted and slurped from the mug. "Gotta meet my boys at noon."

"Okay."

"This place is disgusting. You better have it cleaned up when I get back. And have something hot fixed for dinner."

Corazón swallowed. "Sure, Baby. Just need some groceries."

Mateo grunted and slurped his coffee again. He reached for a metal box on the table. The box sat next to an ashtray filled with the pinched ends of tiny, rolled cigarettes—and next to the plastic-wrapped block of off-white powder I'd noticed a few minutes ago.

Yes, very interesting.

He opened the metal box and I gaped. It was stuffed with cash.

He picked through the mound of money. "Here." He threw a twenty-dollar bill at her and it fluttered to the floor.

"Won't buy much, Baby," Corazón whispered. "Maybe just dinner t'night."

Mateo slammed his cup onto the table. "You complaining?"

"No, Baby. Just sayin'." Corazón squatted to pick up the twenty.

So fast! His foot whipped out *so fast.*

I jumped as Mateo's foot slammed into Corazón's face. She pitched backwards onto her haunches holding her cheek, but she made not a sound. She scrabbled out of range of Mateo's feet, which only seemed to enrage him.

Cursing, he jumped from his seat, grabbed her by her hair, and slammed her head into the wall. Corazón shrieked, but it was apparent that Mateo did not care. Nor would her screams stop him.

Oh, I really don't like you, Mateo, I hissed. *I really, really, **really** don't like you.*

When the chair came crashing down on Mateo's head, I was mildly surprised. I hadn't *planned* to hit him, but I did. More than once.

After I'd hit him a couple of times, the chair splintered and fell apart. I grabbed one of the chair legs and beat him on the head with it.

It kinda felt good, letting all that anger out to play, and I didn't care if it was right or wrong as long as it *felt right.*

Corazón was screaming nonstop—almost as loudly as the mites in my head—however, I don't think Mateo knew (literally) what hit him. When Mateo lay unconscious on the dining room floor, I tossed aside the chair leg. Corazón stared about, her eyes wild.

I slammed the lid closed on the box of money and pushed it toward her. "Take this. Buy a bus ticket out of town and don't come back."

Corazón freaked and backed away, sobbing. I grabbed the box and shoved it into her arms. She promptly dropped it and ran, howling, into the other part of the house.

"Huh." I shrugged, retrieved the box, and followed her. She had locked herself inside the bathroom.

Novel idea.

I knocked on the bathroom door. All was silent on the other side except for the girl's ragged breathing.

"Corazón, listen to me. I know you can't see me, but I'm not going to hurt you. Just listen. You need to get away from Mateo before he wakes up."

I looked around, trying to pick the right words to galvanize her. *You need to blow this popsicle stand? Get outta Dodge?*

I sighed. "What's he going to think when he wakes up, huh? Let me tell you what he's going to think. He's going to think that *you* beat him up. What do you think he'll do to you then? Are you waiting for him to kill you? *Are you?*"

I had to come up with a plan for her. Fast. "Look. I'm going to leave now. You take the money and take Mateo's car. Drive to the Sunport and leave the car on the departures curb—just leave it running, get out, and walk away. Go into the airport and take the escalator down to the arrivals curb. Grab a cab there and have it take you to the bus station. Airport security will tow Mateo's car—it'll be days before he finds it. In the meantime, you'll be long gone."

It was a long speech met with breathless silence. I waited. "Do you hear me? I don't know how long he'll be out. You'd better get moving. I'll put the money on the table before I go."

I set the money box on the table and glanced at Mateo. I *thought* he was out cold. Just in case, I yanked a set of miniblinds off the dining room window and used the cords to tie his hands and feet. It was all very awkward—I'd never tied anyone up before and I wasn't much good at it.

Not sure how long that will last, I thought, *but it will give her a little more time if she needs it.*

Then I went to the front door and made noises like I was leaving. I opened the door, paused, and slammed it shut, but really I stayed in the living room. I still wasn't sure she would have the courage to run.

She surprised me, though.

As soon as the front door banged shut, the bathroom door creaked open. Corazón flew into the bedroom and I heard her opening the closet and drawers, throwing and slamming things about. Five minutes later she wheeled a small suitcase into the living room. She'd tied the mess of her hair into a bun on the back of her neck and put on a clean blouse—one that didn't have her blood on it.

She had her purse and a set of keys in her hand as she tiptoed toward the dining table. Mateo lay trussed (quite unprofessionally, I confess) on the floor, eyes closed, mouth hanging open, but the girl hesitated. She was trembling—and she would have to reach over Mateo's body to get the money box.

Oh, for pity's sake!

I reached over Mateo and grabbed the box for her. "Just take it! Dump the money into your purse and leave the box."

She lurched backwards and uttered a yowl like Jake makes when you accidentally rock over his tail with a rocking chair.

"You're running out of time."

And I am running out of patience.

Her eyes shot around the room trying to find me, but she swallowed, opened the box, and dumped the contents into her bag. It was one of those big, deep bags.

Good.

For a second she studied the plastic-wrapped block on the table.

"You don't want that," I barked. "Now get going."

With one more wide-eyed look around, she grabbed her suitcase and rattled down the front steps. When I heard Mateo's Camaro tear away, I went in search of his cell phone. I found it and made an anonymous phone call to the police.

"Hey, yeah, some guy has drugs just sitting out in the open on his dining room table. Yeah. Looks like heroin or coke or something. I dunno. And he doesn't look too good. Like maybe someone beat the tar out of him—he's out cold on the floor. Here's the address. No. No name. Yeah. Thanks."

Then I walked out of the house, leaving the front door wide open behind me.

The cops arrived, sirens wailing and lights flashing. They were inside the house for maybe thirty minutes before they dragged Mateo out in handcuffs—a very gratifying sight, I might say, and not gratifying only to me. Abe, the Tuckers, Mr. and Mrs. Flores, and Mrs. Calderón all watched the sight from their respective sidewalks.

That rash boldness seemed to own me. I sauntered across the cul-de-sac and stood not far from Abe. I wasn't a bit worried that he or anyone else would notice me. Abe slapped his leg and chuckled to himself and I heard him say two or three times, "Well! Glory to God!" and "Thank you, Jesus!"

I *really* wanted to throw in an "amen," but didn't think it quite prudent.

It wasn't until after the police took Mateo away that I remembered Emilio. What would become of him? Probably CYFD would come pick him up, and that would be a good thing. Surely *any* foster home would be better than life with his uncle, right?

I watched for the kid to come home from school later that day. He slipped in the back door like he normally did and, a few minutes later, jetted back out. He shot around the house once, and I heard him calling Corazón's name. When he didn't find her, he took his usual seat on the curb, but his expression was puzzled and more than a little anxious.

Oh, wow. I wonder if he's worried about Corazón.

It hadn't occurred to me that he might have feelings for the young woman. Then it dawned on me that the two of them had been in similar situations when it came to Mateo and his iron fists. Sort of "the enemy of my enemy is my friend"? I didn't know; I could only speculate.

Emilio placed his hands over his shaved head and stared at the gutter in front of him. Uncertainty radiated from the kid, which made me a little anxious, too. A bit sad.

After all, I'm the one who'd upset the apple cart—even if the cart *was* filled with rotten apples.

I tried to squeeze myself into Emilio's shoes and decided I could appreciate his anxiety. I mean, Corazón never left the house. *Never.* (I was actually surprised that she knew how to drive.) But as soon as he'd entered the house after school, the kid had to have seen the destroyed miniblinds and fractured chair in the dining room. He had to have seen the mess she left in the bedroom as she'd packed to leave.

Was he wondering whether Corazón was hurt? Wondering whether she'd finally had enough? Was he questioning whether she'd be back?

I shivered. Was Emilio fretting over his uncle's response should he come home and find Corazón missing?

That was a lot of worry for a little kid.

Corazón was, I sincerely hoped, far away by now, gone for good. I just hadn't calculated the impact of her absence on Emilio. I hadn't thought of anything while Mateo was kicking Corazón's face. I had just acted.

Well, I'm not sorry. But I was a bit nervous about the repercussions of my actions.

Maybe it was too late to go back and do things differently—but in the here-and-now I could do *something*. While he sat on the curb, I went into my house. Then I walked over to his back porch. I looked around before pulling a big sack of food out from under my baggy shirt.

Look, I have exactly zero experience with little boys—I don't know what they like to eat or don't like to eat. No clue. I just filled the bag with anything I happened to have that looked good to me: half a loaf of bread, a jar of peanut butter, a package of graham crackers, a half-full package of Oreos, a banana, a baggie containing a bunch of grapes, and two apples.

I set the sack on the porch and backed away. Sat on the grass between Mateo's house and the Floreses' house. Waited.

I guess I waited a couple of hours. I don't know what Emilio thought about all that time, but shadows were growing long when he picked himself up off the curb and dragged himself toward the back door. He stopped when he saw the sack on the porch.

He grabbed it, sat down on the steps, and yanked it open. His usual scowl lifted a moment and he actually grinned. Within seconds the kid was stuffing his face with alternating bites of banana and Oreo.

Not a bad combination, I admitted, smiling at his exuberance.

He tore into the grapes next and demolished them. I heard him bite the grapes, several at a time, heard their crunchy sweetness bursting in his mouth. It made my own mouth water. He wiped juice from his mouth and sighed.

It was such an innocent, guileless sigh of contentment.

I don't know why my throat closed up or why tears stung my eyes.

***

"Gemma?"

"Hey, Zander." I had snubbed his phone calls and deleted his voicemails for two weeks, but I couldn't have him coming by anymore, looking for me.

"Where have you been? I've been calling for days! You haven't returned any of my calls."

Before, before the barbecue in the park and before all this happened, I would have been thrilled to hear the worry mixed with a little hurt in his voice. *Before.* However, nothing could be like "before" for me.

"I'm sorry. To tell you the truth—" I couldn't finish the sentence I'd planned. I'd rehearsed saying that I didn't want to see him anymore, but it was more of a lie than I could stomach.

"Tell me what, Gemma?" He was more concerned.

"Zander, I'm sort of in a . . . situation. I won't be able to see you for a while."

That's right. I won't be able to "see" you, but mostly you won't be able to (literally) see me, I added.

Ever.

"What kind of a situation? A problem? Can I help?"

Oh, how I wished he could help! Everything in my heart longed to blurt out my problems. But, no, he couldn't help and I could not involve him. I would rather die than put this good but enigmatic man in the same danger I might soon be in.

"No. Thanks for asking, but no. I'll let you know when things, um, change for the better."

I was going to click off but he stopped me.

"Gemma, I don't know what is going on, but I'm going to pray for you. Right now."

Awkward!

"Uh, I don't think—"

"Just shut up and let me pray, okay?"

I heard him mumble, *something-something "stubborn" something "woman,"* maybe the "somethings" being Spanish? I sighed and waited.

"Father God, I don't know what is going on with Gemma—but you do, because you know everything. I am asking, Lord, in the name of Jesus, that you help her. Show her the way. Give her direction. And point her to the Savior, Lord. I thank you that you hear me, and I know you are already working. I trust you, Lord. Amen."

I didn't say anything. I couldn't, really. I was too choked up.

"Gemma? Are you still there?"

"Uh-huh." A sniff jumped out and I bit my lip to stop another.

Zander's voice gentled. "Whatever it is, Gemma, God has an answer. I promise."

"Thank you, Zander. Goodbye."

I didn't believe him for a second.

⌘⌘⌘⌘

CHAPTER 19

Dear Reader,

Although it feels much longer, it's been only about six weeks since Cushing's men invaded Dr. Bickel's lab under the mountain and my life changed so radically. I am, reluctantly, learning to deal with my new reality.

We face off in daily skirmishes over one thing or another, the nanomites and I. By daily skirmishes, I refer to them objecting when I insist on stretching the limits of my freedom, and to me, in most instances, ignoring their protests.

I believe I am prudent enough when I attempt something new, but I almost always suffer the discomfort of *their* complaints.

Grrr.

To be fair, they are quick to learn and adapt, and I think I see a pattern in their adaptive behavior. I've written how they don't like it when I take a hot shower and they *really* hate when I blow-dry my hair, but they have grown less combative about it as the days go by. It's the same after I try and succeed with a new venture out in public: It takes them a minute, but they eventually adjust to the idea.

At least, sooner or later, they stop griping and haranguing me! And once in a while (I know you'll think this is crazy) I get the eerie feeling, *a creepy suspicion*, that they have intervened. Helped me, in some way.

I can't explain it exactly, but I'm on the alert for it now. If I experience anything more concrete, I'll write about it.

The bottom line, I guess, is that we are not fighting each other as much as we were in the beginning. Yes, I most certainly resent their intrusion into my life, their *hijacking* of my body! If I knew how to rid myself of them, I would do it in a heartbeat.

So while I wouldn't call our cohabitation a "synergistic alliance," we are—*slowly*—learning to "get along." If Dr. Bickel were here, I think he would mark our report cards with "does not play nicely with others," but we are managing, I guess.

Along those lines, I will report that all my attempts to communicate with the nanomites have failed. I don't understand *why* they've failed, since I have followed Dr. Bickel's instructions and have tried every approach I can think of.

Still, for all my efforts, I have received no response from the nanomites, save their initial "alertness" when I say, "Nano." It's discouraging and I think it strange, because I know they are intelligent *and* observant.

Next subject.

I've made some adjustments that should make my freedom of movement easier and less stressful. For instance, the guys came and installed the garage door opener I ordered. I asked for a super quiet opener, but the age of the door itself and the tracks by which the door went up and down were what made the most noise.

Soooo, I bit the bullet and had them install a new door complete with new tracks. The total cost opened a big old sinkhole in my savings account. However, I can now raise the garage door from *inside* my house and I barely notice the sound. I removed the lightbulb from the opener, too, so that the garage stays dark when I'm leaving. Now maybe my ever-probing neighbor—with her face squished against her window—will be less likely to notice when I leave.

Speaking of Mrs. Calderón, that busybody has doubled down on her intrusive efforts. I see her continually peeking out her blinds and she knocks on my door twice a day. I ignore her when she knocks, but I figure it must drive her nuts that she has nothing to report.

Report? She and Genie have been thick as thieves since Genie and I were thirteen. I have no doubt that Mrs. Calderón provides Genie with regular updates about me. Mrs. Calderón feels honored that Genie "counts" on her. She actually feels that she has a special relationship with Genie! What she doesn't understand is that Genie is simply using her. Genie is using Mrs. Calderón to keep tabs on me so that Genie is assured that I'm remaining a properly humbled failure—and so that *I* know that Genie is ever watching, ever-present in my life and affairs.

How do I know this? Here's one instance.

Two years ago, Mrs. Calderón couldn't wait to show me what Genie had sent her as a birthday gift: a lovely, vintage brooch set with sky-blue and amber stones. I had stared at the brooch, at first befuddled and then outraged.

The antique piece had been one of Aunt Lu's favorites. She had sent it to Genie not long before she'd died. I knew how special that brooch was and what Aunt Lu had meant the gift to convey. It was accompanied by a note in which Aunt Lu told Genie how very much she loved her and would always love her. I knew about the note because Aunt Lu, too weak to write it herself, had dictated it to me.

Genie had not acknowledged the gift or the note. Instead, she had given the brooch to Mrs. Calderón, knowing our nosey neighbor would wear it proudly as a token of Genie's "esteem." Genie had given it to Mrs. Calderón knowing she would show it to me. Knowing I would receive the intended message.

As for Mrs. Calderón and her spying, I worry a bit that she has nothing to report to Genie. A complete lack of information might make my twisted sister more curious. More aggressive.

But back to my cool new garage door: It's so quiet that I come and go at night with more confidence, and I make regular after-dark trips to my local Walmart Supercenter and elsewhere. I chafe at my self-imposed nighttime restriction, although I know it's necessary. At night, unless my car is under lights, no one notices that the driver's seat is "empty."

But during the day? I stay home. I don't care to think about the pandemonium a driverless car would cause.

I keep thinking that there *has* to be a way for me to drive around during the day without attracting attention. I just need to figure it out, right? Like I had to figure out the mites' power needs and like I have to figure out "the money thing." I haven't panicked yet, but my unemployment runs out soon.

And then? As I said, it's just one more thing I need to figure out.

No pressure or anything.

***

If I thought the neighborhood was rid of Mateo, I was wrong. Yes, the cops came and hauled him away—and three days later, behind the wheel of a car that was way less cool than his Camaro, he was back.

So were some new faces.

Near sundown the same day, two cars roared into the cul-de-sac, their paint jobs understated but pricy, the throttling engines hinting at the horsepower under the hoods. I counted five men when they exited their parked cars; their movements were deliberate, calculated.

These were not Mateo's rowdy drinking buddies. This was not his crew.

Yes; their heads were shaved and the ink of their tats slithered out from the left side of their rounded t-shirt collars, but these men's faces were older and more experienced. Harder. Colder. They filed into Mateo's house.

Not once since calling the police on Mateo had I thought about the plastic-wrapped block sitting on his table. I did now.

Uh-oh.

Mateo would have to answer for the loss of whatever it was the police had confiscated.

My next thought was, *Where is Emilio?*

The sun had dropped all the way behind Albuquerque's West Mesa and night had cloaked our neighborhood in darkness when I snuck outside and down the sidewalk. I was alongside the shrubs bordering Abe's lot before I made out Emilio's huddled figure, burrowed into the bushes.

I was relieved. *As long as he's tucked in there, he should be okay,* I reasoned.

I turned and walked across Mateo's yard, up to his front windows. I cupped my hands and peered inside.

The mites didn't like it. I snubbed them, as usual.

Mateo was seated in a dining chair facing toward me. Four of the shaved-headed men stood behind him. The fifth—their leader?—was talking in a low, measured cadence.

I glanced at Mateo. I'd never seen him like this, face ashen, eyes bulging. He was scared for his life.

Then the suspected leader turned toward me. I flinched before I remembered he couldn't see me. And, of course, the guy wasn't looking *at* me, just in my general direction.

None of that mattered. I was instantly on my guard. What I saw when he turned confirmed my suspicion that I was indeed looking at the gang's new leader. His body language was confident, his face relaxed.

I didn't recognize the man; in fact, I'd never seen him before—but, oh! I knew that look, that expression. I knew those cold, dead eyes. They belonged to someone who enjoyed power and control, who felt no compassion or compunction when inflicting pain, who viewed emotion as a weakness to be exploited.

I wasn't seeing Genie, of course, but I may as well have been: Narcissism wears the same face everywhere.

And why was *I* privileged to have not *one*, not *two*, but *three* sociopaths in my life?

I strode back home stewing about "Dead Eyes," Mateo's new gang boss, and the damage he might cause our neighborhood. I worried, too, about Emilio.

Someone needs to help that kid.

The pat answer was CYFD. I could make an anonymous call easily enough. They would come out and do a home evaluation and take Emilio into custody. Anything would be better than this, right?

So why hadn't I called them?

They are just another underfunded, understaffed bureaucracy—and they've failed kids before. I know; it's been in the news. What if CYFD **doesn't** *take Emilio? They will tell Mateo they are responding to a complaint, and whether they take Emilio or not, Mateo will be furious. Will he take his anger out on Emilio?*

Then another alarm went off: How else might Mateo react if CYFD came calling? Would he take out his ire on the neighbors in our cul-de-sac? Except for me, all the neighbors were seniors, unable to stand up against Mateo. Would he threaten them?

Worse, would the scary new gang boss do something? I swallowed, cowed by the remembrance of his icy hardness. I abandoned the idea of calling CYFD.

Still, someone needed to look out for Emilio now that Corazón was gone.

Someone?

I was convinced that Aunt Lucy's voice had joined the nanomites and taken up permanent residence in my head: *We are "the someone," Gemma. When God puts a need in front of our face, do we cross the street and ignore it like the priest and the Levite, hoping that "someone" will take care of it? Or will we be the Good Samaritan and have a little compassion? Eh?* **We are "the someone," Gemma.**

I could keep feeding him, I supposed, but "the money thing" again raised its ugly head. For once I pushed concerns for myself aside. I went into my kitchen and took inventory.

Whatever I have I can share, I decided. *I'll figure the money thing out later.*

And I was no longer troubled about Emilio's suspicions of me. The kid, for all practical purposes, was less visible than I was. Who would listen to a boy's suspicions about his neighbor's "state of invisibility?" It was laughable.

While I was thinking on these things, I built Emilio a simple meal. I made sure to include something hot: half of a frozen pizza (I knew he liked pizza, right? and I'd save the other half to bake another time). I added an apple and a banana, a granola bar, a bottle of water, and another bottle re-filled with orange juice.

Next time I shop I'll pick up some small cartons of milk, I told myself.

I went back and forth about bringing him a blanket. I decided on a light but soft stadium throw. It would keep the chill off, but wouldn't be too bulky. I put it into a plastic bag, too.

The kid was still tucked back in the bushes when I took the meal and blanket out to him. The half pizza, hot out of the oven and taped between two paper plates, warmed my chest under my shirt. I walked past him, turned back, and slipped the food out from under my shirt. I set the things down on the sidewalk just out of his view. I let the sack with the bottles in it "thunk" as I set it down. I backed away.

His head popped out of the shrubs at the sound. He grabbed the sacks and then stared at the covered paper plate. The warm cheesy scent of pizza wafted toward me on the cool night air. With something akin to reverence, Emilio picked up the plate, sniffed, and sighed. He scooted back toward his hidey-hole.

And stopped.

"Thank you," he whispered.

I should have just edged away without answering. I should have.

But I didn't.

"You're welcome," I murmured.

***

Along with the money situation, my worries about General Cushing continued to grow. I obsessed about her, dreamed about her sharp, toothy smile. I feared this state of "being in the dark"—I hated not knowing if I were on her radar, if her people were closing in on me.

A few mornings later I climbed out of bed and discovered that a wild, hugely stupid idea I'd mentally tossed around had solidified: While I was sleeping I had decided that today I would put my crazy plan into action.

I tugged on my "quiet" shoes (already comfortably broken in) and headed out the door. I carried a pen and a small notebook in the back pocket of my jeans.

It was my first real venture out in broad daylight.

As I headed down the street, the sun caressed my shoulders and warmed my head. Oh, it felt good to be alive! My heart reveled in the Indian summer weather—week upon week of wonderful sun and mild temperatures before full-on summer gave way to fall. Something in the air and in the slant of the sun hinted at cooler weather approaching, and yet the day was intoxicatingly warm and languid.

I drank it in. I turned my face to the sun and bathed in its rays. I stretched out my legs and jogged part of the distance to my destination, keen to use my body after so many sedentary days spent inside.

The nanomites did not share my enthusiasm. They clicked and chittered at a furious rate. Perhaps, keeping me "optically invisible" was a struggle at the pace I was running. The thought of the mites performing gazillions of computations to make quadrillions of infinitesimal adjustments to trillions of tiny mirrors on an ongoing basis boggled my mind. It had to be a drain on the swarm's power supply. Nevertheless—

"That's *your* problem," I scoffed. "If you aren't up to the task, I suggest you vacate the premises." I shrugged off their disapproval and kept going.

They say that the adaptive power of the human body is astounding. I believe it. The mites' "vocalizations" in the back of my brain (that's the only way I can describe their sounds and where I heard them) pained me less and less each day. They were still annoying, but I realized that, *somehow, in some way*, my body was adjusting to the mites' presence and the pain their sounds caused. What had been a virtual IED exploding in my skull those first few days was now nothing more than a manageable irritation. At the rate things were progressing, I had hopes that the discomfort would lessen further and perhaps end altogether.

Yes, my body was adapting to the mites, and so were my emotions. I was less freaked out about being hidden by the mites and less concerned about "regular" people spotting the occasional brief shimmer as the mites worked their optical magic. At home I accommodated the mites' power needs without much thought, tethering myself to a new, longer, heavy-duty extension cord—as though such a thing were perfectly common. What had been unfathomable just weeks ago was my new norm.

Today, my major concern with the power situation was how long I could be away from direct electricity before the mites ran down their stored energy and started feeding on *me*. Like I said, I could only imagine how much power the mites were expending to keep me hidden out in the open—and I did not want a repeat of that first morning when I almost didn't wake up. I needed to better understand how the mites took in energy and what their storage limits were so I could plan my outings.

This day's venture would be relatively short and simple: I needed information but I did not want to use my own computer or phone (or any in the neighborhood) to get it. I was headed where I could get the info I needed without pointing to my whereabouts. While I was out in the glorious sunshine, I would also test the mites' ability to harness solar power.

Dr. Bickel had lectured me on nanomites' amazing energy capabilities, but how could he have imagined my current situation? I mean, just how good *were* the mites' solar receptors? Were they able to draw *all* the juice they needed from direct sunlight—or were they only able to pull a "trickle charge" from the sun? And would the energy outgo of keeping me hidden outstrip what they could take in during the same time period?

I hoped the amount of electricity the nanomites needed when we returned home would answer some of my questions. As I waltzed along, though, I felt fresh, renewed, invigorated. Practically euphoric!

I slowed and frowned. Was I enjoying the pleasure of being outdoors on such a gorgeous day after being cooped up for weeks? Or were the mites chockfull of energy—perhaps even overfull? Were they— Were they feeding the excess back to me?

Yikes.

Could the nanomites be passing their extra power over to me, actually *overfeeding* me? I had an unexpected and vivid image of *my poor body*, like substandard electrical wire with too much juice flowing through it, heating, smoldering, and bursting into flame.

Holy smokes!

Yes. Quite.

I came to a complete stop and slapped a palm to my forehead: It seemed cool to the touch. Normal, not feverish.

You're okay, I reassured myself. *You're okay.*

Six blocks later I ducked into a small café. I knew the owners, Jay and Bev. I knew they had an office off the café's dining room and that they had a computer and a phone on the office desk.

The breakfast rush was on, keeping Jay and Bev busy out front and over the grill. I timed my entrance into the café to coincide with the arrival of two customers, and caught the door before it started to close. I ducked in behind the new arrivals, sped across the dining room to Jay's office, and slipped inside.

I sat down, opened a browser window, and typed in Sandia's website URL. When it popped up I went to "Contacts" and the employee locator. Then I typed in "Cushing." If she were still at Sandia, even on a temporary basis, they would have her contact info listed here.

Two results came back. One of them was "I. B. Cushing" and included a phone number and mail stop.

Drat.

I suppose I'd held onto the whisper of a hope that Cushing would have slithered back to whatever federal rock she'd crawled out from under. The fact that she was still in Albuquerque, months after the accident and more than six weeks after the raid on Dr. Bickel's lab, did not reassure me. I thought for a few minutes before I picked up the nearby phone and dialed.

I was banking on Cushing not answering her own phone. However, just in case she did pick up the phone herself, I had a plausible wrong-number story at the ready.

I didn't need it.

"General Cushing's office. How may I direct your call?" The woman on the other end was young and efficient.

An intern, I decided, *or a young airman.* In my stiffest and most officious phone voice I replied, "This is Ms. Finch at the Pentagon calling on behalf of Colonel Markey. He has an appointment with the general next month. Would you please give me directions from the airport to her office?"

Without hesitation, the woman rattled off directions to me and I wrote them down. Or started to. I didn't have to finish.

The woman was sitting in Dr. Prochanski's old office.

"Thank you." I hung up and pondered my next move.

How like Shark Face to appropriate Dr. P's office to, *ostensibly,* oversee the lab accident investigation and reconstitute the AMEMS program—when in reality she'd been hunting Dr. Bickel.

She'd found Dr. Bickel but had lost the nanomites. She'd found Dr. Bickel but, if my dear, brilliant friend was to be believed, Cushing would never find his hidden data. Without his data, without knowledge of his ion printhead and the schematics to build one, she would be unable to make more nanomites.

All of the above would be unacceptable to the general, so what was she doing about it?

I needed to know.

I wove my way to the bustling café's exit and pushed my way out, reasoning that people came and went through that door all day long. If it looked as though it had opened from the outside yet no one actually came inside, who would care? People change their minds or stop to answer their phones all the time.

Yes, I was definitely growing more confident.

I walked home at a slower pace because I was planning my next "stealthy" steps. When I went inside, I picked up the extension cord out of habit and waited for the mites to attach and draw from it.

Nothing.

Or was that a resounding *burp* I heard?

After all the energy they'd expended to keep me invisible on the way to the café and back, the mites did not require any power?

I sank into my corner of the sofa to think on and catalogue this discovery.

The mites use solar power remarkably well, just as Dr. Bickel assured me they could. Apparently, they take in enough energy from direct sunlight to function well—more than enough to keep me hidden and keep their storage full.

As the implications of this discovery settled, a lot—no, a *world*—of possibilities opened before me. I breathed out a smile.

Of all those possibilities, my first would be to pay Shark Face a visit.

***

It was still dark when I backed my car out of the garage. My automatic door slid closed   quietly—at a press of the button clipped to my car's visor. I rolled out of our cul-de-sac, past Abe's house on the curve, and away from our neighborhood.

When I had worked on the base, I had used the Gibson Gate to enter. It was the most convenient base entrance from my house, although the MEMS and AMEMS labs were nearer to the Eubank Gate. Today, because I would be walking onto the base, the Eubank Gate was my choice.

I left downtown, merged onto I-25 north, and moved to the far right lane. I took the I-40 East ramp over "The Big I," that beautiful monstrosity of an interchange joining the bisecting interstate highways. Minutes later I exited I-40 at Eubank, drove south to Southern Boulevard, and pulled into the Costco parking lot on the corner of Eubank and Southern. The store would open soon and my car would blend in just fine there.

When I shut off the engine, I took a quick look around—and stepped out, closing the car door in a single quick, fluid move. My exit from the car created a two- or three-second window when someone *might* notice the door open and close with no one actually doing the opening and closing. The real trick would be driving home afterward. I would have to wait for twilight to cover me.

I jogged to the other side of Southern and then across Eubank, timing my moves to dodge the three lanes of commuters already backed up from the base entrance. I set a brisk pace toward the gate, about half a mile ahead.

I took a long look at the gate activity before ducking through the pedestrian entry. It felt strange and exciting, knowing that the airmen checking base passes (some fiercely alert, others equally bored) couldn't see me. I grinned and crossed over to the island separating incoming and outgoing traffic inside the gate.

At the light I cut across the street and paused.

I again watched the stop-and-go traffic coming through the gate. It was fully morning now, and all around me surged the familiar bustle—thousands of people making their way onto the base for another work day. I missed it. I missed earning my way in life and missed feeling that I was a part of something as big as this, even if my contribution had been an insignificant sliver. The only things I *didn't* miss were the bureaucracy and political baloney.

Those I don't miss, I chuckled to myself.

My former office was a short walk ahead. I hung around outside my old building, waiting for an employee to swipe his building access card and pull open the door. A man I didn't recognize obliged me. I caught the door just before it closed behind him and, as soon as the man was far enough down the hall, I followed him through and allowed the door to close and lock.

Of course, I knew my way to Dr. Prochanski's former office. I walked on, confident of my surroundings.

I wasn't, however, prepared to see the woman sitting at my desk. In my chair. I should have been, should have been emotionally ready, but the sight of her stuck in my craw.

She was maybe in her forties and, I thought unkindly, had a mop of black, hideous, over-processed hair. The primal, almost *visceral* urge to yank Miss Usurper from that seat—by the front of her teased-up hair!—took me by surprise. I plopped down in one of the utilitarian chairs near a big planter and gave myself a good scolding.

Not your job anymore, Gemma, I lectured. *Not your desk, not your chair, not your computer, not your business. **Not your circus, not your monkeys**. Get your focus back on the task at hand!*

I swallowed and nodded in agreement, got up and waltzed by the woman. I stuck my tongue out as I passed. I'm not proud of that juvenile act, but I'll admit to it.

The voice I heard echoing down the hall wiped away all feelings toward Miss Usurper. Just as sickeningly sweet, just as deadly, I heard, "Ms. Barela, please come in here."

Ms. Barela jumped as though she'd been shot, grabbed a pad and pen and, her heels clicking on the floor, headed toward General Cushing's office. I stepped out of her way.

She grunted a *very* unflattering comment about the general as she breezed by me, and I just about choked on a giggle. I traipsed at a safe distance behind Ms. Barela, my feelings toward her much improved, and stopped at the doorway to Cushing's office.

Ms. Barela composed herself and entered the general's office. "Yes, ma'am?"

"Call a meeting with my team in thirty minutes. Tell them not to be late."

"Yes, General. Anything else, ma'am?"

"No, not at this time."

Ms. Barela clicked her way back to her desk, grumbling under her breath, and began making phone calls. I listened for a while, but I was distracted, thinking that my timing couldn't have been better.

She's calling her team in for a meeting and will ask for updates, I reasoned. Shark Face didn't know it, but I was going to sit in on that meeting, too.

"Well, I can't help it if you're forty minutes away, Jeff," Ms. Barela insisted. "*She* just now called the meeting."

Ah, yes, I purred. *We're nominating General Imogene Cushing for Boss of the Year!*

Said no one, ever.

I hung around until Cushing's team straggled in. I followed them into the same, *the very same* conference room with which I was so familiar. The unfortunate Jeff pulled up the rear, only three minutes late.

He must have ignored all speed limits, I laughed to myself. I took a seat on the far end of the room, away from the other participants, and made myself comfortable.

The mites, I suddenly realized, were being very quiet—that almost complete quiet when they were "confabbing" or being cautious. I heard only the occasional click or buzz rather than the continuous background hum to which I'd grown accustomed.

Cushing smiled at Jeff as he tried to slip into the room without attracting her attention. "*Thank you* for your presence, Mr. Black."

No one sniggered or cracked a grin. Shark Face's jokes weren't the "joining in" kind. Jeff kept his eyes down and took his seat, duly chastened.

"Well, now. Let's begin, shall we? With you, Mr. Black."

Already off balance, the ill-fated Jeff stammered as he gave his update. Cushing's eyes gleamed with pleasure.

She's enjoying that poor guy's embarrassment, I scowled, empathizing with his discomfort. And as Jeff's report contained nothing of interest to me, I lost myself daydreaming of upset water glasses—or perhaps cups of hot coffee—landing, *inexplicably,* in Cushing's lap.

With one ear I listened to two men update their surveillance of Rick and Tony, heard three scientists report on their ongoing analysis of Dr. Bickel's data (and a disappointing analysis it was), and another three provide a status on the nanobots removed from the AMEMS lab before it exploded.

The accounting of the nanobots (Dr. Bickel's "dumb" bots) was unfavorable, to say the least. With each test result the lead scientist outlined, Cushing's mouth thinned and tightened. It wasn't until the man glanced up and perceived how white and hard her face had grown that his recitation petered out.

I enjoyed watching Cushing's frustration, but I had learned nothing new. It was all information I already had.

The next report had to do with Dr. Bickel's finances—and that earned my complete attention. A man holding a thick folder read from it. "We have dissected Bickel's finances including a number of shell companies and interests through which he operated. He was able to hide many of his activities, but we have uncovered the majority, if not all of them. However, we have not, as yet, identified any local financial connections or resources he may have relied upon, other than the home in which he lived and his work associations, none of which point to accomplices."

I was relieved for Rick and Tony—and for myself—to hear this man's report. So far, this meeting was turning out to be quite reassuring, and I was just toying with how I might empty a basket of soggy coffee grounds onto Cushing's head (and get away with it), when a Miss Trujillo spoke. "We've traced the backpack we found in the lab to REI, ma'am. Definitively."

"Really, Miss Trujillo? Please continue." Cushing's mouth relaxed and her lips curved over sharp teeth.

Backpack? My heart stuttered to a standstill. I hadn't been able to find the backpack I'd bought at REI.

Hide Gemma!

I had a clear memory of the nanomites striking and invading me during Cushing's attack on the lab, but had no further recollections until I'd awakened outside the mountain. The mites had somehow propelled me to the escape cleft in the wall and I'd stumbled through the maze to my outside exit on the mountain—but I had not been wearing the backpack when I'd come to.

With that realization, I turned cold. And remembered.

I emptied the backpack and left it near the stacks of furniture not far from my exit—for me to retrieve on my way out. Just as I always did!

Was there any possibility they could trace the backpack's purchase to me? I licked my suddenly dry lips and leaned forward.

"We've narrowed the purchase period to late June, but we have encountered, er, a delay in going further," the stoic Miss Trujillo reported.

"Explain, please." Cushing was no longer smiling and the group in the room, as one, stilled.

"The transaction was cash, not credit card," Miss Trujillo murmured.

"Store video surveillance?"

"Too far back, ma'am. The files were overwritten. And the clerk we believe served in the transaction no longer works for REI. She has gone off to school, possibly to Europe."

I well remembered the young clerk who had waited on me. We'd talked about her year of painting in France and Italy, how excited she'd been to receive the scholarship to go. Would she remember me?

I already knew the answer.

"What are you doing to find her?" Cushing snapped.

"Ah, um, we only received that information late yesterday and hope to speak with her stateside family today, ma'am."

"You *hope*?"

"I will make the connection today, ma'am," Miss Trujillo corrected.

"I want this effort expedited. It's ridiculous that *this team* overlooked the backpack for weeks. If required, you have my authority to use the entire team to trace the backpack's owner—but bring me results."

"Yes, ma'am."

It was easier getting out of the building than it had been to get in. I just pushed the door open—no access card needed. I stood in the parking lot staring off into the distance, mulling over all I'd heard but, in particular, Cushing's last words: *It's bad enough that this team overlooked the backpack for weeks. Bring me results.*

Had they only recently found the backpack or only lately grasped its significance? Either way, they had in their hands the means to identify me. How long did I have until they did so?

I was still woefully ill-equipped to flee. I estimated that I had, at the most, a few days more to prepare. I would make them count.

After several minutes of contemplating my next moves, I came to myself. I was staring east toward the mountain. Its sloping sides and rounded peaks were painted by the morning's bright sun, making it appear less daunting than it was up close.

Only weeks, really, had passed since I had last climbed the mountain. As I studied it, I was gripped by an intense desire to return, to see what was left of Dr. Bickel's lab.

And why not? Unless Cushing captured me, I could pretty much go anywhere I wanted.

⌘⌘⌘⌘

CHAPTER 20

I drove at a slow, steady speed into the residential area and parked on the same side street I'd used before, the one where I'd found my car on my last trip down the mountain. I crouched between my car and the retaining wall where I was parked and slid my old rucksack over my shoulders. In it I'd packed my leather gloves and "quiet" shoes, three bottles of water, and some lightweight foods: nuts, protein bars, some fruit leather.

Over the top of my clothes and the rucksack I drew on one of Uncle Eduardo's baggy shirts. As the shirt settled on my shoulders and over my body, it disappeared from view, hiding the rucksack beneath it. I slipped out from where I was hiding and into the dusky early light, and moved toward the trailhead.

I had driven here in the dark morning hours. Regardless of when I returned to my car, I could not drive home until after night fell. It would be another long day.

Yesterday, I'd returned home late from eavesdropping on Cushing's meeting, and I'd spent the evening in frenetic preparations. I'd packed and repacked my two bug-out bags, including every dollar of my meager store of cash.

Then I'd handwritten a cryptic note to Abe asking him to take care of Jake. I'd started that note a couple of different times. I'd torn up and burned four failed starts before settling on just the right wording.

Early this morning, after a night short on sleep (and restless sleep at that), I'd thrown my laptop and bug-out bags into my trunk—just in case Cushing's people were waiting when I returned home. From now on, I would keep those items near me, accessible at all times.

The morning lightened, and I avoided others on the trail, stepping aside and standing still until they passed by. I especially steered clear of folks walking their dogs. I bore the scratches of Jake's freaked-out response to my invisible self; I didn't want to see how a large dog might react.

I knew the route by heart and made good time. I scrabbled on my belly under the piñon, down into the arroyo, and under the base's perimeter fence.

I stood up on the other side and exhaled. It was easier making my solitary way toward the mountain than sharing a path with other hikers had been. While I hiked, the nanomites hummed softly and drank in a hefty dose of morning solar power.

I wasn't worried out here in the base's restricted area. No one would notice me or see my flitting shadow. If I happened to run into a base patrol, I would hunker down until they were gone.

I followed the familiar landmarks until I arrived at the PIDAS and lined myself up with the three rocks. I crossed the road and started across the bare dirt toward the fence. Up to now, the mites had been quietly observant. When their nervous chitters broke in, I looked back—and spied the source of their concern: *tracks.*

The mites were able to disguise my footprints where I presently stood, but not my prints farther back—and on the bare, smooth dirt in broad daylight my footprints shouted "intruder!" It was a disconcerting moment, encountering yet another limitation to my invisibility.

Just as I had when I was still visible, I would need to brush away my tracks.

I trotted back, broke off a branch of sagebrush, scuffed my footprints from the road up to the fence line—and stared in dumb wonder at the repaired links in the fence where I'd passed through before.

They (whoever "they" were) had found and repaired the cuts Rick had made in the fence. I pondered this development. No one had reported on this in Cushing's meeting, but they had to know about it. They must have found the point of my incursion early on. Had they also found the door into the tunnels?

I almost turned around right then. I almost ran. Instead, I scanned the area and made myself wait, think, and evaluate.

Were Cushing's people watching the tunnels, waiting for me to return? It stood to reason, but I questioned why no one on Cushing's team had given her an update yesterday if, indeed, her team *was* watching this route into the mountain. Maybe, with this much time gone by, they figured no one was coming back.

No one stupid enough to come back.

I fingered the welded links as I debated whether or not to abort my trek up the mountain.

A light sparked from near my fingertips and I yanked my hand back. Was the fence now electrified? But no, I would have heard its hum as I'd approached if it were, wouldn't I?

The mites, who had been so quiet until warning me about my footprints, clamored for my attention again. I leaned toward the fence and was shocked to see that one of the repaired links looked to be half severed. Without thinking, I reached out to touch it—and again a bright light jumped from my fingertips.

The link snapped apart and I stumbled backwards, landing on my backside in the dirt. I stayed there—recalling Dr. Bickel's lecture on the nanomites.

Members of Delta Tribe each have a tiny laser. Only Delta Tribe.

Were the nanomites "lasering" through the links? I approached the fence again. I hesitated and then stretched my hand toward it, pointing my index finger at the next link up.

A blink later the link "popped." It was sliced through.

Excited about the ability to cut through metal, I was lifting my finger toward the next link, when I remembered what else Dr. Bickel had said about Delta Tribe's lasers.

When connected to an uninterrupted energy source, the nanocloud can generate and direct a laser beam strong enough to cut through steel. It takes them a few moments to bring the laser up to power, but they are quite efficient.

Uninterrupted? Would their solar receptors create enough of an "uninterrupted power source" to prevent the nanocloud from feeding on me? Not for one second did I place any confidence in the mites' altruistic principles: They were programmed to consider the welfare of the cloud above all. I stood there thinking so long that the mites' sudden chatter startled me.

"All right, all right." I elected to keep going, but if I felt at all unwell, I vowed to turn tail and retreat.

I pointed at the next links and Delta Tribe's lasers made short work of them. Before I pushed through the fence, I brushed away the imprint of my backside in the dirt, dragging the sagebrush branch with me. I shoved the fence links into alignment and tidied up around the area.

Walked to the next fence: Rinse and repeat.

Pretty cool, actually.

I felt my forehead. Maybe it would be all right after all. The mites didn't seem to be slowing down or struggling and I felt fine.

Ahead the climb steepened, but I was energized and invigorated. Thirty minutes later, breathing hard but jubilant, I reached the rock outcropping and clambered over and around until I jumped down behind the largest pillar.

Angry rattling caught me utterly unprepared: A snake lay coiled not far from my feet, its thick body poised, tensed, its flat head reared back.

I had nowhere to retreat.

"Nano," I breathed.

I heard them, not clicking or chittering, but humming. The hum grew louder. And then it rose with an intensity that blocked the sound of the snake's rattles, so shrill and loud that my eyes throbbed.

I blinked just as the snake launched itself toward me. A white light surged from my body, converged in a single point in the air, shot forward, and burst.

The smell!

All I could see were bright dots dancing in front of my eyes, but *the smell*! It was ghastly—like burnt hair and seared, scorched rubber all in one. I coughed and gagged on the smoke of it. When the air cleared and my watering eyes could focus, I stared at the snake's charcoaled and still-smoldering carcass:

Two piles of it.

Neatly severed.

Immolated.

Giving Elijah and the prophets of Baal a run for their money.

Other inane nonsense jittered around in my head.

*And how would you like your steak—er, **snake**, sir?*

Well done, please.

And this ridiculous ditty: *If it's smokin' we're cookin'; if it's black, it's done.*

"Nano. Thank you," I whispered. I squeezed past the snake's remains, reluctant to let my feet even graze them.

I stumbled around the wall's curve and fell against the iron door. It could have been Aunt Lucy's shoulder, so glad was I to lean upon a familiar friend. I sobbed with relief and tried not to dwell on what had almost happened, but that one blink, that single frame of the snake's heavy body hurtling toward me kept flashing in front of my eyes.

Eventually I calmed. I drank a bottle of water. I cried a little more. I wiped my face and eyes. Then I put my right hand's fingers on the top right corner of the door and kicked the lower left corner with the toe of my boot.

And went into the tunnels.

Inside it was still. Quiet. My first impression was that no one had been inside the doorway since the last time I'd been here—not that I remembered leaving by this door the last time I'd left the mountain. My exit that night had been accomplished under some kind of autopilot.

I stepped inside the mountain's secret door and watched the mechanism shoot the locking bolts home. After a quick look around, I unlaced my boots and donned the pair of soft-soled shoes I wore when I was out sneaking around in public. I left my boots by the door.

As I trod down the first tunnel, nothing seemed disturbed or changed from before. By the time I entered the large, main tunnel I was more certain that no one but me had gone in or out by the ironclad door behind the outcropping, but that didn't mean they hadn't found the cleft where I entered the lab. I still had a way to go.

I reached the beam and squeezed through the hole behind it then crouched and listened. I heard nothing but the utter silence of the tunnels. I started forward, very glad I was wearing my soft-soled shoes.

The tunnel began its steep, downward descent. I never had liked the feeling of going deeper into the mountain, the sensation of the mountain's weight pressing down upon me, the unsettling impression of the air growing thin and the tunnel walls closing in on me.

It was no different this time. My nerves were on edge. The mites, perhaps feeling my disquiet, hummed softly in my ear.

I regulated my breathing, kept it slow and steady, and counted my steps as a distraction. I had not gone far when the narrow beam of my flashlight glanced off an object lying on the tunnel floor.

Nothing should be here! Had my instincts been wrong?

I scanned the light over the floor until it fell again upon the object against the tunnel wall. It was a book, lying open with its pages face down. I stared . . .

"Dr. Bickel's lab book!" My whisper filled the tunnel and then floated away. I bent and retrieved the precious record. Several pages were bent and dirtied. I smoothed them as best I could and then tucked the book into my backpack.

My heart still hammered in my chest, but it was slowing, returning to normal. I wiped a shaking hand over my eyes.

I had to have dropped his lab book myself. This proves that Cushing did not find this route. She wouldn't have left it here.

I moved forward cautiously, but my senses told me that I was alone in the tunnel. The nanomites, too, were quiet. When I, at last, emerged into the lab, I was convinced that Cushing's people had not found my entrance to the mountain.

The lights ringing the cavern still dimly illuminated the open space and, although I knew it to be impossible, I felt as though Dr. Bickel had to be close by. I wended through the stacks of old furnishings from the sixties and toward the lab.

The remains of Dr. Bickel's small but meticulously organized laboratory lay smashed and broken on the cavern floor. I wandered through the ruin and observed that some of the equipment was missing. Intact parts may have survived Cushing's warmongers and been taken away, but all that remained now were fragments and broken pieces.

Shattered glass covered the floor where the nanocloud's case had stood. The mites chipped a little, but not much. They had to know where we were.

Were they mourning as I was?

Swiping away tears, I made my way over to Dr. Bickel's old living quarters. His desk had been emptied, his computers removed. The desk lay on its side, riddled with holes. His tiny bedroom was stripped. Workers had brought in cinder blocks and cement and bricked up Dr. Bickel's exit to the munitions bunker on the west side of the mountain.

I wandered into his little kitchen, opening cupboards, drawers, and refrigerator. I don't know what I was looking for.

Yes, I guess I did. I was looking for him, for Dr. Bickel. I knew I would not find him. I was longing for the sense of family we'd shared during that summer: two souls without kin who'd found kinship during my infrequent visits to the mountain. I was looking for the kindness Dr. Bickel had shown me in his simple way. They'd removed his body and I would not find him or recapture the sweetness of those days, not here, not anywhere.

I'd lost my parents. I'd lost Aunt Lu. I'd lost Dr. Bickel. I had nothing left I could lose—except my freedom.

Cushing will not get that, I vowed.

I slammed the refrigerator door, yanked open the freezer, and gasped: After nearly two months, the twin parfait glasses were still lovely. I could even make out the strawberries and kiwi slices pressed against the lightly frosted sides.

Grief and anger, long suppressed, refused to stay stuffed inside any longer. Swinging my arms, I swept the counter clean, sending dishes crashing to the floor. Whatever my hands found, I threw against the rock walls. I yelled. I cursed. I screamed at Cushing while I demolished what remained of Dr. Bickel's kitchen.

I pitched a fit even Genie would have been proud of—until, sobbing, I sank to the rock floor of the kitchen. And then I fell into an exhausted sleep against the refrigerator door.

Perhaps an hour later, I woke and rose from the floor. I felt better for having released the pain I'd not allowed myself to feel before. Something else, though, had lodged in my heart during the torrent, something hard and angry. I had only one bitter word to describe it: *Cushing.*

I stretched my cramped muscles and headed toward my exit. I'd seen what I'd come to see and would not return here. As I bypassed the ruined lab area, I wondered why *Cushing* kept power on to the cavern since she had plundered all it offered.

Perhaps she sends her lackeys here every so often, I mused, *to reexamine the place, maybe to bring in fresh eyes to look it over.*

I had another thought: *Maybe she thinks the nanomites could still be here in the cavern, still hiding. They would need power to survive—and they're no good to her 'dead.'*

At the cleft in the wall, I took my last look at Dr. Bickel's lab. I nodded to myself, feeling that anger growing fiercer, my resolve hardening. Everything pointed to Cushing, to her continued search for the nanomites. She still intended to find them, capture them. Misuse them.

"Over my dead body," I whispered.

⌘⌘⌘⌘

CHAPTER 21

I stood in front of my kitchen window surveying the cul-de-sac and neighborhood, still chewing on what I'd overheard in Cushing's meeting and what I'd seen in Dr. Bickel's old lab under the mountain.

Cushing has no idea where the nanomites are, but she is close to zeroing in on me—and if she finds me, she finds them.

The pressing reality of my situation was clear: I needed to leave.

To leave meant to go elsewhere. "Elsewhere" implied a real place and a "real place" required planning and money.

I needed more money, and I needed it desperately—and yet I was as good as broke.

One bit of information I'd picked up during Cushing's meeting had given me hope—although it hadn't dawned on me until a few minutes ago: Cushing's team had not found Dr. Bickel's safe house. His online purchases had been delivered to that house, and Cushing's team had made no mention of it. Was it still undiscovered?

The pounding beat of loud music heralded the arrival of our least-popular neighbor. Mateo rounded the curve in his Camaro and zipped into his driveway. I was surprised to see the muscle car since I assumed Corazón had done exactly as I'd told her and had abandoned Mateo's prized vehicle at the Sunport's departures gate. Airport security would have towed the car and placed it in impound.

Mateo had driven a much humbler vehicle for a number of weeks. Now, obviously, he'd located the Camaro and gotten it out of hock.

I wonder how much he paid in impound fees? A sardonic grin tugged at the corner of my mouth. It wasn't nice of me, but "not nice" was growing on me.

I smiled, too, at the Mateo who stalked up his front steps. He was a changed man, meaning he'd gone down in the world since the day of his arrest. I loved that word "gone" as it applied to Mateo: Gone was his crew. Gone was his old swagger. Gone were the wild parties he used to throw.

Yup, he's definitely been demoted, I gloated. I assumed his demotion was due to Corazón's departure with the drug money and the police visit afterward, confiscating that block of drugs.

Can't say I was sorry.

All we need "gone" now is Mateo himself.

Mateo slammed the Camaro's door behind him and hurried into the house. My eyes searched for Emilio and didn't find him. The kid was clever at keeping out of Mateo's way.

He stayed out of the house whenever Mateo was home and returned when he was away—and Mateo was away most nights lately, leaving at twilight, not returning home until the early hours of the morning.

Eyes narrowed, I mused, *Where does he go? What does he do all night?* Whatever his nocturnal activities consisted of, I was convinced they would not be legal.

My memory of a box crammed with money and of Corazón dumping that money into her handbag was quite vivid.

Money. A little notion slithered into my head. It was a bold little notion, an audacious idea. An idea I entertained only because of the circumstances pressing in on me.

***

Mateo left his house about the same time each night. When his Camaro backed out of his driveway late the next evening, my nondescript old beater was already parked on a curb down the street. To anyone passing by, my car was empty.

The pumping bass signaled his approach. When he flashed by me, I turned on my engine and followed.

It wasn't hard keeping up with him. Mateo drove without caution, without care, his music blaring. He hit Central and turned left, away from downtown. He drove for miles until he was way west of downtown.

I stayed far enough back that I didn't think he would notice me. It wasn't until the traffic began thinning that I started worrying. That's when Mateo turned off his music and slowed. I figured the closer we got to his destination, the more care he would take.

I think I was right.

We turned south and drove a couple more miles. The surrounding area grew darker and more derelict. More oppressed-feeling. I hadn't known that Albuquerque had neighborhoods this bad: boarded up homes, abandoned vehicles, no streetlights, trash everywhere. I stepped off the gas and slowed, letting my car fall even farther back.

Up ahead, in the middle of the next block, Mateo turned into an alley. I knew it would be insane to follow him down the block. Instead, I came to a stop and slowly drove in reverse. At the first corner, I made a quick right turn followed by another right.

I parked on a curb, out of sight should Mateo double back. I didn't like leaving my vehicle where it was, but I didn't have much choice.

I got out and patted the empty shopping bags under my oversized shirt. Satisfied, I retraced my route on foot, trotted farther down the block, and crept into the alley's mouth.

I heard whispers right away, Mateo's and someone else's. I froze in place.

"I'm telling you, someone was following me."

"What you want me to do?"

"I want you to keep *two* guys posted here all night, that's what. Any car comes by and slows down, you send one guy back to me."

"Okay. I'll get Héctor."

The voices moved away from me and I followed. I couldn't see them very well, but they couldn't see me either. I kept the whispers ahead of me until I saw a crack of faint light.

They'd opened a door. The door slammed behind them, cutting off the voices.

I walked by the door and tried to get a sense of the building they'd entered. I stole down the alley to where the building ended. I thought it was an old store of some sort, completely fenced, all the windows heavily barred and darkened.

The nanomites were silent. Perhaps they knew by now that once I'd made my mind up, nothing they did could change it. Maybe they had come to the conclusion that "fighting" me at this time and in this place would only make what I was doing more dangerous —and they would be right.

I didn't need any distractions right now.

I slunk back to the door and waited. Héctor and the other guy would be coming out soon.

They did. When the door opened, I was ready. I slid in behind them as they sauntered through it, so close to them that I could smell them, feel the heat of their bodies as I slipped inside.

"What was that?" one of the men whispered.

"What was what?"

I didn't hear the rest. The door closed behind me and I was inside.

I crept away from the door and through a short, dim hallway. At the end of the hall hung a thick curtain of fabric strips that screened out light from the next room. I peeked into the room and then stepped through the curtain and immediately to the side.

A man cradling some kind of short rifle in his arms jerked his head up and frowned at the curtain's movement. When he saw nothing further, he turned his attention elsewhere.

Dear Reader, I'd never been in a drug house before, so I don't know what I expected. I mean, I'd caught glimpses of meth houses on *Breaking Bad* (not a show I'd recommend or that I watched regularly), but I hadn't been around drugs in real life. I scanned the room to get my bearings.

239

For one thing, I hadn't expected it to be so hot in there. Miserably hot. The building was just one long main room, and every window was sealed shut, covered in sheets of cardboard and strips of duct tape. Ratty, threadbare curtains hung over the cardboard.

Men and women, their mouths and noses covered with dust masks, lined a row of perhaps three tables, placed end-to-end. Each worker had two plates of powder in front of him or her, and they scooped, measured, and mixed the two powders together, and spooned exact amounts into tiny baggies.

The workers placed their filled baggies on a nearby tray that was then passed to a woman who weighed the baggies, zipped them closed, and laid them in small boxes. The work was conducted under the watchful eyes of two armed gangbangers, one at either end of the table.

At a desk over on the other end of the room, two men huddled over a laptop and some kind of machine. One of the men periodically came to the table and collected the small boxes of bagged drugs. Then he would enter numbers into the laptop and hand the drugs off to someone else.

Three additional armed gang members stood watch at various points around the room. All the guards had shaved heads and ink creeping up the left side of their necks. All of them wore the same stony expressions. The guards cradling guns kept their eyes on the workers at the tables, the guys at the desk, and even the two guards at either end of the tables.

More important to me than the guards and the workers at the tables was Mateo. His arms folded across his chest, he observed everything.

And I watched him.

Mateo is in charge here, I decided. What I had planned would likely get him in trouble with Dead Eyes. For a second time.

Mentally I shrugged. I had no compassion to spare for him.

I slipped over to the two men huddled at the desk. Their laptop was connected to the machine, and they were feeding cash into the machine. It shuffled and counted the money and logged it in a spreadsheet on the laptop.

It was all very organized and efficient.

I wandered around in the main room, familiarizing myself with its layout and with Mateo's operation. After watching for a while, I'd noted a restroom and a second door not far from the restroom. I didn't know yet where this second door led.

When a worker needed to use the restroom, he or she had to raise a hand. One of the guards checked that the worker had not hidden any drugs on his person. A guard waved the worker toward the restroom and watched until he returned.

Built into the same wall as the restroom door was a disgustingly filthy kitchenette where the guards got coffee. The coffeepot's glass sides were pretty much black from frequent use and little washing. The kitchenette's sink wasn't much better than the coffeepot. I thought dying of thirst preferable to drinking from the sink's grimy faucet.

Only the one entrance, I also noted. The single entrance/exit simplified the gang's security but turned the building into a death trap for the workers. The whole setup was pretty appalling. The men and women sitting at the table might have agreed to do the illegal work, but I couldn't believe they had agreed to the slave conditions I witnessed.

I didn't want to put any of the workers at risk. I knew Mateo returned home in the wee hours of the morning. I assumed he left at the end of his "shift."

So I waited. I sat down against a wall near an unused corner of the room. I'd been out in the night, away from a power source for a while. I placed my hand over a nearby wall outlet and let the mites feed.

After I'd squatted in the corner for about hour, the two men at the counting table signaled Mateo. I stood, stretched, and sidled over to them. They handed a block of money wrapped in clear plastic wrap to Mateo. He studied the laptop's screen then took the money toward the other door not far from the restroom. I followed right behind.

Mateo opened the door. It led to a simple closet—but the closet housed a safe. The safe stood about five feet tall and, by the looks of it, had to weigh a ton. I peered over Mateo's shoulder as he dialed in the combination.

The door to the safe swung open and Mateo placed the block of cash on a shelf about halfway up the interior of the safe. The shelf already held wrapped blocks of money. Lots of them. The safe had another shelf above the money. I counted a couple of handguns and boxes of ammunition on the top shelf.

My glance dropped to the floor of the safe. As I said, it was a big safe. Four boxes were stacked on the safe's floor. I didn't know what was in them. Just then, Mateo closed the safe's door and twirled the combination dial.

I backed away from the closet. Even when the night's work was over, I was sure they would not leave the money unguarded, but at least the workers would be out of the way. So now, it was just a matter of waiting for the workers to go home.

I returned to my corner. The heat in the room got worse as the night wore on. All those bodies and no ventilation.

Phew!

I kept my head up and tried to remain vigilant. It was hard.

The workers kept packaging the drugs. Gang members I tagged as "runners" moved in and out of the building, bringing money in and taking drugs out. When money arrived, the two men at the counting table put the bills in the machine, packaged them, and handed the blocks to Mateo, who checked the entry logged on the laptop, opened the safe, and stacked the money inside. I watched over his shoulder as he deposited the money.

Around four in the morning, Mateo gestured with his chin at the guards watching the drug packaging process. One of the guards rapped the butt of his gun on the table. The workers finished what they were doing and, one by one, stood up, pushed in their chairs, and waited behind them—like a bunch of schoolchildren at dismissal time.

This "school" had no dismissal bell, though, and the "children" waited with their hands in the air. The two "table guards," under the watchful eyes of the other three guards, searched each worker. As soon as a guard cleared a worker, he or she lined up by the door. No one spoke, not even in whispers.

I pushed myself up from the floor and maneuvered toward the exit so I could better observe what was going on. The line of workers held the curtain of fabric strips aside and I was able to see out the entrance. Through the open door I watched a group of the workers file into a van. When the van was full, it sped off. A second van pulled forward. The remaining workers loaded into the van and it, too, departed.

The guards secured the remaining plates of drugs on the table. They poured the leftovers back into a plastic sack lining a box—a box that looked a lot like the boxes stacked on the floor of the safe.

When the powder had been returned to the sack, one guard tied the sack with a twist tie, and closed up the box. Mateo opened the safe and placed the box atop the other four boxes on the floor of the safe. He closed the safe and directed a few last-minute cleanup details.

A sense of urgency gripped the room. Mateo barked orders to his men who rushed to complete them. Mateo sat down and studied the screen on the laptop while the others scurried around finishing up. I hung near Mateo, trying to read the laptop's screen. Mateo made a few notations in the file and then a printer behind us whirred, spitting out a single sheet of paper.

The outside door opened, and the men cleaning up froze. Even Mateo stilled. Instinctively, I backed away and shrank into "my" corner of the room. The nanomites chittered nervously.

Mateo and his men stood to attention as two guys I recognized strode into the room. The hair on my arms and the back of my neck rose. That's when I knew who was right behind them.

Dead Eyes followed his guards into the drug house. The other two men I'd seen with Dead Eyes when I'd peeked into Mateo's living room window brought up the rear.

Neither Mateo nor his crew moved. No one even twitched. Every face was shuttered as the gang's new leader swept the room with his cold gaze, noting every detail, missing nothing.

When Dead Eyes sauntered up to Mateo, Mateo swallowed and offered the printed sheet to him. No words were spoken. Dead Eyes scanned the sheet and jutted his chin toward the closet. Mateo opened the closet, then the safe. He removed the blocks of money and the box of unpackaged drugs and placed them on one of the tables.

Dead Eyes pointed with his chin again, this time at one of his men. The man took the sheet of paper from his boss and scanned the stacks of money, touching each bundle, counting as he did so. He inspected the box of drugs. He looked at the paper and then to Dead Eyes and nodded his affirmation.

Dead Eyes studied Mateo, and I, from my vantage in the corner behind him, shuddered. Mateo somehow managed to bear the scrutiny with no visible emotion other than the sweat beading on the back of his neck and shaved head.

"I'll pick up this week's take tomorrow, same time." It was the first time I'd heard Dead Eye's voice, and my skin crawled. "I expect the quota to be met."

"It will be," Mateo replied.

"It will be, *what*?"

Mateo cleared his throat. "It will be, *sir*."

Dead Eyes leveled his killing scowl at Mateo. Mateo kept his eyes down, as though meeting Dead Eyes' look might fry him. I don't think he was breathing anymore. I wasn't.

The tense moment lingered until, with a last jerk of his chin, Dead Eyes and his guards ambled toward the store's entrance. The door slammed behind them, and I heard the very faint sound of an engine starting and then fading away.

A palpable sense of relief washed over the room. Mateo pulled a kerchief from his jeans and wiped the back of his neck. He said something to one of the men and his crew shared in a nervous laugh.

Three new guards entered the store and reported to Mateo. They appeared fresh and rested. Everyone else prepared to leave. The atmosphere had all the markers of a shift change: Mateo was leaving the gang's place of business in the hands of these three guards.

That would work for me. I could handle three guards.

Mateo snapped a few last-minute instructions and strode out the door. The rest of his crew, excepting the three guards, followed him. With the departure of all but the new guards, the room stilled. The guards made a pot of coffee and talked together in quiet tones. One of them said something and they all laughed.

I was growing tired from the long night, and I yawned. The coffee smelled heavenly as it brewed. I again squatted in the corner. I didn't have to wait much longer. The men poured coffee into travel mugs and secured the lids. They shouldered their guns and headed for the door. I got up and followed behind.

That's when things went a bit amiss.

I had *assumed* they would take up their posts outside but leave the door unlocked. Even if they locked it, I figured I could unlock the door from inside.

I had figured wrong. The lock was keyed on both sides. They closed and locked the store from the outside—leaving me locked inside.

You idiot!

I railed on myself for not checking the lock as I'd snuck inside the evening before. Already expecting the attempt to be futile, I turned the door's handle anyway, taking care to make no noise. The deadbolt, as I'd known it would be, was in place and the door did not budge. I rubbed my tired eyes and tried not to panic.

It's just a matter of time, I reasoned, assuaging my anxiety. *Someone will come back inside to get more coffee or use the restroom. I just need to wait and not freak out.* But my plans were falling to pieces.

A wisp tickled my cheek. Even as I instinctively brushed the sensation from my face, I understood what it was.

A tiny blue spark spurted from the keyhole followed by an audible click: The door had unlocked.

"Nano. Thank you," I whispered. All my suspicions as to whether or not the mites occasionally helped me had vanished on the mountain with the epic operation now code-named "Serpent Sauté."

Whether or not they "approved" my sometimes-rash actions, the nanomites were proving themselves to be my protectors, if not my allies. I decided that I needed to reconsider our evolving situation when I got home, perhaps even again attempt to communicate with the mites.

But first I needed to *get* home—and before that, I wanted to accomplish what I'd come here to do.

I raced into the main room and over to the closet. Mumbling the combination I'd seen Mateo use on the safe, I turned the dial to each number.

With a sigh of escaping air, the heavy safe door swung open. I smiled at the blocks of cash on the shelf—the answer to my pressing money problems. Could I take it all? Would it all fit in my bandolier-style shopping bags? Would my baggy shirt stretch to cover the filled bags? Would I have to leave some of the wrapped bundles behind?

That last question didn't sit well with me. Dead Eyes was expecting to collect the money tomorrow night.

Why leave a single dollar for these thugs? I eyed the boxes of uncut drugs on the safe's floor with disgust. *Why leave that? Especially that. Why not put a real dent in their operations? Why not—*

I raced over to the filthy coffee station. I rifled through the kitchenette's drawers and came up triumphant. I had what I needed: a dirty, bent book of matches. Only three matches remained in the book. I would have to work smart.

I almost gagged when I entered the bathroom. It, too, had not been cleaned in recent history. The paper towel and the toilet paper dispensers were empty.

No matter. What I really wanted was the empty cardboard TP spool. I yanked it from the holder and returned to the kitchenette. There I found a supply of coffee filters. I crumpled a few of them and stuffed them into the empty spool.

I brought the rest of the coffee filters with me to the printer, where I found several unopened reams of paper. I ripped a ream open and crumpled the ream's wrapping, several sheets of paper, and the rest of the coffee filters and stuffed them into the wastebasket near the laptop.

That was all great, but I needed more, something to ensure that what I started would continue. I browsed through the kitchenette again, finding only one more useful item: the stub of a candle. As I stared around the store, my searching gaze fell on the cardboard-covered windows and the flimsy curtains hanging over them.

"Those," I whispered. I ripped all but one set from their rods and piled them on the floor under the window still hung with curtains.

Then I remembered the thick fabric strips hanging between the main room and the hallway leading to the outside door. The strips were nailed to the doorframe. I tore the strips from their nails and piled them with the rest of the stuff I'd collected.

I carried the wastebasket over and dumped the crumpled paper on the floor and then surrounded the paper with the loosely piled curtains. I dragged a couple of rickety wooden chairs to my pile, leaned them against the wall, and then set an old wooden table over the pile of debris. Finally, I laid some of the curtains over the table and chairs so that they hung down to the rest of the pile.

I returned to the open safe and hauled the boxes of drugs to my makeshift pyre. I opened a box and its plastic sack and poured the contents on the curtains. I sneezed and jumped back when the powder sifted toward my face.

I'd never used drugs—and didn't intend to start now. I pulled the neck of my uncle's oversized shirt up over my mouth and nose and finished dumping the drugs—all five boxes. Even if the building failed to burn to the ground, the drugs would be toast.

Back at the safe, I stripped off my shirt and shook out the fine powder that had accumulated on it. Then I filled my two shopping bags with plastic-wrapped bundles of money. If it didn't all fit, I would burn what was left.

I preferred burning the money to leaving it for the gang's leader.

The thought of Dead Eyes' reaction when he learned about tonight made me tremble. Yes, the man terrified me, but at the same time, he provoked something in me, a deep desire that longed to frustrate him, wound him—perhaps even defeat him. And I wished with all my heart that I could be there to witness his impotent rage when he heard the news.

Who knows? Maybe I could be.

My shopping bags were filled. I again pulled my uncle's old shirt over my head and tugged it around the bags bulging from my sides. It was a tight fit, but as soon as the shirt settled, it and my burdens disappeared.

I tore the two remaining piles of cash apart and spread the bills over the curtains. At the last minute, I chucked the guns and ammunition I found on the top shelf of the safe onto the pile, too. I had no idea what fire would do to them, but decided that it made no sense to leave them out of the fun.

All righty then.

My plans and I were ready.

I returned to the pile of paper, fabric, drugs, and cash. I lit the candle with one precious match. I held the TP roll stuffed with crumpled coffee filters in one hand and the candle in the other. As the paper inside the roll caught, I turned the roll one way and the other, waving it to make the fire burn faster. When the paper was burning well, I dropped the roll in the middle of the pile of rotted curtains.

I was surprised how fast *they* caught—faster than the TP roll had. I held the still-burning candle stub near other fabric edges. They caught quickly, too.

Within a few seconds, any doubts I'd had that the fire might not "take" dissipated. I laid the candle under an edge of the pile and backed away. When the fire blazed up, I retreated toward the door.

The flames ran up the curtains and licked at the furniture I'd piled over and beside it. Tongues of fire gobbled at varnish on the old table and chairs and shot upward. The last thing I saw before I ducked into the hallway were flames streaking up the hanging curtains and the cardboard covering the windows.

I turned the door's handle and counted to sixty to give the fire as much time as I dared. The smoke and smell of the fire were filling the hallway when I eased open the door. I didn't hesitate—the fire needed fresh air. I flung the door open wide and raced outside in the same motion. The fire "whooshed" and billowed from the open door.

I was across the alley when the first guard noticed the open door— and the fire crackling within. He hollered to alert the others.

It was too late, though. As I stumbled toward the street, awkward under my load of cash, I heard their shouts of alarm. I stopped and turned to look.

Smoke and flames pushed the guards back. One of them was on his cell phone, coughing and shouting.

I'd seen enough. My heart pounding furiously, I plodded toward my car. I was glad I'd parked far enough away that no one would associate my vehicle with what happened behind me, but it was a long hike to tote my heavy load.

I opened the back door of my Toyota and crawled inside. There, hunkering down behind the front seat, I removed my baggy shirt and the shopping bags. I piled the bags on the floor and covered them with the shirt. Then I climbed over the seat and got behind the wheel.

Just before I pulled out onto the street, I heard sirens. I kept driving and rounded a corner, moving away from the fire trucks before they came into view.

⌘⌘⌘⌘

CHAPTER 22

My car rolled into the garage near the crack of dawn and I dragged my weary self into the house. My life was taking on more of a nocturnal rhythm with each passing day—and all my nighttime activities were taking a toll on my body. I was exhausted and keyed up, but at least I had money now—more than enough for my foreseeable needs.

I left the bags lying on the floor of my back seat, telling myself I'd take care of them later. I was, at that moment, quite glad I had installed security bars and doors on the old garage and a sturdy new door on the car entrance.

When I woke about six hours later, sanity and a reasonable dread woke, too. I stumbled to the kitchen to make coffee—scaring Jake out of another life on my way there. While my coffee brewed, I chewed the inside of my cheek and checked out my back door to assure myself that the garage was still intact, the stolen packages of money undiscovered. That was when the weight of my actions truly hit me.

What I'd done could have—*must have*—dire repercussions, even grievous ones. No way would Dead Eyes allow anyone to twist his nose as I'd done without bringing down the weight of his wrath somewhere, upon someone.

In my vivid imagination, I saw the money in my car morph into a pulsing neon arrow pointing right at me and shouting, "Here she is! Come and get her."

"I have to hide it. I have to put it somewhere safe, but not here in the house." I was feeling the immensity of what I'd done, but I wasn't experiencing any regret.

As I drank my coffee, I browsed the local news on my laptop. There it was: A fire had destroyed an old, boarded-up neighborhood store in southwest Albuquerque. One of the news stations had photos of the smoking ruin.

"Wow," I breathed, admiring the utter destruction of the drug house. I read every account posted online. It was KOAT's article that caught my attention.

Sources in APD's gang unit believe that the building had housed a drug processing hub belonging to a local gang with ties to a Mexican cartel. A spokesperson for the gang unit, who asked not to be identified, suggested that the fire might have been started by a rival gang out of California seeking to horn in on the market and trafficking routes through Albuquerque. The unit has cautioned APD to be on the alert for gang-related reprisals.

Another gang? The possibility was brilliant—especially since it took the spotlight off me.

Not that Dead Eyes or Mateo would have considered me a threat. I shrugged and sipped on my third cup. I was already talking myself out of feeling guilty.

I finished my coffee and went to the other bedroom, the one that had once been Genie's and mine. I rummaged through the closet and came up with an old suitcase. I hoped it was the right size. I had decided that a small suitcase would keep the cash dry if I decided to bury it somewhere.

I laid the case on the bed and opened it. The case's contents—some of Aunt Lucy's old clothes, special things of hers I should have given away a long time ago—stared back at me. At the time, not long after her death, it had been easier just to pack the items away rather than to grieve over the finality of giving *all* of her away.

I can do this, I told myself. *I've finally let her go. It's okay to let her stuff go, too.*

It wasn't okay, but I made myself act like it was. With suitcase in hand, I slipped out to the garage where I had a stack of boxes from recent online purchases.

I was so nonchalant about leaving the house now. I hardly worried about anyone seeing me—or spotting a suitcase carrying itself to the garage.

I moved Lu's things from the suitcase into one of the boxes. Before I closed it up, I placed a kiss on my fingers and touched them to the blouse on top. Shaking my head, I determined to call one of the local secondhand shops who would come pick up clothes from the curb. I would put the box out on the curb the night before they agreed to come—or right before I abandoned my house.

Setting the box on the garage floor, I pulled my two shopping bags from the backseat and unloaded them, counting twenty-three plastic wrapped blocks of money in all. I had no idea how much was in a block, but I selected one for immediate use. The rest of the blocks I packed into the suitcase and put it in the trunk.

I took the single block of money, my rucksack, and the empty grocery sacks into the house and dropped the block of cash on the kitchen table—next to my laptop.

I still need to trash the hard drive.

The thing was, it wasn't quite time to do that. One last task remained.

I took the bags into my bedroom and started to re-pack them with my "bug-out" supplies. Because of its size, I filled the rucksack with small items. I left space at the top for the bundle of cash I'd kept out of the suitcase. Then I sorted through the rest of my supplies and stuffed what I could into the grocery bags.

Finally, my bug-out supplies were packed and ready, leaving only the suitcase to deal with—the suitcase now filled with blocks of cash. The mites could cover the packed bags, but not the suitcase. I had to move the suitcase elsewhere *and soon*.

With curtains drawn over all my windows, I cut the thin plastic wrapping from the block of money. It fell apart into a wealth of five, ten, and twenty dollar bills. I separated the three denominations and counted how many bills were in each stack. The total came to exactly ten thousand dollars.

Ten thousand dollars! I scrubbed my face. The amount was more than I'd imagined. I calculated how long it and the other twenty-two bundles would keep me going.

Years! my intuition shouted. Yes, I could live for a long time on two hundred and thirty thousand dollars—*if*. If I managed to keep the money by moving and hiding it ahead of Cushing's impending visit.

I was re-counting the block of money when I heard the pounding beat of Mateo's car stereo. I peeked through the curtains and saw his Camaro skid into his driveway. He had hardly turned off the engine before he leapt from the driver's seat and hustled to his side door.

I envisioned the consternation and fury brewing in Mateo's gang, and I wondered what blame might fall on Mateo over the loss of the drug house, the money, and the drugs themselves. I was still watching Mateo's house when a familiar twosome of silent vehicles entered the cul-de-sac.

Dead Eyes.

I swept the money into a plastic sack and dropped the sack behind a bookshelf. Then I slipped out the side door and across the cul-de-sac. A deferential Mateo was waiting on his porch. He held open the door for Dead Eyes and his crew to enter.

I delayed until they were all inside before I snuck up to the living room window to eavesdrop. As my eyes adjusted to the light inside, I saw that Dead Eyes was the only one sitting down—the only one looking relaxed, for that matter.

Mateo was talking, making a valiant effort to control his nervousness. "—got the whole skinny from the crew. They will vouch that we followed normal procedures. The money, the guns, and the product were locked inside the safe when we left. No one was in the house at quitting time except for the three night men."

He shifted his feet. "The guards locked the door and took up their positions outside. They were outside, on their stations, when they all say the door just opened. So much smoke came out the door that they couldn't go back in. They said the fire had already taken over."

"The door *just opened*." Dead Eyes repeated Mateo's words in a soft, sarcastic drawl that made me squirm as much as it made Mateo.

"As you know, *sir*, the door is keyed inside and out. The guards had locked it from the outside." Mateo swallowed and forged ahead. "Even if someone was on the inside when they locked the door, the only way it could open was with a key."

Dead Eyes' tight smile grew tighter. I felt my own nerves quiver in response to the coldness in that expression.

"You said it yourself," he answered softly. "The only way that door could open was with a key. That leaves just one possibility, don't you agree?"

"You mean the guards? But . . ." Mateo chose his words with care, "See, I suspected that at first, too, but Jorge holds the only key. The other two guards swear that Jorge *locked the door* and was at the far end of the alley when the door reopened. On top of that, you and I are the only ones with the combo to that safe."

Mateo hesitated and then added, "I vouch for my men, sir. They are loyal—it had to be an attack."

I had to give Mateo credit—at least he was trying to save his men. And apparently (and fortunately for him), Mateo had his own alibi?

The nanomites, who had been so quiet of late, sounded an alert before I sensed a presence nearby. I stepped away from the window just as Emilio crept up to it.

You stupid kid!

I was yelling at him in my head, so he couldn't hear me, but the mites' chatter grew louder as Emilio cupped his hands around his eyes and stood on tiptoe to peer in the window in the manner I had.

The difference between his doing that and my doing that? I was invisible—*he most certainly wasn't.*

I didn't know if the mites were complaining because I was too close to Emilio or because they were worried he would be spotted. My only concern was that the kid's actions were just plain stupid.

I grabbed the collar of his shirt and yanked him down to the patch of snake grass Mateo called a yard.

Emilio yelped and tried to skitter backwards on his hands. He was maybe a couple of yards away from me when he collapsed and just sat there, frowning and searching in my general direction.

251

"Why you do that?" he whispered, still looking for me.

The mites were blaring their objections inside my head and I had to agree with them. I blew out a big breath and asked myself the same question: *Really, Gem. Why did you do that?*

Emilio crawled up to the house until he was under the window again. I backed off a few feet and was surprised when his wide-eyed gaze followed me.

"Why you do that?" he repeated.

I shrugged and sighed. I guess he heard me sigh because his eyes opened wider.

The mites ratcheted their protests up another notch. I squeezed my eyes closed and rubbed my pounding temples. It had been a while since they'd caused a headache this bad.

"It's true," he whispered to no one in particular. Then he twitched his chin at me and demanded a little louder. "Why you pull me down like that?"

I was growing seriously alarmed at this point. The mites were agitated beyond my control, and if any of Dead Eyes' crew heard Emilio talking to someone just outside the window, they would come investigate.

"Shut up," I hissed. "Do you want them to hear you? Just shut up so I can listen to what they're saying."

Emilio's mouth plopped open and then snapped shut, but he knelt down and was quiet. The mites must have thought I was talking to them, because they, too, simmered down.

I returned my face to the window. Mateo was now repeating what the local news had reported, that the APD gang unit believed the arson to be the work of a rival gang. Dead Eyes looked less than impressed.

Mateo gave it one last shot. "If it wasn't another gang, if my guys were responsible, why would they stick around when they had to know that the blame would fall on them? And why wouldn't they take the guns, too?"

Dead Eyes frowned. Mateo had, at last, scored some valid points with him. Even Dead Eyes' men shrugged, coming to a reluctant consensus.

"Look, I got a source inside the gang unit," Mateo confided, padding his win. "He says the fire chief found traces of *money and drugs* where the fire started—right there with the guns and ammo. They think whoever burned the place piled *everything* from the safe on the floor and burned it all."

Dead Eyes stared at Mateo. "If that's true, then would it be one of our competitors? Wouldn't they have taken the money and drugs, rather than burning them?"

Mateo looked confused. "But if it wasn't my guys and it wasn't another gang, then who?"

Dead Eyes didn't say anything more. He stroked his chin with a forefinger, his appraising eyes considering Mateo. At last, he stood and gestured to his men. "We'll talk again after I've heard from our associates down south, but the situation is serious. If another gang messed with us, they will be sorry that they did. In the meantime, keep your people armed and ready. Ready for war."

I winced. Mateo nodded. "I will."

It was time for us to move—more specifically, for Emilio to get out of sight. "Go," was all I said.

Gesturing for me to follow, he raced alongside the house and turned the corner toward the side door. I sighed and trailed after him.

He sat on the back steps waiting for me, looking for me. When I didn't say anything he whispered, "You here, lady?" Doubt had crawled back into his voice.

"Yes."

The mites were *not* thrilled. "Nano! Silence!" I whispered.

"Who you talkin' to?" Emilio asked, still spooked.

"Don't worry about it."

"Why can't I see you?" he demanded.

I dithered. In for a penny, in for a pound, right?

The mites chirped and I chose to put Emilio off. "It's a long story, and I don't have time for a long story today."

I spun the questions back on him. "What were you thinking, sticking your head up like that? They can't see *me*, but you don't think Dead Eyes would see *you*, poking your stubbly little head up in the window?"

Emilio didn't seem to take offense. "You calls him Dead Eyes? That's a good one," he laughed into his hand.

"Do you know his real name?"

Emilio nodded. "Arnaldo Soto. He's one mean *hombre*. The gang sent him here to take over after Mateo lost some money and drugs."

"Was that when Corazón left?" I should have been more sensitive to Emilio's feelings, but the question just popped out before I gave it much thought.

He lowered his head. "Yeah."

All the pathos in the world was twined around that one weak response.

I sighed again. "I'm sorry she left, Emilio, but Mateo was hurting her. She had to go."

He glanced my way, surprised and a little hopeful. "She left? On her own?"

Now I was nonplussed. "Um, yeah, she did. On her own."

He scratched at his shaved head a minute, thinking. "I thought maybe . . ."

Now I understood. "You thought maybe Mateo had done something with her, that she was, um, dead?"

He nodded just once.

The kid had come home to a busted-up house and no Corazón. I suppose that, with no one to fill in the blanks, he'd drawn his own conclusions. Wrong ones.

I didn't mind setting him straight.

"Mateo woke up in a really bad mood that morning and started in on her. You'd seen that before, hadn't you?"

He shrugged and hung his head, ashamed.

That really ticked me off—it ticked me off that *he* was the one filled with shame for what a supposed *adult*—especially one who'd shirked his responsibility toward a *child*—had done.

I was incensed, and my temper came out in a gush of words. "Look. Mateo didn't beat up on Corazón that day, Emilio. Instead, I beat *him* with a chair. I beat him unconscious. When he was out, I told Corazón to take the money and go somewhere safe. Then I called the police from Mateo's cellphone."

This was a whole new perspective for Emilio, who cocked his head and considered it. "You beat up Mateo?"

"It's not my fault the cops found drugs on the table when they responded to my call. *I* didn't leave them there."

His face split into a grin. "Wished I'd been there to see it."

"Can't abide men who beat on women and kids," I added in a growl, still half-angry.

"Was you sneaking around in the house, then?"

"I guess I was."

He scratched his head again and I wondered when the kid had showered last.

Who would care if he had or hadn't?

"I'm sure Corazón misses you as much as you miss her." Now where had *that* come from? "But she, um, she had to go. She really didn't have a choice. Mateo was going to hurt her really bad if she didn't leave."

Especially after what I did to him, I reflected.

254

The kid nodded and returned to our former topic. "Why was you listening at the window?"

"Who says I was?"

He blinked. "I-I thought I saw you there."

That was news to me. "You saw me?"

"Not you, not the real you, but sometimes you, you wear glitter stuff."

Ah.

"You see the shimmer around me sometimes?"

"Yeah. A little sparkle thing. Not all the time. Just once in a while."

Good to know.

Uncomfortable with our conversation focusing on me, I again turned it around. "I'm more concerned about you, now that Corazón is gone."

How to put this?

"I mean, you are definitely a bright kid and fast on your feet. You stay out of Mateo's way—which is a good idea—but, well, he isn't taking care of you. You need, you know, regular food and stuff. A warm, safe place to sleep. And someone to see to those things."

Emilio folded his arms at that and set his face in lines I was more familiar with: Dark, frowning brows, glowering eyes, and a pinched, puckered mouth. "I don't need *no*body, lady. And you'd better not be calling the welfare people—not if you want me to keep my mouth shut 'bout *you.*"

Well, I'd stepped right into *that*, hadn't I?

"I see." That was all I could think to say.

The corner of his mouth twitched. He thought he had me.

As if.

"So how well have you been eating lately, Emilio? Your bones are going to stick right through your shirt if you don't get some good, hot, meals soon. You know, stuff like all-you-can-eat spaghetti. Hamburgers. Pizza."

Right on cue, Emilio's stomach lurched. He snarled at me in tune with his growling belly, but I'd hit on an idea.

"Winter's coming," I added offhandedly, "and those bushes aren't going to keep you warm much longer. Like I said, you need a better place, a home—a real one. We just need to find someone nice who's willing to share theirs with you."

He snarled again. "My folks are dead and ain't nobody got a 'real home' for me. That 'we just need to find someone nice' is a bunch of—"

He capped his short tirade with a colorful curse word. I dropped down on the dead grass near the steps, sat cross-legged, and thought about what he'd said—not the cursing part, but the part before that. I thought about my own circumstances around his age. How I'd felt.

"How old are you, Emilio?" I finally asked.

"What's it to you?" he spit back.

"Don't be disrespectful," I admonished him. "Answer the question: How old are you?"

He frowned and pursed his lips again. "I'm ten. What of it?"

"Well, I was nine when my folks died," I told him. "I have a sister, a twin. She and I didn't have anybody either, except our Aunt Lucy. See, we didn't really know her when we came to live with her and she didn't know us, but it worked out okay."

Emilio kicked at the step with his toe and I noticed the holes in his shoes.

"Sure, it was hard at first," I soldiered on. "Lucy wasn't used to kids—didn't have any of her own. Didn't know the first thing about little girls, but she promised to love us and to do her best."

"Yeah, but she wanted you, right?"

"Yes. That makes a big difference, for sure," I answered him.

"And she weren't crazy, didn't beat on you. Kick you in the head." He was warming to the topic. "Punch you in the face."

"No. She wasn't crazy and she didn't beat on me," I replied, "But my sister was, and did."

Emilio's head jerked up.

"Even though we're twins, my sister Genie was always different from me. I didn't know why. Now, if I had to put a label on how she is, I'd call it Narcissistic Personality Disorder."

I watched Emilio frown and mouth the long words.

"Yeah, that's all gobbledygook. Psychobabble. It means she cares way too much about herself and nothing for others," I explained. "While we were growing up she was always doing stuff, causing trouble. But she was very good at hiding what she did and good at pointing the blame for what she did at me. If she didn't get her way or she got angry, I was her punching bag."

Emilio's eyes went wide.

"I should probably go," I murmured. I had said too much. More than I'd ever told anyone.

Emilio stood up. "Can I—" He hesitated. "Can I feel you first?"

I didn't answer right away . . . then I reached out my hand to his shoulder. He stiffened at my touch until, with his other hand, he felt mine as it rested on him.

I don't understand what came over me. Perhaps it was the look of wonder on his face, maybe it was more the longing I saw there. I took his hand and drew him toward me, wrapped my arms around him, and squeezed him tight.

How long has it been since I've hugged anyone? The warmth of his thin shoulders felt good. Right.

"I'm sorry for all the things you've gone through, Emilio," I whispered. "I'm sorry you haven't had anyone . . . for a long time."

I choked on the next words. "You do now."

We cried a little then, and I can't imagine how it might have appeared if anyone had seen us—a young boy holding on to and being held by *thin air*.

He stepped back and sniffled when I finally loosened my hold on him.

"You see I'm in a bit of a pickle, don't you?" I tried to make light of our emotional moment by changing the subject. "I can't let anyone see me—er, *not* see me, I mean. So far, nobody but you knows about my, uh, *condition*. It's a long story, but people, bad people, will come looking for me any day. Come looking for something I have that they want."

The nanomites hummed softly. Emilio looked aside and appeared worried.

I caressed his cheek. "I can't be the one to take care of you, Emilio. In fact I'm going to have to leave soon."

Now his mouth was working, protesting.

"I have to hide from those bad people who want to catch me. You understand, don't you?"

He managed to jerk a nod.

"Emilio, do you know my friend Abe?"

He shrugged.

"Well, do you know him, or don't you?" I chided.

"Yeah, I know the old man. He's all right." Emilio chewed the inside of his cheek. "He gives me food sometimes."

"He does?" I was surprised but glad. I wanted to know I wasn't the only person in the neighborhood concerned about this kid.

"Yeah. And your boyfriend do, too."

"He's not my boyfriend," I retorted, biting back the itch to correct his grammar.

Emilio just stared at me. "Whatever," he finally mumbled.

"Listen. I have an idea." I tried to sound upbeat. "I'm going to ask my good friend Abe to take you in. I'm going to ask him to take care of you *for me*, just as if I were doing it. If he says yes, we'll have to get CYFD involved—but only if he's willing," I hurried to add.

Emilio looked skeptical.

"If he agrees, I think CYFD will give him custody of you on a trial basis while he's being approved. I know it will be hard for you to adjust to him, but he's a good man, and he will be good to you. He makes great spaghetti, too."

Had I just committed Abe to something as serious as raising a young boy—without even asking him first? Yet I felt sure Abe would agree to do it, just as soon as I told him—*and showed him*—my situation. And Emilio's.

And as simply as that, I'd made several huge decisions—the scariest one being the decision to let Abe in on my secret. Scary because I loved him. I didn't want him to know things that could get him hurt.

I sighed and took the boy by the chin, as Aunt Lu had done with me many times. "Do you think you can bear it, Emilio? Can you be strong a little longer while we work it out?"

Emilio, his eyes down, nodded.

"Good man. You keep out of sight for now. I'll see what I can do."

I realized as I slipped away that the mites had been, for the most part, silent during Emilio's and my conversation. They were still quiet. If I hadn't known better, I would have called them out for sulking.

But I did know better: They were doing that "confab" thing Dr. Bickel had described. The tribes were consulting with each other, analyzing the data and the potential threat, coming to consensus on the best path forward.

"Nano," I whispered to the mites. "Emilio is a child—not an adult. Don't forget to take that into account. He's a kid and he's easy for adults to overlook. No one will ask him about me—and even if they did, who would give any credence to a kid's tall tale about an invisible woman?"

The answer loomed large in my imagination and set my teeth on edge. *Cushing would.*

⌘⌘⌘⌘

CHAPTER 23

Time was running out—I could hear the clock ticking, sense it winding down, feel it moving inexorably toward the moment Cushing's team would identify me as the owner of the backpack. And show up on my doorstep.

I was almost ready to go. Almost. I still needed to move the cash.

I stayed up late again that night after settling on a course of action to hide the cash. Not wanting to unpack my bug-out bags, I dug out two more fabric grocery sacks and added long straps to them.

All was quiet as I drove through the autumn darkness toward Dr. Bickel's safe house and parked a block away, beside a cinderblock retaining wall. These "screening moves" were becoming natural to me. Then I strolled past the safe house, scrutinizing it for any indication that Cushing's people had been *or were still* there. I studied the house and yard for signs of disturbance or surveillance.

The yard looked well kept. Dr. Bickel had a yard service, paid (he'd said) out of a bank account with enough money in it to keep the yard looking good for years, an account (he'd assured me) that could not be traced to him. Everything to do with the house was taken care of via this account—including mortgage, utilities, and taxes.

All I needed to do was move in and keep a low profile.

No profile would be better.

The safe house was, I conceded, a good solution to my problems, *if*— if Cushing's financial lackeys hadn't uncovered the house's connection to Dr. Bickel.

Keeping my eyes peeled, I walked completely around the block and then up the alley behind the house. Everything looked okay. Undisturbed.

I clambered over the back cinderblock wall, went up to the rear door, and inserted my key in the lock. I swung the door open and pulled back to the alley to wait. An hour later, no jack-booted feds had arrived. With the exception of a barking dog off in the distance, the neighborhood was shrouded in the hush of night, the house enveloped in unbroken quiet.

I slipped through the yard and into the house. It appeared to be just as I'd left it two months ago. I saw no evidence of anyone other than me having been there. A coating of dust lay upon the furniture—a coating, I told myself, that would have been disturbed had the house been searched.

I returned to my car and opened the passenger side door. I stared at the small suitcase I'd placed on the car floor. This was, perhaps, the most dangerous part of "shifting my flag": If the safe house *were* compromised, now or in the future, I would lose the cash in the suitcase.

I'd fretted over that possibility. As a hedge against disaster, I'd crammed two bundles of cash into a large coffee can. I hadn't buried the can in my own yard, though. No, I'd buried it in *Mateo's* neglected backyard.

Wouldn't he be surprised?

Oooooh! And wouldn't he be in trouble if Dead Eyes found it there?

I pulled the now-half-full suitcase out and opened it on the sidewalk where my actions between the door and the wall would go unnoticed by passing cars. I grabbed a stack of money and put it under my shirt, into the shopping bags. When all the money was transferred, I put the case in the car and snuck back into the house.

In the kitchen I scooted the stove away from the wall and used a hammer to break through the plasterboard. Then I stuffed all but one bundle of the money into the hole I'd made, cleaned up my mess, and shoved the stove back against the wall.

The hidey-hole was crude and effective only until Cushing found the house. The word "until" seemed to have found a permanent place in my brain, because I didn't for a moment believe that this place—or any place for that matter—would be safe for me for long, let alone forever.

No place had been safe for Nick Holloway, not even at the end of his story.

No place had ever been safe for me.

No place ever would be.

A black mood descended on me as I sat cross-legged on the cold linoleum. The dangerous feelings I normally resisted seemed to have more power than they usually did.

Dark, stormy questions—for which I had no answers!—pressed me and hammered away at my heart: Would I *ever* be free from the sense of being pursued? Where hypervigilance was no longer necessary? Where I could relax and let down my guard? Where I was truly secure?

Was life even *worth* the never-ending struggle?

I recognized where that last question was leading me. Shoving its insistence aside, I hefted the last bundle of cash and estimated its size. I'd made an observation as I'd climbed over the back wall: One of the top cinderblocks was loose.

I took the package out to the wall. By wiggling the loose block back and forth, it came free at last. My hunch had been right: The block below the one I'd removed had two hollow cavities. I crammed the last bundle into one of the holes and shoved the top block back into position. I would lightly cement it later.

Tomorrow, I decided, *I will make the jump to this house.*

A sense of urgency was growing in my gut. As I drove home, I made a list of the things I'd needed to leave behind, the things Cushing could use to track me if I brought them away with me. At the top of the list were my car, my phone, and my laptop.

I had to leave them behind but I also had to figure out how to replace them in my new identity. The phrase "new identity" expanded the list of things I'd have to abandon very soon: my Facebook, Instagram, and Pinterest pages, my email address, my credit cards, and my online shopping accounts.

My options were shrinking: I had plenty of cash, but I would have no laptop and no online profile. *Without a digital footprint, ordering online was out.* The number of problems and obstacles began to grow—and I still needed to confide in Abe, still needed to beg him to call CYFD and apply to take Emilio in.

The tension I was feeling was making the mites nervous, but I couldn't keep the anxiety from building. I could not ignore the strong impression that I needed to move—*and move now*.

As I opened my side door, I shook off the disquiet, telling myself I was just overtired. Exhausted.

Tomorrow, when I was rested, I would complete my tasks and make the move. *Tomorrow* I would reformat my laptop's hard drive and then smash it to bits. After that, nothing would remain for Cushing to find, nothing that might connect me to Dr. Bickel or that could aid Cushing in her hunt for me.

Before I allowed myself to sleep, I ran through the call logs and address book on my phone. I already knew that once Cushing had her spotlight on me, she would have her team access the logs from my service provider. In that case, nothing on the phone, deleted or not, would be hidden from her—in fact, whatever I deleted or altered *now* would actually be more suspect. I dropped the phone without making any changes.

I would not pick it up again.

I tore through the house, looking at it from Cushing's perspective, determined to destroy anything she could use against me. I was rummaging through the kitchen junk drawer when I saw the cell phone Dr. Bickel had given me.

For use only in a dire emergency, he'd cautioned. But he'd also told me the phone was "secure," that it could not be traced to him. I'd almost forgotten about it. I'd never used the phone and he'd never called me on it. After he'd died, I'd thrown it into the drawer.

It can't be traced to him, but it can't be traced to me, either! It was a stunning, gratifying revelation, and I huffed a breath of partial relief. I scrabbled in the drawer for the power cord and plugged the phone in to charge.

The last thing I did was to re-check the rucksack and bags. What I would be taking away from my home seemed pitifully inadequate: some changes of clothes, extra socks, a nightie, a hoody, hiking boots, toiletries, a little food and water, the Maglite, gloves, a framed photograph of Aunt Lu I kept on my nightstand. My new phone and charger.

Dr. Bickel's lab book.

"More precious than all these supplies," I whispered.

I staged the filled bags, rucksack, and tomorrow's clothes next to my bed. Weary in heart and body, I climbed under the covers and fell into dreamless slumber.

***

Something nudged me awake, and I rolled over and glimpsed the clock through bleary eyes: It was nearly ten in the morning. I had slept hard. As the world snapped into focus I remembered: Today I would make my leap—today I would abandon my home.

Before I pulled the covers back, I was already arranging the day's tasks and rubbing at a familiar spot on my hand.

And then it hit me: *The nanomites woke me.*

My hand was still tingling. Stinging.

The mites were chittering softly, and I knew them well enough by now to distinguish between their typical humming and the nervous chipping I heard now. The mites couldn't 'hear' but they could feel vibrations.

Something was wrong.

I slid from bed and padded on bare feet down the hall to the living room—in time to hear a resounding knock on my door.

Cushing's soldiers would not politely ring the bell. No, for her it would be a no-knock warrant—or *more likely*, she would slap an "imminent national security threat" label on her actions to justify storming the house *without* a warrant.

I told my hammering heart to calm down: whoever *was* at the door? It wasn't Cushing. They knocked again and then rang the doorbell.

Jake, startled out of a dozing pose on the couch, clawed his way into a semblance of traction and scrambled around behind an armchair. I shook my head and placed my eye to the peephole.

Genie!

My impatient twin, dressed to the nines, arms folded, tapped the toe of her three-and-a-half-inch, brand-name heels on my porch.

What is she doing here?

Never mind! Think fast—what am I going to do?

The nanomites were cautioning me, but I needed no warning from *them*: Under no circumstances would I answer that door—not that my inaction would deter Genie for long. What Genie wanted, Genie found a way to get. Too late, I remembered that Genie knew where I kept my emergency key.

"Gemma? Gemma, it's Genie. Open up." More peals on the doorbell. Jake bolted from behind the chair and sprinted for the back door.

Smarter than you look, I acknowledged. But there was no handy cat door for me.

I ran back to the bedroom and scrambled into clothes and shoes. I cast my eyes around the room. My bags! The bed! I tossed the packed bags into the laundry hamper and covered them with dirty clothes. I yanked the bed covers up, tidied the spread, and made a few adjustments to the room to lend to the impression that I wasn't at home.

I swung my bedroom door open and crept back to the living room to wait and watch. I didn't have to wait long.

"Gemma, I'm coming in." And as if to prove her point, I heard her insert a key into the lock on my security door.

I pressed my lips together, angrier with myself than with her. It was *my* fault she had a key. I'd intentionally had the security door locks keyed the same as the front and side door locks. And then I'd placed my emergency key under that old pot by the garage—just as Aunt Lu always had—which, by the way, Genie also knew.

I heard the outside metal door open and then heard Genie insert a key into the heavy front door. I stepped behind it just as it swung open.

"Gemma?" Genie closed the door behind her. "Gemma, are you home?"

She swept her gaze around and sniffed. I scanned my little house at the same time, trying to see it as she would.

Oh, no. My laptop!

There it sat, on the kitchen table under the front window. It was, *of course*, password protected, but I didn't want her to see it, let alone touch it.

I should have destroyed the hard drive last night, I chastened myself, but I had wanted a fresh mind to update this account before copying and removing the file. I'd allowed my fatigue to dictate a lapse in judgment.

I won't do that again, I vowed.

Genie pivoted on her high heels and strode down the short hall toward my bedroom. The moment she turned away, I tiptoed to the table and unplugged and grabbed up the laptop. I slipped it under my shirt.

Genie spent a minute in my room before stalking back into the living room. She wandered around, touching my things, picking up the occasional item to examine it. When she reached the table, she stopped.

The notebook! The one I'd made lists in, the one in which I'd written my crazy, stream-of-consciousness memories that fateful first morning. How had my frenzied preparations to abandon ship missed it? If she picked it up, snooped inside of it—

I twisted my fingers together. *That notebook contains damaging information that could fall into Cushing's hands!*

Genie, however, had fixated on something else: The power cord for my laptop—and the long, heavy-duty extension cord coiled on the floor next to my chair. She bent and touched the extension cord, puzzled. Then she lifted one end of the laptop's power cord. She checked the other chairs around the table, quite obviously searching for my computer.

I was relieved that it was safely camouflaged—then I snapped to how unnaturally silent the mites were, as though they recognized the danger Genie presented. If so, I had to give them props for identifying a true threat when they encountered it.

Are the nanomites familiar with the term 'sociopath'?

Genie dropped the laptop's cord and sniffed again. She swiveled and wandered into my kitchen. While she was rummaging through my cupboards, I slipped the notebook under my shirt to join the laptop.

It *perhaps* made the tiniest sound as I did so.

Genie froze. She strode back into the living room, her head turning, eyes darting about.

The mites hummed a warning.

Shut it! I scolded. I stood in the corner between the dining room and living room and didn't budge. Didn't breathe.

Genie again stomped to my bedroom. On the way back, she checked the bathroom and spare room. She swept her appraising gaze over the living room and once more over my kitchen table. And stopped cold.

I hadn't often seen Genie in doubt. She was too self-absorbed to admit to doubt, uncertainty, or inadequacy and, in my years of knowing her, I had never seen those emotions cross her face. It was gratifying to see that she actually *had* feelings along those lines.

She stared at the table for a full minute, eyes narrowed, as though trying to figure out what was different. Then she snorted and clicked her way through the kitchen. She threw open the back door and marched down the steps toward my garage.

I followed behind, seething, but helpless to keep her from snooping.

That's when I noticed the shiny silver-blue Lexus rental parked in my drive. And Mrs. Calderón peering through her front window and waving to Genie.

Mrs. Calderón. I should have known. I have her to thank for Genie's unannounced visit. She probably called Genie to tell her "how worried she is about me" because I've "become a recluse." I'd like to stuff a cork in her pie hole, I fumed, *and a foot!*

I yanked my attention back to Genie. She hadn't tried to open the garage door; she was merely peering through the barred window, probably to see if my car was there or not.

"Oh, hi. There you are."

My breath caught.

Zander?

It had been a couple of weeks since he'd come around. I figured he'd given up on me, and I told myself that I wanted him to but . . . And what was he doing here now? *Today* of all days?

Genie didn't respond immediately. No, she would resolve on a course of action before she did. I could feel her psyching herself up, as she turned. A beguiling smile wreathed her face.

"Hi, yourself."

No! She was playing *me*!

Apprehension sunk its claws into my throat. Genie had a long, colorful history of taking from me. If something were good, if I cared about it, *if I loved it*, she would take it—just because she could. And if, by some chance, she couldn't take it? *She would destroy it.*

Please! Please don't let her hurt Zander! I don't care what he used to be—that's not him anymore. Please don't let her hurt him! I didn't know what I was admitting to or whom I was asking, but I was far beyond "asking." I was begging.

What happened next was nothing short of amazing.

Zander tipped his head to one side and his calm gray eyes considered her. After a moment, he asked, "May I help you?"

He was significantly less cordial.

My jaw dropped.

"Why, whatever do you mean?" Genie was still playing the role. She smiled that bright, radiant smile, the one that had lured many to shipwreck.

"What I mean is this is Gemma Keyes' house. You aren't Gemma. I'm asking what you're doing peeking in her windows." He glanced toward the open back door, then put his hands on his hips. "And what you're doing in her house."

Too many facets! I didn't know *this* Zander, either—this cool, unshaken man demanding answers from my evil twin. He was neither the "macho, in-your-face gangster" I'd seen with Mateo, nor the kind gentleman he'd been with me. No, this man was unfazed. Authoritative. Impervious. I didn't know whether I was more amazed at his immunity to Genie's wiles or thrilled over his standing up for *me*.

And how in the world had he *known* that she wasn't me?

Genie's smile lost wattage. "If you knew Gemma, then you'd know that I'm her sister."

"Yes, so you're Genie. She's mentioned you. You don't live in Albuquerque, so you've obviously come for a visit. Except I doubt Gemma knew you were coming, or she would be here and you wouldn't be looking for her."

He crooked an eyebrow. "In any event, she *isn't* home at present, so I'm asking—*again*—what you are doing?" He glanced a second time at my open back door. "Did you break into her house?"

I was astounded. *Astounded.*

Genie's expression darkened and she dodged his demand. "Do you know where Gemma is?"

"Miss, I appreciate that you are Gemma's sister, but I believe you have entered her house in her absence without her permission. You're a lawyer. I'm sure you understand what will happen when I call the police."

Not *if*, but *when*. My heart swelled—and then clenched. *No! Don't call the police, Zander! Don't!*

"And you are?" Genie, mistress of aggression, swaggered toward Zander—intent on invading his personal space—but I'd seen him nose-to-nose with a hardened gangster. Genie may have met her match.

Woot!

Zander didn't budge. If anything, he leaned forward, mirroring Genie's posture, enunciating each word, "I'm her pastor."

Folks, I did not see that coming.

I had never thought of him as *my pastor*! I hadn't decided exactly *what* he was to me, *but absolutely not that.*

Genie's lips parted a bit. She was as surprised as I was, but nowhere as disappointed.

"I see."

No, she didn't.

"I suggest you take your leave, Miss Keyes. I'll let Gemma know you were here. In her house."

Genie's lip curled. "You do that."

Without another word, she straightened her shoulders and clicked to the sedan parked in my driveway. Her head swiveled toward Mrs. Calderón's window. The face peering through it disappeared.

I stood in my back doorway, stunned and hurt. My heart had been lifted up and then slammed to the ground.

I automatically moved toward the front of the house as Zander came inside. The mites were chirping softly, concerned, but not overmuch. Just being themselves around other people, I guess.

Zander stood in the living room. "Gemma? You can come out now. She's gone."

He thought I was hiding from Genie. I was disappointed and, frankly, I didn't care anymore. I would be gone soon, anyway.

"Don't turn around," I whispered.

He jumped a little and started to turn.

"No. Don't."

That stopped him.

"Keep facing that way, please—*ow!*"

In less time than it took for me to speak ten words, the mites went from unruffled and unconcerned to ballistic protest. They were stinging me!

"Nano. Stop it!"

Zander's head swiveled a little before he caught himself. He took a breath. "I'm sorry; were you talking to me, Gemma?"

The mites switched from stings to stabbing noise. They were voting a great, big, fat *no* on Zander. I ignored them as best I could, but it was hard—the shooting pangs were blinding.

"No, don't worry about it," I temporized. What was I going to say next? Did it matter? It didn't feel like it mattered anymore. I kneaded my aching eyes and throbbing temples.

"Thank you for getting rid of Genie." I glanced out the window, but her car had long since roared out of our cul-de-sac. "How . . . how did you know she wasn't me?" I was a little curious about that.

Zander shrugged. "Call it discernment."

"Um, discernment?" I shook my head. I didn't understand.

He must have sensed my confusion. "She might look like you on the outside, but she isn't you on the inside. At all. I could feel that."

"Oh."

It was an odd situation, Zander talking to me over his shoulder. I didn't know where to go next. He did.

"Gemma, you haven't told me much about Genie, but I got the distinct impression that she had hurt you in the past. Hurt you deeply. Am I right?"

I sighed and gritted my teeth. The stabbing pains in the back of my head were like sharp knives.

He turned his head toward me, just a little. "As soon as I realized who she was, I wanted to get her away from you. I don't want her to hurt you again, Gemma."

"I-I, um, thank you." Tears clogged my voice. I couldn't stop them; I hurt everywhere.

"Gemma, may I please turn around? I haven't seen you in so long."

"No."

No, Pastor Cruz, I bristled. *No, you can't see me anymore.*

An edge crept into his voice. "Gemma, tell me what is wrong! I am worried sick about you."

I urged myself to buck up. Be tough. Realistic. "Pastor Cruz, I thank you for everything you've done for me the past few months. You've been a great, um, friend and all—"

"*Friend?*" His voice was incredulous.

"All right, you've been a great *pastor.*"

I didn't realize I was signing up to be "pastored," but all right. **Whatever.**

He put a hand to his face and chuckled a little—which really teed me off.

"What's so stinking funny?"

"You, Gemma! Didn't you hear what I said earlier? I just wanted to get her away from you, away from your house, away from *us*—so I told her I was your pastor. Surely you didn't want me to say I was your, er, *friend?* Maybe more than a friend?"

Soooo much. So much was prancing and gamboling about in my tiny pea brain—like a happy, singing episode of *My Little Pony*, complete with pink and purple dancing unicorns. So many words and thoughts competing with the nanomites and their incessant, mushrooming clamor.

"You said that 'I'm her pastor' part to get rid of her?" My jaw was clamped so hard it was difficult to get the words out.

"Of course. I don't know your sister, Gemma, but one up-close-and-personal encounter told me a lot. I don't mean to disparage her, but she's sort of scary, don't you think? I don't want her to scare you anymore."

Oceans of emotions collided and jumbled up in my heart, overwhelming me. I was distracted, though. The mites simply *would not* shut up.

"Gemma, may I turn around now?"

The mites lodged their collective vote by ratcheting up the racket. I bit back a groan. Besides, I hadn't completely bought into Zander's, "Maybe more than a friend" bit—after all, I grew up in church, remember? *He was a full-on believer; I wasn't.* End of story.

There could be no "more than friends" between us. Not ever.

Nothing had changed. If anything, the situation was worse.

"No, Zander. I can't let you."

The mites' hum intensified and strengthened, as when they'd fried the rattlesnake behind the rock outcropping: The many hums were becoming one, and I grew alarmed.

A disturbing question rose to the surface. *Would they hurt Zander?*

I couldn't stop the single sob that burbled out. My head was caving in from the pain, the mites' hammering dissonance was intensifying—and I was growing weaker. I could barely stand.

Zander persisted, and asked over his shoulder, "Can't you at least tell me why? Can't you tell me what is going on?"

I wanted to. I wanted so badly to tell him. Tell him everything. But I was so tired.

When I didn't answer, he added, "This is driving me nuts, Gemma, this secrecy thing you're doing, not allowing me or anyone to see you. I know we don't have a long history, but I hope you trust me. I hope you know I only want what is best for you?"

I didn't respond. It couldn't have been later than noon, yet already I was weary. Worn, inside and out. Exhausted. Out of habit, I picked up the extension cord.

The mites did not "latch" on.

A slow comprehension rolled over me: The mites were draining me. *Intentionally draining me.* Could they sense that my resolve to keep them a secret was slipping? Did they think that Zander posed a risk so great that they were taking steps to shut me up? Shut me down?

I struggled to stay focused as the drain overspread my body. I knew I couldn't win against them, but my stubborn heart refused to bend to their will.

*Nano, you know **nothing** about the human need for freedom—especially our most basic and primal need, **the freedom to choose**. What you are doing to keep me silent and compliant? What you are doing to shut me up? It won't work. It won't have the effect you hoped for.*

Just the opposite.

You will never control me.

I would rather die.

I whispered to Zander. "If I tell you, *if I show you*, you can never tell anyone. Ever."

The mites kicked into a higher gear. My head was bursting, and I beat it with my hands; I beat it in a feeble attempt to stifle the pain.

"Nano, no! I'm going to tell him—*you can't stop me*. Stop hurting me! STOP IT!"

I crumbled to the floor, sobbing, "Nano! STOP IT!" I curled into a ball, hugging the agony to myself.

The roaring noise faded; in its absence, the room spun and whirled. The mites' silence, though, was not enough: No strength remained in my body, not even enough to lift my head or a hand.

The mites' attack had crushed me. They had gone too far. The tide was sucking and pulling at me as it withdrew. I quivered helplessly; my life was draining away.

From a far distance, I heard Zander's panic-stricken voice calling my name. His voice grew fainter.

So this is it.

My lungs no longer moved. I could hear my heart thundering, fast and frantic. Tiny points of light exploded behind my closed eyelids. I had a sense of floating, of flickering.

Wisps of cool air tickled my arm and touched my fingers.

The thudding of my heart slowed. The breeze on my skin slowed. My thoughts slowed. One nagging regret lingered. *I'm not ready to die. Not ready.*

The breeze caressing my skin turned, reversed direction. A warm oily pressure followed it up my arm, into my shoulder. Heat overspread my chest and face. The heat rolled across my body into my other arm, down my legs to my feet.

I shuddered and gasped. Life-giving air entered my lungs.

"Gemma! Gemma, where are you?" He was feeling around on the floor, very near me.

"Here . . ." I didn't expect him to hear me; I couldn't manage more than a whisper.

"Gemma?"

I squeaked something unintelligible.

His hands found my arm, my shoulder. He said something in Spanish that conveyed alarm. "Gemma, are you all right?"

Surely he knew I wasn't *all right*, didn't he? I guess it was just the first thing that popped out of his mouth.

"Help . . . sit up . . ." I whispered.

Zander slid an arm under me and lifted me up. I wobbled against his shoulder and chest, but I was breathing, drawing in oxygen. *Life*. Life was trickling back into me.

I don't know how long Zander propped me up so I could breathe easier. I drifted in and out of consciousness until I strengthened and my thinking became coherent again. Zander was praying in a soft voice for me, but I knew it would take hours to fully recover from the mites' drain.

Speaking of the mites, they were quiet. Eerily so.

Another confab. Another threat analysis. Another decision forthcoming. I should have been concerned, but I didn't have the strength to be.

Zander supported me for a long while until I was able to shift my weight to lean against a leg of the table.

"Bet you're . . . pretty freaked out?"

Zander sat back on his heels, but he didn't let go of my hand. Maybe he thought he'd lose track of where I was if he let go.

"Um, yeah. I'm not taking that bet."

I laughed, then coughed and convulsed. I hardly had the strength to breathe in. Breathe out. "W-water?" I gasped.

"Um . . ."

I was right—he was afraid to let go of me. Afraid this all wasn't real.

"I'll be . . . here . . ." Three words and I was empty again.

The warmth wasn't flowing through me anymore. The nanomites had stopped fetching power for me.

Why did they drain me and then, at the last second, revive me?

I felt certain of the answer. *They brought me back from the brink, but are keeping me down until they decide on an appropriately "safe" course of action.*

I sneered at them. *Tiny tyrants!*

"Hand me . . . that . . ." I couldn't finish my thought.

"Hand you what?" Zander squeezed my hand. "Don't faint on me, Gemma. What do you need?"

"Cord," I wheezed.

He picked up the end of the extension cord with his other hand and held it in front of me. "This? I—"

The mites shot down my arm, out my hand and into his, through his body, and onto the cord. Zander jerked and tried to yank his hand from mine, but the mites kept the connection.

Energy flowed into me. It coursed from the cord, through Zander, through our joined hands, into my body. Zander couldn't let go of my hand or the extension cord, no matter how badly he wanted to—and I figured he wanted to pretty badly right about then.

So. The mites must have finished their confab.

"About time," I whispered to them.

Bad bugs!

"What is it?" Zander gasped. "What is that feeling?"

"Electricity. They need. I need. They . . . drained me."

He was quiet, probably sorting through prospective funny farms, wondering which one took applicants for my kind of "funny."

But he asked again, "Gemma, are you going to be all right?"

"Yes. After. While. Takes. A minute."

Give or take a couple of hours.

"Will you still be, um, invisible?"

I nodded then remembered he couldn't see my nod. "Yes."

"Will you tell me?" He didn't finish his sentence, but he didn't need to. I listened. The mites said nothing.

"Yes," I whispered again. "I'll tell you."

⌘⌘⌘⌘

CHAPTER 24

Eventually I grew strong enough to move to my spot on the sofa in the living room. Zander decided I wasn't going to "disappear" and went into the kitchen to fix us something to eat.

I lay unmoving on the sofa but I was listening—and not to the nanomites. It was pleasant, hearing Zander open cupboard doors and bang pots and pans.

Nice. But don't get used to it.

After eating, I had enough strength to begin my tale, the same one I've recorded here for you, Dear Reader. The telling of the gist of it didn't take long, but answering questions, filling in details, and repeating certain aspects took hours.

Under Zander's probing queries, I even talked about Genie. My small admission to Emilio had opened a crack in the dam I'd built around my childhood. Once I began unburdening myself to Zander, that dam gave way. I think I found it easier to talk about my sister and the childhood she had terrorized when I knew Zander couldn't see my face or my tears.

When I finished, I was even more exhausted, my voice scratchy and rough.

"You've been carrying this secret for a long time, Gemma." Zander's eyes were sad. It hurt that my words had grieved him. I didn't want that.

"I'm sorry, but, well, I've never been able to tell anyone. Until now."

"Not anyone?"

"I had no one."

He just nodded.

"Zander." I had to say it. I had to get it out of my mind and into the open. "Earlier when you said that we were maybe more than friends? You know we can't be *that*, right? So there's no point in talking like we could be."

He considered before answering. "Yes, I agree. There are reasons we can't be together."

"Because of my 'condition' or because I can't . . . won't buy into your faith?"

Again he thought before he spoke. "What if I said your spiritual 'condition' was as much an obstacle as your physical one?"

He fumbled for my hand and I gave it to him. "I want to tell you something, Gemma, something I believe will make a difference for you."

He hesitated. I thought I knew what was coming. "I can't, Zander. I can't join your church." It was a settled decision, one I'd made years before.

"I'm not asking you to join my church. I want to tell you about Jesus."

"I can't share your religion then. Whatever." I was too tired to argue.

"I dislike religion, Gemma. Religion does a lot of damage to people. It takes what should be the simplest, purest expression of God's love, something even a child can understand, and replaces it with some kind of formula—a complex and impossible set of rules and behaviors—when it is really about God's gift of grace and his power to transform us."

I tried to huff, but came out more like a sniff. "God's power to . . . transform? That's exactly my point. Aunt Lucy took us to church for years. It never helped the one person who needed such a thing."

He looked puzzled. "Who are you talking about?"

I waved my free hand—not that he saw me do so. "*Genie*, of course. My sister is messed up, Zander. Sick. You only met her once and yet somehow you noticed it. She's, um, very good at hiding what she is. If anyone needs 'transformation' as you call it, *it's her*. We went to church for years. It never helped her one bit."

Zander's lips pursed and he rubbed them with his other hand. I got the sense he was trying to frame or word something complicated. Turns out, it wasn't so complex—he was trying to say something difficult to hear.

Difficult for me to hear.

"Gemma, you are as much in need of God's grace and forgiveness as Genie is."

I was stunned. And hurt. "Why would you say such a thing to me?"

His gray eyes were direct. "Because it's true, Gemma. You aren't perfect. Maybe you aren't as 'messed up' as Genie? Maybe not as messed up as I was. But you're still messed up."

"That's ridiculous. I—" I frowned and bit my lip.

He took a deep breath. "Look. God knows how messed up we—all of us—are, so there's no sense in trying to deny it. We can't hide the truth from him, because he sees everything. We are actually hiding the truth from ourselves, not from him."

I disagreed. I shook my head.

But he couldn't see me and continued, "Our 'mess' is what the Bible calls sin. It includes the things we know are wrong but do anyway, the things we aren't proud of but that we excuse, that we laugh off or brush aside with an insincere, *nobody's perfect* or *I shouldn't have done that—but oh, well.*"

I had a sudden, vivid recollection of the many things I'd excused lately . . . and not so lately. I was perturbed by how many things.

Zander wasn't finished. "The worst kind of sin, though, is more insidious. It hides inside of our comparisons of ourselves to others. It says, 'I'm not as bad as *her*,' or 'He's *really* a bad person but I'm nothing like that—*so I must be all right.*'

"It's the sin of hubris, Gemma, the sin of pride and its close cousin, presumption. Presumption justifies our actions when we rank another person as *beneath or below* us. Presumption tells us that it's okay to talk down to a weaker individual or to treat them badly based on our own sense of superiority; pride allows us to denigrate another human being—someone made in the very image of God—for their weaknesses and flaws."

He looked at me, his words more pointed. "When we *presume*, we excuse bad behavior and even rationalize our taking the law into our own hands. Hubris blinds us, Gemma. We don't see our own faults because we're too busy finding the faults of others."

Ouch.

"But the church let us down, Zander. Let *me* down. Everyone believed Genie's lies, believed what she said about me, all those things she did and blamed on me! Do you know how many times *I was punished for what she did?*" My voice sounded shrill, even to me.

Zander's eyes grew sadder, the tiny lines around them more pronounced. "I'm so sorry, Gemma. So very sorry. The church is full of imperfect people just like us. I'm sorry they failed and hurt you. If they knew the truth, they would be appalled at what they'd done. But blaming *them* doesn't fix *your* problem, does it?"

"My problem?"

"Don't *you* also have flaws and blind spots?"

I was silent. He was kind but persistent.

"Come on, Gemma. Have you never failed anyone? Have you never hurt or . . . betrayed anyone? Those offenses and failures must be paid for, and you can't do that. Only Jesus can do that. You need him."

He looked down. "Gemma, you are braver than you think you are. You have overcome so much! But until you admit that you need to be rescued as much as Genie does, you will remain far from God, and far from what you desire the most."

Before I could reply he asked, "Look at me, Gemma." He traced up my arm until he reached my shoulder and ran his fingers up my neck and my cheek until he touched my eyes. He fixed his gaze where his fingers rested.

I stared at him. He stared back. "Don't shut out the God who made you, Gemma. He has a plan for you. I'm not saying everything that happens *is* his plan. I'm saying if you seek him, you'll find him.

"And if you find him, he will work even *this*," he ran his hand back down my arm—my invisible arm—and rubbed it gently, "for good. According to his will. *I trust him.* And I'm willing to wait for him to reveal his will."

We didn't say anything more for a long while, lost as we were in our own thoughts. Zander held my hand and I was glad that he did, in spite of the insurmountable gulf between us. The sun was sinking when he broke the brooding silence.

"Are you certain this Cushing woman is coming for you?"

I was not thinking just then about Cushing, but about Zander. Through my entire recitation—as I had explained about Dr. Bickel and the nanomites and what they had done to me—he hadn't once expressed doubt. Astonishment, yes, even incredulity, but not doubt in *me* as I presented the facts. He had asked for details but he had not called my integrity (or sanity) into question. Even now, he accepted at face value the threat I told him Cushing represented. He was merely asking for clarification.

"Yes, I'm certain. The clerk at REI will remember me. We had a nice conversation about her year abroad. It won't take Cushing's people long to show the girl a picture of me. And Cushing knows me; she's the one who had me fired. Yes. She will come."

"What will you do?" It was then that I heard the pain in his voice and saw it in his eyes.

"I have to leave. Tonight. I have . . . somewhere in mind, a safe place," I whispered. "I'm weak, though, and before I leave I have stuff to do. Right now. Will you help me?"

"Anything," was his instant response.

"Afterward, I need to talk to Abe."

"Does he know?"

"No. I'm glad you'll be with me when I tell him. Show him."

At my direction, Zander tossed Dr. Bickel's lab book, my notebook, and the marked-up copy of *Memoirs of an Invisible Man* into the fireplace. He doused them with some charcoal lighter fluid before he put a match to them. We watched, mesmerized, as the flames licked at the books and reduced them to pages of ash and a lone, crusted metal spiral.

When the fire had completed its work, Zander pressed his lips together. He took up the poker and beat the pages until they were dust. "So Cushing can't reconstitute anything," he said through tight lips.

"Thank you."

I grabbed the cell phone Dr. Bickel had given me. Zander helped me don the filled rucksack and shopping bags. In my weakened condition, my burdens might as well have been bags of bricks.

Zander stood back to view the results. My baggage stuck out from the rest of me, bulgy, awkward, and parts of the bags were visible upon my invisible body as the mites scrambled to cover them.

"This is kinda weird looking, y'know?" he cracked, but his gray eyes swam with worry. "Don't you want me to carry something?"

"No, thank you. Watch this." I pulled my uncle's old shirt over my head.

He watched the shirt settle about my shoulders and cover the bags. Watched the quick flash of shimmer as the mites made the shirt and all under it as undetectable as I was.

He gaped. "Um, whoa. I mean *wow*. That's *crazy*."

"Yeah. Tell me about it."

"Are you ready?" he asked.

"One sec," I replied. I picked up the laptop and stuffed it under the shirt where it, too, disappeared. I crossed my arms across it and held it tight.

"Nice trick," he mumbled.

"I can't leave it here."

He nodded his understanding.

"Can you walk with me to see Abe?" I needed to talk to my friend, beg him to take Emilio, but it would require more exhausting hours of explaining and answering questions.

We crossed the cul-de-sac together, Zander with his hands in the front pockets of his jeans and me with one unseen hand leaning on his shoulder for support. As we reached the other side, Abe came out to greet Zander.

When we were close enough, Zander said quietly, "Hey, Abe. Can we go inside?"

"Sure, sure. You see our girl yet?"

"Uh, not exactly."

I had to smile a little.

While Abe was putting coffee on, I snuck into his guest room and unloaded my "burdens." I came out as Zander was, awkwardly, trying to prepare Abe for my revelation. He was working hard to gently break it to Abe—but how do you "gently break" something like this? He was making a hash of it and confusing Abe instead.

I stood in the hallway and said his name. "Abe."

Abe looked for me then jumped up and backed away. It took a while to explain things, took him touching me, my face, my arms, my hands. Took many an earnest, "Dear Lord in heaven" and "Bless God, I don't know about this. I just don't know, Gemma," before he settled.

The nanomites? I heard not a click or hum from them during my conversation with Abe. Had they given up trying to break me to their will? Did they now trust me, trust my judgment? I didn't know the answer, but I was grateful for the silence. I could not withstand another battle with them.

I had known my "condition" would be a lot for my old friend to take in. It was. I had known my request concerning Emilio would be harder. It was.

"Emilio knows all of this?" Abe peered in my direction, still shocked. Not at all comfortable.

"He knows about my situation. Not the why or how."

"And you want me to take the boy." Because he couldn't make eye contact with me, Abe stared at Zander. My old friend looked so tired!

"I can help you, I hope, but from a distance." It was a feeble offer at best.

Zander grasped Abe's shoulder. "I'll help you, Abe. I'll be Emilio's big brother. I'll come get him and run him ragged for you. Take some of the strain off your grocery bill—'cause let me tell you, that kid can eat."

We shared a nervous laugh.

"And you think CYFD will just hand him over to me?" Abe demanded. "Just like that? What about Mateo? What do you think he's goin' to say about it?"

Zander spoke up again. "I'll tell CYFD what I've seen—Emilio sleeping in the bushes, Mateo slapping and kicking him. Your testimony and mine should get the boy removed from Mateo's care. And you let me handle Mateo. I can deal with him."

I'd seen Zander and Mateo facing off. I believed Zander—as long as Dead Eyes didn't get involved. I didn't want Zander anywhere near that man.

"Besides, Abe," Zander added, "We'll pray on it. God will make a way."

I wasn't sure about *that*.

Abe asked, "Well, and I suppose you want me to keep that charming cat of yours for you, too?"

I cringed. I'd forgotten about Jake! "He was Aunt Lu's cat. I—" I couldn't finish. I kept remembering how he'd howled and mourned for her when she died.

"Don't you worry about His Ugliness. I'll take care of him. For Lu."

Gratitude brought me to tears. "Thank you." It was all I could offer.

I had been answering Abe and Zander's questions for an hour when we heard a light tap on the front door. It was late evening now.

Abe and Zander looked at each other. Abe hobbled to the door but did not turn on the porch light. Zander switched off the lights in the living room. Then he and I stood behind the door as Abe cracked it open.

Emilio hunched in the dark shadows of the covered porch. "Lookit," was all he said. He pointed. We joined Abe in the door and stared.

At least five vehicles with darkened headlights halted around the cul-de-sac. At a signal, armed men and women raced toward my little house. Abe closed the door behind us, and we huddled in the shadows with Emilio. Without speaking, we watched Cushing's people break through the doors to my home. I'd been expecting it, but I was still horrified.

Abe shifted his weight from foot to foot, fretful and apprehensive. "Dear Jesus! O Lord!" he prayed over and over.

Emilio came near me and felt around until he found my arm. He slid his hand into mine and squeezed it. I squeezed his back.

"Them the bad people you talked 'bout?"

"Yes."

"We won't let 'em git you."

"No," Zander agreed. "We won't."

More tears clogged my throat.

Two trucks with banks of spotlights in their beds arrived. A generator's motor cranked up and the spotlights snapped on. The lights lit up the cul-de-sac like a night game at Isotopes Park, home of Albuquerque's minor league baseball team.

A single vehicle rolled to a stop in the middle of the cul-de-sac and Cushing herself emerged from the back seat. Men and women jerked to attention as she passed by. When I spied her, marching toward my driveway, I realized I had been holding my breath. It whooshed out.

"That's her," I whispered.

In a way, I was relieved that I hadn't been wrong about Cushing coming for me. Relieved that I hadn't overestimated her or how swiftly she would act. I wouldn't doubt myself in the future when it came to her.

At that moment I was giddy with relief that Zander had parked in front of Abe's house instead of mine—and I was just as thankful that I had carried my laptop and shopping bags on my person when we came over. If I had left them in my house? The prospect was too sickening to consider.

And I wondered what my neighbors were thinking. When the police had arrested Mateo, the residents of the cul-de-sac gathered openly on the sidewalk to watch and speculate amongst themselves. Not so this time. No, like the four of us cautiously observing from the shadows of Abe's porch, my neighbors were also being careful.

Something about Cushing's team did that, made you want to keep well back—out of the way and out of their notice.

Mrs. Calderón peered from the safety of her living room window. The Tuckers stayed on their porch. The Floreses were out of town, but Mateo, arms folded defiantly, stood on his porch, too.

No, not you, Mateo. Not this time anyway. I scowled as I watched him through narrowed eyes.

"Will they come around to us, asking questions about Gemma?" Abe sounded concerned.

"Listen," Zander hissed to all of us. "If they do come around, we don't need to lie. They will ask if we've seen her. We can tell them the truth: that we haven't *seen* her, right?"

"Well, you haven't," I grumbled.

Abe shook his head and snorted, but Emilio giggled.

About then a sleek rental car glided around the curve past Abe's house. A silver-blue Lexus. I felt like I'd been punched in the gut.

Genie. Belicia Calderón had, no doubt, called her as soon as Cushing's people approached my house.

An agent waved Genie off. Then, as he got a good look at her through the window, he shouted and pulled his firearm. He held it on her and yelled for her to get out of the car and get on the ground.

I laughed into my hand. "Oh, wow! They think Genie is *me.*"

Tough luck, Genie!

A raft of agents surrounded Genie now. They forced her to kneel on the rough asphalt and put her hands behind her head. Even from a distance I could see her—*feel her*—pulsing with frustrated rage.

The agents rifled through her purse and pulled her ID. One of them handed it to Cushing. She studied it and then gestured the circle of agents away. She nodded for Genie to get up. Genie harrumphed, lowered her hands, and got up from her knees.

"I have to hear what she tells Cushing," I told Abe and Zander.

"Are you strong enough?" Zander asked. He peeled Emilio off me and hugged him to his side.

I shrugged. "Yes."

I have to be.

I whispered to the nanomites as I stepped from the porch. "Nano. I'm going near Cushing to listen in." I paused at the bottom of the steps. "No tricks from you. I can barely stand as it is, so be quiet *and play nice* so I can hear what they say without getting caught."

The mites were silent. I heard nothing from them as I came from behind Genie. I positioned myself a few feet off her shoulder so I could watch her and Cushing at the same time.

". . . And you're Gemma Keyes' sister?"

"Yes. We're twins. I've already told you that." Genie sniffed. She eyed Shark Face and was not impressed.

Cushing's black eyes bored in on Genie. "You live in Virginia, yet you are *here*. Why is that?"

"It's a free country. I visit my sister once in a while. What of it?"

Cushing didn't appreciate Genie's attitude. For once I did.

"Miss Keyes, we are investigating an incident of national security. A serious incident."

I told you! Didn't I? Didn't I tell you she'd dress it up as "national security"? My fingernails dug into the palms of my hands. I had to bite my lip to keep quiet.

"I would think you would be more concerned about your sister's involvement in such a situation," Cushing added.

Genie smirked. "Whatever my sister's involvement in your '*serious* national security incident' might be, I can guarantee that it is minimal—at best. She is not what you'd call the sharpest tool in the shed."

I was *not* too tired to slap her!

Cushing's face gave nothing away as she studied Genie. "I see. Yes, I believe Gemma likes to give that impression, Miss Keyes. However, I've become convinced that she is, ah, *sharper* than you credit her."

Genie looked as though she didn't want to believe the general, but Cushing's unwavering gaze gave her pause. "Hmm. So you say."

Two of Cushing's agents approached. "Please excuse me one moment, Miss Keyes." Cushing turned to the agents. "What have you found?"

"Nothing, ma'am." The speaker was the unfortunate Jeff, the latecomer to the staff meeting, accompanied by Agent Trujillo of the REI backpack investigation. "There's evidence that she's been in the home as recently as a few hours ago, but she is not there now."

Zander and I hadn't exactly cleaned up after we'd eaten—I imagined the scraps of food on our plates pointed to "as recently as a few hours ago."

"Computer?"

"Not in the house. She has a laptop—we found a power cord—but it's gone."

"Have the cyber people look up her IP address and dig into her online activity."

"They are already on it, ma'am."

"Car?"

"In the garage."

"So she's on foot."

"We've established a perimeter and a sweep of the neighborhood."

"Very well. You know what to bag from the house."

She dismissed Jeff and Trujillo and turned back to Genie. My sister did not like to be kept waiting. She was positively vibrating with impatience.

"Have you seen Gemma since you've been in town, Miss Keyes?"

"No. I arrived last evening and came over this morning, but she wasn't home. She doesn't, um, answer her phone when I call."

"Why is that, Miss Keyes?"

Genie's eyes narrowed. "I'm sure I can't speak for her, *General*." She raised her chin. "I only came to town because I haven't been able to reach Gemma for some time, and her neighbor, Mrs. Calderón, hasn't seen her for weeks. Mrs. Calderón might have more information than I do."

Genie pointed at Abe's house. "Oh, and Gemma is friends with the old man who lives across the street."

Thanks, sis.

After that Cushing's team organized themselves to interview all the neighbors. I managed to drag my spent body to the curb where the impromptu interviews were taking place.

Abe stuck with the response Zander had suggested. "I ain't actually seen Miss Gemma for weeks now," he told a male agent with wide-eyed simplicity. "Why, I ringed her doorbell, and she wouldn't even open— jes' talked through the door, she did. She was sick. Nasty cold and all."

"And you haven't seen Miss Keyes since around September 15?"

Abe scratched his nose absently. "I ain't got a date in mind," he muttered, "but tha' sounds 'bout right."

For an educated, well-read man, Abe's intelligence had declined significantly. I might have laughed, but I was shaking too hard, the ill effects of the mites' assault reaching deep into my bones.

"And you haven't talked to her since?" the agent prodded.

Abe tucked his chin to his chest, thinking, and I drew in my breath. I knew he wouldn't lie.

"Well," he said, "Truth is, she hain't called me in weeks."

The agent nodded and turned to Zander. "What about you? How well do you know Ms. Keyes and when did you last see her?"

Zander answered the questions dispassionately, almost carelessly. "I'm an associate pastor at Downtown Community Church. Abe, here, attends DCC, too. He asked me to introduce myself to Miss Keyes, so I did."

He shrugged. "I don't know her well, but she attended our church as a child. Haven't seen her, though, in several weeks. Haven't spoken on the phone, either."

Breathe, I told myself.

Mateo, arms folded, stonewalled the agent interviewing him. "Don't know the woman. Don't care," was the extent of his comments.

"Are you certain?" the female team member persisted.

"Which part of 'I don't know the woman' do you not get?" Mateo snarled. The agent backed away.

And I was very proud of Emilio's responses.

"I don't know the lady real well," he offered, suddenly a little shy, "but she was nice to me. No, I ain't *seen* her. Maybe she moved or something?"

Since everything I intended to take with me was already sitting in bags in Abe's guest room, I guess I had already moved. Or something.

During those interviews, Genie leaned against her high-end rental car cataloging the proceedings. Her conversation with Cushing still rang in my ears, but I did not underestimate my sister's willingness to assist Cushing in her search for me—if, at some point, Genie decided that her cooperation would further or complement her own objectives.

I was beat. I collapsed on a big landscaping rock in my front yard. While I kept one eye on Genie, I listened to Cushing calmly issuing orders to her team. As "in control" as the general managed to sound, the rigid set to her back and the edgy, too-careful responses of her team told me how frustrated she really was.

I studied Mrs. Calderón, who, from behind a barrier of yellow tape, held lively court with two agents. They eventually came and reported to Cushing.

"The next-door neighbor tells us, and I quote, 'I haven't seen Gemma Keyes in weeks, even though I know she is in there. She ignores me and she will not open the door when I knock and ring the bell. She is very rude,' end quote."

The agent cleared his throat. "The woman is positive that Keyes was living in the home as recently as today. She insists that Keyes was in the habit of going out when no one was noticing because," he consulted his notebook, "and again I quote: 'Gemma drives around at night, and I know she does because the car isn't parked in exactly the same spot in the garage every day. I *know* (the neighbor asserts), because I *check.*'"

Cushing pursed her lips and the agent cleared his throat. "This neighbor adds, 'Gemma picks the mail up after dark, and she puts the garbage out during the night before collection day and puts the can back the night after.'"

Cushing arched one eyebrow. "Who is this exceedingly observant woman?"

The agent pointed. Mrs. Calderón, from the sidewalk in front of her house, her red wig slightly askew, drew her mouth into a wide smile and waggled her fingers at Cushing in coy greeting. Cushing's plump lips parted and she returned the smile, her sharp white teeth gleaming in the artificial light, her black eyes fixing my neighbor like a collector would fix a bug with a pin.

Mrs. Calderón's smile faltered and her waggling fingers sank to her side. She backed away and waddled up the walk to her house.

"Interesting," Cushing murmured.

I swallowed, horrified at the level of detail Mrs. Calderón had collected and reported—not just to Genie but now *to Cushing*. Even as her team bustled around her, Cushing tapped one finger on her chin, her eyes focused elsewhere.

It made me nervous. It scared me.

She's thinking, putting things together.

I reviewed what Genie had said to Cushing. What the two agents had reported to her. What my friends and neighbors had told her people.

I didn't like where it all pointed.

Ain't actually seen Miss Gemma for weeks now . . . No, I ain't seen her . . . I haven't seen Gemma in weeks, even though I know she is in there. She ignores me and will not open the door when I knock and ring the bell . . . she picks the mail up after dark and she puts the garbage out during the night before collection day and puts the can back the night after . . . .

From the beginning, my greatest advantage had been that Cushing did not know where the mites had gone or what they had done to me. My invisibility had been an incredible defense against Cushing.

I felt Nick Holloway's angst creeping up my spine.

Cushing's people packed up the spotlights and left quite late that night. Her team had trashed my home, taken away a lot of stuff in large sacks, and plastered yellow "Do Not Enter" tape over my doors. The neighbors gradually dispersed, too.

I was relieved to see them all go.

I staggered back to Abe's. I needed to get my things and say goodbye, but I was exhausted.

I found Emilio shivering on the curb.

"What are you doing out here?" I scolded gently.

"Wanted to say g'bye 'fore you go," he chattered.

"Come on." I took him by the hand and led him into Abe's house.

"I found Emilio on the curb." That's all I said. Emilio's shivering said the rest. Zander glanced at Abe.

Abe nodded resolutely and put his hand out. "I don't think we've been properly introduced, but I'm Abe."

"Yeah, man. I know."

"And you are?" Abe kept his hand out.

I nudged Emilio. "Shake his hand, please. Tell him your name."

Emilio looked down but shook Abe's hand. "Emilio Martinez," he answered in a low voice.

"Well, Emilio, you look cold. Would you like a hot bath? Some hot chocolate?"

Emilio shrugged. I nudged him again.

"He's asked you two questions. Don't you think you should answer?"

Emilio sighed. "Yeah. I'd like that."

"Yes, please," I insisted.

He sighed again. "Yes, please."

"Got a bed for the night, Emilio?"

Emilio shook his head.

"Right. Well, it's sure too cold to be sleeping outside, so we'll get you fixed up. Come with me and tell me if you think this bedroom will work for you."

"I should, um, get my things out of the room first," I suggested. I followed Abe as he ushered Emilio down the hall. I grabbed my three bags and left Abe and Emilio looking over what I hoped would be Emilio's new bedroom.

God willing.

I made a face and dragged my things into the living room. Zander was quiet and so was I. We listened to water running in the bath until Abe reappeared.

"You got him to take a bath?" I was surprised. Amazed, even.

"No kid can resist a bubble bath," he chuckled.

"Didn't know you stocked it, Abe," I teased.

He smiled. "It was Alice's. Has to be near-on to twenty years old, but it still made bubbles when I poured it under the tap. Smelled good, too. I forgot how good." He moved toward the kitchen. "Need to fix that boy some vittles. He peeled off his shirt and I thought his ribs were goin' to jump through his skin."

A fresher, cleaner Emilio eventually wandered into the living room wearing one of Abe's t-shirts. It covered Emilio's knees—and his ribs.

"Here, boy. Got you some food." Abe pointed to a plate on the table.

Emilio lost no time cleaning the plate of its contents. Then Abe asked him to climb into bed.

"You got school t'morrow?"

"Yeah."

Abe grimaced and then took a breath. "I'd appreciate it, young sir, if you would answer my questions with 'yes, sir,' or 'no, sir.' Can you do that?"

Emilio dithered and studied the pattern in the old carpet under his feet.

This is it, I thought. *Make or break time for this child and his future with Abe.*

The moment stretched out, but finally Emilio looked up. "Yes. Yes, sir."

I think Abe, Zander, and I all smiled at the same time.

Well done, Emilio, I cheered.

"May I tuck him in?"

The words jumped out of my mouth without thought, but Emilio looked toward me with an eagerness that surprised me.

"Sure. If that's what he'd like."

"Yeah! I mean, yes, sir."

I took the boy's hand and led him into the room. I sat on the bed and bounced a little. "What do you think? You like the bed? Will you be warm enough?"

"Yeah. It's big, too."

I tucked him in and sat on the edge next to him. "I'm not leaving Albuquerque, at least not just yet. I have a place where I'll be safe for a while. I'll keep in touch with you. You and Abe and Zander."

"You gonna be okay?" He sounded a little anxious.

"Yes. I'll be all right. How about you? Will you be all right?"

He thought a moment. "Yeah. I'll be okay."

I stayed a while, Emilio's hand nestled in mine, until his even breathing told me he'd slipped off to sleep.

When I returned to the living room, Abe asked me to sit down. "See here, Gemma. Why can't you stay in my house, with Emilio and me, 'stead of runnin' off to this other place you got in mind?"

Zander nodded. They'd been talking and agreed on Abe's offer.

"I would love to, Abe, but I should be clear with you." I took a minute to frame my thoughts. "See, Cushing has no moral qualms. None at all. She wants the nanomites and will do whatever she needs to do to get them."

I wished the two of them could have seen my eyes, seen the concern in them. "The people I-I care about are just leverage as far as she is concerned—*perfectly expendable leverage*. Yes, I might 'hide out' here for a while, but if she even suspected the strong ties we have? She would take you away. *Emilio, too*. Whether you could help her or not, she would take all of you—and who would stop her? Who could? I can't have that. *I won't*. Do you understand what I'm saying?"

Sobered, they nodded.

"You will be safer if I am somewhere else and if you possess what they call 'plausible deniability' when it comes to my whereabouts and activities."

Zander, Abe, and I spoke for only a few minutes afterward, and Zander helped me put the bags on again. He and I laughed together as Abe, with wide eyes, watched Uncle Eddy's shirt settle over my body and "disappear" the bags slung across my chest.

"I have the bare necessities with me, and I'll be in touch," I assured them. I looked at Zander. "I will find a way for us to communicate. Not often, but something safe."

"But where are you going, Gemma? Tonight, I mean." He was frowning, unhappy and worried with my decision to leave.

"I told you. I have a place. It's safe. For now."

That was all I told either of them, Dear Reader. I had already placed them in more danger than I cared to dwell on. I would not give them information for Cushing to crush out of them.

Abe held out his arms. "Can this old man get a hug?"

I let him hug me and I hugged him back. Then I collapsed in his arms, sobbing. "Thank you. For Emilio," I sniffed. "For Jake."

Zander put his arms around both of us. "I'll be praying for you, Gemma."

"Thank you."

I straightened under my load and walked away.

⌘⌘⌘⌘

Chapter 25

I tore the tape from the side door of my house and slipped inside. I purposely hadn't said anything to Abe or Zander, but I was too worn to go another step.

Besides, I figured of all the places in Albuquerque, my house was probably the safest place for me for one night. In the morning, I would covertly board a city bus and get off within a few blocks of the safe house.

I pulled the laptop out from under my shirt, set it on the table, and staged my baggage near it. Before I left in the morning I would, at last, format my hard drive, pull it from the laptop, bash it to bits, and leave the pieces for Cushing as the gesture I hoped she would take it for: *In your sharky face, General Cushing, **ma'am***.

I didn't turn on any lights, just wandered into the living room. I kicked at the trash that Cushing's team had made of my things and collapsed into my corner on the sofa. I wanted a few moments to say goodbye to my house and my memories of Aunt Lu.

I must have dozed off for a while but then I awoke, alert, my mind churning. I was doing that thing again, sitting alone in the dark, "figuring things out"—and coming to terms with the fact that my life as Gemma Keyes was over. Nothing would ever again be "normal" for me.

Maybe there isn't an answer for you, a voice suggested, but I recognized my old friend, hopelessness, raising his nasty head.

I squashed him. My life might be drastically different now, but it was far from hopeless and far from over. I had options. And friends.

I have friends, I repeated, *people who love me.*

I would "figure it out" as I went along, just as I always did.

Something rustled nearby. Jake's green eyes glowed through the dark as he stared toward me.

"Came to say goodbye, too, did you?" I whispered.

He didn't blink, but just stared. After a moment he yawned, a big, full, fang-exposing yawn. Then he shook himself.

"Gee, thanks. I'll miss you, too."

He hissed and trotted away. I heard the cat door *snick* as Jake pushed through it.

Goodbye, Jake.

My thoughts turned to Zander. Earlier today, Zander had spoken things that pierced my toughened skin. Things that made me uncomfortable with myself and with many of my actions.

Have I been so self-absorbed, so concerned with Genie and what she did to me that I've never examined my own actions—my own life—in the same light?

And Zander's words challenged decisions I'd made as a girl because of my bad experience in church. He'd talked about things I'd given up on.

Things . . . that needed careful reconsideration.

Transformation, he'd said.

The nanocloud had certainly transformed me, but that wasn't the transformation Zander had meant. *A transformation of the heart and soul,* he'd said. *It's about letting God peel off the old, ugly, scarred man and letting him give you a new life, a life Jesus died to give you.*

I sighed, not convinced, and dragged myself from the sofa to a chair at the table. I booted up my laptop and commenced to update this, Dear Reader, my written account—*the single document on my laptop's hard drive*—and the sole reason my laptop had to be destroyed.

Deleting the file and reformatting the disk could not wholly erase the file. Destroying the hard drive was the only way to keep my account from Cushing's prying eyes.

I didn't need to demolish my external hard drive—it contained nothing Cushing could use against me or to find me—but I dared leave no trace of *this* file—my complete and up-to-date account—where her people could find its bits and bytes and reconstruct it.

I will, after I update this record, save a copy of the file to a flash drive and take it with me. Then I will delete the file on my laptop, empty the recycle bin, and smash the hard disk.

As the boot completed, my laptop pinged a new email. I hadn't received many emails of late, but I didn't much care. Tonight I was divesting myself of Gemma Keyes. As soon as I was finished here, she would be gone.

I almost ignored the ping. Shrugging, I opened my email for the last time. My inbox showed one new email. I didn't recognize the sender but the subject line staggered me. Ice-water chills poured over me in waves, scrambling my skin.

Sorry about the spam.

I couldn't move.

"No, no, no, no, no. Not possible! Not!" The mites stirred, uneasy with my dismay.

I clicked into my spam folder and sorted through the junk mail. Nothing of note.

Frantic, I started at the top and checked again. Nothing.

My hands were wet with perspiration but I was freezing. I scrubbed my hands on my jeans and then hugged myself. I stared again at the new email: *Sorry about the spam.*

It's how he contacted me the first time, I told myself. *Who else could have sent it?*

"But it's not how we communicated after that," I whispered. We'd used a message in my draft folder with the subject line *Position Description* to communicate.

But I purged that file not long after I realized Cushing would, sooner or later, be looking at me, snooping in my life!

Hands shaking, I clicked on the draft folder. There, in the folder I had *emptied*, was a lone draft message with subject line *Position Description*.

The date stamp read *today.*

I clicked on the email and scanned the hasty, garbled message.

G,
Yes, alive. Top S. mil installation don't no where.
1 guard @night; 3 rotate nights. Taught all Samba.

I was dizzy, light-headed. "But why in the world would he teach them—?"

Guard lax. Left smart phone on card table; went to answer phone at desk. Enuf time 4me to get to anon email account.

He put more care into the next lines, signaling their importance.

Told you I uploaded research to secure place in cloud. As you said: No such place. "Cloud" still real server. Vulnerable. Uploaded all— every part of life's work—to only place could never be hacked. You know. Safe

The message ended there.

He ran out of time to write more. My finger traced the words on the screen, re-reading and reading between the lines. His last words had been enough to trigger a memory.

. . . as I said, Gemma, five tribes. Alpha Tribe holds the nanocloud's collective memories and learning. Think of them as being the library— the historians—of the nanocloud.

Right then, I knew. I knew why the nanocloud clung to me and refused all my commands to leave. I understood *what I carried*, and the great—the awesome—responsibility thrust upon me.

I put my face in my hands and bowed over my laptop, pondering, for the second time, news of Dr. Bickel's return from death to life.

He's alive? My sweet, brilliant, mad scientist is still alive?

I read his message once more, then purged the folder and the trash— even though my efforts wouldn't keep Cushing's IT people from finding and reading Dr. Bickel's message on Google's servers.

Too late, Cushing, too late, I gloated. *I know he's still alive and you can't undo that.*

For a while I let my thoughts roam over happier days spent in the lab under the mountain—Dr. Bickel's childlike pride in the nanomites, his struggle to hold his cards right, his ego and mercurial temper (always followed by mortification), his shy pleasure when he brought out one of his fantastical desserts.

"Oh, Nano," I whispered. "We need to find him. We need to find Dr. Bickel and get him out. Somehow! We need—"

I covered my eyes with my hands, overwhelmed by the futility of such a task.

The room behind my closed eyes brightened. I lowered my hands and gaped at the laptop's screen. On a bright silver background, in bold, flowing blue words, I read,

WE CONCUR GEMMA KEYES.
STAND BY.
SEARCHING MESSAGE ORIGINATION.

⌘⌘⌘⌘

The End

The Adventure Continues in
Book 2: *Stealth Power*

ADDITIONAL READING

The Center for Integrated Nanotechnologies (CINT) fact sheet. Retrieved February 1, 2015, from LANL.gov.

Che, X., Salaymeh, A, & Reynolds, R. (2014). Monitoring the vital signs in a complex social system: An example using cultural algorithms. *International Journal of Swarm Intelligence Research, 5*(1), 55-107.

Cheng, S., Shi, Y., & Qin, Q. (2013). A study of normalized population diversity in particle swarm optimization. *International Journal of Swarm Intelligence Research, 4*(1), 1-34.

Cramer, G. (2012). *Quantum stealth: The invisible military becomes a reality.* Retrieved December 24, 2014, from Hyperstealth.com.

Estimating a timeline for molecular manufacturing. Retrieved January 06, 2015, from Center for Responsible Nanotechnology.

The future of stealth camouflage in special operations. February 5, 2014. Retrieved April 9, 2015 from Business Insider.

Kadkol, A. & Yen, G. (2012). A culture-based particle swarm optimization framework for dynamic, constrained multi-objective optimization. *International Journal of Swarm Intelligence Research, 3*(1), 1-29.

Kirtland AFB—Nuclear Weapon Storage. Retrieved March 9, 2015, from VirtualGlobetrotting.com.

Manzano Base. Retrieved March 12, 2015, from Wikimapia.org.

Microsystems & Engineering Sciences Applications (MESA) fact sheet. Retrieved December 12, 2014, from Sandia.gov.

Nanoscale 3D printing. Retrieved January 5, 2015, from Wikipedia.org.

Research Advance in Swarm Robotics. Volume 9, Issue 1, March 2013, Pages 18–39. Retrieved January 20, 2015, from ScienceDirect.com.

Sandia recognizes five green-certified buildings. News Release: September 08, 2009. Retrieved December 17, 2014, from Sandia.gov.

Shi, Y. (2014). Developmental swarm intelligence: Developmental learning perspective of swarm intelligence algorithms. *International Journal of Swarm Intelligence Research*, 5(1), 36-54.

Swarm intelligence. Retrieved December 4, 2014, from Wikipedia.org.

Weapons of Mass Destruction: Manzano. Retrieved December 17, 2014, from GlobalSecurity.com.

What is Nanotechnology? Retrieved January 06, 2015, from Center for Responsible Nanotechnology.

Yen, G. & Leong, W. (2011). A multiobjective particle swarm optimizer for constrained optimization. *International Journal of Swarm Intelligence Research*, 2(1), 1-23.

SCRIPTURE QUOTATIONS

ABOUT THE AUTHOR

Vikki Kestell's passion for people and their stories is evident in her readers' affection for her characters and unusual plotlines. Two often-repeated sentiments are, "I feel like I know these people," and "I'm right there, in the book, experiencing what the characters experience."

Vikki holds a Ph.D. in Organizational Learning and Instructional Technologies. She left a career of twenty-plus years in government, academia, and corporate life to pursue writing full time. "Writing is the best job ever," she admits, "and the most demanding."

Also an accomplished speaker and teacher, Vikki and her husband Conrad Smith make their home in Albuquerque, New Mexico.

To keep abreast of new book releases, visit her website, http://www.vikkikestell.com/, or find her on Facebook at http://www.facebook.com/TheWritingOfVikkiKestell.

OTHER BOOKS BY VIKKI KESTELL

A PRAIRIE HERITAGE

Book 1: *A Rose Blooms Twice* (free eBook, most online retailers)
Book 2: *Wild Heart on the Prairie*
Book 3: *Joy on This Mountain*
Book 4: *The Captive Within*
Book 5: *Stolen*
Book 6: *Lost Are Found*
Book 7: *All God's Promises*
Book 8: *The Heart of Joy—A Short Story* (eBook only)

GIRLS FROM THE MOUNTAIN

Book 1: *Tabitha*
Book 2: *Tory*
Book 3: *Sarah Redeemed*

The Christian and the Vampire: A Short Story
(free eBook, most online retailers)

Faith-Filled Fiction™

Made in the USA
Columbia, SC
02 June 2018